THE
REPLACEMENT

THE
REPLACEMENT

SUSAN *WALES* AND
ROBIN *SHOPE*

Revell
Grand Rapids, Michigan

Published by Fleming H. Revell
a division of Baker Publishing Group
P.O. Box 6287, Grand Rapids, MI 49516-6287
www.revellbooks.com

Printed in the United States of America

Library of Congress Cataloging-in-Publication Data

Wales, Susan.
    The replacement / Susan Wales and Robin Shope.
      p. cm.
    ISBN 10: 0-8007-3111-5 (pbk.)
    ISBN 978-0-8007-3111-3 (pbk.)
     1. Investigative reporting—Fiction. 2. Women journalists—Fiction. 3. Politicians—Fiction. 4. Missing persons—Fiction. I. Shope, Robin. II. Title.
PS3623.A3585R47 2006
813'.6—dc22   2006006884

This book is dedicated to an exceptional literary agent,
Beth Jusino,
who found beauty in the ashes and had the perseverance to
sift through them!
For her genius, excellence, time, talent, and patience . . .
Beth, we could fill this page with your superlatives.

Acknowledgments

Our thanks to the exceptional team at Fleming H. Revell of Baker Publishing Group for the opportunity to write this series; especially to Jennifer Leep, who discovered *The Chase*. Many thanks to Jennifer for her perseverance and the grace she gave to us. A big thanks to our editor Kristin Kornoelje, who has demonstrated Job's patience, and the virtuous woman's creativity and work ethic. Your price is far above rubies! Thanks to the world's greatest proofreader—Donna Henry.

Susan Wales thanks . . .
Special thanks to my friends Tisi Aylward and Laura Burkett for their suggestions, and my friend Terry Steele for Jill and John's song "Here and Now."
My love and gratitude to my husband, Ken, who makes so many allowances for my career and believes in my talent, to my parents for their gift of storytelling, and to my daughter, Megan, and granddaughter, Hailey, who provide the inspiration.

Robin Shope thanks . . .
Big thanks to my family, Richard, Kimberly, and Matthew, who hold open the door so my words can spill onto the pages. I do this for you.

1

Rain fell in ropes and wind shuttled through them,
webbing the city in its ephemeral weave.

Julia O'Faolain

With umbrellas in bloom, tourists flocked to Capitol Hill. Journalist Jill Lewis peeked out a side door at the crowd. Sightseers on tiptoes wobbled for glimpses of senators. A faithful few marched on the fringes, wigwagging protest placards high. Visitors aimed cameras, hoping to capture an important face in their lens. A Brownie troop pranced down the steps in a crooked line. "Stay together," their leader ordered. Media neophytes with sun sticks and video cams jockeyed for position while reporters clutched microphones. Like Jill, they longed for words worthy of history books.

Jill pressed her forehead against the door. From out of nowhere, a dark, hairy arm reached over her head and pushed the door. Whoosh! The door flew open. Jill was catapulted into the April drizzle. Before she hit the slippery concrete, the arm hooked her, snapped her back like a fish on a line, and slammed her against the wall. Without so much as an apology, the arm's owner bolted into the crowd.

"Jerk," Jill muttered.

Digging in her purse, she found a pair of oversized sunglasses and slid them onto her nose. Jill prayed no one would recognize her but had barely ventured a dozen steps when someone did.

"Hey, Jill. Jill Lewis! Over here!" The animated voice belonged to Dan Peek, an ambitious intern from the *Gazette*. "What's a hotshot reporter like you doing out here with the wannabes?"

Jill's umbrella shot up, blocking her from the bigmouth's view. Unfortunately, she couldn't swing it around soon enough to hide from curious onlookers. She turned back around and shot Dan an exasperated look.

Dan skulked away, mumbling apologies, as tourists gawked at Jill. Some even asked, "Who is she?" An occasional segment on CNN or Fox did not a household face make.

Suddenly the double doors of the building swung open, snapping everyone's attention to the front entrance of the Capitol.

Bodyguards bearing chests like concrete barriers burst through the doors and funneled pathways through the mob for the lawmakers. Distinguished senators appeared next, smiling and waving; some paused for obligatory handshakes and photo ops.

After a while, two security guards stepped up to lock the doors. Jill groaned. "Where is he?"

Her afternoon wasted, Jill decided to return to her office to try and salvage the day. Navigating puddles down the steps, she looked up just in time to see a plaid umbrella soar over her head. Ducking the plaid blur, she watched helplessly as its owner grappled for it in the wind, stumbling in his pursuit.

He bumped into Jill on his way down the steps. Arms flailing, she found an anchor—the arm of a man with a crew cut.

"Thanks," Jill began, but the man jerked his arm away. Then to her surprise, he reared it back and shoved her. Tumbling backward, Jill wailed as her head smacked hard into the concrete.

"Hey, what do you think you're doing?" a bystander yelled at the man. He and another guy lunged at the attacker.

Undaunted, Crew Cut grabbed the stray umbrella and swung it like a bat, keeping the challengers at bay. In the scuffle, his boot rammed Jill's knee, its sharp point puncturing the skin.

Jill screamed but was quickly silenced when a whack intended for her defenders crashed across her face. Dazed, she caught sight of the skull and crossbones tattoo on Crew Cut's forearm.

Two police officers arrived just as Crew Cut slithered into the crowd. One cop took off after him; the other helped Jill to her feet.

"I'm Officer Ware of the U.S. Capitol Police." He tipped his hat. "Your name please?"

"Jill Lewis."

"Ms. Lewis, would you like to sit down? Do you need any medical attention?"

"No, uh, thank you," Jill said as she looked over her bleeding knee.

A woman stuffed a wad of tissues into Jill's hand. Jill thanked her and used the tissues to blot the blood that dribbled from her knee. Another lady emptied ice from a Coke cup into her husband's handkerchief and gently pressed it onto Jill's purpling face. A man opened a bottle of water and insisted she take a sip.

The other police officer returned, huffing and puffing. "I lost him."

"Go talk to the other witnesses, I'll finish up here," Officer Ware ordered. He flipped his pad open. "Ms. Lewis, can you give me a description of the man who attacked you?"

"He was a large, bull-faced man. Dark eyes and skin, with a crew cut. His arm was muscular and hairy, dark hair. Oh, he had a large tattoo on the inside of his right forearm."

"What kind of tattoo?"

"A skull and crossbones."

"Now, tell me what happened."

The second officer stepped up in time to hear Jill's account of the incident.

Afterward, Officer Ware looked to him for verification.

"Her statement matches most of the eyewitness accounts," the other officer confirmed.

Jill raised an eyebrow. "Most?"

"A couple of people suggested that when you grabbed his arm, he thought you were attacking him."

"But he was at least three times my size."

"When somebody grabs you, for some it's just a natural reflex to strike back."

Jill stiffened. "You think it was self-defense?"

At this point, Officer Ware stopped writing. "Not necessarily. I'll file a report. If you want to come down and look at some photos, here's my card."

Jill snatched the card. "Thanks a lot."

Officer Ware flipped his notebook closed. "Thank you, Ms. Lewis. If anything comes of it, we'll—"

A voice suddenly squawked over the radio dangling on his belt. "All officers in the vicinity of the Capitol, do you read? Over."

Ware yanked his radio and replied, "Ten-four. Officers Ware and Bonner."

A static voice garbled the information. "We have an 11-8, a possible 914 H on the sidewalk below the Capitol. All officers report at once. Over."

The two officers gave Jill a parting nod and dashed down the steps.

Hobbling after them, Jill grabbed her cell phone and dialed her editor. Rubric's voice boomed through the telephone line. "I've been waiting for you to call. What did Senator Brown say?"

"Quick, get a photographer over to Capitol Hill." Translating the police codes, Jill told him, "A man just collapsed on the sidewalk with a possible heart attack."

"Who is he?"

"I don't know yet, but if he's a senator, we've got our front-page story."

"And if he's a tourist?"

"Bury him on the back page."

"Then what do you suggest for a headline?"

Her attention distracted by the commotion below, she pushed through the wall of rubbernecks to the front and gasped. Sprawled out on the sidewalk was the victim. The man with the plaid umbrella.

"What is it, Jill? Answer me!" Rubric hollered.

"Somebody's giving him CPR," Jill said and inched closer for a better view of the victim.

"Who?"

"The senator . . . Senator Brown."

2

*In journalism there has always been a tension
between getting it right and getting it first.*

Ellen Goodman

Cameras flashed in Jill's eyes as she searched the faces of the photojournalists behind the press line. She spotted a photographer from the *Gazette* and waved to him. He flashed her a thumbs-up and continued to snap shots of the ambulance bumping across the curb heading straight up the walk.

The scene erupted into chaos as people shouted and ran in every direction. Squad cars shot up, and cops popped out of them to shoo the encroaching crowd. Jill lingered on the sidelines, watching, praying. The EMTs strapped the senator in place on a gurney and started an IV. They loaded the patient into the back of the ambulance. The emergency vehicle made a hard left onto the street. Amid blasts of horns and lights, it raced at breakneck speed toward the life transport helicopter hovering nearby.

As the rain melted away, people shut their umbrellas. Jill's view unblocked, she caught the eye of Senator Brown's chief of staff, Eric Richter, pacing on the sidewalk below. She waved at him, and he motioned her over.

Up close, Jill was shocked by Eric's appearance. His jacket and tie were crumpled. His hair dripped sweat, curling haphazardly around his face. He stared blankly at Jill through red and puffy eyes.

"Can we talk for a minute?" she asked, gently touching his arm.

"Sure, until my car gets here." Unashamedly, he wiped tears off his cheek with his shirtsleeve.

Jill embraced him. "Eric, I'm so sorry. Are you okay?"

"I'm trying to be strong for the rest of the staff. Jill! What happened to your face?" Eric asked.

"I fell. It's nothing, really. Is there anything I can do for you, Eric?"

"Just pray, Jill."

"What happened?"

"I'm not sure, but I heard a paramedic say something about a heart attack."

"Did the senator have a history of heart problems?"

"No. Brown had a complete physical a couple of months ago, and the doctors at Bethesda gave him a clean bill of health. Frankly, I was shocked, but the senator said it was his good genes. And sure enough, when the tests results came in, there were no obesity-related illnesses. Have you seen him lately?"

"I haven't, but I was supposed to see him today. He stood me up."

"You should've gone through me if you wanted to see him," Eric fussed at her, seemingly irritated that he'd been bypassed.

"But I didn't ask for the meeting. The senator called me late yesterday. He sounded panicked and said it was urgent that he speak to me today. And you wouldn't believe how I had to juggle my schedule to make it happen."

"Did he say why he wanted to see you?"

"I was hoping you could tell me."

"I don't have a clue. You're sure it was today?"

"Positive."

"Wait. I can clear this up in a minute. I've got Brown's schedule in my BlackBerry." He whipped the PDA out of his pocket and scanned the calendar. "Sorry, Jill. There's nothing down here for you today or in the future," Eric said. He appeared dubious of her claim.

"I guess we'll have to wait until . . ."

"If . . . he recovers. Excuse me, Jill, here's my car."

Eric sprinted onto the street as security waved a shiny black Expedition through the traffic.

"Which hospital?" Jill called out to him.

"Bethesda."

"Call me!" Jill yelled and gave Eric a wave.

"I . . . I'll try." The SUV pulled up to the curb, and a junior aide jumped out to open the door for him.

Jill watched until the vehicle sped away and mouthed "Bethesda" to the *Gazette*'s photographer. She wandered around until she found a shelter under an overhang. Her fingers moved adeptly as she punched her front-page story into her BlackBerry for the early morning edition. *"Another historic day in Washington unfolds as a powerful man lay fighting for his life on the Capitol steps."* Jill added the details, wrote the story, and hit send.

Within minutes, Rubric text-messaged her. "Welcome back to the front page, Jillie!"

Smiling, Jill shoved her BlackBerry into her purse and looked up at the sky. Overhead she heard the clatter of helicopters. Crammed with reporters and cameramen, the whirlybirds spun their way toward the breaking news. But Jill was first at the scene.

"Jill!"

Jill cringed at the sound of her ex-boyfriend's voice. Then forcing cheerfulness and a smile, she said, "Hello, David."

"I saw you talking to Eric on the sidewalk, but then I lost sight of you. How about dinner tonight?"

"Sorry, but I have to get back to the office."

David tagged along behind her as Jill sloshed down the steps, detouring around a news crew that was setting up equipment.

He pointed to the camera crew and asked, "Just how much is it going to cost them to get your pretty face on TV?"

"Being in front of a camera every day isn't my thing. Although, they could've gotten me pretty cheap at one time. But you wouldn't know that since you didn't stick around after the *Gazette* fired me. What was it you called me, a 'political liability'?"

"Still holding a grudge, I see."

Jill stopped and spun around. "Not at all. I'm thankful. Things worked out for the best."

"You're beginning to sound like your mother."

"Thank you."

"What? I never thought you'd take that as a compliment." David eyed Jill suspiciously.

She only smiled and shrugged her shoulders.

Momentarily flustered, he quickly moved on to politics. "Uh, Senator Brown's death will shake things up in the political arena."

Jill turned around and started down the steps again. "He's not dead yet."

"Ha! Did you see him? I've got a better chance of getting you to go to dinner with me than Brown does of surviving."

Jill paused on the step. "Then this is a sad day for the Democrats."

"Are you joking? As far as the Democrats are concerned, Brown's death would be what your mother calls the providence of God."

"I'm sure the Democrats would've eventually pressured Brown to stop his filibuster frenzy closer to the elections."

"We've tried, but it's hopeless. Brown owes too many favors to the unions and special interest groups. If we don't cooperate with the Republicans and get some important legislation passed, there won't be one blue state on election eve."

"Maybe the Democrats pushed him down the steps?" Jill suggested with a suspicious smile. She set her briefcase down beside her.

"If anyone's to blame for his death, it's Brown himself. Have you seen him lately? The man's a puff pastry . . . at least a hundred pounds overweight."

"But Eric Richter just told me that a few months ago the doctors at Bethesda said Brown was in excellent health."

"Surely you aren't gullible enough to buy Eric's spin on Brown's health?"

Jill decided to take advantage of David's chattiness. "Who's going to replace Brown as minority leader?"

"I just got off the phone with my boss, and Senator Jacobs says his replacement is Tommy Harrison."

"Harrison? But he's so conservative. And didn't he almost switch parties last year?"

"Yes, but he's a genius and the only Democrat who can successfully negotiate with the Republicans."

"But once the elections are over . . ."

"That's the easy part. Analysts predict Harrison will lose his reelection bid by a landslide." David gently touched the bruise on her cheek. "Hey, what happened to you, anyway?"

Jill swatted his hand away and picked up her briefcase. "I was next to Brown when he fell, and he almost took me with him."

David winked. "You're lucky he didn't fall on you. Are you sure we can't continue this conversation over dinner?"

Without a word, Jill waved good-bye at David, leaving him on the steps while she ran off to hail a cab. In the cab she typed another story. *"As Senator Brown fights for his life, speculation over his replacement takes center stage."*

Back at the *Gazette* Jill stopped by the employee lounge and grabbed an ice pack out of the freezer before seeking refuge in her corner office. She tossed her rain-soaked coat on the sofa and crumpled in her desk chair. She slid out of her soggy shoes and had just placed the ice pack over her face when she heard someone open her door.

"What'd you do, Lewis, give Senator Brown a heart attack?" The voice belonged to Annabelle Stone, the *Gazette*'s illustrious publisher.

Startled, Jill sat up and dropped the ice pack.

Auburn hair flying and rippling down her back like a dusty windstorm, Annabelle circled the room. She spotted the remote and snapped on the TV, jockeying back and forth between CNN, MSNBC, Fox News, and all the major networks.

"That must have been some meeting." Annabelle whistled.

"There was no meeting. Senator Brown stood me up."

"I hope you spoke with his aides to find out why he wanted to see you. This could be big."

"Eric Richter didn't know a thing about our meeting."

"Mmm. Start talking to some key Democrats to find out who Brown's replacement as minority leader is going to be—in case he doesn't make it."

"I know who his replacement's going to be—Senator Thomas Henry Harrison IV from Alabama."

"What Democrat are you cozying up with, honey? 'Cause whoever he is, he's sold you an igloo down in Miami Beach."

"Just think about it. The election's coming soon . . ."

Realization popped on the publisher's face in the form of a big smile. "Say no more, my darling girl. I get it. Harrison's the Democratic Party's one-night stand. They'll dump him afterwards."

"No, the Democrats won't even have to do the dirty work; the voters of Alabama will do it for them."

"It's a brilliant political move. Wish I'd thought of that." Noticing Jill's face for the first time, Annabelle gasped. "What happened to you?"

"I was right in front of Brown when he started falling and knocked me over. I grabbed an arm. Unfortunately that arm belonged to some maniac. He shoved me, kicked me, and finished me off with an umbrella." Yanking off her hosiery, she balled it up and tossed it into the trash can.

"Well, it doesn't look that bad. Have a seat in that chair right now and write your story while your memory's still fresh."

"Done. Rubric has it along with photos for the morning edition." Jill paused briefly to check her voice mail, searching for the most important call of all. To her disappointment the message wasn't there.

"What do you think is wrong with Senator Brown?"

"Eric Richter thinks it's his heart."

"That'll be no surprise to anyone. Brown is a big blob of blubber teeming to explode. Oh, Rubric suggested that we send his young intern over to the hospital. Do you think he's ready?"

"I don't know . . . He's so young and just not really . . ."

"Savvy?"

"Exactly."

"Then I'll need you to go with him. And get a doctor to look at those bruises while you're there." Annabelle breezed out of the office.

About to protest because of her injuries, especially her drum-beating headache, Jill thought better of it. She needed to question the senator's other aides to see if anyone was privy to the reason he wanted to see her. She called Dan, the intern. "Get a car and meet me in the garage in fifteen minutes."

Jill dug through her purse for her BlackBerry but couldn't find it, so she snatched a steno pad and a couple of extra pens off her desk. Sliding her feet back into her heels, she yanked her coat off the sofa and went downstairs. "What happened to you?" Dan asked, holding the door open for her.

"I fell."

"Oh. Sorry about that."

"Thanks. It's no big deal." She settled into the front seat.

"You know this is providential."

"That remains to be seen."

"I mean the opportunity to work with you."

"Don't thank me, thank Annabelle. It was her idea."

Dan was silent as he slid into the driver's seat.

She poked him in the arm. "But I agreed it would be great to have my favorite intern along."

An effervescent smile popped back on the intern's face.

"Did you see what happened at the Capitol today?" she asked him.

"Nope. I left before the senator fell."

"Well, that's a good lesson for you, then. Reporters should be the last to leave. Always stay until the bitter end. When I started out, I waited hours, sometimes days, or even weeks for a story."

"Now they fall at your feet." He smirked.

"Very funny. But not true. I'd hung out at the Capitol for hours today. Investigative reporting is a lot like fishing; it's a waiting game that takes incredible patience."

As Dan slogged the car down the flooded streets, Jill plotted the course of their investigation on the steno pad. "If we're going to work together, first you should know the chain of command. You report to me, and in turn, I report to Rubric and Annabelle. Until you learn my style, you're to discuss every decision with me. And I expect total honesty and loyalty. Understand?"

"You got it."

"Good. I've written down the investigation's objectives for you."

He glanced down at her pad of paper and grimaced. "Don't you have a PDA? Want me to help you set up one?"

"Sometimes pen and paper suffice, especially when your PDA is lost in the purse of no return."

"Oh, so Jill Lewis is human after all."

"I can be disorganized, but I don't expect you to be. First, we'll check in at the hospital PR office, but we'll have to go behind the scenes to find out the doctor's prognosis for Brown."

"How do we do that? They don't allow reporters beyond a certain point."

"Why do you think I brought your good-looking mug along? It's no secret that nurses warm up to cute guys."

Dan looked like he was trying to hide a smile, but he didn't quite succeed.

At the hospital, Jill and Dan maneuvered their way through the crowd in the lobby. Security was tight, but the throng of reporters vying for the first story taxed the hospital guards.

"We'll have the exact same story as the rest if we hang out here," she said and looked around, searching for a way to slip past the lobby. Just then a reporter from another news agency got into a shoving match with a security guard, pulling everyone's attention toward the scuffle.

Jill saw her chance. Hooking Dan's arm, she ducked into a side corridor, dragging him behind her. They smiled at one another as they rode the elevator to the fifth floor. Finding the door to the chapel open, they tiptoed inside. A stylish woman was kneeling at the front, her hands clasped together in prayer.

"The senator's wife," Jill whispered.

"How'd you know she'd be in here?"

"Where would you be?"

Suddenly distracted by a commotion behind them, they turned around to see a young man enter the chapel.

"Mom, the doctor needs to see you," he announced in a loud whisper.

Jill and Dan watched the young man help his mother to her feet. As Mrs. Brown left the chapel, a flash of recognition appeared in her eyes when she passed by the pew where Jill and Dan sat. She nodded at Jill.

Jill nodded back at her and turned toward Dan just as he

aimed a digital camera at the grieving pair. She knocked the camera away. "Just what do you think you're doing?"

"Making headlines. Why'd you stop me?" Dan yelped. "A front-page picture of the grieving family leaving the chapel is something even the TV news wouldn't have. And why didn't you talk to her? We could've had quotes in the story."

"Let's go. Now!"

Once in the hallway, Jill grabbed his camera and deleted the pictures of Mrs. Brown and her son. She dropped the camera in his hand when she was finished.

"Guess I screwed up, huh?" Dan said.

Jill glared at him and pointed him toward the elevator. "Meet me in the lobby."

Shoulders slumped, Dan boarded the elevator.

Despite her injuries, Jill flung open the door to the stairwell. She needed a time-out. She walked down the stairs until a sudden bolt of pain seared through her knee. She stopped. To regain her balance, she hugged the rail. Slowly, she dragged herself down one flight of stairs. "Ah, only twenty more steps," she whispered to herself as she calculated the distance to the elevator from the fourth floor landing. But just as she reached for the doorknob, a sudden wave of nausea crashed inside of her, doubling her over. The walls began to spin. Dizzy, she slumped against the door and slid down to the floor. She closed her eyes and hugged her knees to her chest.

Above her, a door banged open and closed. Jill's eyes fluttered open, and her heart raced to the rhythm of the footsteps. "Hello! Please, I need some help down here. Fourth floor." Jill's words echoed through in the stairwell, but the footsteps stopped abruptly.

"Please don't go. I'm down here . . . on the fourth floor. Help me . . . please."

The sound of the footsteps resumed, moving closer and closer. They came slowly at first, then faster until at last the feet stopped before her. Slightly opening her eyes, she made out the boots through a film of hazy gray. Crew Cut's boots! She opened her eyes and lifted her head until she found herself face to face with a blur, a large blur. Eyes focusing, she saw it was Crew Cut. Or was she hallucinating?

"Please, can you help me? I'm . . ."

Crew Cut flashed a smile, revealing bleached teeth.

"Who are you?" Jill demanded, her voice bouncing throughout the stairway.

No response.

Jill spoke quickly, slurring her words. "I didn't attack you on the Capitol steps this afternoon. I was falling, and I reached for your arm. That's all. I'm sorry."

Crew Cut hesitated for a brief moment, but then he barreled past her, knocking Jill's head against the wall. She heard his footsteps pounding down, down, down. She listened as a door opened and slammed shut. The stairwell became silent. The footsteps were gone.

Jill crawled over toward the door. Coaxing herself to stand, she grabbed hold of the doorknob and struggled to open the door. But it was locked. She jiggled it, but it wouldn't turn. She banged on the door and screamed, "Help!" But no one heard her. Exhausted, she knelt down on the floor and leaned back against the wall to decide what to do next, but her mind was so fuzzy she couldn't concentrate.

She wasn't sure how long she'd been there when a shaky voice from below called up to her. "Jill, are you there?"

"Dan, up here, on the fourth floor."

Sprinting up the steps two at time, Dan found Jill struggling to get back on her feet.

"You're hurt."

Jill winced and took hold of Dan's outstretched hand. "I'm not sure I can walk. Now my ankle's hurt too."

"Did you fall?"

"I guess so. I'm not sure." She paused. "A guy was just here. He shoved me."

"Who was he?" Dan got her to her feet and put his arm around her waist. He easily pushed open the door she had struggled so hard to open.

"I think he was a guy I saw earlier today." She pointed to her face. "The one who did this."

"I thought you said you fell?"

She winced. "I did."

Dan looked confused. "Are you sure you're all right?"

"No."

"I'm taking you to the emergency room," Dan said as he punched the elevator button to the lobby.

Jill hesitated. She had to admit she felt really ill. Maybe she had a concussion from her fall this afternoon. Crew Cut did knock her pretty hard, and that would explain the nausea too. She wouldn't mind something stronger for her headache either. But then she remembered she hadn't eaten all day and protested. "No, it'll be hours before they see me."

"Think about it, Jill. Emergency room? Doctors? Nurses? Imagine the scoop we'll get there."

"The heart trauma center is in an entirely different location than the ER. I think I'll go home so I can get something to eat and get some sleep. Will you call me with any updates?"

"You're leaving me in charge here?" Dan's eyes grew wide.

"You can handle it, can't you?"

The intern beamed and nodded his head.

Dan helped Jill get into a cab. On the ride home, she worried about leaving Dan there alone. Annabelle would be furious if she ever found out, but what choice did Jill have? Every inch of her body ached. She just hoped the kid didn't blow it.

Looking out the cab's window, she was thankful the rain had stopped. The quiet moment gave her time to think about Crew Cut. Who was he? And why did he keep popping up wherever she was? Was it a coincidence? Had he really been on that stairway? She tried to capture the details, his boots, his face, and his features.

Back at her apartment, Jill felt much better after a bowl of chicken noodle soup. Then she drew a bath and climbed into the tub. Leaning back on her inflatable pillow, she felt soothed by the warm lavender water. Before bed, she packed her ankle and the right side of her face in ice, gulped down some pain medication, and then slipped under the covers.

Grabbing her cordless phone off the nightstand, she stared at it for a long while. *Should I call him? Should I call John?* She longed to hear his voice, but she decided against it as her mother's advice lilted inside her head. *"Men are hunters. They want to pursue, not be pursued."* She chose sleep.

Minutes later when the phone rang, hope sprang alive in the darkness. "John?"

"Jill! They wheeled Senator Brown into surgery a couple of minutes ago."

She sat up and rubbed her eyes. She was confused for a moment, trying to figure out who was on the line. "Dan?"

"Yeah, it's me."

Jill willed her mind to sharpen and free itself from sleep numbness. "Bypass surgery?"

"According to the doctors, the senator had a massive stroke."

"No kidding. What's the prognosis?"

"Fifty-fifty. They're going to try to repair a blood vessel in his brain."

"Where did you get your information?" Jill asked, hopscotching her TV back and forth from CNN to Fox News.

"The senator's son, the one from the chapel, and I were in the same elevator, so I asked him about his father, and he just flat-out told me."

"Good job. Call the story in to Rubric and stay in touch with any breaking news."

"Jill, wait! How are you feeling?"

"Fine."

"Are you still upset with me over that camera thing?"

"Why shouldn't I be?"

"I just wanted to prove I was a real go-getter."

"Then get a job at the *National Enquirer*."

"Jill, I'm really, really sorry. I've already blown it twice today."

"And the day's not over yet."

After the phone call ended, Jill felt relieved that things were under control at the hospital. She knew if they weren't, Annabelle would kill her for deserting Dan. But Dan was a good kid. She agreed with Rubric that Dan had a bright future as long as he could bridle some of his youthful enthusiasm.

Jill turned off the TV and the lights. She shimmied back down in the covers, praying she'd hear from John Lovell soon. Perhaps he'd had a change of heart?

3

New love is the brightest, and long love is the greatest; but re-vived love is the tenderest thing known on earth.

Thomas Hardy

"Good morning, Jill. That new intern is a real go-getter, isn't he?" Landry paused for effect as she watched Jill hobble off the elevator the next morning.

"What's Wonder Boy done now?"

"He just called for you and Rubric to tell you that Senator Brown survived his ten-hour surgery."

"If Dan wants to impress me, he'll have to tell me something I haven't already heard on the morning news," Jill said. She was surprised Landry hadn't commented on her injuries. The half hour Jill had spent on her makeup must have done the trick.

"Oh, there's more," Landry added. "Dan also said to tell you that Senator Brown was placed on life support following the surgery."

"That's not unusual after a serious surgery. It could be temporary." She started walking toward her office but then turned back to Landry. "Is Rubric in yet?"

"No, but you can reach him on his cell phone. I just called him to tell him the news."

"What was his reaction?"

"Enormously pleased. He says Dan's going to give you a real kick in the pants. Good thing you had that front-page story this morning. Great job, by the way."

"Thank you."

Jill grumbled to herself all the way down the corridor to her office. "Rubric is obviously worried about me if he's trying to pit a lowly intern against me, although I have to hand it to him, the guy's good. I'm slipping, and everybody at the *Gazette* is noticing. And it's all John's fault for distracting me."

Jill limped into her office, shutting the door behind her so hard that one of her journalism plaques fell off the wall.

"Bad morning?"

Jill stopped abruptly, still clasping the doorknob. Glancing over at her desk, she caught sight of a man's hand resting on the arm of her chair. After the way this morning had begun, she almost expected Crew Cut to be back again, this time to break her leg. Peeking around the chair, Jill was mortified when she recognized John Lovell's lanky frame. Sipping a tall café latte, he turned around in the chair, folded the morning edition of the *Gazette*, and placed it on her desk before he got to his feet.

"You're back," Jill noted matter-of-factly as she walked right past him.

John grabbed her arm to pull her toward him and gave her a big hug.

Stiffening in his arms, she pushed him away.

"What's wrong, Jill?"

"Nothing. I'm just surprised to see you."

"Why? I told you I'd be back."

"But you didn't tell me it would be over two months before you did."

Sheepishly, John said, "We've worked together before. You know how it is on an undercover job." Changing the subject, he said, "If you have a hammer, I'll help you get that award back up on the wall."

"Don't bother." Jill picked up the fallen plaque and stuffed it in a desk drawer.

"Oh, there's a café mocha on your desk for you. I hope it's still hot."

Jill mumbled a thanks but left it there.

"I stopped by to tell you good-bye before I left for my assignment, but you weren't here. Didn't you get my message?"

"Oh, I got it." She sat down at her desk, pulled the top drawer toward her, and took out the pink slip. Unfolding it, she read aloud, "Jill, I've been sent out of town on an investigation. Will be in touch. Love, John." Jill crumpled up the pink slip and tossed it at the trash can beside her desk. When she missed, John grinned, picked it up, and tossed it back at her.

Jill stood up and walked over to her window.

Stepping up behind her, he remarked, "It's a beautiful day, isn't it? Spring's my favorite time of year in Washington."

"Is that why you came back?"

"No, I came back to see you," he said as he put his arms around her waist and kissed the back of her neck. "Will you have dinner with me tonight?"

"Tonight?"

"I know it's late notice, but I'm hoping you don't have any plans."

"Well, I do."

John frowned.

"What did you expect me to do after you disappeared for two months? Sit home every night and wait for you to call?"

"I'm sorry, Jill. I'll always come back to you. Eventually. I love you." John took her into his arms and was about to kiss her when he noticed the faint bruises on her face. "What happened to you?"

"I fell."

"Have you had a doctor look at this?" He outlined a bruise with his fingertip.

"It's fine, really."

As he leaned over to kiss her, Jill held up her hand. "First, we need to talk."

"I couldn't agree more. There's so much to talk about. Are you sure you can't wiggle out of your plans and come to dinner with me tonight?" John picked up the morning edition of the *Gazette* and pointed to her front-page headline. "Let's celebrate."

"You'll need to convince me."

Without another word, John took Jill in his arms and kissed her.

Jill trembled as shivers zigzagged up her spine, melting every ounce of resolve and anger.

They both jumped when Annabelle suddenly blazed through the door.

John dropped his arms from around Jill.

"Annabelle?" Jill gulped. She was surprised to see the publisher at this early hour.

Totally ignoring Agent Lovell, Annabelle grabbed the remote and turned on Jill's TV, adjusting the volume twice as high as it should be.

"What's going on?" Jill asked.

Annabelle pointed a sharp red nail at Jill like a weapon. "What's wrong with you, Lewis? Playing spin the bottle on my nickel when a big story's breaking?"

"I already know—the senator's on life support."

"Bet you didn't know his family has already decided to pull the plug."

"That was on TV?"

"No, Dan told me. He said the hospital spokeswoman is going to hold a press conference in about ten minutes."

"Dan called you?" Jill felt her face flush. *So Dan has broken rule number one in record time.*

Annabelle nodded and fanned herself with the Hermes scarf elegantly draped across her shoulders. "Well, hello, Agent Lovell.

I thought you were up in Deviland, ridding Wisconsin of the bad guys."

"That's Delavan," Jill interjected, not about to let Annabelle poke fun of her hometown. "And he's already gotten the bad guys. That case is officially closed."

Annabelle ignored Jill. Her eyes were on John as he ambled over to shake her hand.

"Hello, Annabelle. I was just leaving," he said, grabbing his coat off the back of Jill's chair.

"Don't leave on my account. You're always welcome at my newspaper, Agent Lovell."

"Thank you, but I have a meeting. Good-bye ladies, nice to see you both. Jill, I'll pick you up at seven."

"Wait! You don't know where I live." Jill pulled away and quickly turned to her desk to scribble her address on a piece of paper.

"I'm FBI, remember?"

She smiled and stuffed her address into his pocket just in case.

The moment John left, Rubric stuck his head in the doorway. "So Lover Boy's back in town."

Jill pointed at Rubric. "Eavesdropping outside my door again, I see."

"Oh, stop it. Let's get to work," Annabelle commanded as she clapped her hands together. "All this lovey-dovey stuff is giving me indigestion. Jill, see if you can reach Eric Richter and find out what's going on with Brown. See if he can confirm the Harrison rumors."

"Harrison!" Rubric slammed the morning edition down on Jill's desk.

While Jill made her phone call, Annabelle brought a surprised Rubric up to date on the Harrison rumors.

Eric answered the phone on the first ring.

"It's Jill. I just wanted to call to say how sorry I am, Eric."

"Thanks, Jill." He spoke in a low voice. "I'm waiting outside his room for the family. Several members of the staff want to go inside to spend some final moments with the senator. They'll probably pull the plug in the morning, but he's already gone."

Jill sighed. "How sad. What was the final diagnosis?"

"He suffered a massive stroke. They tried to repair a broken blood vessel in his brain, but there was too much damage done by the time they got in there."

So David was right. Eric had been spinning Brown's good health. "Will you please give my condolences to Senator Brown's family and your staff?"

"I sure will, Jill. Thank you."

"I'm sorry to ask at a time like this, but is there any truth to the Harrison rumors?"

Eric's voice dropped to a whisper. "I've had discussions with several key Democratic leaders. Harrison will definitely be Brown's replacement as Senate minority leader. Until he loses the election, that is."

"What do you think about Senator Harrison?"

"It's no secret he and Brown clashed like gladiators, but the man's brilliant. The Democrats despise him, but they also respect him, and of course the Republicans think he's the greatest Democratic senator who ever lived."

"I'd like to ask a favor, Eric. If you can pull some strings and get me an interview with Harrison, I'd be forever grateful."

Eric was quiet for a moment. "I can't make any promises, but I'll be in close touch with him during the transition. I'll try to put in a good word for you."

"Take care, Eric. Let me know if there's anything I can do."

"Okay, I'll be in touch."

When Jill hung up the phone, she heard Annabelle and Rubric arguing.

"Tommy Harrison's nothing but a Republican disguised in donkey ears."

"Don't get yourself so worked up, Rubric. I hope you took your blood pressure medicine today."

"I'm not crying over George Brown!" Rubric barked. "The man's got the scruples of a rattlesnake."

"For heaven's sake, you two! Show some respect, the man's dying." Jill felt very tired. *Did I once really love this job?*

"Rubric's still holding a grudge over that bogus story Brown gave him once." Annabelle chuckled.

"What bogus story?"

"Brown told Rubric that he'd agreed to be John Kerry's running mate. Rubric published it, and then Kerry named Edwards. Rubric's never forgiven Brown."

Rubric rolled his eyes. "What did Eric Richter say?"

"Brown's replacement's going to be—ta-da—Tommy Harrison."

"But how can the Democrats be so darn sure Harrison will lose his election?" Rubric asked.

"He's running against a Republican, and not just any Republican—Andrew Friedman," Jill said.

"The Atlanta Falcons place kicker? The kid who played for Alabama? The guy who won practically every game with his phenomenal sixty-yard field goals! Ha! The only vote that Harrison will get in the whole state of Alabama is his mother's." Rubric laughed. "Jill, get an interview with Tommy Harrison right away and find out who the man really is and what he thinks about all this."

"I've already made the call."

"Good. I want to know every opinion Harrison wrote as a judge. And every bill he's either supported or vetoed as a senator," Annabelle ordered.

"While you're at it, kid, look for anything questionable in the man's background—booze, drugs, gambling. Go as far back as childhood," Rubric added. "If we're lucky, we'll turn up a few broads in the mix."

Jill frowned.

"Did you hear me, Jill? Dig in the dirt. I want dirt, acres and acres of it," Rubric reiterated.

Just as Jill was about to protest, her phone buzzed.

"It's Senator Morrissey," Landry announced.

"Leave it on speaker phone," Annabelle ordered as she pushed Rubric back into his chair and sat down herself. "Let's all hear what Niall has to say."

Obediently, Jill pressed the button and said, "Senator Morrissey, hi, it's Jill Lewis. How are you?"

"I'm fine, and you? Would some information on Tommy Harrison interest you?"

"If those rumors are true, I'm very interested."

"Oh, they're true all right," the senator assured her.

"I thought so. I heard the Republicans were already popping the champagne bottles."

"When they hear what I'm going to tell you tonight, they'll try to re-cork those bottles. Heck, they'll hold a revival to raise Senator Brown from the dead."

"You've certainly spiked my interest, Senator. How soon can we meet?"

"How about tonight? Can you meet me at the Indian restaurant on Massachusetts Avenue? You're familiar with the Bombay Club?"

Jill felt the energy crackling in the air as her two colleagues salivated along with her for the news. "What time?"

"Seven."

Jill remembered her date with John. When she'd told John she had other plans, she'd been telling a little white lie, but now it was true. It was as though God were encouraging her to dust even the smallest cobwebs from her soul. "Is it possible to meet any earlier?"

"Sorry, but I can't make it any earlier."

"How about breakfast tomorrow?" Jill flipped through the calendar on her desk.

Annabelle waved her arms wildly.

"Senator, please hold on a minute, and I'll see what I can arrange for tonight."

Jill put the phone on hold, but before she could explain, Annabelle yelled at her. "I don't care if you're having dinner with the president! Cancel it."

Jill's stomach lurched. She glared at Annabelle and pressed the phone button. "I can delay my other appointment. Seven's fine."

"Why don't I send a car for you, and my driver can drop you off at your next engagement."

"Great," Jill said and provided her address for the driver.

"Hallelujah!" Annabelle shouted when Jill hung up. "I want a whole series of articles on Harrison, announcing him as the frontrunner to replace Brown in tomorrow's edition. From what Morrissey insinuated on the phone, I think we'll get the scoop on Harrison. Maybe he isn't as conservative as we've been led to believe."

Jill wrinkled her nose. "Even if that's true, why would Morrissey squeal on his own party?"

"Oh, he's probably got the goods on Harrison, and it's much easier for a senator to talk to the press and let us do his dirty work," Rubric reminded Jill.

"Morrissey's never been one to make waves," Annabelle pointed out to Jill.

"And he's always been sympathetic to the Republicans on certain issues too," Rubric added. "Remember, he just doesn't serve labor. He's got a large conservative Catholic constituency in Illinois to please."

Annabelle tapped the crystal on her Cartier tank watch. "I expect that Harrison article on my desk by five o'clock," she said. "After your meeting with Morrissey, call Rube. He'll know where to find me."

Annabelle winked at Jill and sailed out of the office with Rubric, leaving behind the scent of her costly perfume.

4

If you stop to be kind, you must swerve often from your path.

Mary Webb

Millie, Jill's assistant, trotted into her office with a stack of files Jill had ordered. "Harrison's voting records. I'll get to work on his judicial opinions."

"Thanks, Millie."

Jill spun back around to her computer and tapped on her keyboard. She sighed while searching the Internet for any unusual information on Harrison. His name was on literally thousands of sites. Jill began sifting through all the pertinent information.

Half an hour later, Millie stuck her head inside Jill's office and held up some files.

Jill glanced up from her computer. "Any luck?"

"I've got Harrison's judicial opinions for you." Millie walked over and plopped the files high on Jill's desk.

After Millie left, Jill dialed several informants and offered each a generous payment for any forthcoming information on Harrison.

In a moment, Millie popped into Jill's office again, this time her arms weighed down with even more files. "More of Harrison's judicial opinions," she said, stacking them on Jill's credenza.

Jill thanked Millie as she scooted back to her office next door.

Delving deeper into his judicial opinions, Jill found them shocking. As a judge, Harrison's writings were the most liberal she'd ever read. Coupled with his ultraconservative voting records, things didn't compute—who was this man? An imposter who portrayed himself one way and voted another?

As a judge, his sanctions on big businesses were brutal. A staunch environmentalist, he set pollution fines at least five times higher than those other judges imposed. Two of the largest nuclear power plants in the United States were located in Alabama—TVA and the privately owned Farley plant—and Harrison fined them over minor disputes most judges would have ignored. His sentences were lenient, especially where young people were concerned. When it came to the death penalty, Jill couldn't locate a single death sentence imposed.

In stark contrast to his judicial opinions were his congressional voting records. He voted against both military funded abortions and partial birth abortions. His votes on environmental issues were split about fifty-fifty. He recently backed an ultraconservative candidate for the Supreme Court. From his voting record as a senator, Jill discovered that he appeared to have become friendlier with big businesses in sharp contrast to the war he had once waged against them in Alabama as a judge.

Perplexed, Jill dialed Rubric. "This Harrison research is making me crazy." She explained the contrast between the Alabama senator's voting records and his judicial career.

"Which party do you think he's fooling?" Rubric asked.

"Both? He appears to be his own man, but it's too soon for me to make that call."

"Maybe Morrissey will provide the answers for you tonight."

"I hope so. I sure can't figure out this guy. Either he's truly ethical, representing the views of his conservative constituency, or it's all a sinister ploy used by the Democrats to gain the Republicans' trust."

"I believe you've found your story, Jill."

"Temporarily, but eventually I'll have to expose the real Harrison—if I can figure out who that is."

"You will."

More discouraged than ever, Jill hung up the phone. For the tenth time she tried to call Harrison's office to set up an interview with the senator, but like each time before, his assistants told her they were deluged with calls and would be in touch. She'd have to camp outside Harrison's office if she had any hope of catching him. A few brief words with him in the hallway were preferable to the empty promises from his office staff.

The next hour she banged out the salient points from the research material to write an article titled "A Donkey Disguised in Elephant Clothing?" Her next piece on Senator Brown's condition and the prospect of taking him off life support in the morning was somber.

When finished, Jill emailed her articles to Rubric and the copyeditor for corrections. Before she left for the day, she phoned Dan and left him a blistering message on his voice mail: "Don't you ever call Annabelle again, or you're out of here." Noticing she still had a handful of hours left to prepare for her date with John, Jill tried to slip out the door unnoticed. There had to be a dress with her name on it at Sak's, and she was determined to find it. Just as she pressed the elevator button, she heard Landry call to her from the front desk. "Oh, there you are, Jill. I just rang your office."

"What is it now?"

The receptionist pointed her pen at a mousy young woman sitting in the far corner of the lobby, nervously thumbing through a magazine.

"What does she want?" Jill whispered.

"Who knows? But she says it's urgent."

"Why is it always urgent?" she mumbled as she walked over to the young woman. She extended her hand and a fake smile. "Hi, I'm Jill Lewis."

"Oh, Ms. Lewis, it's an honor to meet you." The young woman jumped to her feet, dumping her magazine onto the floor. She vigorously shook Jill's hand throughout the exchange. "I desperately need your help." She bent down to retrieve the latest copy of *The New Yorker* and whispered, "My life's in danger."

"I'm sorry, I didn't get your name," Jill said as she caught a glimpse of Landry's smirk.

"Allison Cooper. Ally."

"Nice to meet you, Ally. Unfortunately, I'm on my way out the door. I'll ask the receptionist to ring my assistant so she can schedule an appointment for you next week."

"But, Ms. Lewis, I can't wait that long!"

Jill shook her head. How many times had she heard this line before? At times, Jill felt like a magnet for all the weirdos in Washington. She spoke firmly. "I'm sorry, but I have an appointment. You'll have to come back another time." Jill turned to walk away.

"Ms. Lewis, I don't think you understand. You've got to help me!" The young woman skirted around her, blocking her exit. "I have no one to turn to and nowhere to go except my apartment, and I'm not safe there. Since I've been in Washington, I've read your columns faithfully. I just know you can help me."

For the first time, Jill took a good look at the girl. She looked familiar. Jill knew she had seen her before, but where?

"Please, Ms. Lewis."

Jill's heart softened at Ally's words. "Come on back to my office, and I'll see what I can do."

Landry made a sucker face at her, but Jill just shrugged as she walked past the receptionist and led the frightened girl down the corridor to her office. "Have a seat," Jill said, pointing toward the sofa. She threw her coat over her chair and tapped her BlackBerry.

Wide-eyed, the young woman whirled around Jill's office. "Wow! Nice office."

"Thanks. I'll tell my mother and sister you said so; they insisted on decorating it for me."

"It's beautiful . . . And this view! I can see the Capitol from here."

Jill tried to size up what type of woman Allison Cooper was. She couldn't be older than twenty-two. Judging from her clothes—a faded gray cotton skirt and a dingy white blouse—the girl was on a meager salary. A simple silver cross dangled from a filigree chain around Allison's neck. The symbol caught Jill's eye and struck a chord in her heart. "Where are you from, Ally?"

"Youngstown, Ohio."

"Ah, the murder capital of the world."

Ally nodded. "People always said Youngstown had a lot of mob-related stuff going on, but I just assumed it was a rumor until they busted the city officials a few years ago."

"What brought you to Washington?"

"One of my instructors at business school mentioned there were tons of high-paying secretarial jobs here. Besides, I'd read somewhere that the men in Washington outnumber the women five to one. Is it true?"

Jill smiled. Ally was beginning to relax. "I'm not sure, Ally. I—"

"Do you have a boyfriend?"

"Let's stick to the matter at hand." Jill turned back to her calendar. "Can you meet me here in the morning at eight?"

"I can't. Tomorrow's my last day on a temp assignment, and tomorrow night I've got to pack. I'm taking the noon train the next day to Youngstown to see my family."

"Looks like your calendar's full. When will you be back in Washington?"

"I don't know if I'll come back at all."

Jill sighed. "Then I suppose I can spare a few minutes now."

She pulled a small tape recorder from her desk drawer and then sat down beside the young woman. "Mind if I use this?"

"That's fine."

"Start from the beginning and tell me why you're afraid."

"Until a couple of weeks ago, I was a file clerk, but then I was accused of misplacing a file. It must have been an important one, because the boss and everyone else in the office freaked out when I couldn't find it."

"They fired you?"

"How did you know?"

"Just a lucky guess."

"It was totally unfair. I didn't lose that file."

"What made them think you took it?"

Ally shrugged.

"You must have some idea. Did your job require a security clearance?"

"Hardly. I was only a lowly file clerk at the Parks Service in the U.S. Fish and Wildlife Department."

"Maybe someone inadvertently returned a classified document to the wrong file room. Have you ever seen a file marked classified or top secret?"

"If I have, I didn't know it."

"You'd know it. The cover sheets are brightly colored, and they're stamped classified or top secret."

"No, this file didn't look like that at all. It had a standard Fish and Wildlife cover sheet."

"So you saw the file?"

"You're not gonna believe this, but right after I was fired I was getting my things together when I spotted the file behind my file cabinet."

"Then why didn't they let you keep your job?"

"Because I never told them I found it."

"Why?"

"I know it was stupid of me, but I was so upset about being

fired, I just wasn't thinking straight. Besides, I wanted to know what the big deal was about that file. But later, when I saw what was in it, I got scared. I figured if I turned it over to them, they'd know I'd looked inside and would still want to get rid of me."

"But hadn't they already fired you?"

"I meant get rid of me, as in 'bang, bang.'"

Jill resisted rolling her eyes. "May I see the file?"

"I didn't have time to stop by and pick up the file after work."

"What was in the file?" Jill asked.

"A lot of stuff about snakes. I want you to look at it, Ms. Lewis."

"I'll be glad to, but if this file wasn't marked classified, it's probably nothing."

"Then how do you explain why they were so upset when the file was lost?"

"I'd guess a supervisor probably asked for the file, and when it wasn't there, he likely complained about the inefficiency of the file room. Somebody usually has to pay, and this time it was you, the file clerk."

"But they're still after me." Ally's voice was quiet but forceful.

"How do you know?"

"There's a car that follows me, always the same one, a green Navigator. I also get lots of hang-up calls. I'm terrified."

Jill didn't know whether to take the girl seriously or not, but she figured she should err on the side of caution. "If you think you're being followed, you should take every precaution. I think you've made a wise decision to go home, at least for a while."

Ally sighed. "I wish I'd never taken that stupid file."

Jill felt unnerved when Ally's gaze settled on her, almost as if she expected Jill to do something. "No one's going to murder you over a missing file."

"Then you don't believe me."

"I believe you, but haven't you blown this a little out of

proportion? I won't know that until I read the file. I do understand your fears, though."

When Ally didn't respond, Jill asked, "What would you like me to do?"

"Could you write something in the *Gazette* about this? That way they won't be able to hurt me because it will be out in the open." She paused. "Unless they make it look like an accident. They do that when it's too obvious to murder you. I've seen it on *Law and Order*."

Her mention of the TV show suddenly made Jill doubt her sincerity. She shut off the tape recorder and grabbed her briefcase. "Come on, Ally. I'll walk out with you." The two women headed toward the lobby. "Before you leave, get the file to me. I'll see if I can sort it all out for you."

"Thank you so much, Ms. Lewis," Ally gushed, the relief evident on her face.

Jill pushed the elevator button a couple of times as though it would bring the car faster. "So where's this file now?"

"At the Trailways Bus Station in a locker. I've watched a lot of crime shows, and I saw that on TV. This guy, he stole a lot of money from this lady, and then he stashed it at the bus station in a locker. That's how I got the idea."

Jill suppressed a giggle. "I'm impressed."

Ally spontaneously hugged her. "Thanks, Ms. Lewis—uh, Jill. I knew I could count on you."

Jill rode the elevator with Ally to the lobby and then headed to the garage to get her car. Soon she was driving toward home in her Range Rover. Jill decided she'd put it off long enough and should call John to inform him of the delay. She dialed his cell phone.

"John here."

"You sound just like Craig Martin." Jill smiled at the memory of John's undercover alias that he used when she first met him at the *Lakes News* in Delavan.

"You're still in love with him, aren't you?"

"True, but I love you too." With John's jovial mood, she felt more at ease. Maybe things were okay between them after all.

"Glad to hear it. Where are you?"

"On my way home."

"Good. I don't want you to be late for our big date."

"Well, that's the reason I'm calling."

"Why am I not surprised?"

"I'm sorry, but I've got to meet Senator Morrissey tonight at seven o'clock. I tried to switch it to breakfast, but Annabelle was in my office when he called and—"

"Jill, slow down, you don't have to explain. We could wait until tomorrow night."

"No way. I've waited two months for this dinner. Besides, the senator is sending a car for me, and his driver can drop me off by eight o'clock. I just need to know where."

"I've made reservations at the Inn at Little Washington, but it's at least an hour and a half drive. We might need to choose another restaurant closer to where you're meeting."

"Our meeting is at the Bombay Club on Connecticut Avenue."

"Then how about Citronelle's? Around eight o'clock."

"Great. See you at eight o'clock." Jill shut off the phone.

The blast from a cabbie's horn drew Jill back to the present. "Sorry!" She waved an apology and jerked the Range Rover back to the side of the street to wait for a spot to jump back into the lane.

As she pulled back onto the road, the blare of a car's horn made her bang on her brakes. At the sound of tires squealing, Jill tightly closed her eyes as she braced for impact. When none came, she opened her eyes and turned her head to see a green Navigator. It was inches away from her. The driver revved his engine, acting as though he was about to come through her at any moment. Seeing a break in the traffic, Jill pressed on the accelerator and floored it.

Hadn't Ally said a green Navigator was following her?

5

*What makes us so afraid is the thing we half see, or half hear, as
in a wood at dusk, when a tree trunk becomes an animal and
a sound becomes a siren. And most of that fear is the fear of not
knowing, of not actually seeing correctly.*

Edna O'Brien

Jill walked into her apartment and picked up the Tiffany clock
beside her overstuffed chair. Only an hour left to get ready.
Could she make it? Of course! She had been in tighter spots
than this in her life.

Inside her closet, she pushed through three six-foot rods
of business and casual clothes, all generously provided by her
mother for fear her daughter might end up naked—or worse
yet, not be attired in the latest designer clothes.

Jill clicked on the TV, intent on hearing the latest news about
the senator's condition as she quickly removed her nail polish
and repainted her nails soft pink. Pink! The hot pink shawl her
mother had sent her from her trip to India would make a nice
accessory. After her nails were dry, she kneeled down to pull
the rumpled shawl from her dresser drawer. "Ouch!" she cried,

grabbing her injured knee. She pulled herself to her feet and tossed the pink wrap over the ironing board.

"Perfect. This is a hot pink kind of night. Thanks, Mom."

Her mother! She'd forgotten to call her to tell her that she was going out with John tonight, the man her mother knew as Craig Martin. Jill ran for her cordless phone and dialed Pearl as she plugged the iron into the outlet with her other hand. Muting the TV, she kept her eyes fixed on the screen, watching for the late-breaking story.

After several rings her mother answered, somewhat distracted. "Uh, this is Pearl."

"Mom, it's me."

"Who?"

"Only two people call you Mom . . . I'm your firstborn. Remember me?"

"Oh, Jill." Her mother heaved a sigh.

"Are you sitting down?" Jill asked as she pressed the wrinkles out of her shawl.

"Not only am I sitting down, but I'm at my bridge table right in the middle of playing a grand slam. I'll call you in the morning, darling."

"But Mom, I've got news."

"What could be better than a grand slam? Your news will just have to wait."

"Wait? But I've waited a couple of months to tell you this."

"Then you can wait a few hours longer. I've got to run, darling. Talk to you later. Bye-bye."

Jill heard the phone click. She frowned at the phone a moment, then quickly dialed her sister, Kathy. Jill had to tell someone that the handsome FBI agent had come back into her life.

Kathy's phone rang and rang, and finally a babysitter picked up and said Kathy and Jeff had left early to drive to Chicago for dinner with a client.

Jill decided not to let her frustration get her down. She finished pressing the shawl and placed it on a hanger and hung it on the back of the door. She turned up the volume on the TV so she'd be sure to hear any breaking news about the senator above the commotion of the shower.

Jill slid into the shower. The drum of the warm water worked magic on her sore muscles. After washing her hair, she turned off the shower and heard the house phone buzz. "Now who on earth could that be?"

She pressed the button on the intercom. "Hello?"

"Good evening, Ms. Lewis. There's a driver to pick you up downstairs. Says you're expecting him. From Morrissey's office," Ralph the doorman announced.

"Well, he's forty-five minutes early. Tell him I'll be down in about twenty—no, make that thirty—minutes."

Jill rushed back to the bathroom, then dried her hair and twirled it into a simple French twist, fastening it with a pearl and rhinestone comb. She picked up the crystal and silver decanter filled with Lady Primrose talc and sprinkled it all over her body before picking up a bottle of perfume.

Jill stepped inside her closet. She looked around and finally pulled out the black dress she'd worn on her special night with her former beau, David. No time for superstition; it was the greatest dress in her closet. Why not?

Wiggling into the dress, Jill slipped on a pair of black heels. She reached up to pull an evening bag off the closet shelf and stuffed a small tape recorder inside for the session with Senator Morrissey. Lastly, she fastened pearl and pink tourmaline earrings on her ears. Jill grabbed her pretty-in-pink shawl on her way out and hurried downstairs to meet the driver.

"Hi, I'm Jill Lewis," she introduced herself. Where did the senator find these goons? Jill figured she'd cast this one in *The Sopranos.*

"And I'm Rock." Extending his massive hand with fat, stubby

fingers, the monster of a man shook Jill's dainty one, crushing her fingers with such force it brought tears to her eyes.

Undaunted by his frightening appearance, Jill scolded him. "I'm sorry I'm late, but you should've called me to tell me you'd be early."

"I didn't mind waiting." He politely opened the car door for Jill. As she took a seat inside the limo, he offered, "Please help yourself to anything you'd like."

"Thank you," Jill replied.

As the limousine pulled away from the curb, Jill kicked off her shoes and scrunched her toes into the soft, thick carpeting. Settling into the backseat, she surveyed the elegant interior of the car. Fresh roses were fastened in a container on the burl wood table. Jill leaned over to sniff them. Sparkling crystal glasses and crystal decanters with silver tags lined the bar. Nice. She poured herself a glass of Perrier and added a twist of lime. Quite comfy now, she flicked on the television to watch the news, but soon her thoughts wandered to John.

Jill had pined over John for months, but he'd ended her misery when he'd shown up at her office, professing his love for her. But then he'd disappeared again. Two months without a word—totally unacceptable, and when she saw him tonight she'd tell him so. Time to slow this spaceship to happily-ever-after and get back down to earth. Jill closed her eyes and rehearsed the lines of the script she'd prepared to deliver to John tonight. But the rehearsal was suddenly canceled by the car's jerky stop.

Catching a quick glimpse out the back window, Jill yelled, "Driver!"

To Jill's dismay, the car turned onto the expressway ramp heading north. Her mind raced. Had she willingly stepped into a trap? *Why didn't I question the driver when he came so early?*

"Driver!" she yelled a second time, this time much louder. When he didn't respond, Jill unfastened her seat belt and quickly scooted up toward the driver.

"Driver! Driver!" she yelled, pounding on the window that separated them. "Where are you taking me?"

The tinted window slowly lowered a couple of inches. "To Senator Morrissey."

"At the Bombay Club on Connecticut Avenue. It's back there." Jill pointed.

"Didn't the senator tell you? There's been a change of plans."

"No, he did not. Stop this car immediately!"

"Ms. Lewis, I have my orders. Call Senator Morrissey. He'll explain."

Jill wasted no time. Frantically she dialed the senator's cell phone. It clicked over to voice mail on the first ring. After leaving a message, she banged on the window again. "I can't reach him. Do you have another number for the senator?"

This time the driver responded by lowering the window halfway.

"Senator Morrissey said he could be reached on his cell phone. Ms. Lewis, I'm going to have to ask you to sit down and fasten your seat belt."

"Oh, all right." Exasperated, Jill complied. After a few minutes she called out to the driver. "Since the senator's phone isn't on, you either tell me where we're going or else let me out of this car."

"Relax, Ms. Lewis. You left a message. I'm sure we'll hear from the senator shortly."

"Shortly isn't soon enough. I'll have to reschedule my meeting with the senator. Did he inform you that I have an urgent appointment following our meeting?"

"He did, and I've been instructed to drive you there too."

"Do you know where Citronelle's is?"

"Of course."

"Then turn this car around and take me there, right now." Her hands began to shake.

"Sorry, Ms. Lewis, but I only take orders from my boss."

By now Jill doubted that this guy even worked for the senator. "I'm going to wait five minutes, and if we haven't heard from the senator, you're going to take me back to the city or else I'm dialing 911."

Looking down through the window, she suddenly caught a glimpse of the chauffeur trying to conceal a steel gray object on the seat beside him.

"Is that a gun?" she yelped. Now she sounded stupid. Of course it was a gun. "Okay, I'm not waiting five minutes—stop this car right now or I'm calling the police!"

"Listen, Ms. Lewis, there's nothing to be scared of. Carrying a gun is part of my job. And I can't just turn around. We're on the expressway."

Jill didn't think the guy looked like someone who was afraid to break a traffic law. "Then pull off at the next exit."

The driver didn't respond, only closed the window separating them.

Just then she heard a phone ringing on the front seat. Banging on the window, Jill yelled for the chauffeur to lower it again. Slowly the window inched down, just enough for Jill to hear the driver say, "This woman gives new meaning to the words *drama queen*. I'll put her on."

Who is he calling a drama queen?

He passed the cell phone to Jill through the window, and she quickly put it to her ear. "Hello?"

"Jill, this is Senator Morrissey. What's wrong?"

"Senator, I'm so relieved to hear your voice." She dropped her voice to a whisper. "Your driver's got a gun."

"Of course he's got a gun; he's one of my bodyguards."

"But where's he taking me? You said we were meeting at the Bombay Club, but we're heading north."

"I'm sorry, I should've called you. My chauffeur is driving you out to my boat at the Annapolis Yacht Club. Didn't he tell you?"

"He said to talk to you."

"Let me explain. Several things have developed since we spoke earlier today, and I'm afraid I can't afford to be seen with you in public. That's why I was forced to arrange this meeting at my yacht."

"Did you forget I have another appointment?"

"I'm sorry, Jill, but it's urgent that we meet tonight. You have my word that my driver will get you to your appointment as soon as we're done. I'll see you within an hour."

"Thank you, Senator." *Great. John will probably have gone home by the time I get there. See ya in another couple of months.*

"Ms. Lewis, are you all right?"

"I'm sorry, Senator. Someone has been following me, and I thought—"

"Well, you're safe with Charles. I'll see you shortly. And Jill, it will be worth your time."

The line went dead.

Jill slipped the phone back through the window to the driver, and he rolled up the glass partition again. *Wait a minute! Charles . . . the driver's name is Charles? He told me his name was Rock!* Jill pounded on the window. "Hello? Hello?"

"Is everything okay?" the driver called to her on the intercom, not bothering to lower the window this time.

"Would you please get the senator back on the line for me?"

A few seconds passed before the driver told her, "His line's busy. Why don't you just sit back and enjoy the scenery?"

"Enjoy the scenery? It's dark outside."

"The lights are pretty," he shot back on the intercom.

All the stress of the day came crashing down on Jill, and she began to do what she should have done long before—pray.

6

*The cream of enjoyment in this life is always impromptu. The
chance walk; the unexpected visit; the unpremeditated journey;
the unsought conversation or acquaintance.*

Fanny Mae Fern

When Rock finally turned the long car into the Annapolis Yacht
Club, Jill sighed, but her relief was short lived. Without warning,
he suddenly swerved the big black limo to the left and then accelerated right past the club, tossing Jill to and fro on the backseat.

"Hey! What do you think you're doing? The yacht club's
back there," Jill said.

Rock kept right on driving toward the marina until coming to a screeching halt in front of a magnificent yacht. From
where Jill sat, she could tell it was one of importance due to the
prominent spot in the harbor. The ship, shrouded with a misty
veil of fog, leisurely swayed with the current. Jill's eyes grew
wide as she studied the ghostly outline of glimmering lights on
the ship's mast.

The limo driver blew the horn loudly.

*What if the senator's not on board the ship? What if the voice
on the cell phone was an imposter? What if they murder me and*

dump my body in the sea? No one will ever know what happened to me.

"Wait here," Rock ordered, stepping out of the car. "Senator Morrissey will be here shortly to take you aboard." The door slammed behind him.

Jill made a quick call to her office and whispered a message on Rubric's voice mail: "I'm at the Annapolis Yacht Club in a limo parked in front of a yacht supposedly belonging to Senator Morrissey, but if anything happens to me, I was driven here by a large thug with dark hair and a big hairy mole on his face, who calls himself Rock, a.k.a., Charles."

Clicking off her phone, Jill was relieved to see the senator's form sprinting from the boat toward the car. She felt silly that she had gotten so worked up over nothing.

Jill looked up and noticed the senator carried a package in his arms. Files? As the form drew closer to the car, the driver rushed over to open Jill's door.

A jittery Jill stepped out and saw the roses in his arms. *Why is the senator bringing me roses? Obviously, he's going to ask a very special favor of me.*

Jill made out the man's face in the shadows—it wasn't the senator at all! There stood John, looking striking in a dark suit. He made her heart flutter, he was so handsome.

"John! What are you doing here?"

"Don't look so disappointed."

"No, I just thought—where is Senator Morrissey?" she asked, glancing around.

"Probably sitting down to dinner with his wife at the Bombay Club."

"What's going on?"

He kissed Jill instead of answering.

She pushed him away and wagged her finger at him. "You've got a lot of explaining to do, mister."

John grinned and held the roses out to her like a little boy who'd picked his first bouquet. "There's nothing to explain. I wanted to surprise you, and that's not easy to do when your girlfriend's the top investigative reporter in the country."

"Well, you did it." Intoxicated by the scent of the roses, Jill said, "They're beautiful."

She passed the roses and then her hand to John, who led her across the parking lot toward the boat.

"Wow! That's some dress."

Jill spun around so he'd get the full effect. The fishtail skirt of her black silk chiffon dress lapped at her long, shapely legs as she swung her hot pink shawl around John's neck, pulling him close to her. "You like it?"

"My heart rate just climbed over two hundred."

"We're almost even. Mine hit five hundred in that car. I was convinced I'd been abducted." Jill lightly pounded his chest with her fist.

John pulled away. "Come on." He curled his fingers around hers and lifted her hand, kissing her fingertips.

The limo driver smiled and waved good-bye as he got back into the limo.

"Who's the limo driver—an actor?"

"A friend from the bureau, Charles Rock."

"Oh, dear. After that little performance of mine in the car, he probably thinks you're with a crazy person."

"No way. He knew the plan. I also warned him you were a drama queen and that you'd probably try to jump out of the car."

"Drama queen?"

"Uh-huh. Spielberg's still crying that he didn't discover you first."

Jill scrunched her nose. "Well, your little plan worked. What could be more romantic than dinner on a yacht? Is the boat yours?"

"On my salary? It belongs to my boss, Bill Tucker. When I

told him my plans for tonight, he insisted his wife, Lynda, make all the arrangements for the yacht club to cater our dinner on the boat."

"Amazing."

"It gets better. Bill also arranged for one of the sailors at the club to captain so I can give you my undivided attention."

Just as John led Jill up the ramp, she heard their song "Here and Now" playing softly in the background.

"Our song? You remembered that snowy night in your cabin?"

"Of course I remembered. It was the song playing on the radio the first time we danced."

Jill smiled in sweet recollection. "The memory of that moment has played over and over . . . Sometimes I thought we'd never be together again."

"There were times I had my doubts too. But here we are."

"I guess nothing is impossible for God . . . even a romance as complicated as ours," Jill said, ditching the script she'd prepared.

She kicked off her heels before stepping onto the polished wood floor of the yacht. Shoes in hand, she stepped onto the deck with John and gasped. Aglow with hundreds of candles, the boat sparkled like a jewel as it rocked to and fro on the black velvet landscape of the sea.

A waiter appeared out of nowhere with two glasses of champagne poised on a gleaming silver tray. John gave a stem to Jill and kept one. "To us." They clinked their glasses and then sipped the champagne while John gave her a tour of the boat.

Peering through the glass of the cabin, Jill admired the tall flickering tapers in the ornate silver candlesticks and more of her favorite roses centered on the table that was exquisitely set for two with the finest silver and china laid upon crisp white linens.

John gave the captain orders to take the boat out into the moonlit bay. Without waiting for consent, he took her glass and set it with his on a nearby table, and spun her around the deck.

"I didn't think you liked to dance."

"There's a lot you don't know about me."

"And I want to know everything," she replied in a true reporter fashion. "Like your favorite food, what you liked to do as a little boy, who was your best friend, and—"

John put his finger to Jill's lips. Under the moon and the stars, they danced to the rhythm of the boat rocking upon the water, until the waiter announced dinner was served.

Inside the cabin, Jill and John reminisced about their quirky courtship as the feast commenced with carrot soup, followed by a tricolor salad with fried goat cheese medallions and pine nuts. Next, the waiter brought them delicate china plates of sumptuous roast duck à l'orange on a bed of wild rice served with crisp julienne vegetables and sweet potato puree in orange cups.

Talk came easily to them as they crunched French bread smothered in herb butter and tasted the fine wine. Dessert was best of all—chocolate mousse served with steaming hazelnut cappuccino.

"Mmm," Jill mumbled between mouthfuls of decadent chocolate.

"Enjoy it while it lasts. After tonight, we'll be eating hot dogs until my next paycheck."

"A hot dog eaten with you would taste like chateaubriand."

John reached over and pulled the mother-of-pearl comb out of Jill's hair. Her blonde hair cascaded down her shoulders. "I've been waiting to do that all night," John confessed as he led Jill out under the moon and the stars on the top deck, where the music played softly in the background.

He took her hand in his. "Will you marry me, Jill?"

The steel in her veins dissolved into mush as she looked into his eyes and saw his deep love for her reflected there. She wanted to shout the "Hallelujah Chorus," but she couldn't find her voice. She simply whispered, "Yes."

On cue, John pulled out of his pocket a perfectly square blue box tied with a white satin ribbon. He flipped the top of the ring box open, waiting for her reaction.

Jill gasped at the large emerald ring that lay nestled inside. The ring, a bit ostentatious, was certainly not what she would've chosen.

"Do you like it?" John asked.

Seeing his earnest face, Jill had only one answer. "I love it." She pushed the ring past her knuckle and exclaimed, "It's beautiful . . . and it's . . . oh my, is it plastic?" She began to laugh.

"After emptying two dozen boxes of Cracker Jack, I found out the hard way they don't put rings in them anymore."

"Then where'd you find it?"

"The party favors section at the corner drugstore. It came in a package of six, so don't worry if you lose it. I have five more of them at my hotel. You'll get your real ring this weekend."

"Oh, John, I'll cherish this ring forever."

"I'm not sure it will last forever, but I'm glad you like it. There's a real emerald ring waiting for you in Chicago. But don't be disappointed, I must warn you it's a lot smaller than this one."

"Whew, that's a relief." Jill pretended to struggle to hold up her ring finger.

"You won't to have to struggle for long. I've bought two airline tickets to Chicago so we can pick up my father and drive to Delavan this weekend to announce our engagement to your family and give you your real ring."

"This weekend! I can't wait to see my mother's face."

"Would you mind if we kept this a secret until we tell our families?"

"I'll . . . I'll try, but I can't make any promises." Jill shut her eyes. "I'm not dreaming, am I, John?"

7

An engaged woman is always more agreeable than a disengaged.
She is satisfied with herself. Her cares are over, and she feels that
she may exert all her powers of pleasing without suspicion.

Jane Austen

A few hours later, music blared from the clock radio beside Jill's bed. "Five o'clock already?" Rubbing her eyes, Jill suddenly recalled the night before. Was it a dream? Afraid to look for the evidence, she kept her left hand buried under the covers and touched the back of her ring finger. It was there! It was true—John had proposed.

She glided into the kitchen for raspberry tea and schlepped her teacup in her right hand with a devotional book tucked under her other arm. She settled in her overstuffed chair, warmed by the sunrays from the nearby window. For the next half hour she enjoyed her quiet time. Following the devotional, Jill changed into her jogging clothes, and she was off to the park.

Within moments her feet were pounding the trails. The air was crisp, and the jogging path was deserted. Jill ran alone at a fast clip until, seemingly from nowhere, she heard the quick steps of another jogger pounding the pavement behind her, keeping perfect time. She increased her speed, but much to her dismay, her pursuer sped up too.

Slowing down, she heard the jogger behind her slow as well. His breaths were deep and long. Who was following her? Not Crew Cut again? She formed a fist and considered turning around to deliver it into someone's face. Instead, Jill picked up her pace down the winding path, praying she wouldn't start hyperventilating. The damp air pierced her throat, making it burn.

Crossing the trail to the other side, she hoped to run into another jogger, but the path was empty. Footsteps still followed. *Do not panic*, she told herself. She knew that she needed to slow her heart rate down so her reaction time would be maximized. Under her breath she counted the beats as sweat bubbled on her brow and rolled down into her eyes.

Her mind began to clip off stories of joggers attacked in city parks. Hadn't a young intern been murdered here a couple of years ago? It had taken the authorities a long time to discover her body. Passing through a clump of trees, she shivered. Up ahead, the trail split, so she went one direction and then quickly switched to the other side—right into the overgrown bushes.

"Slow down, speedy, I'm losing you," a male voice called out to her.

Jill stopped and listened. She propped up against a tree to catch her breath. The familiar voice brought a smile to her face.

"John, you scared the heck out of me!" she wheezed in between breaths.

"And you put me through an unbelievable obstacle course. I don't know when I've had such a good workout." John held his side.

"I thought I was running for my life." The sun shone brilliantly through the trees, splintering rays of diamonds across John's face. "How'd you find me?"

"I was less than a block away with coffee to take to my fiancée when I spotted her running from her building."

"A likely story."

"It's the truth."

"Then where is it?"

"Splattered across the sidewalk a few miles back."

"Oh no. Hey, what are you doing here, anyway? I thought you had a meeting on the yacht this morning with your boss, Bill Tucker?"

"It was postponed, along with my . . . promotion."

"Promotion? John, that's wonderful! Why didn't you tell me?" She patted him on the back.

"I wanted to wait until it was official."

"You're going to be the bureau chief before you know it!" She threw her arms around his neck.

Hands clasped, the couple crossed the street, heading toward the corner Starbucks. Jill dug a twenty out of her pocket and announced, "My treat."

"That's a good thing, since I spent all my cash on the coffee on the sidewalk. Hey, how about buying me a newspaper too? I'd like to see exactly what you've been up to lately."

Jill dropped some quarters into the newsstand and handed him the morning edition. "Ta da! See my headline." Her smile slid into sadness. "They're pulling the plug on Brown's life support this morning."

"That's too bad. Great reporting, though." He smiled at her. "Now speaking of reporting . . . How many people have you told about our engagement so far?"

"You don't trust me?"

"Let's just say I know you too well," he teased, twisting a lock of her blonde hair around his forefinger. "Hey, want to see my townhouse in Alexandria? As soon as we get back from Delavan, I'll give you the nickel tour. Then you can help me decide if we want to live there or if we should buy a new place together."

"I'd love to see your townhouse. How about tonight?"

"Jill . . . I'm sorry, not tonight."

"Then, how about a quiet evening at my place? I've taken a few cooking classes, so you don't have to worry that I'll poison you."

"I'm afraid I'll be dining in the friendly skies on the afternoon flight to Miami, but I'll be back in time for us to fly out next weekend."

"Next weekend? I thought you said this weekend."

John took her hand and kissed her fingertips. "I did, but I'm not going to make it back. Next weekend will be here before we know it, and we'll take a long weekend in Delavan to celebrate. Oh, this news should cheer you up. Guess who's coming with my dad when he picks us up at O'Hare?"

A smile pulled at the corners of her mouth. "Gracie? So that's where our dog is."

"Oh, so she's our dog now?"

"Now that we're engaged"—Jill pointed to her ring and reminded him—"what's yours is mine and what's mine is yours . . . or however it goes."

"Gracie was yours first, and she'll always be yours, but I have to admit I've become attached to that dog. I can't wait to get her back."

"Why don't you make arrangements to fly her back with us from Chicago next weekend?"

"I'll be away too much the next few months. My dad's around a lot, and it's better for Gracie to be with him."

"Bring Gracie back anyway, and I'll keep her for you. She'd be great company for me. And while you're at it, why don't you make plans for us to elope?" Jill teased half seriously and tossed her empty coffee cup in the trash bin at the corner.

"Elope and forfeit Miss Cornelia's wedding write-up in the *Lakes News*? I don't think so. I thought we could discuss the wedding plans and choose a date with our families next weekend."

"When would you like to get married?"

"If it were up to me, I'd wake the justice of the peace and marry you this morning before I leave for Florida." John took her hand again and held on to it. "How about you, Jill? What kind of wedding do you want? Do you like big weddings? Small weddings?"

"Personally, I think big weddings are a waste of time and money, but my mother . . ."

"Say no more."

"A real wedding in a church surrounded by family and friends is one very special gift I can give my mother. It's the least I can do, if you're okay with it. She believes being the mother of the bride is one of motherhood's greatest perks. I don't want to disappoint . . . within reason."

"Whatever you and your mother decide is fine with me . . . as long as I'm invited."

"It would be just like my mother to leave the groom out of the wedding." Jill laughed. "Do you have any other requests?"

"I'd like to get married in a church with all my family, and I definitely want you to be my bride. Other than that, let your mother have her fun."

"You're going to be sorry you said that."

He laughed and squeezed her hand.

Jill asked, "Hey, what's going on down in Florida, anyway?"

"Nosy Nellie."

"That's how I make my living . . . remember?"

"Jill, you know I can't tell you. You're going to have to learn to live with that."

"That's not going to be easy for me. You know I'm naturally curious."

"You'll get used to it."

"Please tell me you'll be safe?"

He sighed. "Remember, I'll always come back to you . . . eventually. In the meantime, when we're apart, you can pray for me."

"You can count on it."

An hour later a professionally dressed Jill sailed through the doors of her office. "Morning, Landry."

Landry paused to swallow a bite of bagel. The ever so prim and proper receptionist erased a cream cheese mustache with her napkin and looked up at Jill. "Good morning, Jill. Rubric is asking for you. He says it's urgent and that you should see him right away."

"Rubric always says it's urgent."

Landry rolled her eyes. "Well, you could keep him waiting if you'd like to tell me about that cute guy who was in here the other day. Who is he?"

"An FBI agent," Jill said, longing to show Landry her funny little plastic ring. She slipped her left hand into her pocket.

"How did you meet him?"

"We worked together on an investigation." Jill propped her hand on her hip.

"Well, I'm happy for you, Jill. And you don't have those little worry lines between your eyes anymore. Is it Botox or is it love?"

"Ha-ha. Very funny." Jill turned to go find Rubric.

"Oh, Jill, before you go, your mother's called at least ten times this morning."

"Did you put her through to my voice mail?"

"I tried, but your mother said she doesn't like to talk to machines. You need to get her into the twenty-first century, Jill."

"That's a scary thought."

"She did say it was urgent that she speak to you. You'd better call her."

Jill hurried down to her office. She put her purse and laptop on her desk and was about to dial her mother when Landry buzzed her. "Surprise, surprise! Mrs. Pearl Lewis is on the line for you."

"Okay, put her through."

Jill heard her mother's voice on the line.

"Darling! Where were you? I've tried your cell phone all morning, but I got your voice mail again and again. I'm dying to hear your news."

"You weren't dying to hear it last night. Did you make your grand slam?"

"Not only did I make it, but can you believe Eleanor had the audacity to double me? It was so exciting. But I'm sorry I was unable to talk to you, darling. I couldn't sleep all night wondering what you had to tell me. Now, what's the big news?"

"Get my room ready. I'm coming home a week from Friday, and I'm bringing someone very special with me for you to meet."

"Oh? Who?" Pearl tried to sound nonchalant, but Jill picked up on her mother's excitement.

Perhaps she'd tantalize her mother with a tidbit of information. "I think I may have finally met Mr. Right. His name is John Lovell."

"I don't believe I've ever heard you mention this young man before."

"You're right; I've never mentioned this name before."

"Well, I can't wait to meet him."

"If you're free next Saturday night, John wants to take our entire family out to dinner."

"I have no plans that I can't squirm out of, especially for an event as special as this. I'll call Kathy and Jeff to make sure they're available. But isn't this a little sudden, Jill? After all, not long ago you were pining over that darling Craig Martin. Do you ever hear from him?"

Jill chuckled. "It's as if Craig Martin never existed."

"Please don't do anything rash, darling. Just remember that you're on the rebound. You should proceed with caution."

"Mother, aren't you the one always saying I'm at that age where I can't afford to be so finicky?"

"Ah, did I say that? Well, I shouldn't have."

"No, you were exactly right, Mom. I was way too picky." Jill struggled to squelch her giggles.

"What does he do? Has he been married before? Does he have children? Where's he from? Who's his family?"

"Slow down. You can ask him all those questions on Saturday."

"You can tell me a little bit, can't you?"

"Let's see. John's a government employee, and he's never been married, but I haven't met his family yet."

"Hmm." Pearl hesitated. "This is marvelous news. Although I'm not sure if a government employee will be ambitious enough for you. But I won't draw any conclusions until I meet him."

"That's generous of you, Mother."

"Why don't I have the dinner right here? After all, our home is far nicer than any restaurant. I'll hire a caterer. Hmm, I wonder if your grandmother Muv would fly up for the party? I don't see why not. And maybe I could hire a string quartet for some music."

"Whoa! We don't want to run this one off, do we?"

"Don't be ridiculous. You want to impress him, don't you?"

"Absolutely not."

"But, I—"

"Remember your advice, Mom? Men are hunters, and they don't like to be pursued. Let's play it cool, okay?" Jill suggested, remembering visits of boyfriends from her past. On the other side of the phone, Jill could hear the buffet drawers being opened and closed. In her mind's eye, she imagined her mother with the phone tucked up under her ear, examining her finest Irish linens.

Pearl was silent for a few moments before Jill heard the buffet drawer being slammed shut. "Very well. I'm so glad you're coming home, darling. At least let me get one of the guest rooms ready for your boyfriend."

"Don't worry, Mom, it's all arranged."

"Very well. What time should I expect you to arrive next Friday?"

"Probably late Friday night, but we won't leave until Monday."

"Splendid. Then the two of you will go to church with me on Sunday. Oh, I hope he's a Christian?"

"Yes, he is. Don't worry, Mother. I'll see you next Friday. Love you."

It was hard for Jill to get her mind back on her work after that phone call. She could hardly wait for the weekend, but if she wanted to keep her job she was going to have to concentrate on Senator Harrison. Jill began paging through the mounds of research Millie had left for her. Before she got too heavily involved in it, she decided to walk over to Rubric's office to check in to see what he considered so urgent. She picked up a stack of the Harrison research to carry along to read in case Rubric was on his phone, which he often was.

Jill paused just long enough to snatch a couple of bagels from the office's kitchenette before poking her head into his open doorway. Her mentor sat in his leather swivel chair with his feet propped up, as though it were his throne. He looked up and motioned Jill in. While he finished his phone call, Jill rummaged through the jumbled office for a place to sit. There was none.

"Why didn't you call me after you met with Morrissey last night?" Rubric questioned, slamming the phone down.

"Because I didn't have any news for you." Jill juggled her files as she plopped a cinnamon and raisin bagel slathered in cream cheese in front of him.

"Nothing?"

"It's not good . . . at least for you, but definitely good for me. Can you believe my fiancé put Senator Morrissey up to calling me with the bogus information so he could surprise me?"

"Were you?"

"Stunned."

"Annabelle and I knew. John called and asked us to make sure you got to that Morrissey meeting."

"And neither of you told me? Thanks a lot, Rubric."

"A big investigative reporter like you, and you didn't suspect a thing." Rubric laughed. "Ha! I've got a good feeling about this John Lovell. He's the first person I've ever known who could pull off a surprise where you're concerned. Come on, let me see that big rock on your finger."

Jill held up her hand and then burst out laughing at the expression on Rubric's face. "Got you this time."

"Since when do they put such nice rings in Cracker Jack boxes?"

"They don't. John found it at the drugstore."

"Hey, big spender."

"Stop it, Rube. I'll get my real ring next weekend. Which reminds me. I'll need some vacation days, next Friday and Monday morning."

"Fine with me, as long as you keep your cell phone hot."

Jill set her files on his desk then moved a stack of papers out of Rubric's worn green chair, dumping them on the leaning piles on the sofa. She spread a newspaper out on the seat of the soiled chair and sat down. "Now tell me what's so urgent this morning."

"What's going on with the Harrison story? I need something to placate Annabelle."

"Since Morrissey didn't have any information, that was a setback, but I hope to find something in the mounds of research Millie has piled up on my desk, or at least to hear from one of my informants." Jill pulled her pile of research back down into her lap.

"There's something about Harrison that just doesn't set well with me," Rubric said.

"What do you mean?"

"I get so tired of seeing his mug all over the place. He's a media hog, and he hangs out with all those Hollywood types. Surely there's some Democrat who despises him that will spill his guts. What have you found so far?"

Jill nibbled on her bagel between citing some of Senator Harrison's judicial opinions she'd highlighted. "Decidedly liberal, but his voting record reveals that Harrison represents the conservative views of the people in the State of Alabama, not his own."

"I've read Harrison's bio. Pretty impressive. Alabama born, honor graduate, a highly decorated stint in the navy, second in his class, and the law review at Harvard. But what do we know about his personal life?"

Jill pointed at the research in her lap. "It says here that Harrison married a debutante, Catherine Delaney Hadley, the daughter of a wealthy Alabama businessman from Montgomery."

"Now I smell a story. What about his family? Were they rich too?"

"Southern aristocracy, but the money's all gone." Jill read aloud another article to Rubric. "'Harrison and his wife, Catherine, returned to his hometown, Roanoke, Alabama, to take care of his ailing mother, Elizabeth, and the Harrison family home, both deteriorated by years of his late father's neglect and drunkenness.'"

"Didn't I tell you I smelled a money marriage?"

"You may be right. Listen to this: 'With Catherine Harrison's money and exquisite taste, the senator's ancestral home and his mother's health were lovingly restored to their original splendor.'" Jill held up a picture of the palatial antebellum home for Rubric to see.

"Here, here! The question is—is the senator happily married?"

"It says here, 'By all accounts from friends and family members, the Harrison marriage was happy and produced a son and daughter.'"

"Was?"

"Wait a minute," Jill said, thumbing through the paperwork. "I must have missed something. There's nothing here that tells what became of Catherine Harrison."

"Let's ask Annabelle, she'll know." Rubric buzzed the publisher.

"Hello," Annabelle's voice trilled over the speakerphone.

"Hey, what happened to Senator Harrison's first wife?"

"Mmm, she died so long ago that Harrison rarely mentions her. I seem to recall one of my friends told me it was pretty gruesome, something like a car accident."

"Did he ever remarry?" Jill asked.

"No, but who could ever replace Catherine? She had beauty and brains, all wrapped up in a big bow of Southern charm."

"You knew the Harrisons?" Rubric asked.

"Catherine Hadley and I both made our debuts at the International Ball, but we lost touch after that. So until a few years ago, I never knew she married Tommy. At one of my parties, he picked up a silver frame and pointed out his late wife in my old debutante photo."

"That must have made him sad," Jill mused.

"No, we had a good laugh over it when I told him about Catherine's bet."

Rubric's ears perked up, and he leaned in closer to the speakerphone. "Bet?"

"At the deb parties that summer, Catherine spoke of nothing but the heartthrob she'd left behind in Alabama and . . ."

"So what, don't all girls talk about their boyfriends all the time?" Rubric said.

"Not when they're dancing with handsome men who had titles of prince and baron before their names. Even so, Catherine bet us all one hundred dollars that Tommy would be more famous than any of our dancing partners."

"That must have cost her a bundle," Rubric quipped.

"What?" Annabelle's voice grew loud and animated. "Tommy's not only the most eligible bachelor in the country, but he's also a senator. And I might add, richer than Trump. Catherine didn't lose; she won her bet. Oh, there's another line. Ciao."

Rubric grinned as he clicked off the speakerphone. "Too bad you just got engaged, Jillie."

Jill raised an eyebrow. "Daddy always said, 'Marry a rich man and you'll earn every penny.' And what do I need with more money?"

"Mmm, never heard that one before. But Tommy . . . he's got the power too. Wouldn't you like to be the wife of a rich and powerful senator?"

"I'd rather be one myself, thank you."

"Don't get any ideas. And keep me posted on this case."

Jill said good-bye to Rubric and returned to her office to check her voice mail. There were three messages. Before she could put the phone back in its cradle, she heard Landry's voice over her intercom.

"Guess who's on the phone?"

"John?" Maybe his plans changed, and he was calling to tell her they'd have dinner tonight after all.

"Nancy Drew."

Jill groaned and picked up her phone. "Hello, Ally."

"Jill, I have to see you right away."

Jill scanned her calendar. "Can you be here in half an hour?"

"I can't be seen there."

"What do you mean?"

"I'm in a hurry. I'll explain when I see you. Can you meet me at the McMillan Reserve in Rock Creek Park in half an hour?"

"Ally, I have a deadline. I can't go traipsing off on a whim."

"This is no whim. My life is in danger!"

"Okay. Okay. I'll meet you at the benches near the play area at the southeast end of the park in half an hour."

"Just hurry. My train leaves at noon."

Jill put down the phone. This nonsense in her life right now was unwelcome, but she was obligated to follow this through in case Ally really did have some pertinent information.

It was a perfect day and everyone was out, so finding an empty cab was a challenge. Time ticked away as she waited in the taxi line, so she hopped a bus. It was crowded with tourists and city dwellers. Finding a seat on the aisle, she soon found it enjoyable watching people.

At her stop, she disembarked and crossed the street. Finding the park was easy. Finding the right bench was more difficult. They were all filled with mothers keeping an eye on children at play. But the farthest reach of the park was empty.

"Hi, Jill," Ally called out. The girl was wearing a black warm-up suit with grimy running shoes. Her hair was slicked back in a ponytail that accentuated the dark rings around her eyes. She was pulling a huge suitcase.

"Ally, are you okay?" Jill patted the girl's shoulder.

"No, I'm not."

"I see you're packed and ready to go."

"I've got to get out of Washington before they . . ." She dropped her face in her hands and began to sob.

Jill tried to comfort the girl and pulled a tissue from her purse. Ally took it and blew her nose.

After she regained her composure, Ally continued. "Last night, after I was at your office, I got another anonymous phone call, and this time it's not just the file they want—they want me."

"Take a deep breath and get your thoughts together. What did the caller say?"

"He threatened me. He said they'd murdered the senator, and if I didn't hand over that file, I'd be next."

Jill did her best to bite back her exasperation. "Senator Brown wasn't murdered, he died of a stroke."

"Yes, he was too murdered. The man who called me last night distinctly said, 'We've murdered the senator, and you're next.'"

"Whoa. Let's back up here. You got a phone call from some-one you refer to as 'they.' First, who are 'they,' and second, why would 'they' call you?" Jill rubbed her forehead, feeling a head-ache coming on.

"If I knew their names, I'd go to the police. I told you, they called me to get their file back. Now that they know we've talked, you're in danger too."

"Don't be ridiculous. These people have no idea I'm looking into this matter."

"Oh, they know."

"What makes you think that?"

"Because the man on the phone last night said, 'Not even Jill Lewis can help you.' They knew I went to see you yesterday."

If Ally was telling the truth, then Jill had reason to be concerned. But she just wasn't convinced of Ally's sincerity.

"When the voice on the phone told me that they had murdered the senator, I suddenly remembered that George Brown was one of the senators mentioned in the file."

"You're just remembering that now? A tad convenient, don't you think, since his name has been all over the newspapers the past few days?"

"You don't believe me."

"I didn't say that. But who would want to kill Senator Brown? I mean, the man had his enemies, but they were all politically motivated, none life threatening."

Ally stopped talking and dug inside her purse. "Look, I don't want to do this anymore." Finally, she pulled out the key and held it up in the air. "Here's the key to the locker where I stashed the file. I've written the number down for you on this piece of paper. This has the number on it along with the numbers where you can reach me in Youngstown. Maybe the answer is in the file." The young woman plopped the key into Jill's right hand and stuffed the paper into her left one. "Read the file for yourself. I'm washing my hands of this whole stinking mess. I'm outta here and on the nooner to Youngstown." She jumped up to leave.

"Wait, which Trailways Bus Station?"

"First and L Street. It's all written on the paper. By the way, I'd like to give you the key to my apartment too. I know we've just met, but I might need your help if I decide to stay in Youngstown. Would you mind emptying out my apartment and sending my things to me?"

Jill hesitated and mumbled under her breath, "Now I'm your best friend?"

Ally dug in her purse for her apartment key.

"I'll need your apartment address too."

"It's already on the paper."

Jill held up her hands. "Don't you have a friend who could do this for you?"

"It's not that much. I just had time to pack a few clothes is all."

"Oh, all right, give it to me. There's an intern at the office who can take care of it."

Ally smiled nervously. She handed Jill the second key.

The women stood to their feet. Jill gave Ally a quick hug. "Call me when you arrive in Youngstown. Have a safe trip."

"Thanks. You be careful too," Ally said, picking up her suitcase and dragging it toward the street.

Jill waited with Ally a moment for her bus to arrive. As Ally wrestled her suitcase up the bus steps, Jill remembered something the girl had said the day before.

"What did you say the make of the car was, the one that's been following you?"

"A Navigator, a green SUV."

Jill's heart flip-flopped. Was it a coincidence that the car that had almost pushed her off the road the day before fit the description? Except that it had turned out to be a red Honda. *Don't get paranoid on me, Jill.* She hailed a cab and hopped inside, looking back to make sure she wasn't being followed.

Back at the office, Jill debated whether or not she should discuss Ally Cooper with Rubric. He'd think she'd lost her mind if she mentioned Ally's suspicions that Senator Brown was murdered. Nah, she'd get the file first, maybe send a runner over to the bus station to pick it up later today. At the moment, she had to get organized to write another front-page article on Brown and the exposé on Harrison.

As an afterthought, she picked up the phone and called Dan Peek. In case the file contained some incriminating information, she'd feel more comfortable with the intern retrieving it.

"Are you available to run an errand for me?"

"So you aren't mad at me anymore? After that message you left I thought—"

"Just get down here."

"See you in five."

Jill slipped the key out of her pocket and held it tightly in her hand.

"Hey," Dan said as he appeared at her door.

Jill frowned. "Hey, yourself. Good job on the Brown investigation. But remember, you're supposed to call me first, not Annabelle."

"Will do."

"You're a stringer; I'm the one who's supposed to relay the news to the publisher."

"Sorry, Jill. Thanks for the second chance. How can I make it up to you?"

"Following orders might be a good start."

"Okay. I just want to prove myself. I want to fit in here. Did Rubric tell you he's offered me a job after graduation?"

"He did. In the meantime, how'd you like to do a little job for me?"

His face lit up. "Of course!"

"Good. Your mission is to fetch something for me. Here's a key." Jill handed it to him and scribbled the locker number and the address on a piece of paper. "Run over to the Trailways Bus Station at First and L Street and bring the contents of this locker back to me."

"What's in there—a dead body?"

She rolled her eyes. "Don't be so dramatic, Dan. It's only a file."

"I'm on my way out to class, but if you need it today, I'll get it after my classes are done."

For a moment Jill hesitated, then said, "Tomorrow's fine. I've got plenty of work to keep me busy today."

"You've got my word. You'll have that file on your desk by seven o'clock sharp."

"Great. If I'm not in, put it in the top right-hand drawer of my desk."

"You got it."

"Thanks, Dan. And if you follow my orders, the next time I might even give you an undercover assignment."

The young redhead smiled at Jill and saluted her before he ambled out the door.

As Jill sat down at her computer, an uneasy feeling settled over her. Maybe she should go herself to retrieve the file. No, it'd remain safe inside the locker, and she'd have it soon enough delivered by Dan Peek's capable hands. Surely he wouldn't mess up a third time.

Jill tried to put those thoughts from her mind so she could finish her article on Senator Brown. When it finally came together, she emailed it to her copyeditor.

A short while later, Rubric stuck his head into Jill's office. "Did you make the deadline?"

"Have I ever missed one?"

"No."

"Then that's your answer."

Jill picked up her coat and briefcase and walked out of her office with Rubric.

"Anything on Harrison yet?" Rubric asked as the two of them boarded the elevator for the parking garage.

"I'm working on it."

"What about the girl who dropped by yesterday? What kind of story was she proposing?" Rubric asked as he walked Jill to her car.

"I'll know by tomorrow morning," Jill assured him as she unlocked her car door.

"Do you think there's a story there?"

"Maybe. If it's true, it could be pretty sensational." Jill hopped up into her Range Rover, and Rubric closed the door. She opened her window.

Rubric stuck his head partially inside her window. "Then it's probably a fake."

Jill was halfway wishing she'd gotten her hands on that file today. Maybe she should rendezvous with Dan and get the key so she could read through the file tonight? Nah, she was too tired, and Georgetown was too far. "Good night, Rubric."

"Sweet dreams, Jillie," Rubric said as he walked away. "But if you don't dream up an article about Harrison, you might be writing obituaries—again!"

A few blocks away, she stopped at the Firehook Bakery and Coffee House to pick up a key lime tart for her Bible study. Tonight the group was meeting at the home of a friend to begin a new study.

Jill chastised herself for not getting her hands on Ally's file so she could review it tonight. Perhaps she should drop off the pie and skip the Bible study. She could meet Dan to pick up the key. For a moment, Jill struggled with temptation. But then she remembered her commitment to this Bible study. Successfully resisting her greatest sin, workaholism, Jill parked her car. Ally's file would have to wait until tomorrow morning.

It was after the eleven o'clock news when Jill got home, so she went to bed right away. Tomorrow was going to be a big day, and she wanted to be at her optimum.

But Jill's morning didn't go by as smoothly as she hoped. Instead of driving, she hopped on the metro to save time. Dan had promised to deliver Ally's file by seven o'clock, and it was already seven thirty as Jill hurried past the newsstand in the lobby.

Her friend Helen, who ran the newsstand, stuck her head out the door.

"Whoa! What's the hurry? If you don't slow down you're going to slip on this marble in those high heels."

Jill paused to hug Helen. "John's back! But I've got deadlines, so the details will have to wait."

"Didn't I tell you he'd come back?"

"You did, and I'll tell you all about it at our breakfast," Jill promised as she dashed to the elevator.

"John's return calls for a celebration! Let's have Krispy Kremes with our breakfast too. My treat," Helen called out after Jill before the elevator doors slammed shut.

"Good morning, Landry. Hold all my calls, please," Jill said as she walked into the office of the *Gazette*.

Landry nodded at her between bagel bites and phone calls.

Immediately, Jill got to work. She frantically shifted through the papers in her drawer but couldn't find the file. Next, she searched the top of her desk, her in-box, and all her other drawers. Ally's file was simply nowhere to be found. Picking up the phone, she called Dan's cubicle. No answer. She called another intern and learned that Dan hadn't come in yet. She left instructions for Dan to see her the minute he walked in the door. Jill hung up the phone. She quickly buzzed Rubric. He hadn't come in either. Next she tried Landry.

"Hi, where is everybody this morning? Have you seen Dan, or did he leave anything for me at the front desk? And how about Rubric?"

"No, sorry. I haven't seen either one of them."

"I have Dan's cell number, but do you have any other numbers for him?"

"I think so. Hold on."

In less than a minute Landry came back on the phone to give Jill Dan's home number. Jill left messages for Dan to call her at both numbers. She felt irritated that she hadn't remembered to instruct Dan to call her if he ran into any problems. And what about Ally Cooper? Had she arrived in Youngstown? If she had, she hadn't let Jill know.

Worry wouldn't help a thing. Just last night in Bible study, they'd studied the verse admonishing no worry. She turned her attention to the Harrison research. As the pages of her research unfolded, Jill found herself fascinated with a man riddled with contradictions. Wouldn't she love to crawl inside the senator's head for a couple of hours?

Intrigued, Jill hadn't realized how much time had passed when she heard a knock at her door. According to her watch, it was one o'clock, so it was probably Millie.

Sure enough, her assistant slipped in to bring Jill's lunch. If it weren't for Millie, Jill would have starved to death long ago. Millie set down a pastrami sandwich and a Diet Coke in front of Jill.

"Thanks, Millie. I had no idea it was this late. Wait a minute, will you?"

Jill picked up the phone and called Landry to see if anyone had heard from Dan yet. No one had.

She turned her attention to Millie. "How's it going? Have you found anything on Harrison's wife's automobile accident yet? I'm curious to see if the senator was driving. And if so, was he driving under the influence?"

"It's on my to-do list. Right now I'm buried in his legal opinions, but I can change course."

"Forget it. Truthfully, if there were anything suspicious about her accident, it would've come out in his election campaign."

"You're right. Buzz me if you need me, Jill." Millie returned to her office.

Jill sat back in her chair and took a bite of her sandwich. She was getting nowhere with the Harrison research. What she really needed was an interview with the senator himself. Unfortunately, he had two-headed monsters guarding his phone system and his door. Jill figured his office was probably surrounded by a moat filled with reporter-eating dragons too. There has to be another way to get through to him.

Since Eric was in the midst of funeral arrangements for Brown's funeral, it was probably too crass to call him to remind him of his promise to set up the interview with Harrison. That left David. Although she preferred to break off all ties with her ex-boyfriend, Jill knew he was well connected to Harrison, and picked up the phone and dialed his cell phone.

David answered immediately. "Jill. So you've decided to have dinner with me after all?"

"Actually, I'm calling to ask a favor."

"So that's what I've become to you now . . . a reliable source? Oh well, at least it's a start. I see the news tip I gave you a few days ago has already ended up on the front page."

"Yes. Thanks to your tip, I was the first to break the Harrison story. Now I'd like an interview with him."

"Listen, I'll make a deal with you—if I can get you an interview with Harrison, will you go to dinner with me?"

"Deal," Jill agreed. She thanked David and hung up the phone.

Despite how David had treated her in the past, he had been her boyfriend for five years, and he deserved to hear the news of her engagement to John from her, so a quiet dinner was probably a good idea. She continued her research for a while, but then, eyes blurry from all the reading about Harrison, she straightened up her office and got ready to leave.

On her way out, Jill passed Rubric in the lobby.

"Were you aware that Dan Peek never showed up for work this morning?"

"No."

"Not only did he not show up, but yesterday, I sent him on an extremely important errand that he promised to have completed by this morning."

"He's under a lot of pressure at school and probably just over-slept."

"I hope you're right," Jill said. Rubric seemed unconcerned, so she wasn't going to worry about Dan anymore—the file, yes, but Dan, no.

8

A ruffled mind makes a restless pillow.

Charlotte Brontë

After a meager supper of tuna salad, Jill washed her face and brushed her teeth and dug into her chest of drawers for a worn pair of flannel pajamas that she often referred to as her "security jams." Twirling her funny plastic ring around and around, she told herself that she needed her security jams tonight because she had only been engaged for twenty-four hours and her fiancé was already gone again, miles away from her. At least he'd be home next Friday. Less than two weeks. She'd survive.

That wasn't the only thing that was nagging at her, though. What if Ally Cooper's wild tale proved to be true? The whole thing was preposterous, but Jill felt edgy. Deciding not to go there, she willed herself to think happy thoughts.

She imagined what an exciting week her mother was enjoying. *Mom's probably polishing the silver, fluffing up the pillows, relandscaping the lawn, redecorating the whole house, or something nutty like that for my boyfriend's visit.* She giggled thinking about seeing her mother's face when John, a.k.a. Craig Martin, walked in the door.

Pulling her down pillow over her head, she fell asleep. A few hours later, her phone jangled loudly, waking her. In a sleepy daze, she opened her eyes, trying desperately to make out the numbers on the lighted dial of her bedside clock. Four a.m. *Ugh! Already?*

She glanced at the caller ID; it was just as she figured . . . unknown. But maybe it was John returning her call.

Half awake, she mumbled into the receiver, "Hello, darling."

"This ain't darling." The voice belonged to her informant, code name "the Pied Piper." "I've got the goods on Harrison for you. Three o'clock Friday afternoon in the Pullman Bar at the Churchill Hotel."

"I'll be there."

"Don't forget the money."

"Give me the details."

"Cash only . . . unmarked hundred-dollar bills."

"How much this time?"

"Five g's."

"You're joking."

"I can promise you, it'll be worth it—and more." *Click.*

Jill lay back in bed. Her throat was scratchy sore and her head hurt. The result of standing in the rain the day of Brown's death? Shaking her head, she wheezed and sneezed, grabbed a tissue off her nightstand, and blew her nose. Hard to imagine she ever felt like a princess only a night ago.

Filled with anticipation, Jill got up extra early the next morning. She hoped that the Pied Piper would provide some explosive information about Harrison for her. Grabbing her phone, she called Rubric to arrange for the cash she needed for Piper. There was no answer, so she left a message at the office and on his cell phone. She made a cup of tea and carried it to her closet.

Jill decided to pay close attention to her clothes today. Around

Washington, one never knew where its elite might drop in for happy hour. As she flipped through the clothes in her closet, she spotted a black Armani pantsuit hanging with a pleated blouse. Jill slid a pretty lace camisole and then the soft pink blouse over her head. Zipping the silk pants, she slipped a snakeskin belt through the loops and fastened the gold and enamel buckle. With pearls around her neck and on her ears, she pulled her jacket off the hanger and put it on, draping a pink and black scarf around her shoulders. She pinned the scarf to her jacket with a circle of pearls set in gold. Glancing in the full-view mirror, Jill looked the part of a successful Washingtonian.

Jill arrived at the *Gazette* and went straight to the front desk, only stopping long enough to inquire if Landry had heard from Dan.

"No news."

"Is Rubric in yet?"

"He had a meeting this morning, but he'll be in by noon."

That was a relief. Jill could go straight to accounting with her cash request form to get the process rolling for Piper's money. Although she needed Rubric's signature on the form, she knew it would be much better for him to read Piper's five-thousand-dollar demand than for her to tell him. She stopped by her office to fill out the form.

As soon as Jill sat down at her desk, she booted up her computer and pulled up the cash request file. Before she began typing in the pertinent information, she pushed her chair back from the desk. The whereabouts of Ally's file still nagged her. She looked again in all the obvious places for the file, just in case Dan had dropped in after hours. It wasn't there. With her search on hold, she completed the form and dropped it off in accounting and knocked on the door to Rubric's office. There was no answer, so she peeked inside.

Relieved to find his office empty, Jill left a copy of the form on his desk. No need to leave a note for him to call her. Just one glance at that form, and he would holler so loudly it would alert her, as well as everyone else at the *Gazette*, that he was back in his office.

Jill hurried back down the corridor and tacked a Do Not Disturb sign on her door and blocked her phone, and then jumped right into the Harrison research. If Piper came through with the goods on the Alabama senator, she had to be ready to write the story. A couple of hours into her research, she took a break and left another message for Rubric to call her. Again, there was no answer. Before she could hang up the receiver, she heard a tirade with her name attached in the hallway outside her office.

"Jill! Jill Lewis! Jill, do you hear me? Answer me!"

It was Rubric, of course.

"I'm in here. Come in," she hollered.

"I don't believe it. Has the whole world gone mad?" Rubric screamed as he blazed into Jill's office.

She looked up at him. His hands were balled into fists, his face was redder than raspberries, and his whole body trembled.

"Hello, Rubric. Where have you been?"

"Since when are you my keeper?"

"Why didn't you call me? I left at least a couple of messages for you."

"I just walked in the door, and I had to go straight to accounting to approve your money. What happened to the old days when we could give someone a hundred bucks for some dirt?"

"Inflation, Rubric. Besides, we're dealing with the Pied Piper, and you know his info is always pure platinum."

"But five g's? I want you to tell this little pansy Piper that if he doesn't deliver, this may be the last stash he ever gets from us."

"There's no reason to get so upset until we hear what he has to say. If you don't chill out, Rubric, you're going to have a stroke."

"The only thing that's going to make me feel better is if you come back with a smoking headline."

Jill got up from her desk to head to the lobby. Rubric followed her.

"I'll find some stuff so hot it will burn a hole right through the front page." She stopped her fast-paced walk for a moment. "Hey, Rubric, did you know that Dan Peek didn't show up for work this morning?"

"Again?"

"Not only did he not show for two days in a row, but I had sent him on an important errand. He's really left me in the lurch."

"I suppose you want me to fire him?"

"That's not what I was thinking. I was more concerned that something may have happened to him."

"The kid's under a lot of pressure at school. Or maybe his girl broke up with him or something. He'll be back eventually."

9

Surprises are like misfortunes or herrings—
they rarely come single.

L. E. Landon

A half hour later Jill pushed her way through the early cocktail hour crowd to the Pullman Bar. She had chosen the appropriate outfit to wear because she noticed admiring stares from the men in the bar. Jill looked around and saw her informant on a stool and hunched over the bar with his back to the room. She stepped up behind him and nonchalantly took the seat to his left.

Piper slipped her a note. As he walked away, she opened the note and read it. *Take a seat at the far booth away from the windows.* A little dramatic even for the Piper, but she'd play along.

Jill waited a few minutes after ordering her water with a lemon twist, and then walked toward the back. To her surprise, there were two gentlemen seated in the booth. Turning around, the Piper had a surprise for her. "Jill, I'd like you to meet my friend, Senator Tommy Harrison."

Jill's jaw dropped.

"Miss Lewis, this is an honor indeed." The handsome gentleman sprung to his feet and shook Jill's hand.

"Why, uh, thank you, Senator." Regaining her composure, Jill slid in across from him and asked, "How are you?"

"I've been better, but it's a pleasure to finally meet you. I'm a great admirer of your work."

The Pied Piper slid out of the booth.

"Wait," Jill stopped him. "I think I owe you something." She held out the briefcase.

"No. This one's on me." He pushed the case away. "I just told you to bring the money so you would understand the importance of this meeting."

Jill watched him leave and tucked the briefcase next to her. *Piper, you just made Rubric a happy man.*

Jill turned her attention to the senator. He wasn't very tall. Perfectly fit, he had light brown eyes and an intoxicating smile. Tanned and impeccably dressed, he exuded an incredible amount of charisma. Jill agreed with his many female admirers—Senator Thomas Henry Harrison was an eligible bachelor indeed.

"Well, Senator, I have scores of questions for you, but you obviously wanted to see me, and I must say that surprises me since I called your office a dozen times requesting an interview and never heard a word."

An even bigger smile lit up his face; his eyes crinkled at the corners, and deep smile lines etched a perfect frame around his mouth. "It's no secret I'm the favored candidate to replace Brown. The press is crawling all over my office, and as you experienced, my assistants are very protective. But I wanted to see you personally because I have a favor to ask you."

"Me?" Surprised but pleased, she silently thanked God for her good fortune. Senator Harrison was sitting before her, ready to write her headline. She tried to remain calm and professional. *Don't blow this.*

She narrowed her eyes at him. "I don't get it. Why not call me directly? Why use a middleman?"

"Your informant called to say you were looking for some dirt on me. I knew you'd been calling my office—"

"Wait. I'd prefer to call what I do as procuring background information, not dirt."

"Background information? Now that's a polite way of putting it. I preferred a discreet meeting. This seemed to be the best way to make that happen."

Harrison's smile unnerved Jill. Was he flirting? She hoped not. Perhaps it was only his legendary Southern charm.

"What can I get you to drink, Ms. Lewis?"

"Diet Coke with lime, thank you."

Waving a waiter over to their table, the senator ordered Jill's soda and then a bourbon and Coke for himself. The waiter hung around after he'd taken the order just to chat. Senator Harrison was positively magnetic—just not magnetic enough to defeat his opponent, a former jock Republican in Alabama.

In a few moments, the waiter had their drinks in front of them.

"Peanuts?" The senator held out the round dish to her.

"No thanks."

Scooping up a handful of nuts, he dropped them in his drink. Jill blinked. It seemed an odd gesture for such a refined man. Then she remembered her childhood days in the South.

She smiled. "The farmer's lunch."

"Is there anything you don't know, Ms. Lewis?" he said, raising his eyebrows.

"My grandmother lives near Mobile in Alabama. By the way, call me Jill."

"So Jill, you grew up with peanuts in your Coca-Cola bottle?"

"You bet. I spent every summer with my grandmother until I turned twelve and wanted to hang out with my friends at the lake in Wisconsin." Uncomfortable that the conversation was becoming personal, Jill changed course. "It's no secret I'd love a story from you, Senator Harrison, but what could you possibly want from me?"

"The same."

"What kind of story?"

"You'll see. First of all, don't you find it strange that a conservative Democrat like myself is being considered as Brown's replacement for Senate minority leader?"

Before Jill could reply, the waiter stepped up with another bowl of peanuts and placed them on the table.

Harrison nodded, swirling the peanuts in his drink.

"I'm listening." Jill took the tape recorder from her purse and set it on the table between them. Harrison reached across the table to shut it off, knocking the bowl of peanuts over in the process.

"Nothing personal, but I would prefer that you not tape this conversation."

Jill reluctantly pulled the recorder off the table and slid it back inside her purse. Next, she took out the steno notebook and flipped it open. "Why do you believe the Democrats want you to replace Brown as their Senate minority leader?" she asked.

"We can discuss that later. First, I have a much more important matter to talk about with you."

Jill scrunched her forehead.

"But I can tell you that whoever wants me in that position was willing to do anything to get Senator Brown out of the picture, even commit murder."

"The autopsy report ruled that Senator Brown suffered a stroke." Jill agonized that she didn't have in her possession Ally Cooper's file before this meeting. Twice in one week she'd heard someone say Brown was murdered.

Without a word, Harrison pulled several disks and a couple of hard copy files out of his briefcase. He ceremoniously laid them on the table in front of Jill.

Jill read one of the labels aloud. "MST?"

"The murder weapon."

"Never heard of it. What is it?"

"A powerful drug developed by a biotech company for the treatment of brain cancer."

"Does it work?"

"Miraculously, in laboratory rats. Within a few weeks after the lesions in the brains were injected with MST, the tumors virtually disappeared. And most of the rats from the clinical trials are still alive."

"And in humans?"

"How much do you know about clinical drug trials?"

"Not a lot."

"Well, the real challenge of a Phase I drug trial is adjusting the dosage from the laboratory rat to the human subject. I'm afraid the human dosage proved fatal in the first MST drug trial."

"What about subsequent trials?"

"There was only one human trial for MST. The FDA halted any further trials."

"But you stated that was one of the major challenges of a drug trial, adjusting the dosage. If the drug was so successful in laboratory rats, why wasn't the company allowed another clinical trial?"

"There were extenuating circumstances. It wasn't just the fact that the test subjects died . . . it was how they died."

"I'm waiting." Jill cupped her chin on her hands.

The senator sighed deeply. "Within minutes after the MST was administered, some of the participants in the trial suffered a massive stroke. The results were very similar to what happens in a brain aneurysm."

"Sounds like the plot of a science fiction movie. Are you saying someone got their hands on the substance and used it to kill Senator Brown?"

"I'm sure of it."

"Why are you telling me this? Shouldn't you go straight to the FBI or the CIA?"

"Remember a few years back when the Ukrainian leader, Viktor Yuschenko, was poisoned with dioxin by the CIA in that country? I believe that someone in a high-ranking government position could be involved in this plot. I'd rather do this investigation alone if you're not willing to help me, but I hope you'll partner with me in finding the truth."

"What role would I play?"

"To write a story about my suspicions that Brown was murdered. I believe it would force the FBI to order a second autopsy to test for any traces of these substances in Brown's body."

"May I have permission to use your name?"

"Not a chance. Just say 'a high-ranking politician suspects.'"

"And you're sure that would be enough to establish doubt that the senator's death was due to a stroke?"

"Only if we act swiftly. I've heard that the family plans to have his body cremated."

"Why not go directly to the family? Surely if anyone would want the truth, it'd be them. Or go to the FBI yourself. You're a credible source, Senator. Certainly they'd agree to the autopsy to look for traces of the substance."

"I told you my concerns about approaching the FBI. I have to go public. It's the only way I can ensure that something will be done and that I'll be protected. As I said, I suspect a high-ranking individual, but it could be more far reaching. At this point I don't want to involve the family either. I'm not sure they'd believe me. Will you write the article?"

"Oh no. I won't write any story based on an assumption."

"Isn't that what you do?"

"Not without substantial proof and credible sources. I'd like to help, but I could lose my job, and ultimately my career."

"But you can write a story that states that a high-level source suspects foul play, and that should halt Brown's cremation until the FBI orders a second autopsy."

"That's assuming that the FBI will take the bait. Anyway, I still need a motive."

"Oh, I've got a motive for you. Brown's largest campaign contributor is Creation Pharmaceutical in his home state of Ohio."

"So what? Who'd wish him dead?"

"Some would say I did."

The hairs on her arm bristled. "You?"

"Therein lays the motive. After a disastrous FDA trial for MST, Senator Brown lobbied relentlessly to close Bio Tech Labs, the company that developed the drug in a small swampland in my state."

"Why?"

"I was noticing your snakeskin belt. Are you a fan of snakes?"

She frowned at him. "Excuse me? What does that have to do with MST?"

"Trust me. It does."

"In that case, I'm only a fan of the dead ones. Why do you ask?"

"I'm not sure you'll enjoy this investigation then, because snakes are at the front and center of it. Senator Brown claimed that the drug was a threat to national security and pressured the FBI and the FDA to intervene immediately. He instilled a lot of hysteria about who might get their hands on the substance or, worse yet, the formula, since the venom is from a snake whose natural habitat is the Middle East."

"A snake?" She wrinkled her nose. "It sounds like Brown's concerns were a little over the top."

"Probably pure hysteria, nothing more, but I never denied that the drug had potential for evil if it got in the wrong hands."

"Was Senator Brown successful in shutting down the company?"

"No. Bio Tech struggled, but they survived. However, Brown was able to garner enough support to pressure the FDA to halt the trials, and even the manufacture of the substance. It's costing my state jobs." Harrison stared down at his drink.

"So you were lobbying for this company? From what you've told me about this drug, why would you do that?"

"Because this substance had amazing results in laboratory rats, so MST has great potential. If Bio Tech Labs was given the opportunity to adjust the dosages in the drug trials, then MST would have great potential as a cancer drug. But Brown used this debacle not only to halt the research and manufacture of MST, but also as an opening to keep Bio Tech from putting another successful drug on the market."

"Why?"

"It's strictly financial. Bio Tech Labs had completed an FDA trial for another drug, a vascular-targeting agent for cancer that has the potential to save thousands of lives; and Brown's largest political backer, Creation Pharmaceutical, developed a similar but inferior vascular-targeting drug. Their drug was already on the market and is making millions."

"With Bio Tech Labs' vascular-targeting drug out of the way, Creation would have no competition for their drug that is inferior to the one developed by Bio Tech."

"Exactly. And had Bio Tech Labs been able to complete their FDA trial on MST and not suffered such huge losses and setbacks, they would have had the resources to launch the marketing for their drug. If this miracle drug went on the market, Creation Pharmaceutical would stand to lose millions."

"So Senator Brown was protecting his state interests."

Harrison nodded his head. "And he was paid handsomely for it by Creation Pharmaceutical to the tune of a couple of million dollars for his recent political campaign."

"Ah, so we definitely have a motive."

"True, but Jill, now that this drug has been used for murder, I'm not so sure that Brown had the wrong idea about MST."

"Are you saying that you now think that Bio Tech Labs is a real threat to our national security?"

"Not Bio Tech Labs necessarily, but MST," Harrison said. "Since the company is located within my state, I know the high-ranking officials in the company, but they employ hundreds of scientists and other employees, and it's obvious that this drug has fallen into the wrong hands. I think Brown was murdered with this drug as he was coming down the steps of the Senate building, and I want you to help me prove it."

"That's a big assignment," Jill said. "Before I agree to any of this, could you explain to me how Brown could have ingested MST?"

"A scratch on the skin with a sharp object is all it takes, but as big as the man was, they'd have to give him a larger dose; it's possible he could've been injected."

"Wouldn't death be instantaneous? Brown lived for hours after his collapse."

"For some, but there are several issues. First of all, the person's health and immune system are factors in how they'll react to the drug. Other key factors—the person's weight, the amount of poison ingested—are all predictors of the quickness of death."

"This is one case of where Brown's extra weight probably helped him."

"I'm sure it was a factor, even though the killer probably factored that in the size of the dose. Of course, immediate medical attention is factored in as well. The IV slipped into his vein helped to dilute the toxicity of the poison somewhat. But his dosage must've been high enough that death was the eventual result. The doctors were treating Brown for the stroke, not the poison, but even had they known about the poison, he would've died anyway."

"You've got my attention, Senator."

"Good. The FDA ordered that all the MST be destroyed, and it was, but someone must have confiscated a supply of the drug or sold the formula, or maybe it's even being manufactured elsewhere."

"That's a frightening thought. You obviously fought hard to keep the company open. It's not easy for a man in your position to admit he's wrong."

"I still stand by my belief that Bio Tech Labs should remain open, but the FBI must open a major investigation at once. We're dealing with a deadly substance here."

"I'd like to help, but without using your name, I can't write that article without more data to substantiate your suspicions."

"Yes, but if the people behind this learn of my accusations, how long do you think I'll live?"

Jill stared at the senator. "People don't go around killing senators. The risk is too great."

"But senators can have accidents that can't be proved otherwise. Had I not raised the possibility that Brown was murdered, would anyone have given the cause of his death a second thought?"

"Probably not. But if what you told me is true, why would you be in danger? Since you support the development of this drug and the company that developed it, I would think you'd be safe."

"It's the unknown, Jill. If Brown is cremated before the story is published, we'll never know if Brown was murdered or not. Once the information is out in the public arena, I won't be at as great a risk."

"Fair enough," Jill replied. Then she thought for a moment. *But can I persuade Rubric to convince Annabelle to publish the speculative article?* "I'll try. If my editor gives the okay tonight, you'll have your story in tomorrow's edition. May I have a copy of those substance reports?"

"They're all right here." Harrison patted the disks he had placed on the table earlier.

She started to leave the booth. "I'll be in touch."

Harrison reached out and lightly grabbed her arm. "Just be careful. This could be the greatest story of your career, Jill, but also the most dangerous."

She pulled her arm away but stayed seated in the booth. "Maybe I should conduct a standard interview with you to run in addition to the article on Senator Brown and the MST. So as not to raise suspicions of anyone who saw us here today."

"Good idea." Harrison settled back into the booth. "What would you like to know?"

"Now that it's likely you'll be Senator Brown's replacement, how do you feel about the possibility of losing your seat in the next election?"

"Heck, I love a woman who's direct." He chuckled. "Truthfully, I seriously considered changing parties, which would have guaranteed my reelection."

"Do you really believe that a candidate from any party, Democratic or Republican, can win against a football hero in Alabama?"

"A girl who understands football. You're quite a woman, Ms. Lewis. What I was trying to say is that the Republicans made me a deal. If I switched parties, they'd support my candidacy and then there would have been no football hero opponent."

She scribbled on her steno pad. "Thanks for the explanation." Jill held up the envelope. "If what you say is true, these people, whoever they are, would've gotten away with murder. If your documentation backs up what you've told me, and if the story is printed, you'll win your election for sure, even as a Democrat in Alabama versus a Republican football hero."

"You think that's my motive? Reelection?"

"Part of it." Mildly impressed with this man, she still was cautious. After all, it was politics. She'd been set up before. She glanced at her watch. "I've got to move along if we're going to have any hope of getting this article published in tomorrow's edition."

The senator stood and shook Jill's hand. "Ms. Lewis, it's been a pleasure meeting you."

Jill nodded. "Is there a number where I can reach you tonight if I need to get in touch with you?"

"It's all in there." He tapped the envelope.

Jill grabbed her things, including the money that the Piper had turned down. "Thank you, Senator. I'll be in touch."

"Thank you, Ms. Lewis. I look forward to reading your morning headlines at the breakfast table." Before he left, he smiled at her with such radiance that it made Jill feel warm inside. *I'll give you this, Senator Harrison—you are one fine-looking man!*

10

*No first step can be really great; it must of necessity
possess more of prophecy than of achievement.*

Katherine Cecil Thurston

Jill ran against the stream of workers leaving the *Gazette* for the
day. Inside the elevator, she dialed Dan once more and stomped
her foot in frustration when there still was no answer. "I need
that file." Jill's heels clicked on the marble lobby when she left
the elevator. "Landry, did Dan Peek ever show? And what about
Ally Cooper? Has she called?"

"Nope." Landry waved a pink slip in the air. "But here's a
message you'll want to see."

Jill raised her eyebrows.

"Your boyfriend."

"Why didn't you put him through to my voice mail?"

"Your voice mail is long winded, and he said he was in a
hurry."

Jill frowned. "And you wanted to snoop."

"Hey, I love romance. I'm between boyfriends. Can't I live
vicariously through you until that changes?"

"Sure." A smile flowered on Jill's face as she snatched the pink
slip from Landry's fingertips and sailed back to her office to savor

her message. She read and reread the pink slip. "Miss you. Love you. See you Friday."

Friday's a million years away with all I have to accomplish in the interim. After she dropped the briefcase of money on the floor, she dumped the contents of her own bag onto her desk. Quickly dialing Rubric, Jill announced, "I'm back, and I need to talk to you."

"I hope it's good."

"Oh, it's good. Give me fifteen minutes."

Although Jill believed Harrison was credible, she refused to blindly trust his accusations. The next few minutes she shuffled through the files and read the reports, which she found surprisingly thorough and well documented. When she'd read enough, she picked up the briefcase filled with money and marched up the hall with Harrison's reports tucked under her arm. The moment he saw her, Rubric jumped to his feet. "What'd you find out?"

Without a word, Jill laid the briefcase across his desk.

"What's this?"

"Your money."

"So the Pied Piper stood you up? Losing your touch, eh, Lewis?"

"First of all, the Piper didn't stand me up, and furthermore, he gave me what just might be the best story of my career."

"Don't tell me he wants more money." Rubric groaned as he sat back down, stretched his legs, and propped them up on the desk.

"No. He made a very special delivery—Harrison."

"You're joking."

"No, Harrison wants us to do a story."

"What kind of story?"

Jill dumped some papers off the chair onto the floor and sat down. Leaning closer to Rubric's desk, she whispered, "Harrison suspects Senator Brown was murdered."

"That's preposterous."

"Really? It's the second time I've heard this rumor in three days."

"Why wasn't I told about the first time?"

"I did mention to you I had a tip. Remember?"

"The dizzy file clerk from U.S. Fish and Wildlife? Well, you can forget Nancy Drew."

"But she claims to have information stashed in a locker at the Trailways Bus Station."

"Then get your hands on that stuff tonight," he barked, "and then we'll talk."

"Well . . . actually, I'm not sure I can do that."

"Then we're not printing anything until we have the file in our possession and verified for authenticity—unless you've got some other documented proof."

Jill shook her head in frustration. "But Harrison says the story has to appear in the morning paper to stop the cremation and force a second autopsy on Brown's body."

"Or your accusations will go up in smoke?"

"Very funny." Jill shoved the Harrison envelope to Rubric.

"What's in it?"

"The murder weapon."

"Yeah, right."

"Read for yourself. It's all in a report Harrison gave me. It's a drug, MST."

"Then how do you explain that the autopsy said that Brown died of natural causes?"

"The autopsy is perfectly accurate. Brown died from a stroke. But it was a stroke that was induced. By the MST. Just examine the report on the FDA trial of this drug. It's all right here." Jill tapped the file with her fingernail.

"Have you read it?"

Jill nodded.

Rubric breezed through a couple of pages with Jill reading over his shoulder.

"Sounds plausible," Rubric reluctantly admitted. "But this doesn't prove anything. It's only a theory."

"Pretty scary stuff, though."

He looked up from the papers and glared at her. "I want that file."

"So do I, but Rubric, you might as well hear it from me. I've blown it."

"Then you're fired."

"Let me finish. I met the girl for the second time in the park. She handed over the key to the locker where she supposedly stashed the file."

"It wasn't there?"

"I don't know."

"What do you mean you don't know?" Rubric raised his voice and drank from an open bottle of Maalox on his desk.

"I sent Dan Peek to pick it up for me. You're always telling me to delegate, remember? He was off to class and said he'd bring it to me on his way the next morning."

"Are you crazy? What was the first rule I taught you when you showed up at the *Gazette*?"

"Never delay authenticating a lead."

"So what's your excuse?" Rubric bellowed.

"I was busy. And I wasn't sure I believed the girl."

"And Dan hasn't shown up? Get him on the phone."

"I've tried to reach Dan half a dozen times already."

"What about the girl?"

"All I get is her voice mail. She took a train to her parents' home in Youngstown, but when I called their number this morning, there was no answer, not even a machine."

"I want to know the moment you hear from either one of them."

"We can't wait for them. We've got to take the first step. You've got to trust me on this one."

"After you let that file slip through your hands? No way."

"But if Brown's body is cremated, we'll never know the truth."

"Another autopsy may prove nothing."

"But how will we know if we don't try?"

"Annabelle will never go for it. We need proof, or at least a hard motive."

"Oh, there's a motive." Jill came around and cleared out a spot to sit on Rubric's desk. "Brown was secretly waging a battle to close Bio Tech Labs, the pharmaceutical company that manufactured the drug MST."

"Now you're talking." He scooted forward in his rolling chair.

"Yeah, and listen to this. Bio Tech Labs is located in Alabama, Harrison's state."

"Maybe Harrison knows more than he's telling you?"

"That's possible. He is a politician, after all. But I don't see why Harrison would want this autopsy if he were behind this."

"Maybe Harrison's afraid he'll be implicated in the murder and is running interference." Rubric lit up a cigarette.

"If Harrison was involved, he'd want the body cremated, especially since there's not the least bit of suspicion surrounding Brown's death. The senator died of natural causes, a stroke, case closed."

"Surely someone from the FDA, Bio Tech Labs, or even a family member will eventually suspect foul play when they hear Brown died from a stroke."

"These drug trial results aren't released to the public. Apparently, it's not unusual for terminal patients to die as a result of drug trials with no thorough explanation given, other than it failed."

"If they're not released, then how did Brown and Harrison know about them?"

"Interesting point," Jill said.

"What about lawsuits?"

"The participants who take part in these drug trials are terminal, and they sign up if it offers them the slightest ray of hope. They're required to sign papers exonerating the drug company of the outcome."

Rubric lit up another cigarette, but Jill yanked it from his mouth and crushed it in his beloved ashtray in the shape of a man's head in a top hat. Rubric had swiped it from Diamond Jim's Steak House, his favorite haunt, over thirty years ago, and it had become his most prized possession.

"What'd ya do that for? You know I never use this ashtray," he scowled as he waved away the smoke from his face. "Who does Harrison think is behind this?"

"He doesn't have a clue."

"Then he's lying. Tommy Harrison's got the clout to go to the FBI. Why'd he come to you?"

"Harrison's convinced a high-level government official's involved, so he's afraid to go to the FBI."

"Bull. You've let some smooth-talking politician outsmart you."

"Consider what happened in the Ukrainian elections. The man's own government poisoned him. Listen, Rube, if we don't act fast, we'll lose our evidence."

Rubric sat silently for a moment, reviewing the files. Finally he spoke. "Go ahead. You've convinced me. Write your story."

Jill jumped up and then paused before leaving. "What about Annabelle?"

"I'll handle the old gal, but I'd better see that mysterious file you mentioned on my desk by eight o'clock tomorrow morning, or you'll be lucky to get a job in your hometown scrubbing floors at the Delavan newspaper."

"Let's just pray that we'll hear from Dan soon."

"You pray and I'll worry." Rubric reached across his desk and pulled a cigarette out of the crumpled pack as Jill sprinted out the door to go write her shocker of a story.

11

Courage can't see around corners,
but goes around them anyway.

Mignon McLaughlin

Jill's assignment was to arouse suspicion about Brown's death in her article. A couple of hours later the story was written. Hopefully, by tomorrow, the Feds would be all over Bio Tech Labs, and Brown's body would undergo a second autopsy. Brushing her hands together, she smiled, knowing she'd done her job.

Rubric signed off on it with his approval. "I put my head on the chopping block for you this time. You'd better have Nancy Drew's file on my desk first thing in the morning, or you're fired."

"Then find your little buddy Dan for me," Jill called out to Rubric as he left.

Waiting for Dan to show was driving her batty. Turning off her computer, Jill remembered she not only had Ally Cooper's Washington address but her apartment key as well. Jill knew there was no way she'd drive her car into Ally's high-crime neighborhood, so she hailed a cab.

Along Ally's neighborhood streets, she saw security bars covering some of the windows. Banged-up cars lined the curbs as stripped vehicles sat on cinder blocks in some of the driveways.

"Wait for me, okay?" Jill handed the cabbie a fifty.

A TV blared, and somewhere a dog barked as Jill knocked at the door of the brownstone. In a few minutes Jill heard a raspy voice through the door. "Who is it?"

"Hello, I'm Jill Lewis with the *Washington Gazette*. Does Ally Cooper live here?"

"Go away. I already told the man that she's not here."

"What man?"

"I don't know. Just a man who was asking for her."

"May I speak to you for a minute, Mrs. . . . ?"

"O'Reilly."

"Hi, Mrs. O'Reilly. May I ask you a few questions?"

The elderly woman cracked the inside door and peered out.

"Ally gave me a key to the rear entrance of her apartment."

"My son gave me strict orders. No one's allowed inside unless he's here."

"If you'll unlock the gate to your backyard, I can go around to the back and let myself in."

"I said no one comes in without my son being here."

"Okay," Jill said, exasperated. "When will your son be back?"

"I'm not sure. He lives in Maryland and only comes out on weekends a few times a month."

Jill sighed as she dug a fifty-dollar bill out of her wallet. Holding it up as bait, she asked, "Now will you let me come inside?"

"Make that a hundred and you're in, Ms. Lewis."

"Thank you," Jill said as she passed the old woman a crisp bill.

"This'll help with my prescriptions. Follow me." Mrs. O'Reilly led Jill around to the side gate.

Jill found Ally's apartment at the far end of the courtyard and pushed open the creaky door. Someone had obviously beaten her here—the modest abode was in shambles. Had someone ransacked it, or did Ally do this to the place? The sofa bed was yanked out, and the sheets had been ripped off the thin mattress.

Inside the bedroom closet, Jill found a box of clothes. A few hangers gripped the metal rod. Dresses that were ripped to shreds were dangling from some of the hangers. At the far end of the room was a desk and a TV set, both pushed over onto the floor.

Both of the garbage bins, one in the kitchen and another in the bathroom, were empty. Sighing heavily, she knew that whatever answers may have been here were now gone.

"The apartment's been ransacked. We need to call the police," she told Mrs. O'Reilly.

"I don't want any police nosing around here."

"The man who was asking for Ally, did you let him into the apartment?"

"Of course not."

"Did he offer you some money? With the high cost of prescription drugs, who could blame you?"

"I already told you, I didn't let him in." A glaze of fear covered the old woman's eyes.

"Mrs. O'Reilly, we need to notify the police. To collect compensation for the repairs, you'll need a police report for the insurance company."

"It's that bad, huh?"

Jill nodded, dialing the police. Jill stepped down to the curb to talk to the cabbie. "Here's another fifty. Will you stay?"

"You keep paying, I'll keep staying." The driver stuck the bill in his visor.

Jill returned to the front door, where Mrs. O'Reilly was waiting. Jill took a seat on the cement step as the landlady slowly stooped to sit next to her.

"I hope it won't be a long wait," Jill said.

"In this neighborhood, we'll be lucky if they show up at all," the landlady grumbled.

Sure enough, over an hour passed before the squad car pulled up in front of the brownstone. The officers gave their names, and after Jill briefed them, they asked to see the room. This time Mrs. O'Reilly led them through her small, tidy house and across the thick seventies shag carpeting.

Writing up a report didn't take the policemen long; there wasn't much to see.

"There's no sign of forced entry," the older officer said. After scribbling down a few sentences on a blotter, he asked, "Anything else you can tell us before I sign off on this report?"

"Didn't you find anything?" Mrs. O'Reilly asked.

"No, ma'am."

"Officer, a man was here earlier asking to see this apartment," Jill said.

"Oh? Can you give us a description of this man?" the officer asked.

Jill gestured toward Mrs. O'Reilly.

"My eyes aren't as good as they used to be, but he was a large man—not fat, but muscular, with dark hair."

"Large but not fat. Dark hair." The cop stifled a smirk. "Do you recall if he had any distinguishable features?"

"Only that he had the whitest teeth I've ever seen."

"Mmm, sounds like Crew Cut to me," Jill mumbled.

"Okay, thank you, ma'am," the cop said. "I think we've got what we need."

After the police left, Jill said good-bye to Mrs. O'Reilly and got back in the cab. Relief flooded her as she left the neighborhood behind. But her relief didn't last long; the cab had barely gone a block when there was a light tap on the bumper.

Glancing in the rearview mirror, the cabbie complained, "What's that guy doing? Can you see if he's on a cell phone?

Hang up and drive!" He waved at the car, but the car stubbornly clung to the cab's bumper. "Hey buddy, go around!" the cabbie yelled.

The next hit was harder and done with definite intensity. The first bump had been no accident.

"Are you okay?" the cabbie said as he looked back at her through the rearview mirror.

"I think so."

"Hang on," the driver warned as he made a hard left and zipped down an alley. Approaching the end, he waited for a hole in the traffic to make his way back onto the street again. In the interim, the pursuing SUV spotted the cab and turned into the alley. With the SUV closing in, the cabbie decided to make his own hole in traffic. The pursuer tailgated right onto the street.

The cabbie careened in and out of traffic, knocking Jill from one side of the seat to the other. "Whoa!"

The chase continued for blocks as they headed west toward the interstate. Getting on 395, the two cars looped around Arlington Cemetery.

"I think we lost Jeff Gordon," the cabbie said.

Jill looked around. "So it seems."

"We did it! We outsmarted those bandits!" The cabbie laughed, smacking the steering wheel.

"Ah, perhaps you should look to your right then," Jill suggested, seeing the green SUV out her window.

"No worries." He wove into a line of cars that were at a dead stop, forcing the SUV to pass them. The cabbie laughed. At the last minute, he turned into a city parking lot toward the *Gazette*.

As they neared Jill's destination, the cabbie spotted the vehicle again. "Now he's getting on my nerves. Hang on." As he sped down the narrow lane, his rig clipped a few trash cans. The cab came to a screeching halt at a dead end. Before Jill could catch her breath, the driver backed up and spun the car around to swerve around the corner to another alley.

Skidding to the end of the alley, the pursuing car rammed the cab and held it against the brick wall. For a moment all was quiet, so Jill decided she should try to escape, but just as she opened her door, the cabbie rammed the gear stick into reverse and accelerated into the end of the alley. As the car lunged forward, Jill fell backward in the seat. Before a bordering building clipped off the door, she scrambled back to close it.

"What did ya do to tick that driver off, lady?" The cabbie shook his head.

Finally at her destination, Jill paid the driver and gave him a two-hundred-dollar tip. Safely inside her own car, Jill called Rubric to report the state of Ally's apartment and the chase with the infamous green Navigator.

"I'm supposed to feel sympathy for your close call?" Rubric barked. "Sounds like an everyday occurrence in that side of town to me."

"But why would the SUV follow me?"

"In that neighborhood, you have to ask? When you find a real story, then I'll listen. Until then, hasta la vista," Rubric said as he slammed down the phone.

Maybe Rubric didn't appreciate that each clue was a dot that when joined with the others was beginning to paint a picture. But there was someone who might appreciate the dots ... Tommy Harrison. In fact, he'd brought most of the dots to her canvas.

Tommy! Jill suddenly remembered she'd forgotten to call him to tell him they were running the story. She quickly dialed him on her cell phone.

When Tommy answered, she heard a partying crowd in the background.

"Senator, it's Jill Lewis. I'm sorry. I got really busy and—"

"Slow down, Ms. Lewis. I've been waiting for you to call. Did you run the story?"

"Front page, tomorrow's early edition."

"Thank you. Oh, and Jill, when the sun comes up tomorrow, I hope you're going to be prepared for the fallout." The phone line clicked.

12

*Our whole life consists of despairing of an answer
and seeking an answer.*

Dorothee Solle

The next morning, all the news stations were calling to book Jill for interviews, so after a few calls she let it ring. Throughout her morning run, Jill couldn't identify her concerns, but something gnawed at her. Straying a few yards from the jogging trail, she paused to check her phone for messages. Nothing there but calls from bird-dog producers and reporters, nipping for a few minutes of her time. Suddenly, the reason for her feelings crystallized. Were she and John working the same case? He'd had to leave just before the news of her investigation broke.

Jill left the park and headed to Starbucks for a tall latte. Outside on the terrace she dropped her coins in the metal newsstand and grabbed a copy of the morning edition to read while she waited in the line. Ah, there it was, her headline that would rock the nation: "Senator Brown's Death Suspect." By this time she guessed that Senator Harrison had seen it. Now they had to wait for the FBI to respond and launch their investigation.

After her latte, Jill went to her apartment to get ready for work and arrived at her office just before seven. "Have you seen Dan Peek?" she asked Landry at the front desk.

Busy with phone calls, Landry put a line on hold and replied, "No one has heard from Dan, and frankly, even Rubric's worried. He went out looking for him."

"Maybe he came in after hours."

Landry shrugged and went back to her phone calls.

Jill escaped to her office and shut the door. Both Dan and Ally were missing. Had she made a mistake by not taking this investigation more seriously? Had her lack of caution put them both in danger? Frantically, she pulled out her top desk drawer and searched for Ally's file, hoping she had overlooked it. She emptied the drawer but found nothing there except a couple of reference books and her health insurance file. Next she checked her other drawers, her credenza, and the top of her file cabinets. She scoured the room. Nothing. The file simply wasn't there. No sign that Dan had been there either. It was eerie how everyone who touched the file seemed to vanish.

Twisting her hair back, Jill threaded it with a pencil to keep it in place. She frowned as she pictured Rubric roaming the streets in search of Dan. She couldn't sit at her desk any longer and do nothing, so she walked down to the intern's bull pen at the end of the hallway. The supervisor, a thirtysomething athletic type, looked up at her and smiled.

"Have you heard from Dan?"

"Not a word. Shall I call you when he shows up today?"

"I'd appreciate that very much." Jill scribbled her number on a notepad, ripped it off, and handed it to the supervisor. "My cell phone number."

Now enough time had passed so she could officially file a missing person's report. But first Jill wanted to contact his family. She walked down to personnel and nodded to the clerk. "Good morning, Ed. Would you please pull Dan Peek's file? He's one of our interns."

Ed nodded. "Rubric came by earlier and took his file, but I have a duplicate. You've got clearance. Wait here and I'll get a copy for you."

When he returned, he handed Jill the file and pushed a form on a clipboard toward her. "Sign here."

"Thank you." She signed her name on the form and returned to her office with the file.

Jill scanned the file but found no local contact listed, only a widowed mother in Little Rock as his next of kin. She thought of Dan's mother, so recently widowed, and decided to rethink her plan. It wouldn't hurt to delay a few days before she contacted Dan's mother.

As she shuffled the papers back in the file, Dan's photo slid out onto her desk. She stared at his smiling face. His curly red hair was the perfect frame for his freckled nose and green eyes. Instead of putting the photo back into the file, Jill slipped it into her briefcase. Once the file was together, she took it back to personnel with a promise to return the photo later.

When Jill walked back into her office, she heard her buzzer and pushed the button.

"Jill, the switchboard's jammed with calls for you or Rubric about your story. Rubric isn't in yet. Do you want to talk to anyone?" Landry asked.

"Tell them we'll release a statement later today."

Jill decided to make use of Rubric's absence. She donned a large pair of Chanel sunglasses and slipped by the front desk. She hailed a taxi to the Trailways Bus Station.

At the door of the bus station, Jill saw buses rolling in from every direction. She pushed through the revolving door and noticed passengers standing in line for tickets. The smell of body odor mingled with eggs cooking on a grill and stale cigarette smoke made her gag.

Jill walked over to the row of metal lockers stacked on top of one another and stared at them. She pulled out the paper with the locker number written on it and went up to the locker and jiggled the door. Maybe Dan had already come and gone. If he had, where was he? And where was the file? Jill went over to the stationmaster's office and spoke to a man at the front desk. "How do I rent a locker?"

"They're self-service. Another company owns them; we just lease them the space. You put your money in and then take the key."

"And if you lose your key, does your office keep a master key?"

The man stared at her. "They won't install those fancy new biometric locks like the ones on the lockers at the airports since we don't have that much business here. But since 9-11, the rules have changed. We're able to open any locker in case of a security threat, so depending on why you need to get in there, I just might be able to accommodate you."

"A young lady left some vital information for me in one of the lockers here. She gave me the key, but unfortunately I've misplaced it. Now she's disappeared, and it's crucial for me to get inside that locker. The information in it could provide the answers to her whereabouts. I believe her life is in danger, so I have to get my hands on that information."

"Do you consider this a threat to national security?" He looked skeptical.

"It could be."

"Well, neither you nor I can determine that, can we?"

"Not until I see the file."

He shook his head. "I'm afraid you'll have to get a court order, ma'am. Or if you really believe it's a security threat, I would suggest that you contact the FBI."

"Okay. Oh, there's one more thing I'd like to ask," Jill said, pulling out the snapshot of Dan Peek. "Would you mind looking at this photo and telling me if you've seen this man in the past couple of days?"

The man behind the desk studied the photo intently. "Can't say that I have. I'd remember that carrot top. You might check around with the other employees at the ticket counter."

She reached back in her bag for a card. "Here's my card with my contact numbers. If you do see this man, please give me a call."

Jill flashed Dan's photo to all the employees with no success. With nothing left to do at the bus station, Jill went outside and gulped the fresh air before hailing a cab.

"Where to, lady?"

"The *Washington Gazette*."

Once she settled inside the cab, her cell phone rang. "Hello?"

"Where in the heck are you?" The voice belonged to Rubric.

"On my way to the office. Any word from Dan?"

"Nobody in Washington has seen him. And where's the file that was supposed to be on my desk this morning?" Rubric hollered.

"Dan promised I'd have it on my desk. But I've looked everywhere for the file. It's just not there."

"No Dan, no file. Not looking good for your career, Jill. If you want to keep your job, I suggest you find them both."

"There's still time."

"Oh, yeah? Every newspaper, network, and cable company in the country is calling about your story. What am I supposed to say to them?"

"I'm sure you'll think of something."

"Like I did when a lawyer for Senator Brown's family called this morning?"

"They called? Are they open to the autopsy?" Jill's voice was filled with hope.

"Absolutely not. And I gave the family my word—if there's no validity to your front-page claim, I'll personally escort you out of this building and change the lock."

"Thanks for the vote of confidence," Jill said. "But I'm not worried." Her voice held more bravado than she felt.

"You'd better be worried, and you'd better start praying that you can persuade the FBI to order another autopsy, because I can assure you the Brown family won't order one."

"I've prayed all morning for the FBI to call."

"You must have the hotline to heaven."

"The FBI called too?"

"Yep, they'll be here in half an hour."

"I'm on my way."

Hurriedly, Jill dialed Senator Harrison's private cell phone. "Good morning, Senator."

"Jill, the Hill's buzzing about your story."

"What's everyone's gut reaction?"

"That it's highly probable Brown was murdered. It worked, Jill. Congratulations."

"That's great news. And congratulations to you."

"Now the hardest part of all—to sit and wait for the FBI to launch their investigation."

"Your wait may be over," Jill informed him.

"What do you mean?"

"The FBI's on their way to my office now. That's not all. Brown's family has already spoken with my editor. I'm confident that you'll get your autopsy, Senator."

"Did the family approve it?"

"Not exactly, but I'm confident that the FBI will."

"I owe you, Jill."

"No, I owe you for an amazing story, but before we break out the champagne, let me get through this meeting with the FBI."

He chuckled. "When this is all over, I'm going to repay you with a big steak dinner at my farm in Middlesburg."

"A simple thank you is enough."

"Well, we'll see if I can't convince you otherwise. Listen, I've got to go. I'll catch you later."

"Wait! Before you hang up, I have a question for you. Is there any connection between U.S. Fish and Wildlife and Bio Tech Labs?"

"I should say so. I have plans to attend a cocktail party tonight, but if you'd like, I'll meet you afterward for a drink or a late supper, and we'll discuss it."

She definitely got the feeling she was being hit on. "Can you tell me over the phone?"

"It's pretty involved, and besides, if we get together, you can brief me on your meeting with the FBI."

"Okay," Jill acquiesced. "Call me on my cell phone, and I'll meet you somewhere."

Jill clicked off her phone and rode the elevator up to her office. Landry told her the FBI agents were waiting for her in the conference room.

The agents, a woman and two men, were gathered around the massive table with coffee in front of them.

"Hello, everyone, I'm Jill Lewis."

The agents stood. The older agent shook Jill's hand and introduced the other agents. "I'm Abe Masourian of the FBI. I've been assigned to lead this investigation. Ms. Lewis, this is Agent Sally Weinstein and Agent Jimmy Allen. We prefer to be on a first-name basis."

"It's a pleasure to meet all of you."

After shaking the agents' hands, Jill distributed bound copies of the research reports to each agent.

Once they were seated, Jill stood to make a brief statement. "Thank you for coming. These reports show probable cause for a connection between the death of Senator Brown and a drug called MST developed by Bio Tech Labs."

"Are you insinuating that someone at Bio Tech Labs had the senator murdered?" Abe, the older agent, asked.

"I'm only recommending that the FBI order a second autopsy

to confirm these suspicions that Senator Brown was murdered with MST."

"But you suspect Bio Tech Labs is behind this?" Abe tried to force an answer from Jill.

"It's highly probable. Brown was instrumental in halting Bio Tech's MST drug trial."

"What's MST?" Jimmy, the younger agent, asked.

"A drug that Bio Tech Labs developed to treat brain cancer. You'll find the information on page ninety-five. To summarize, laboratory rats treated with MST have survived the cancer. This is extraordinary since the life expectancy of a malignant brain tumor patient is minimal."

"Has the drug been tested on human subjects?" Sally Weinstein asked.

"Yes, but the challenge is adjusting the dosage from the laboratory rats to human subjects. In its first drug trial, the dosage tested resulted in the deaths of a number of participants within hours after the drug was administered."

Abe apparently saw the shock on Jimmy's and Sally's faces and turned to them to explain. "Remember, these cancer patients have only a few months to live. They sign up for drug trials because they have nothing to lose."

"Abe's right," Jill said. "It's not unusual for terminally ill participants in a drug trial to die, but when these MST deaths occurred, Creation Pharmaceutical saw an opportunity to bankrupt Bio Tech Labs."

"Do they have a competitive drug?" Abe asked.

"That's the clever part. Creation used MST as a smoke screen. It was Bio Tech Lab's vascular-targeting drug that Creation wanted off the market. They are earning billions of dollars from their vascular-targeting drug, but the medical journals have touted that Bio Tech's is far superior."

"So Creation saw an opportunity and went through the back door, so no one would suspect them," Jimmy said.

"What part did Senator Brown play in this?" Abe asked.

"It's outlined in the report. Creation Pharmaceutical is located in Brown's state of Ohio, and they've contributed millions of dollars to his reelection campaigns through the years."

"They were calling in a favor," Abe said, nodding his head.

"But how could Brown halt the trials on a promising drug?" Sally asked.

"Every participant dying of a stroke gave Brown the ammunition he needed to claim the lethal drug could become a potential target for biochemical warfare. And since 9-11, creating hysteria over the fact that MST contains a snake venom indigenous to the Middle East isn't too difficult."

"But since the report wasn't released to the public, how did Brown know about it?" Sally pressed.

Jill shook her head. "I'm still working on the answer to that question."

Abe pointed to Jill's reports. "You've given us a motive, but this will remain a conspiracy theory until we've had time to analyze these reports, do some field tests, interview witnesses, and gather all our evidence."

"Read quickly. The senator's body is being cremated tomorrow."

"I can assure you we'll halt the cremation immediately, but until we've had time to look over the reports and conduct an investigation, we won't make a decision on the autopsy," Abe said. "We'll be in touch with you, Jill." He started to turn around but then turned back to Jill. "By the way, we'd like to talk to your source."

"That's impossible," Jill said.

"Well, we may have to subpoena you then," Abe warned as he and the other agents packed up and left. When they were gone, she grabbed the phone to dial Senator Harrison with the good news. Afterward she wrote tomorrow's headline: "FBI Halts Senator Brown's Cremation Until Further Investigation."

Rubric was beside himself with excitement when he came bounding into her office just as Jill was slipping her laptop and a few hard files into her briefcase.

"Are you leaving? I came in here to tell you to take the rest of the afternoon off," he said. "You can take off tomorrow too."

"Thanks, but what I'd really like is to hear if you found out anything about Dan."

Rubric's forehead creased in worry. "I've got nothing. I checked the campus infirmary and a few hospitals. Nobody there had seen him. I even spoke to his roommate. Hadn't seen him since the morning you gave him the key. His roommate showed me Dan's class schedule. He was supposed to go to his internship class. His books were missing, so his roommate assumed Dan had probably made it to class. But he'd never come home that night."

Jill felt her heart drop.

"I checked out all his favorite hangouts according to his roommate," Rubric said. "I showed his picture in his dorm to a bunch of kids, but no one had seen him. My last stop was the campus safety office. A guy there told me that if I call back on Monday they could fax over any campus accident reports."

Rubric looked pretty down, so Jill gave him a pat on the shoulder. "We'll find him, Rube. Don't worry."

Rubric didn't say a word, just walked out of her office.

Jill stood there for a moment, trying to process what Rubric had just told her. Her cell phone's ring jerked her out of her thought. It was Tommy Harrison.

"Hi, Jill. If you can meet me at seven, I'll have dinner for us at my apartment."

She hesitated for a moment, reconsidering if she should have dinner with him in his home, then agreed.

"Good," he said, sounding pleased with himself.

"This isn't a date, Senator. It's a business meeting," Jill reminded him.

"Who says work can't be fun?"

"*Fun* isn't exactly a word I would use to describe myself."

"Oh, but I love a challenge."

Jill sighed as she wrote down Harrison's address on her notepad. She'd already survived a car chase today. How difficult could a middle-aged woman-chaser be?

13

Now the serpent was the most cunning of all the wild animals that the Lord God had made.

Genesis 3:1

"Welcome, Jill, please come in," the senator said, stepping aside to allow her entrance. Dressed casually in blue jeans, a polo shirt, and Gucci loafers, he held an intricately cut crystal glass of bourbon and Coke. He led Jill to his elegantly appointed living room.

Her eyes were immediately drawn to a glittering panoramic view of Washington.

"This is magnificent," Jill said, noticing that the living room was decorated in a pleasing Southwestern décor.

"Thanks. I live here when Congress is in session. What can I get you to drink?"

"Water, please. Do you spend weekends at your farm in Middlesburg?"

"Yes, but after we recess, I go back to my home in Alabama and I hole up there until the Senate reconvenes."

"I'm sure your other homes are lovely. Personally, I'd never want to leave this view."

"Said the city mouse to the country mouse."

"I'd hardly call you a country bumpkin."

"Don't let the facade fool you. I'm happiest at my farm and in my pastures in Alabama. Please, have a seat. I want to hear all about your conference with the FBI today."

"You already know the outcome. First, I'm anxious to learn about the connection between Bio Tech and the U.S. Fish and Wildlife."

Harrison put her water down before her and picked up a silver tray of cheese and crackers on the coffee table and offered it to her.

"Thank you," she said, helping herself.

He speared a piece of cheese and grabbed a cracker off the tray before settling into a leather chair to explain. "Exotic animals and reptiles shipped into this country must go through the port in Miami to be inspected by U.S. Fish and Wildlife."

"For what? Drugs?"

"And a number of other things: legality, disease, and proper shipping standards to ensure the goods or the receiver are not put at risk."

"Snake venom is inspected too?"

"No. Drug protocol calls for absolute purity. Since venom is easily contaminated or diluted, to ensure strictest quality control measures Bio Tech Labs has skilled herpetologists on staff who milk the snakes in their labs."

"Bio Tech uses real snakes?"

"No, they use rubber snakes."

"Stop poking fun at me. Snakes are one topic I've managed to avoid until now. Once I get involved with this investigation, though, I plan to become an expert on the Saw-Scaled Viper and MST."

"I don't doubt that for a minute. Why do you think I called you?" The senator winked at her.

Purposely, she looked the other way.

A young man in his twenties in a crisp white chef's apron popped his head around the corner. "Excuse me, Senator Harrison, but dinner is served."

"You really shouldn't have," Jill said in protest. "I assumed you were ordering takeout when I agreed to dinner."

"Not in this house. Jill, meet Ryan Stiles, my right-hand man. Whenever I'm home, he cooks for me."

"Which is almost never," Ryan added, winking at Jill and offering her his hand. "Hello, Jill, nice to meet you."

"Nice to meet you, Ryan."

"Ryan is also my computer techie and my driver. He's only worked for me for a short while, but I can't imagine what I ever did without him."

"Hope you like red snapper," Ryan said. "The senator caught it on his recent fishing trip to the Florida Keys."

"I love red snapper."

Harrison led Jill to the dining room and pulled a chair out for her at a massive glass-topped table. Jill sat down in the striped Chippendale chair as the senator took his seat beside her. He blessed the food, intriguing Jill all the more.

Ryan served a romaine salad with strawberries, pecans, and vinaigrette dressing. After sampling a bite of the salad, Jill said, "This is absolutely delicious."

"Thank you. Those pecans are from my farm in Alabama."

Ryan returned to open the costly bottle of wine and poured a small amount into the senator's wine glass. The senator closed his eyes and tasted it. "Perfect."

They discussed the investigation extensively over a delicious dinner of red snapper on a bed of wild rice served with steamed asparagus and spaghetti squash with crusty French bread.

"I must admit, since you told me that venom is a component of modern medicines, I've done some research. It was shocking to me. I guess we should think twice before we kill a snake."

"Snake venom has become a lucrative business in the United States."

"I really had no idea."

"It's true, and it takes a lot of milking to procure enough

venom to manufacture an antivenin or enough venom for an ingredient for a drug."

"I'm interested in this particular venom, the one that's used in MST," Jill said.

"The venom of the Saw-Scaled Viper has a cocktail of enzymes that contains miraculous properties."

"Until today I'd never even heard of a Saw-Scaled Viper."

"They're carpet vipers, found in the rocky areas of the deserts of Africa and the Middle East."

"What do they look like?"

"They're small, about eight to ten inches, but they're mean little devils. Gray or brown with brownish blotches and a wavy white stripe, they have a dark marking on their heads in the shape of a cross."

"I'll let you know if I run into one."

"Oh, you'll know it. They'll rub their serrated scales together, creating the sound of a saw cutting wood when they sense you're near."

"So that's how they got their name. Are they similar to a rattlesnake?" Jill asked.

"Yes, but these vipers are a heck of a lot more venomous and aggressive than rattlesnakes. Vipers leap and strike, making it impossible for the prey to get away from them."

Jill raised an eyebrow.

"I'm not joking. These are aggressive snakes. They've even been known to chase their victims."

"Well, then I hope I never see one. How deadly is the venom?"

"I'm afraid that's the worst news of all."

"It can't get any worse than a snake that chases you. But go on, I'm a big girl; I can handle it."

"The Saw-Scaled Viper is considered one of the world's deadliest snakes. More people die from its bite than any other snakebite in the world."

"You know a lot about these snakes."

"I hope I know everything. I've worked closely with the folks at Bio Tech Labs," he said. "Now tell me why their connection with U.S. Fish and Wildlife is so significant?"

Before Jill could respond, Ryan came in the dining room with a silver pie server in one hand and a key lime pie in the palm of the other hand.

"Don't tell me you picked the limes when you were in the Keys?" Jill teased the senator.

Ryan laughed as he served the pie. "The senator's a fisherman, but I bought these limes at Whole Foods, and don't you let him tell you any different."

Inserting a silver fork into the pie, Harrison waved to Jill to continue.

"A couple of days ago, a young woman from U.S. Fish and Wildlife came to see me. She made the same claim you did."

"That Brown was murdered? You're joking."

"At first I didn't believe her, but she said she had proof."

"What kind of proof?"

"A file that apparently contained a memo about snakes and even mentioned Senator Brown."

"Do you have a copy of this file?"

"Someone is delivering it to me, possibly tomorrow." Jill glanced at her watch and said, "Speaking of tomorrow, it's late. I should go."

"Not until you tell me about your meeting with the FBI."

She shrugged. "There's not much to tell. I gave them all the facts you presented to me, and they halted the cremation. You did my homework for me, Senator. Thank you."

"Thanks for running the story and then presenting the documentation to the FBI. Now we just have to wait for them to give the nod for the second autopsy."

"You presented some very convincing evidence, Senator. I don't think we'll have to wait too long." She stood up from her chair. "It's been a lovely evening, but I've got work to do."

"Wait here. I'll get my keys and walk you down to the lobby."

When he left the room, Jill surveyed the photographs on top of the piano. Two young faces, obviously Harrison's children, smiled back at her from a majority of the frames. The boy was a youthful version of the senator, with thick brown hair and an intelligent face. The young woman was blonde and quite svelte, a pretty little thing. Jill picked up a frame of the senator with his son just as the senator walked back into the living room.

Startled, Jill dropped the frame. Bending to retrieve it, she scooped it off the floor, quickly setting it back on the piano. "They're lovely children."

"Caught you snooping, huh?"

Jill blushed.

Harrison chuckled. "They're both away at school. Ready?"

Since there were no photos of the senator's wife, Jill assumed the couple had either been divorced at the time of her death, or else the senator was so grief-stricken he couldn't bear to see his late wife's face. Jill was tempted to ask him what happened to Mrs. Harrison, but she lost her nerve in the elevator ride down to the lobby.

After Jill handed her parking ticket to the valet, Harrison smiled at her. "I really enjoyed having dinner with you tonight."

"It was strictly business, Senator."

"Perhaps we can change that." He leaned toward her as if to kiss her, but she scooted away as the valet pulled up in her car.

Jill hopped in her car as the valet held the door for her, but the senator stepped up to close it.

"Good night, Jill," he said.

Glancing back at the senator in her rearview mirror, Jill mumbled, "If there's a snake in this investigation, it isn't the Saw-Scaled Viper; it's you, Senator Harrison."

14

To see coming toward you
The face that will mean an end of oneness is—
Far more than birth itself—the beginning of life.

Holly Roth

The next few days Jill appeared on all the networks to discuss her front-page story. Senator Brown's possible murder riveted the nation, and everyone was speculating about who wanted him dead. Jill had just returned home after another grueling day when her phone rang. She considered letting the call go to voice mail but picked it up at the last minute. "Jill Lewis."

"Hello, Lois Lane, newswoman extraordinaire."

"John! Are you back in town?"

"I sure am, with two first-class tickets to Chicago in my pocket."

Friday morning Jill saw him from a distance. Dressed casually in jeans and a white shirt, John was leaning up against a pylon at the airport, absorbed in reading the *Gazette*. Twisting the plastic engagement ring on her finger, she smiled, hoping he wasn't an illusion. John looked up from the newspaper as though he sensed she was near. As their eyes met, she paused and then ran into his arms.

"I missed you, Jill," John whispered, planting kisses on her face. "I wanted to call, but there was never any time."

"I was pretty busy myself."

"I can see that," John said, grinning and pointing to the newspaper. "Congratulations! I've been reading your articles every day."

"Let's just hope I get that second autopsy. But this is our weekend, no business. I'm all yours except that I promised Rubric I'd keep my cell phone hot and check my email twice a day."

"Ah, Rubric. Is he coming along on our honeymoon as well?"

"Oh, please."

When the gate agent announced it was time to board the plane, John picked up his carry-on and took Jill's bag from her. Curiosity over John's investigation was driving her batty, but Jill dared not ask—yet. She'd wait for the right time and sort of slip it into the conversation. First they had more important things to discuss on the flight, like wedding dates, honeymoon destinations and china patterns.

When the plane landed at O'Hare, they walked hand-in-hand to baggage claim. Jill felt nervous, being only yards away from meeting her fiancé's father. *Will he like me?*

John pointed out his father, who was waiting behind the wall of glass along with dozens of others looking for their loved ones. John waved wildly, then pointed at Jill before giving her a bear hug, nearly knocking her off her feet. Jill blushed and then waved back at the older version of her fiancé. John's father was tall, lanky, and handsome in a rugged sort of way. His wavy hair was distinguishably grayed at the temples, but those same twinkling periwinkle blue eyes were unmistakable.

Moments later, Mr. Lovell walked up to greet them.

"Jill, this is my father, John Lovell Jr. Dad, this is my bride-to-be, Jill Lewis," John said and proudly pulled Jill front and center, making her feel as if she were a rare pedigree at a dog show.

"Mr. Lovell, this is such an honor." She reached out her hand.

"Don't give me that Mr. Lovell stuff. Everyone calls me Big John."

Before Jill said another word, Big John gave her a hug. With Jill under one of his arms, the older man greeted his son with the other arm. The father-son embrace was so tight that Jill feared she'd be smothered between them.

Dropping the bags at a bench near the curb, Big John turned to his son. "John, you've found a mighty pretty face to sit across from you at the breakfast table every morning."

"She's a smart one too," John said proudly as he pecked Jill's other cheek.

"Careful! I bruise easily."

Mr. Lovell went to get the car and pulled up to the curb a few minutes later. The couple heard Gracie before actually seeing her. Nearly unrecognizable, Gracie was easily three times larger than the last time Jill saw her. John lifted the back door to the SUV. In an instant, Gracie was out and all over him, wild with slobbery licks. Her tail hit the car so fast and hard that Jill expected some dent damage. It was a sweet scene, seeing John and Gracie together again.

"Gracie," Jill called out to the dog.

At the sound of her voice, Gracie froze. Then the dog bounced toward her and stopped to smell Jill's feet. Her black nose followed Jill's body up to her waist, where she finally recognized the scent. Wiggling her posterior, she shot her front paws up on Jill, causing her to fall back into Big John's arms.

"Oops!"

"Gracie, down!" John called, pulling at her collar.

"It's all right, really," Jill said, hugging the dog.

"I'm looking forward to meeting your mother tomorrow," Big John said. "John says she's quite the charmer."

"Mom can get a little carried away with company coming, although I've warned her not to overdo. But you're going to love her."

"John says you're surprising her with the news of your engagement. I hope she won't be offended that my son's not asked her for your hand. Where I come from, that's a no-no."

"Oh, she'll love the surprise much more. She's quite fond of your son, but she only knows him as Craig Martin, the name he used in our undercover investigation. Mother is under the impression that John Lovell is a new beau, so this is going to be a surprise when she sees Craig."

"I hope so," Mr. Lovell replied, turning the steering wheel north toward the Wisconsin border on the interstate.

When Jill saw the Welcome to Delavan sign, she became giddy. Her hometown was like a time capsule with the old buildings, old water tower, and art deco clock tower. The cozy storefronts were just as she remembered, lined with rows of vintage lampposts draped with American flags whirling and unfurling in the breeze.

At last, they were at the front gates of the Lewis estate and drove down the long cobblestone drive shaded by a canopy of trees. After his dad parked the car in the driveway, John got Jill's luggage from the trunk. Jill noticed her mother's car was gone and apologized. "We're early, and Mother's not here to greet you. I'm sorry."

"No problem. I'll meet her tomorrow."

"Yes, please come by for breakfast tomorrow, say around eight o'clock."

"We'll be here," John told her and then kissed her good night. In line right behind his son, Mr. Lovell was next to give her a good night peck. Gracie had to have her kiss in the form of a slobbery lick.

Jill hurried inside. From the kitchen window she watched

the taillights disappear down the drive. She helped herself to a quick supper, and then lugged her suitcases up the steps to the second floor. Just as she finished unpacking, she heard her mother and ran downstairs.

"Welcome home, my darling! Where is your young man?" Pearl was coming in the back door from the grocery store.

Jill answered as she began to empty the paper bags. "John was sorry to have missed you, but I've invited him for breakfast at eight."

"I just don't know if I can wait another day to meet your Prince Charming. Why don't you call him and ask him to drop by for dessert and coffee?"

"Oh, it's too late. I'm exhausted, and I can't wait to crawl in bed so I'll be fresh for tomorrow."

"Did you find the baked-potato soup in the Crock-Pot?"

"It was delicious, thank you."

"Now tell me all about John."

"He's kind and considerate with a great sense of humor. We have provocative discussions, and each time I'm with him I fall more in love with him."

"Go on . . . I want to hear every detail."

"It will have to wait until tomorrow. My current investigation has really zapped my energy. I've had to pull several all-nighters."

"Get some rest then." She patted Jill's cheek affectionately. "I wish you didn't have such a stressful job. You should move home and enjoy a tranquil life."

"Good night, Mother." Ignoring her suggestion, she kissed her mother's cheek before heading off for the stairs.

"Good night, darling," Pearl called after her.

Away from Washington, Jill got the first peaceful night's sleep that she'd had in days.

Returning from her jog the next morning, Jill found her mother in the kitchen.

"Morning, darling, I didn't hear you slip out earlier. This is the day that the Lord hath made, let us rejoice and be glad in it."

Jill moaned. "Mom, let's try not to recite a verse of Scripture each time we open our mouths today."

"Are you worried I'm going to embarrass you in front of your young man? I thought you told me he was a Christian."

"He is, but . . ."

"Don't worry. I'll behave myself." Pearl pulled at Jill's faded jogging clothes. "What happened to the cute Juicy sweats I gave you for your birthday?"

"They're too dressy and too tight for me to wear on a run. You'll have to accept that I'm more into comfort than fashion, Mom."

"I'll just order another a couple of sizes larger for you to run in, and you can wear your other one around the house. What color would you like?"

"Please don't bother."

"I insist."

"Then you decide." Jill looked at her mother, who of course looked perfect in her Escada warm-up suit and her spotless size-five Nikes. Jill chuckled. Only her mother wore pearls with a warm-up suit. Naturally her hair was perfect without a single strand out of place.

"You'd better get dressed in case our guest comes early. Oh, that obnoxious little man from your office, what's his name? Rubric? He called you this morning to remind you to turn on your cell phone. Can't those newspaper people ever leave you alone?"

"Thanks for the message. What's this?" Jill picked up a tablet with a list of names written in Pearl's stylish handwriting.

"Oh, I thought it might be nice to have a few people over for brunch on Sunday to meet John."

"A few?" Jill began adding up the guest list in her head. "Like maybe the whole town, Mother? An intimate little get-together with five hundred people?"

"Stop being silly, Jill. Anyway, I've already called the caterer. It's all arranged."

Looking out the window, Jill spotted John and his father coming up the driveway. "Uh, I'm going outside for a few minutes."

"But Jill, you need to shower before our guest arrives!"

Jill was already out the door, running to greet both men stepping out of the car with Gracie in tow. "Morning. Come on inside."

"Good morning," John said, kissing her cheek. "Dad, you go ahead with Jill. I'll be in right after Gracie takes care of business."

The handsome older man followed behind Jill up to the side door of the house. Like a flash, the door jerked open, causing the hydrangea wreath to madly sway from side to side. Pearl appeared smiling on the other side of the door.

Pearl's demeanor suddenly changed. Examining the fiftysomething man from head to toe, she narrowed her eyes at him.

"Mother, this is John Lovell Jr."

"Oh, hello," Pearl said between clenched teeth.

"John, this is my mother, Pearl Lewis." *Mother can't really think . . . ? She does!* Realizing that Pearl had mistaken John's father as her beau, Jill decided to have some fun and play along.

"Nice to meet you, Pearl. Please call me Big John. All my friends do." He shook Pearl's hand vigorously.

Raising her voice, Pearl said, "Well, come on in, Jill, and you too, Big John." Stiffly, she offered Big John an armchair to sit in while directing Jill toward the couch. "Coffee for anyone?" she asked.

"I'm fine, Mom. How about you, Big John?"

"Coffee sounds good."

Jill fought the urge to giggle. Her mother had undoubtedly mistaken this handsome older man as Jill's newest love interest. Jill couldn't resist continuing the charade.

"I need your help in the kitchen, darling," her mother said. "Now, please."

"If it's all right with you, I'll just stay out here with John."

Pearl shook her head and walked into the kitchen. The sound of slamming cabinets soon followed.

A few minutes later, Pearl was back—this time with the phone in her hand. "Jill, it's that darling little man from your office. Better take it in the kitchen. He says it's important, so it's most likely of a private nature."

"So Rubric's darling now instead of obnoxious?" Jill asked as she followed her mother to the kitchen to take the call.

After assuring Rubric she'd keep her cell phone on and charged, she turned around to face her mother. Usually those looks dropped Jill to her knees, but this time she chose to ignore it. Huffing a bit, Pearl reached for the mugs, accidentally crashing two against each other, badly chipping one. Disgustedly she tossed it out and reached for another. "Darn! I loved this old set too."

"I'll start the water, Mom." Filling up the kettle at the sink, Jill looked outside to see her John playing with Gracie on their walk back from the fence line.

"Jill," her mother said.

Quickly pulling the curtains together to shut out the view, Jill turned around. "Yes, Mother?"

"How long have you known this, uh, John character?" Pearl set out a half dozen of her home-baked blueberry muffins.

"Long enough to know he's the man I want to marry."

"I never pictured you with . . . him, an older man. Although I must admit, he's quite handsome." Before Jill could respond, Pearl continued, "I'm sure he's been married before, hasn't he?"

"Yes, but his wife died of cancer."

"Praise the Lord!" Pearl exclaimed.

"Mother!"

"I meant that he's not divorced—or worse yet, married. Divorced men have baggage, and some even have children. I know what this is about . . . I recently read a study on this very thing.

You're replacing your dead father with an older man. Big John is your new father figure."

Just as the microwave timer pinged, Jill heard someone come in through the back door. "Hello! Anyone home?" John called out. Gracie bounded in, perfectly aware she still owned the place.

Pearl's face brightened. "Jill! That sounds to me like Craig Martin's voice. And Gracie!" Pearl nearly sprinted into the hallway to hug him.

John winked at Jill.

"Jill, look who's here! It's Craig Martin! You look so young, and wow, what great shape you're in. Say hello to Craig, Jill," Pearl said.

"Hey you. Come on into the kitchen and have some breakfast," Jill said.

Following the singing teakettle into the kitchen, Pearl asked, "What brings you here, Craig?"

"Yeah, Craig, why are you here?" Jill said with a laugh.

John was smiling broadly. "Should I tell her now?"

Jill nodded.

"Mrs. Lewis, the reason I'm here is . . . I've come to ask you for your blessing. I want to ask for your daughter's hand in marriage."

Pearl's mouth flew open as she turned around and looked at Jill. "Haven't I always told you not to give up five minutes before the miracle happens? If we stop trusting God, then sometimes we find ourselves in a big mess like this one." Turning to John, Pearl said, "Yes, you have my blessing!"

John shot Jill a puzzled glance as Pearl shoved her into his arms. He kissed her.

"What's going on in here?" Big John asked, walking into the kitchen.

"Big John, I'm so sorry, but I must speak. Before Jill met you, she was in love with this man, the one she's kissing."

Jill and John pulled apart. "Mom, meet John Lovell the third," Jill said, pointing to Craig.

"You're John Lovell? If you're . . . then who are you?" Pearl pointed to the older man.

"I'm John Lovell Jr."

"Is this some kind of reality TV program?" Pearl asked.

Within a few minutes Jill had the situation explained.

After playfully batting Jill in the arm, Pearl stepped forward to give the older man a big hug. "I'm so sorry about the confusion, but this is a wonderful surprise. Will you forgive me for being rude, Big John? We adore your son, and I've never been happier for my daughter."

"I can assure you I'm just as happy about this as you are," Big John said. "Jill is a lovely young woman in every way. And I can see for myself where she gets it too."

Pearl blushed demurely. "Thank you. Come on, everyone, gather around the table and enjoy some coffee and muffins while I put breakfast on the table. Jill, check the frittata in the oven. The fruit salad's on the table, and I'll make some more coffee."

When breakfast was served, Big John said the blessing and they dove into the delicious food. The four of them discussed family, the wedding, and various other topics.

After breakfast Pearl invited Big John to take a tour of the home, leaving Jill and John alone at last. Noticing that Gracie was snoozing in the sun over by the window, Jill asked, "Would you like to walk down to the lake, John?"

Hand in hand, they started the descent down the hill from the house to the lake. They sat in a swing on the long pier and watched the flow of the water. Each wave crashed into three others, leaving zigzag lines of whitecaps. This lake held many memories for them, a few from their investigation they'd prefer to forget, but Delavan would always remain special. This was the place they fell in love.

"I have something for you," John said as he reached inside his pocket.

Jill turned to face him.

"It's time to replace that plastic ring you've been hiding from your mother."

"John, it's not that I don't love it . . . It's just that it's something special between us, and I don't want anyone to disparage it. That's why I haven't shown it to my mother."

"No need to explain." John's hand pulled out a velvet box. He took the heirloom ring out and slipped it on her finger.

"Oh, it's stunning." Jill gasped as she looked at the oval-cut emerald flanked by two sparkling diamonds set on a platinum band. "This is the most beautiful ring I've ever seen."

"It was my grandmother's, then my mother's, and now it's yours. If you haven't changed your mind about marrying me, that is."

"Are you kidding? I'll tell you a million times . . . I'll marry you, marry you, marry you."

John kissed her fingertips. "I hope you like it, but if you don't, I want you to pick out whatever ring you like . . . within my budget, of course."

"No, I meant what I said. It's beautiful and I love it. It's vintage, my very favorite style."

"I believe you." Just as John leaned in for a kiss, his beeper went off and he groaned after looking at the number. "Uh-oh, I'm afraid this call is an emergency from the bureau. Excuse me a minute." John walked toward the house.

Jill sat swinging, but the chain creaked so loudly that she slowed it with her feet so she could hear what John was saying. But his voice was too muffled for her to make out the words. In minutes John came back. "Is there a problem?" Jill asked.

John sat down beside her and took her hand. "I'm afraid so. I have to fly back to Washington tonight and then on to Florida. I'm booked on a red-eye to Miami."

"You have to leave?"

"I'm sorry, Jill."

"Then I'm going to fly back with you. Mom will understand."

"Are you sure?"

Jill nodded.

Inside the house they found Pearl and Big John at the kitchen table, laughing and talking over coffee as the sunlight poured in the floor-to-ceiling window.

"Ta-da! My ring," Jill said and held it out for her mother to see.

"Oh, darling. It's gorgeous." Pearl jumped up and gave Jill a big hug and then turned to John. "Welcome to the family!"

"Thanks," he said. "I hate to spoil this happy moment, but I've got to leave earlier than planned. The bureau has called me back to Washington tonight."

Jill turned to her mother. "I've decided to go with him, Mom. I hope you're not upset."

Pearl looked disappointed for a moment, then put a smile on her face and waved her hand in dismissal. "You might as well go back with John if that's what you want to do, Jill. I can't very well throw an engagement party without him, now can I? I'll call and cancel faster than the plans were made."

Jill squeezed her mother tightly. "I'm sorry our visit was cut short."

"I am too, darling, but I understand. Anyway, you've left me with many things to do in your absence. We'll visit daily by phone about the wedding."

Just then Jill's phone rang, and she pulled it out of her purse and headed into the other room to answer it. "Hello?"

"I hope I'm not interrupting anything."

"Senator Harrison. What can I do for you?"

"Having a nice weekend?"

"The best. I'm with my family."

"Give them my regards."

"Thank you, I will."

"I thought you'd like to know the FBI contacted me today. They want to question me first thing Monday morning."

"That's a good sign," Jill noted.

"Either that or you told them I was your informant."

"I'll never tell. No matter how much they torture me," Jill joked.

"Is it possible we could talk before then? Maybe sometime Sunday?"

"I'll try to call you Sunday afternoon."

"Please do. It's important," Tommy reiterated.

"Okay." She hung up, then jumped when she turned around and saw John standing in the doorway.

John raised an eyebrow at her. "Rubric again?"

"No, Senator Harrison."

"What did he want?"

"A meeting with me to discuss my investigation."

John shook his head. "The guy's bad news."

"What do you mean?"

"Just trust me, Jill, don't get involved with Tom Harrison personally or professionally."

"But I'm already involved with him on my investigation."

"Then do your business and then get uninvolved."

The flight from Chicago to Washington was bumpy, so neither John nor Jill slept. Turning on the cabin light to admire her beautiful emerald engagement ring, Jill leaned onto John's shoulder.

"Got any special honeymoon requests?" he asked.

"Somewhere warm with cool breezes, and a turquoise ocean framed by white sandy beaches with watercolor sunsets," Jill said. "Oh, I want to take scuba-diving lessons."

"Mmm. That sounds great. Let's get them to turn this plane around and go there right now."

Jill smiled. Closing her eyes, she transported herself to such a place. She lay on warm sands snuggled next to John.

When John had enough of her uncharacteristic silence, he whispered in her ear, "Is there something bothering you?"

"What could possibly be bothering me? I've never been happier."

"I know you haven't been frolicking on that imaginary beach in your mind all this time. You might as well come out with it."

Jill sat up straight. "Okay, but I'm a little hesitant to bring this up again since I know you can't talk about all the machinations of your career. John, is there anything else you can tell me about Senator Harrison?"

"I guess I asked for it. But I can't comment."

"But does your current investigation involve the Alabama senator? If it does, can we trade information?"

"I've given you my opinion of the man."

"Yes, but what does he have to do with your investigation?"

"Nothing. When I told you to stay away from him, it was strictly based on the rumors I've heard around Washington."

"But you didn't say he wasn't involved in your investigation."

"Because I can't. The sooner you learn this, the easier our relationship will be."

She folded her arms across her chest. "Fine. But I need Harrison for my story, so I've got to spend some time with him."

"Do what you have to do professionally."

By the look on his face, she knew she had pushed too hard. So much for this "two shall become one" stuff! As long as John was FBI, there would always be a part of him that was off-limits to Jill. Could she accept all his secrets?

"Hey, let's talk about our honeymoon some more. How does Hawaii sound?"

Once they exited the plane in Washington, John paused only long enough to kiss Jill good-bye. Then looking in her eyes, he whispered to her, "Remember, I'll always come back to you . . . eventually." He sprinted through the airport to catch his flight to Miami.

His parting words worried Jill. *Why did he say that now? How long will it be before I see him again?*

"Stop worrying," she scolded herself as she twisted the engagement ring on her finger. *We've got the rest of our lives to spend together.*

15

God's gifts put man's best dreams to shame.
Elizabeth Barrett Browning

Jill's morning was veiled with sadness. Already she missed John. She was glad when she remembered it was Sunday. Church was a spirit-lifter for Jill. Within an hour she was dressed and power walking down H Street toward 16th Street to St. John's Church on Lafayette Square. Slipping through the red door, she tiptoed down the aisle of the sanctuary and then stopped halfway to squish into the pew beside a pleasant older couple. Upon recognizing Jill, several people nodded and smiled a warm welcome. Jill acknowledged the couple and then bowed her head in prayer.

Hearing a small commotion at the back of the church, Jill turned to catch sight of Senator Harrison heading in her direction. What was he doing here? Jill watched him walk straight up the middle aisle toward the front. He paused briefly at her pew, acknowledged her with a dazzling smile, and continued on down the aisle.

Whew! Relieved that her pew was packed to overflowing and there was no seat for him, Jill watched as the senator took a seat down in the front. How convenient—where everyone could see him. Once Harrison settled into the pew, Jill watched a small gathering of worshipers rush to greet him and shake his hand. No wonder the man had an ego the size of Texas.

The organ rang out, and Jill rose with the congregation to sing a hymn. When the sermon began she forgot all about Senator Harrison as she became absorbed in Rev. Hayes Perdue's poignant sermon.

After the service, Jill remained in the courtyard, chatting with a small circle of friends, showing off her ring, and discussing the sermon until she felt a tap on her shoulder.

"Hello, Ms. Lewis. How nice to see you again."

Jill's friends waved good-bye and walked away, not wanting to intrude.

"What are you doing here?" Jill asked.

Harrison chuckled softly. "Don't look so worried. I'm not stalking you, I'm a member at St. John's."

"I've never seen you here before."

"How would you know if you'd seen me or not—we just met. Besides, when I saw you, I thought you were stalking me."

"Oh, please, everyone in America knows who you are," Jill reminded him as she stood on her tiptoes and looked around the grounds of the church.

"Looking for your boyfriend?"

"Photographers."

"The president's not here today, so the cameras aren't either. I see you're here alone. I assume those big plans you said you had for the weekend didn't go well?"

"Au contraire." Jill held up her hand for him to see her ring.

"Then I guess your fiance's not a Bible-toting man, huh?"

"That's none of your concern."

"I beg to differ. As a Christian brother, I'm obligated to remind you that the Bible does say, 'Do not be unequally yoked.'"

"If you're worried about my soul, don't be. John's a believer, he's just out of town on business."

"If I'd put that ring on your finger, I wouldn't let you out of my sight for a minute."

"Some of us have to work for a living, Senator."

He held up his hands in mock surrender. "I'm sorry, I was only teasing."

"Senator, please, if we're going to work together, you're going to have to stop this . . ."

"This what?"

"Flirtation."

"I prefer to call it admiration."

"Well, whatever you want to call it, stop it."

"All right. Truce?"

She nodded her head. "Should we cancel our lunch date? I'm not sure it's wise for the two of us to be seen in public together."

"It's too late to hide now. The FBI's already brought me into this investigation, so the pressure's off. You no longer have to protect me." The senator gestured to the long black Lincoln that pulled up to the curb. Ryan Stiles hopped out to open the car's door for them.

"Hello, Miss Lewis, nice to see you again," Ryan greeted her warmly.

"Thank you, Ryan, it's nice to see you too."

"Where to, boss?" Ryan asked the senator.

"We're headed to 3001 Connecticut Avenue."

As the car pulled out into traffic, Jill asked, "What's there?"

"Let's just call it lunch-'n-learn."

Jill wondered just what this man thought he could teach her. John was right; she should stay away from him. Well, at least after the investigation was done. Harrison, in the meanwhile, had some vital information she needed, and he appeared just as eager to solve this case as she was. Resisting the temptation to judge him, she vowed to get through this investigation.

When the car finally came to a stop, Jill laughed as she read the sign. "We're having lunch at the National Zoological Park?"

"Home of the city's best hot dogs." Harrison stepped out of the car and helped Jill from the backseat.

"Ryan, give us a couple of hours, and I'll call you when we're ready to leave."

The meaty aroma from the hot dog stand wafted toward them, making Jill ravenous, but to her disappointment, the senator waved her past the big red hot dog cart with the mustard-colored wheels.

"Hey, what about our lunch?"

"Homework first," he told her, escorting her down Olmsted Walk. "Lesson number one. Cut the 'Senator' and call me by my name."

"You Southerners have so many names. What am I supposed to call you? I've seen you on *Hardball*, and Chris Matthews calls you Thomas Henry. Bill O'Reilly on Fox News refers to you as Thomas, and Diane Sawyer calls you Tommy."

"My friends call me Tommy."

"Tommy it is."

"In spite of your suspicions, I wasn't stalking you. You promised you would call when you came back to Washington this afternoon, so we could talk before I meet with the FBI tomorrow. The fact that you showed up at my church earlier today was, let's say, a God thing. What have you told the FBI about my involvement?"

"Trust me, I'd go to jail before I'd reveal the name of a source. But since the FBI's already involved you, why don't you decide if you want to tell them we're working together or not?"

"Good, then the power remains with me. I'll tell them tomorrow that we're working together," Tommy said as he stopped in front of a large brick building with an octagonal dome on top. He pointed to the sign: Reptiles & Amphibians.

"Oh no," Jill said, shaking her head. "I'm not going in there."

"Come on, you don't want to flunk Snake 101. I want to make sure that you get a good, long look at the Saw-Scaled Viper."

"That won't be necessary. I've seen enough photos of that little viper online."

"It's one thing to see it on a page; quite another to see it in the flesh. Is Jill Lewis admitting she's afraid of a little snake enclosed behind thick glass? What do you know?"

"Oh, all right. Let's go. I'm right behind you."

Just outside the entrance, a zookeeper dressed in khakis and wearing a stick-on tag that read "Hello, my name is Bruce" held a long, thick snake up for a group of children. A brave few were stroking it. Jill and Tommy paused to listen as Bruce explained to the kids, "There are many different kinds of snakes in the world. Most of them are quite harmless. But there are some snakes that are poisonous. If you see a snake, don't touch it or try to pick it up yourself but leave the area and alert an adult about the snake. Now, are there any questions?"

Several hands shot up in the crowd. He pointed to a little girl's waving hand.

"What's the name of the snake?"

"Ralphie," Bruce replied. "He's a king snake. See how his eyes are to the front of the head? That's a good indicator that Ralphie is a nonvenomous snake. There are a lot of folks who get bitten trying to determine if the snake is poisonous or not, so don't try to figure it out yourself."

"Don't worry. You won't see me touching a snake," Jill mumbled under her breath.

Bruce motioned the gathering crowd inside the reptile house. "You're in for a real treat. It's feeding time. Go on back to the tanks and watch the snakes as they eye their prey and then devour it. You'll find it fascinating."

"Fascinating? It's downright disgusting, if you ask me."

"I think you're enjoying yourself. Come on. Let's take a look at the Saw-Scaled Viper." Tommy led Jill straight back to the tank of poisonous vipers.

She gazed at the coil of snakes. Yep, there they were—the

bone-chilling reptiles that not only slithered through her dreams but were at the centerpiece of this investigation too.

"The Saw-Scaled Vipers are smaller than most other snakes, but they pack lots of power and poison," Tommy explained. "Hey, look. They're feeding the snakes over to our right. Let's watch."

Jill made a face but followed him over to the tank that housed the largest poisonous snake in the world right after the king cobra—the black mamba. The mamba was a long and skinny thing, quite agile in movement. His yellow slanted eyes sent more shivers over her body. Jill watched as the zookeeper deposited a white rat into the tank. Right away the defenseless rat sensed danger and tried to burrow. Having time to play, the mamba watched the rat for a short time before slowly uncoiling.

Jill jumped as the snake reached and grabbed the rodent with lightning speed, sinking its fangs into the soft flesh. The rat twitched and shook its limbs violently in death throes before falling motionless.

"Bon appetit," the senator whispered as the snake began to swallow the rodent. Jill winced as she watched the rodent's form slowly moving through the snake's body.

Jill went back for one more look at the Saw-Scaled Vipers. One of the vipers spotted Jill and swirled up closer to the glass. The snake leaped at her, furiously swiping and striking, its venom dripping down the glass. Jill's scream echoed throughout the reptile house and brought Tommy running to her side.

"What happened?"

"Let's get out of here."

"I've seen a snake strike dozens of times, and it's still a thrill." Tommy seemed mesmerized by the snake.

"You actually enjoy this?"

"Nature fascinates me. I love to camp, hunt, and fish, anything outdoors. How about you?"

"My idea of camping is a suite at the Ritz-Carlton. Come on, let's get out of here."

Tommy and Jill walked a far distance from the reptile house to a park bench where they could sit down and collect their thoughts. "So what do you think of the Saw-Scaled Viper?"

"I hope I'll never lay these eyes on one again." Jill turned to look at the senator. "How long do you think it will take the FBI to discover that Senator Brown was murdered?"

"Ah, so we're back to the investigation, I see. First, they'll have to establish that MST was the cause of death. To do that, they'll have to perform a second autopsy."

"They'll order a second autopsy," Jill replied confidently.

"They've called an investigation after your front-page story, so they already suspect that Brown didn't die of natural causes, and that's why I'm being questioned. The FBI considers me a suspect in his murder."

"That's no surprise since you and Brown were openly hostile to one another."

"Whether they suspect me or not, I'm sure the FBI will question me relentlessly for hours about Bio Tech Labs. By tomorrow afternoon they will have subpoenaed all the company's files."

"Let's assume they discover that Brown was poisoned with MST. Will they launch a full-fledged investigation?"

"Oh, believe me, I think they already have."

"You have nothing to hide."

"True, but I want this case solved. I believe we're dealing with a potentially hazardous threat that could wipe out a lot more people than a suicide bomber. And that is motivation for the FBI to take this seriously."

"If only I could find Ally Cooper and get my hands on that file she confiscated from U.S. Fish and Wildlife."

Tommy sighed. "I agree. It would be nice to have something to back my claims. Do you believe what she told you was true?"

"I wasn't sure until I met with you, and then every piece seemed to fit together so perfectly."

"Where is the file now?"

"In a locker at the Trailways Bus Station. I sent an intern with the key to pick it up for me several days ago, and I'm afraid he's disappeared."

"You realize that your intern's life is in danger, if he's not dead already. Have you filed a missing person's report?"

"My editor, Rubric, filed one informally with the police department and also with the campus security police at Georgetown, where the intern is a student."

"We've got to get that file. Do you have an extra key to the locker?"

Humiliated by her oversight, Jill mumbled, "No." *How could I have been so sloppy on this investigation? Simple—I've had my head in the clouds since John showed up in my life again.*

"Did you tell the FBI about this file?"

"No, I didn't want to mention it to anyone until I'd had a chance to validate it. I had to tell my editor, but he's the only other person who knows about the file. And he's just as eager as I am to get his hands on that file."

"Why didn't you tell me about this sooner so I could've helped you get that file?"

"Can you pull any strings for us?"

"Strings, no, locks, yes." He flashed her a charming smile.

"A senator can't go around picking locks."

"They can if people's lives depend on it. I'd rather risk my career ripping off the red tape than save it waiting for the bumbling bureaucrats to cut it. Now, how about a hot dog?"

"How about two, smothered in onions with a glob of mustard?"

"You don't have to eat onions to keep me away from you."

But Jill wasn't so sure, so she got her hot dogs just like she wanted them. Tommy ordered a chili dog and a side order of greasy French fries drizzled with cheese. They balanced their food with icy Cokes and walked over to the picnic tables under the shade of a willow tree.

"This is so much fun." Jill smiled at Tommy.

"You're a low-maintenance woman."

"Is that a nice way to say I'm a cheap date? Uh, I meant a cheap appointment." Wiping mustard from her mouth, Jill wished she could also wipe the red blush off her face. "That was delicious. Would you like some cotton candy?"

"Allow me." Tommy got up and brought back two swirls, a pink one for Jill and blue one for him.

Snatching a piece of the pink confection off the cone, she said, "When I was a kid, my grandmother told me that clouds were made of cotton candy, and I believed her until I was almost twelve."

"Where did you grow up, Jill?"

"Wisconsin, but I spent my summers with my grandmother."

"Where does your grandmother live?"

"Fairhope near Mobile." Jill instantly regretted mentioning her grandmother.

"Mm, I remember you said that when we met, but I don't know any Lewises from Mobile."

"She's not a Lewis, she's a Winthrop."

The senator folded his arms and smiled. "You're Claire Winthrop's granddaughter, aren't you?"

Jill nodded.

"The Bedingfield-Winthrop Foundation does a lot of good in the world, especially in Alabama. You should be proud of your Southern roots."

"You probably know more about my roots than I do. My mother wanted my sister and me to have a normal childhood, so she never discussed the family business with us." Jill stopped and then gasped. Pointing straight ahead she whispered, "That's Crew Cut!"

"Who?" Tommy looked confused.

"Hurry, he's getting away!" Jill yelped as she saw Crew Cut turn around and run. She started to go after him.

Tommy held her back. "Wait here," he ordered as he took off after the man.

A few minutes later, he jogged back, out of breath. "I lost him. Now, explain to me why I was running after him in the first place."

Jill gave her brief history with Crew Cut, beginning with the first time she saw him, the day Senator Brown collapsed on the Capitol steps.

Tommy's mouth tightened in a grim line. "I'm betting Crew Cut is our hit man. Jill, I think you need a bodyguard."

"In my ten years as a reporter, I've never had a bodyguard. I'm not starting now."

He grinned at her. "I love a feisty woman. Come on, let's get out of here."

While Tommy called Ryan for the car, Jill's mind raced. As obnoxious as Tommy could sometimes be, she had to admit at times he was utterly charming. Twisting her engagement ring, she felt guilty for enjoying her afternoon with him.

Back in the car Tommy told her, "I need the location and the number of the locker where this mysterious file is supposedly stashed." He held up a Swiss army knife for her to see.

"You have a Swiss army knife with a USB memory drive?"

"It's the latest toy, the Cyber Tool. Ryan is up on all that high-tech stuff, and he got it for me."

Jill dictated the locker information to Tommy to type into his BlackBerry. He then reached inside his briefcase and pulled out half a dozen CDs. "The personnel files from Bio Tech Labs; everyone's there from the janitor to the CEO. Use that suspicious mind of yours and tell me which one of these employees or board members might be suspect."

"Will do." Jill stashed the stack of CDs in the middle section of her purse.

When the senator dropped Jill off at her apartment, he made a promise to her. "If the file is in that locker at the Trailways Bus Station, I'll have it on your desk by morning."

Jill didn't doubt him for a minute.

16

Because we are always staring at the stars,
we learn the shortness of our arms.

Mary Roberts Rinehart

Jill left for the office earlier than usual. No doubt Ally's file would be on her desk, and she couldn't wait to discover what secrets were written inside it. She maneuvered her Range Rover down the back streets of Washington in an effort to get to her office in record time.

"Morning, Landry," Jill called out as she swooped by the front desk on the way to her office.

"Wait a minute," Landry called out to her. "The way you slide by me every morning you'd think I was home plate."

Jill turned around. "What is it?"

Landry wrinkled her nose. "Rubric wants to see you in his office right away."

"What's up?"

Landry shrugged her shoulders.

"Call him and tell him I'll be there in five minutes."

Racing to her office to look for Ally's file, Jill was just turning the doorknob when Rubric stepped from behind, making her jump. Dropping a key into her hand, he grinned. "For you."

"Don't sneak up on me. And where did you get this?" Jill asked, turning the key over in her hand.

"Dan."

"Where is he?"

"In the hospital. He was hit by a car before he ever got to the bus station. Come on, let's run over to Trailways and pick up that file."

"Wait, is Dan okay?"

"He will be, but he's been in a coma, and his leg is broken in three places."

Jill grimaced. "How'd you finally find him?"

"One of our stringers finally found him at Georgetown Hospital. He was listed as a redhead John Doe."

"Why didn't the stringer look there earlier?"

"He did, but he swore none of the John Does registered were Dan."

"I hope you fired him."

"No, it was an honest mistake. Dan's head was so banged up they shaved off his red hair, and he was so pale, the stringer thought he was an old man. At least he had the sense to go back and look at all the John Does again today. And sure enough, that old man turned out to be Dan."

"When did the accident happen?"

"The same morning he was supposed to pick up the file, an SUV ran him down."

"SUV? Then this was no accident."

"So what are you doing to find out who these people are?"

"I'm counting on Ally Cooper's file to tell me."

"What if this missing file turns out to be a dud?"

"I have other leads. In the meantime, let's go to the hospital and talk to Dan."

"I've already been there. He didn't see a thing. If he had, he wouldn't remember it anyway."

"Did anyone see it happen?"

"A couple of witnesses hung around until the cops got there. It's all here in the police report." He held up a folder, which Jill promptly snatched out of his hand.

"First, let's go and see if this girl's mysterious file even exists."

"You're too late, Rubric. I've made other arrangements for the file to be picked up this morning. I expect it's already on my desk."

"Let's have a look at it then." Rubric swung the door to her office open for her.

Jill blazed through the door with Rubric, who watched as she hurriedly shuffled through the papers on her desk, scattering them everywhere. The large desk was piled high with mountains of research, memos, and junk mail. She yanked open the drawers and dug through them but found nothing. The file just wasn't there. Again.

Jill looked at the clock on her desk. "It's still early. They'll drop it off later, I'm sure."

"Depending on someone else is what got us into this mess in the first place. Let's go get it ourselves."

She crossed her arms over her chest. "I knew you'd find a way to blame me."

"You should've never let that key out of your sight. Oh, forget it, I'm going to go ahead and get a car out of the garage."

Rubric left as Jill took another couple of minutes to straighten the jumble of papers and files. She hesitated when her phone rang. After four rings, figuring it could be Tommy, she snatched up the receiver. "Jill Lewis."

"Still dreaming about that honeymoon?"

"Nothing but." She wondered if John could hear the smile in her voice.

"I should be back by the end of the week. We've been engaged over a week. Want to celebrate this monumental anniversary at the Inn at Little Washington?"

"Oh, John, you're so romantic. I love you."

"Me too. Catch you later. Gotta go." He sounded rushed.

A dazed Jill put down the phone and glanced at her watch. For a newly engaged couple, that had to be the world's shortest phone call. She wondered what mysterious case was keeping John so busy. She still suspected they were working the same case.

Hurriedly, Jill grabbed her things, made her messy office a quick promise to return and straighten it, and charged out the door.

At the curb, the company car was gassed with the motor running. Jill walked up to Rubric and said, "I'll drive. You read. I brought the police report along."

They both got in the car, and Rubric read the report as Jill pulled out of the lot. "Here we have the results from the lab about the car scrapings. The paint is from a brand-new seven-passenger Navigator. The model number is from one of these five-digit model numbers, all made in Michigan."

"That sounds like the same SUV Ally claimed was following her. I think it's been after me too."

"Here's a list of places where this particular color and model has been sold over the past year. I'll give this to you to investigate."

"Good. I also want to question the witnesses to the accident."

"It's all here as part of the report, but remember—where witnesses are concerned, they all seem to remember things differently."

"Did anyone get the license plate?"

"It says here there wasn't one, only a dealer's card."

Rubric shut the folder, leaned back in his seat, and closed his eyes. Suddenly remembering something, he raised up in his seat. "I forgot to ask about your weekend. I'll bet Pearl made the wedding announcement in the town square complete with confetti and a marching band."

"You should've seen her face. I'm not sure who's happier about my engagement, Mom or me. But I do know who's happier about the wedding plans."

Rubric shuddered. "I can only imagine."

"Yeah, it's a nightmare. She called me on my way to work this morning to give me an update on some of her grandiose plans."

"I'm breaking out in hives just thinking about it," Rubric said.

"Can you believe she's ordered a pair of swans to swim in the pond during the wedding reception?"

"What's wrong with ducks?"

"Didn't you know? Ducks aren't monogamous, but swans are."

"So those philandering duckies have to go? Now I've heard it all." He slapped his knee.

"No, you haven't. It gets worse. There's not just one wedding gown; she's insisting I wear one for the ceremony, and another for the reception. Oh, and did I mention the fireworks display she's planning just before we leave for our honeymoon?"

"Color coordinated, I'm sure. I'm guessing she's arranged for you to leave for your honeymoon in a phantom fighter jet?"

"How'd you know?"

"Just a lucky guess, I suppose."

She laughed.

"Spare me any more of the gory details." Rubric pulled a handkerchief out of his pocket and wiped his sweating brow. "Can't you just elope?"

"In my dreams."

"Hey, have you seen my ring?" Jill held her hand up for Rubric to see and nearly swerved into the other lane. Horns blared as she almost sideswiped a BMW.

"Sorry, Rubric. What do you think?"

"What do I think? Newly engaged women and cell phone talkers should be banned from roadways. When's the big day?"

"Probably September, but as soon as I know I'll email Annabelle to tell her you need the day off too."

"Oh no, you won't. I don't do funerals or weddings."

"But Rubric, you'll have to make an exception. I want you to give me away."

"I'd be happy to give you away, just not at the wedding."

"No, I'm serious. I'm counting on you."

"Aw, Jill, don't do this to me. There's no way. I'd rather have quadruple bypass surgery than attend a wedding." Looking at his watch, Rubric complained, "Can't you drive a little faster?"

"I'm checking to see if anyone is following us."

"It's probably the wedding police."

"Stop, Rubric, I'm serious." Jill filled Rubric in on the events that had transpired, beginning on the steps of the Capitol and ending with seeing Crew Cut at the zoo.

"I believe we've got ourselves a doozy of a case here." He pulled a toothpick out of his pocket and stuck it between his two front teeth.

"I couldn't agree with you more."

"What's your opinion of Tommy Harrison?"

"A man with an ego, but he's passionate about his beliefs, which I admire. Then there are times he can be pretty obnoxious. And John says he's untrustworthy."

"Do you trust him?"

"Harrison hasn't earned my trust yet."

"Just don't become another casualty of his Southern charm."

Jill frowned at Rubric as she pulled into the bus station parking lot. Buses were rolling in from every direction.

Jill's cell phone rang. "Private number. I'd better answer it." She turned on the phone. "Hello?"

"Jill, it's Tommy. I'm afraid I have some bad news."

"How bad is it?" Her stomach tied in knots.

"The locker was empty."

"Then someone got there first?"

"Ryan didn't think so. When he arrived, he found the lock intact, but when he opened the locker, it was empty. Did this Cooper girl dream up the whole thing?"

"I was never sure I believed her. Whether she was telling the truth or not, the fact remains, without the file we don't have any proof."

"Forget it then, and let's go onto Plan B."

"What's Plan B?"

"I haven't figured it out yet."

"Well, when you do, let me know. Thanks for calling, Tommy."

She hung up and then opened her car door to get out.

"What?" Rubric demanded.

"The locker was empty."

"Humph. I knew that girl was as phony as a politician's promise."

Jill wasn't quite ready to give up on Ally. "Maybe she inadvertently gave me the wrong locker number. Now that I have the key, I'm going to try to open every single locker."

Rubric slapped his forehead. "Why do I ever get in a car with you? It happens every time. I've lost my mind and almost my life a few blocks back. Take me back to the office, will you?"

"Take a cab," Jill said. She walked over to the nearest row of lockers. There were at least two hundred of them, all locked, resembling miniature caskets. Ignoring the curious stares of the onlookers, Jill did exactly as she'd said and tried the key in every single rental locker, while Rubric sat with his legs crossed at the ankles, absorbed in a day-old *Gazette*.

Eventually Jill reached locker 107. The one with the broken lock compliments of Ryan. An hour later Jill sighed as she pulled the key out of the last one. "I give up. Might as well return the key. It looks like Ally Cooper has made a fool of me. Now I just have to figure out why."

She and Rubric headed to the car. As she got in on the driver's side, Jill said, "I don't know if I should be upset with Ally Cooper or if I should assume something terrible has happened to her."

"Dan turned up this morning. I'm sure Ally will show up next."

"In better condition than Dan, I hope. And when she does, I'll have a busload of questions for her."

Jill and Rubric rode in silence back to the office. She was turning into the garage as the parking attendant flagged them down. "Ms. Lewis! There was a man who parked his car in the garage who was looking for you."

"Is he still here?"

"You just missed him."

"Do you know what he wanted?"

"He said it was urgent and asked for directions up to your office."

"Who do you think he is?" Rubric asked Jill.

"I don't know," Jill replied and then turned around to inquire of the parking attendant. "What kind of car was he driving?"

"Sorry, I don't remember." The man scratched his head.

"Was he a young guy?"

The man shrugged.

"How tall was he?"

"He was a big guy, one of those people who works out."

"Did he have really white teeth?" she asked.

"Yeah, do you know him?"

Jill looked at Rubric. "Crew Cut."

17

He [the snake] said to the woman, "Did God really say,
'You can't eat from any tree in the garden'?"

Genesis 3:1

Back in the office, Jill and Rubric stopped by Landry's desk.

"Did any packages come for me while I was away?" Jill asked.

"Let me check." Landry shuffled through the deliveries. "Nothing here with your name on it."

"Any calls for me?"

"Just the producers from networks and cable news shows, begging for interviews. I sent all ten thousand calls to your voice mail."

"If anybody else calls, tell them I transferred to Antarctica and there's no email or phone service in my igloo."

"Landry," Rubric barked, "call the parking lot attendant and have the videotape prior to ten a.m. pulled from the garage's security cameras, and bring it to Jill's office."

"You got it."

Rubric hurried Jill into her office. They checked every inch for packages, folders, or envelopes.

"There's nothing out of the ordinary here," Rubric noted.

"That's a relief. I want to spend the day reviewing these Bio Tech personnel files."

"Good. After those surveillance tapes arrive, call me," Rubric said before he left.

Jill pored over the research and began to piece together the evidence on Senator Brown's death. After compiling a list, she pulled the Bio Tech personnel files out of her briefcase and inserted the first one in her computer. When Landry came into her office with the surveillance tapes, she welcomed the break from her monotonous resume research.

Jill popped the first one into the VCR. Businessmen and women were weaving in and out of their cars. Jill sat close to the screen to scrutinize the content, being careful not to miss a single detail. Then, from the corner of the screen, a bulky man with a familiar stride and a very short haircut walked to the center.

Reversing the tape, Jill watched again from the man's first entrance on the screen. He was clearly aware of the cameras and adept at keeping his head shielded. This alone alerted her. People in normal circumstances ignored the cameras, and if they didn't, they usually looked directly into the lens. Crew Cut was a camera dodger, but this clip from the camera wouldn't prove it in a court of law. Under oath, could she swear it was Crew Cut? No. Did she feel certain her safety was in question from seeing this? Yes.

After shutting off the tape, Jill yanked it from the VCR and set it on top of the TV. Next, she inserted the tape from the entrance, then the one showing the exit of the garage. A couple of Navigators, but both were light in color. Crew Cut was no dummy. She phoned Rubric with the disappointing news that there was nothing conclusive on the tapes.

Jill looked at the clock on her desk. It was 10:30 a.m. She thought a Coke and a brownie from the vending machine in the lounge might perk her up a bit. By the time she arrived in the break room, several co-workers had already gathered for a midmorning coffee break. Pushing aside her concerns about Crew Cut, Jill decided it would be a fun distraction to chat with her friends.

"Good morning," Jill greeted everyone.

"Look, everybody, it's Jill!" Landry hollered.

"Are we glad to see you!" Millie, her assistant, effused, as she along with several other co-workers rushed up to greet Jill. "Somebody left you a box of Krispy Kreme doughnuts over there," Millie said, pointing to the large box on the counter.

"Oh no!" Jill slapped her cheeks with both hands. "I was supposed to meet Helen for breakfast this morning to celebrate my engagement. Guess Helen gave up on me and sent the doughnuts up here instead. Let's not let them go to waste."

"Wait a minute. Did you say engagement?" Millie said.

A moment of silence followed before everyone squealed and rushed up to congratulate her.

Landry hollered, "Who's the lucky guy? Wait. Don't tell me. If it's that super hunk, John Lovell, I'm so jealous. Wish I'd found him first."

"You guessed right!"

"Let me see that rock," Landry said, grabbing Jill's hand.

Jill held her hand out for Landry to see.

"Oh, it's beautiful. It's an antique."

"It was his grandmother Lovell's ring, and then his mother's. I'll be the third Mrs. Lovell to wear it."

"Oh, that's so sweet," cried Millie, who was straining to see the ring.

"When did he propose?" someone asked.

"A few nights ago."

"We've got to plan a girls' night out to celebrate!" Millie said.

"We can start celebrating right now with your box of Krispy Kreme doughnuts," Landry suggested.

"Yeah, too bad we don't have any champagne," Millie said.

"I just made a fresh pot of coffee," one of the copyeditors piped up.

Jill smiled and trotted over to the cabinet to pick up the box of doughnuts. "Whoa, there are lots of gooey doughnuts stuffed in here, girls," Jill said, putting the box down on the table.

As Jill untaped the sides of the box, everyone gathered around the table in anticipation of a favorite doughnut. With her mouth watering, Jill slowly opened the lid, careful not to risk losing a single bit of frosting to the underside. "This is my party, and I just want to say that if there's a chocolate custard filled one in—"

Jill froze. Coiled into a circle and masquerading as a round cake doughnut was a Saw-Scaled Viper, forked tongue twitching, scales sawing. All eyes fell on the snake as it flew forward and opened its mouth instinctively, fangs ready to plunge into Jill's flesh.

Pandemonium broke out in the break room, followed by screams as the women scattered like roaches under a light. Jill knew that the women's hysteria was what saved her from the snakebite, because the viper became so confused that it writhed and turned, striking in all directions, not knowing where to strike first.

All the women ran out of the room, Jill right behind them. Once out of the break room, Jill peeked through the window on the door.

"Where's the snake?" Landry whispered to her.

"It's not in the box. I don't see it on the table either. Must be on the floor somewhere."

By now Rubric was there, holding his prized baseball bat signed by super hitter Barry Bonds. "Quick! Somebody bring some newspapers. Stuff them under the door so the snake can't escape!"

A few minutes later a band of policemen, firemen, and paramedics arrived simultaneously. Office workers stuck their heads out of the doorways to check out all the commotion and to watch the firemen as they went into the kitchen, closing the door behind them. Jill waited along with a growing crowd, listening to cabinet doors being opened and closed. While she waited, she placed a call to Agent Abe Masourian of the FBI.

"I see it!" yelled a male voice.

A whacking sound rocked the door, followed by applause from the assisting firemen. In another moment the men emerged from the room. One fireman dangled the body of the dead snake from a snake hook. The viper's head was enclosed in a container carried by another fireman.

Several policemen took reports from everyone present in the kitchen. When satisfied they had all the information, they spread out to the offices to question the staff members to see if anyone saw who delivered the box of doughnuts or anyone who looked suspicious.

"This is one engagement party I'll never forget," Landry said.

Rubric ordered everyone back to work and then walked with Jill down to her office. "Jill, go home for the day."

She shook her head. "This is all my fault. We knew that Crew Cut was delivering a package here. I can't believe I fell for this."

"Stop it, Jill. Nobody expected—"

"That doesn't matter. If I'm not more careful, I'm going to have a very bad accident. For the first time I've realized how many risks I take—risks that could cost me my life."

"Stop it, Jill. Go home and get some rest."

"But I have all these personnel files from Bio Tech Labs to review. I keep avoiding them, and they're haunting me like an overdue term paper."

"Look at them at home."

"I may take you up on that offer." Just as Jill began gathering her things, there was a tap at the open door.

"Yes?"

"FBI, Jill."

Jill dropped her briefcase and invited Agent Abe Masourian to sit down.

"Ms. Lewis, I just received a call from the lab; they've positively identified the snake in your doughnut box as the Saw-Scaled Viper."

"I already told you that."

"So you're familiar with the viper?"

"I can't say I know him well, but we've met."

The agent's face remained expressionless as Jill continued. "I've read extensively about the species since I first learned its venom may have killed Senator Brown. This isn't the first time I've seen that creature up close."

"Oh? Was there another time the snake showed up in your food?" Agent Masourian asked.

"No, of course not. Senator Harrison and I visited the snake house at the zoo."

"Why would you go there with the senator?"

"For hot dogs," she said. "Haven't you heard? They're the best in the city."

The agent did not look happy. "Ms. Lewis, tell me everything that happened today."

Abe took copious notes as Jill retold the event and then said, "I'll never eat another Krispy Kreme doughnut. At least not until tomorrow morning. Oh, I have a tape you might be interested in seeing." She pushed the tape back into the VCR and pressed play. When Crew Cut appeared in the video, she pointed to the screen. "This is the man who was the courier for the package."

"The tape is pretty grainy," Abe noted. "But we can do some amazing adjustments to the pixels back at the lab. Mind if we take the tape?"

"Of course not." Jill pulled the tape out and handed it to him.

Agent Masourian stood to go.

"We want you to take extreme caution, Jill—with everything you do and everywhere you go," Abe warned her.

"I will."

Jill walked him out to the lobby.

After she said good-bye to the agent, Rubric came running toward her, toting his prized baseball bat. "Jillie! Good, you're still here. I want you to take this home with you."

"What am I supposed to do with it?"

"You never know when you might need it to smash a snake."

"Thanks a lot."

"Don't mention it. Now, get out of here."

"Okay. But tomorrow I want to drop by Senator Brown's office to talk to his chief of staff, Eric Richter. I still want to find out why Brown wanted to see me, and I hope Eric can tell me if the FBI plans to order a second autopsy."

Jill stepped into the elevator with her arms loaded down with work and the bat tucked up under her arm. Rubric called out a final "Be careful!" as the doors shut.

Once she arrived home for the night, Jill felt a strong desire to talk to John. She didn't care what her mother said about men being the hunters, so she dialed his number. Disappointed when his voice mail picked up, she climbed into her bed and sat cross-legged. Flipping through some bridal magazines, Jill smiled. It was a nice change to look at smiling models instead of coiling snakes. For the remainder of the night, she had not another thoughts of snakes—only visions of lace, flowers, cake, wedding gowns, and especially honeymoons.

18

Once someone like her got a leg in the conversation,
she would be all over it.

Flannery O'Connor

Early the next morning, Jill spotted Eric Richter, Brown's chief of staff, in the corridor of the Richard Russell Building. She waved at him from a distance and ran to catch up with him.

To Jill's surprise, he turned and went the opposite direction. Figuring he didn't see her, she went after him. When she was only a few feet away from him, she smiled and said, "Eric, you're just the person I wanted to see."

His mouth tense, Eric said, "I heard you left town. Can't say that I blame you."

"Only for a weekend to visit my family," Jill said as she put her hand on Eric's shoulder. "Look, we've been friends for a long time, and I understand why you might be a little upset."

"A little? Jill, if you were my friend, you would've talked to me before you printed those accusations."

"I'm sorry, Eric, but you know the rules. I was dealing with evidence from an informant."

"No, you were manipulated by Harrison, who's making one

last attempt to get his name in the history books before he goes back to Podunk, Alabama. If you had called me, I could've warned you and possibly saved your career."

Shocked that Eric knew her source, Jill balanced herself against the wall. "Where did you hear about Harrison?" she asked.

"Well, the two of you haven't made much of an effort to hide."

"Eric, I'm meeting with him for the same reasons you are."

"I have to work with him in the transition, and I sure as heck don't like it. But you've been seen with him all over this town."

"And?" Jill asked. She was sure Eric was bluffing.

"Here he was, a junior senator in Washington for the first time, the representative of one of the poorest states in the country, and he has the audacity to think he can harass his party's leader?"

"Maybe he was just trying to represent his state."

"You're taking up for the little weasel now? His real agenda is and always has been to make a name for himself. And he's succeeded in the tabloids, but apparently that's not enough for him. Now that he's snagged a few headlines in the *Gazette*, even that's not enough for his ego. Harrison is aiming for the cover of *Time* magazine."

Eric's words were louder now, attracting stares from the people arriving for work. He pulled Jill by the arm into a side hallway to continue their conversation.

"The way Harrison pestered Senator Brown all the time, he reminded me of one of those little yappy dogs who won't shut up. You know the kind that tries to attack a dog four times his size. Brown kept knocking him away, but he kept coming back, ready for more. For a little dog, he's got a nasty bite, but he's never won a dogfight, and he's sure not going to win this one." Eric licked his lips in satisfaction.

"So that's what this is all about . . . You're blaming Harrison for Brown's death. Do you believe he murdered him?"

"There was no murder, Jill, but I wouldn't be surprised if Harrison's continued harassment of Brown didn't contribute to his stroke."

"I'm sorry. Does Harrison know you feel this way?"

"I wouldn't give that schmuck the satisfaction of knowing that he bothered Senator Brown. And I'm warning you to stay away from him if you want to keep your job at the *Gazette*. If Harrison doesn't get you fired, your editor has promised Margaret Brown he's going to fire you if the second autopsy proves inconclusive."

"So you believe the FBI will order a second autopsy? Wonder what's taking them so long?"

"I don't know. Look, I've got to get to work." Eric started walking away.

"Chill out, Eric. I'm only trying to help." Jill followed after him.

He turned around. "What I don't understand is why you're insisting on subjecting Brown's family and the country to this unnecessary ordeal."

"I want to know the truth. Don't you?"

"I know the truth. Senator George Brown died of a stroke. What's your problem?"

"Brown made a call to see me on the day before his death. I'd prefer not to discuss it in the hallway. May we step inside your office?"

Eric waved her on down the hallway into the office.

"It's pretty empty in here," Jill noted.

"The transition team's in place. It's just my assistant, Janet, and me left. We're packing the office to make room for the newly appointed senator," Eric explained as he led Jill into the late senator's private office, pulled out a chair for her, and took a seat behind the massive desk in Brown's leather swivel chair.

An average-sized man, Eric was dwarfed by the late senator's oversized chair. Jill shivered as she imagined the elephant's dose of MST it must have taken to kill a man the size of Brown.

"What do you plan to do once this job is over?" Jill asked.

"I have some job leads, but there's still plenty of work to do around here for a while. Now tell me your conspiracy theory."

"You've read my story. What I need to find out is why Senator Brown wanted to see me."

"First, I'd like to hear why you think Brown was murdered. I'm sure there's a lot more to it than was printed in the paper."

Perhaps if she gave in a bit, he'd offer up the information she needed. Jill pulled out a couple of files from her briefcase and set them on the desk. "How much do you know about MST?"

"Only what Brown told me, that one of its chief components is the venom from the Saw-Scaled Viper."

"Yes, but Senator Brown's charges about MST being a threat to national security were exaggerated. Purely political, in my opinion. Wasn't Brown's real goal to keep Bio Tech's vascular-targeting drug off the market?"

"A deadly snake, the Middle East, and a drug trial debacle that resulted in the deaths of many of the participants. I'd say he was more than justified," Eric said smugly.

"Brown saw an opportunity to slip through the back door; to cripple Bio Tech in an effort to prevent their vascular-targeting drug from going on the market, especially since it's far superior to the one manufactured by Creation Pharmaceuticals. Ever heard of them?"

"They're one of Brown's campaign contributors."

"_____ door." Jill whipped out an Excel list of Brown's _____ aced it under Eric's nose.

_____ ross the desk to her. "I've got this list in my

_____ n't seen this one." Jill pulled out Creation _____ nual report. "Creation has made billions off _____ ng drug."

_____ en it. What's your point, Jill?" Eric asked, _____ maller and smaller in the chair.

173

"Bio Tech's new vascular-targeting drug will wipe Creation's off the market. Here are the reports from several medical journals. How's that for a motive?"

"A motive for what?"

"For Senator Brown trying to cripple Bio Tech Labs, protecting both his and Creation's interests. In turn giving Bio Tech a motive for murder. The facts are all here." Jill pounded her fist on the file.

"If we hadn't been friends for so many years, I'd throw you out of this office right now."

"I'm sorry, Eric, but you need to hear me out, please." Jill pulled a document out of her file and slid it across the desk to him. "These are the reactions from the snakebite of the Saw-Scaled Viper. Look familiar?"

Eric flipped through the file and said, "I read your article in the paper, remember?"

"Do you recall the day of Brown's collapse you told me you were puzzled because the senator had a recent physical? You mentioned that he had low blood pressure and low cholesterol, so what did the doctors say caused his stroke?"

"They said it was likely caused by a congenital defect in an artery."

"Yes, that's one of the causes of a stroke, but there are others: an aneurysm, which is similar to a weakness in the artery, high blood pressure, and a snakebite with a certain type of venom."

Eric was quiet for a moment. "I admit that your information is compelling, Jill, but why can't you acc_____ ept th___ _enator had a weakness in an artery instead of pr_____ posing ____ conspiracy theory?"

"Because there's a motive for murder, _____ and it's a big

"Thanks for the explanation, but I've re_____ ally got to ge now."

"Not so fast—it's my turn."

"You've got five minutes," Eric said, po_____ inting to his watch.

"The day Senator Brown called me, he seemed troubled. He also intimated he had a story for me. If you could give me a clue what that story might have been, it could be vital in solving his murder."

"If the senator was murdered. You know everything I know that was going on in the Senate. They were voting on the confirmation of a couple of cabinet members, a few bills, but nothing that would push anyone to murder him."

"A reliable source said the Democrats were unhappy that Brown wouldn't cooperate with the Republicans."

"True, but politicians aren't mobsters; no one's going to murder him for that."

"Eric, if I could get a copy of his phone records, I could prove to you that Brown called me. I could also review them to see who he was talking to in the days that led up to his phone call to me."

"I'm sorry, Jill, the FBI subpoenaed most of our records, and the copies of the disks are already packed away in storage."

"Where's your storage?"

"In the back."

"All I need are the phone records for the week before Senator Brown's collapse. Do you have time to get them for me now?"

"It's not as simple as it looks. I have no way of knowing which phone line he called you from—if he called you—so I'd have to locate them all."

"How many phones did he have?"

"George carried a couple of cell phones. I think one of them was in his wife's name, actually. Add those to his office and home lines, and it could take some time to locate the records."

"I'll wait. It's important, Eric," Jill said.

He didn't speak for a moment, only stared at her. Then he said, "Oh, all right. I'll go check. Wait here."

Eric left the room. Within seconds he was back. "On second thought, why don't you come with me?"

She frowned. "After all the years we've been friends, you don't trust me?"

"Sorry, Jill, you're a reporter first, a friend second. Reporters aren't born to be trusted; they're born to snoop."

"But we all know that politicians can be trusted."

"You said it," he said with a grin and unlocked the door to the storage room and turned the light on inside.

Jill followed him. As he looked through the file boxes, she took the opportunity to scan them too. He pulled out several plastic containers filled with disks and stacked them on a worktable in the center of the room. The two of them crossed over to another aisle. In the corner, Jill looked up on the top shelf and spotted a box labeled "MST." She pointed to it. "Look up there. There's a large metal box that's labeled 'MST.'"

"You're hallucinating."

"I am not. Look up there and see for yourself."

"I was a fool to bring you back here," Eric groaned.

"If that box contains MST, it could be the best decision of your career."

Eric pulled out a small stepladder and stood on it. He reached for the large metal box and gently shook it. "It's heavy."

"Be careful!" Jill warned as she reached up to help him bring the box down. "If this contains MST, it's dangerous and a threat to everyone in this office. Not to mention in violation of the FDA's order to destroy all samples of MST."

Together they gently set it down on the floor of the storage room and examined the outside of the box.

"I'm not so sure if this box contains MST. It's highly unlikely that Senator Brown would have any samples of MST in this office. How would he have gotten his hands on it? And why is it here?"

"Rumor is that he used his political clout to convince the FDA to halt the drug trials," Jill reminded Eric. "Maybe that's why these samples are here. He probably used them in his presentation."

"Okay, okay, Jill, you've made your case. I'll try and open it. But I've never seen this box before, so I don't have a clue where to look for the key," Eric said, studying the lock.

"I don't want you to open it. It's not safe. I want you to call the FBI and turn it over to them."

"Let's just leave it on the floor right now until we find the rest of the phone records."

"Okay, but hurry. The sooner we get that box out of here, the better."

Above all, Jill wanted those phone records, so she obediently tagged along behind him while he searched the shelves for them.

After they located more phone records, Eric picked up the mysterious box and carefully set it on the desk. He tugged at the lock. They both jumped back when it popped open.

"Oh my gosh . . . you were right."

"I knew it! It's MST. There must be over two hundred vials here. We've got no choice; we have to call the FBI. I have the senior agent's number right here in my phone."

Eric frowned. "I can see you're going to make that call whether I like it or not."

"The FBI will need these for evidence. Then they'll need to be destroyed," Jill said. "For now, they need to be locked away in a highly secured facility."

Jill called her lead contact on this case at the FBI. While they waited for them to arrive, Eric's assistant, Janet, made copies of the phone records for Jill.

"Why am I not surprised to see you here, Ms. Lewis?" Agent Masourian teased when Janet escorted him and his partner, Jimmy Allen, into Senator's Brown's office, where Jill and Eric waited. "Where there's anything to do with this snake, there's Jill."

"You're right about that," Jill said. "I'm beginning to believe that I should wear a vial of antivenin around my neck."

"Not a bad idea."

"Eric, this is Agent Abe Masourian, the senior agent assigned to the investigation of Senator Brown's death, and this is his partner, Agent Jimmy Allen."

"We've met. Nice to see you again, Abe, Jimmy," Eric said as he stood up and shook their hands.

"What happened this time, Jill?" Abe flipped open his notebook.

"I came to ask Eric for copies of Senator Brown's phone records so I could prove to him and anyone else who didn't believe me that the senator called me the day before he died."

Eric shrugged his shoulders. "I'd even told Jill on the day Brown collapsed that I didn't have a clue. I didn't even know Brown had an appointment with Jill."

"So where'd you find the MST?"

"In the storage closet on the top shelf. It's full of vials of MST."

Both agents studied the contents of the box.

"Eric, we'll have to take these vials back to the lab," Abe told him.

"That's fine. We don't want them in here."

"Have you ever seen this box before?" Abe asked Eric.

"No, not until Jill pointed it out to me today. How about you, Janet?"

"No, I've never noticed it."

"Neither of you know how Senator Brown had these in his possession?"

Eric and Janet shook their heads.

"I don't think we have any other questions at the moment."

Janet left and was back in an instant with another man, a tall man about forty years old. Jill stared at the immaculately dressed stranger in a dark Brooks Brothers suit with a red and blue wide-striped tie. He had a square jaw, cropped blond hair, and a well-toned build.

"Jill, Eric, this is our division chief, Bill Tucker," Abe said. "Agent Tucker, this is Jill Lewis from the *Washington Gazette*, and Eric Richter, chief of staff for the late Senator Brown. You've met Janet."

"Yes." He smiled at Janet and turned around. "Jill, Eric, it's nice to meet you both." Agent Tucker shook hands with them as they exchanged greetings. He then turned to Jill. "After your little doughnut incident and now this, I decided I'd better get over here and check on you. John forgot to mention how beautiful you are."

"Thank you, Agent Tucker. John's told me so much about you. I'm glad to finally meet you."

"John's like a brother to me, so I insist you call me Bill."

Jill nodded her head. "Thank you, Bill. John said you and Lynda got my note, but I'd like to thank you personally for helping him with his surprise proposal."

"So you were surprised?"

"It was the most wonderful surprise of my life. And John said it was you who suggested your boat . . . It's exquisite."

"Lynda and I are glad we could play a small part in your happiness. To be perfectly honest with you, John is the reason I rushed right here. Are you okay, Jill?"

"You don't have to worry about Jill. She always keeps a cool head," Abe told Bill.

Bill laughed. "Then I should recruit you for the bureau."

"I'm flattered, but I think one FBI agent in the family is enough."

Overhearing the conversation, Eric said, "I didn't know you were engaged. FBI agent, huh? Now that's the perfect match."

"Isn't it? And Jill will be the first wife who understands why her husband has to leave in the middle of the wedding reception," Bill teased.

"Don't even think about it," Jill retorted.

Bill's smile vanished. His tone grew serious. "I should tell you that John heard about the doughnut incident. He nearly walked off the job to come here to check on you. He made me promise to take good care of you. So, if this escalates, I'll order some protection for you."

"That won't be necessary, Bill."

Bill turned to Eric. "As long as I'm here, I'll have a look around the office."

Since John hadn't returned her frantic call from yesterday, Jill had wondered if she weren't just talking into a recorder somewhere on another planet. At least now she felt comforted that Bill had spoken to him, and John was keeping close tabs on her. He'd appointed a guardian angel for her—Agent Bill Tucker, one of the top men in the bureau.

19

Nobody can take away your future.
Nobody can take away something you don't have.

Dorothy B. Hughes

The message light was blinking when Jill walked into the office. "Let this be you, John!" Before she had a chance to listen to them, her phone rang. She answered cheerfully, hoping it was John. At the sound of a strange male voice, the pen fell from her hand onto the desk.

"Did you like your doughnuts, Jill?" a chilling voice rasped.

"Who is this?" Jill demanded.

"Someone who wants to help you find your little friend Ally."

With all her heart, Jill wanted to believe the caller, but by the mention of the doughnuts, she was doubtful his motives were altruistic. "Where is Ally?"

"I know where she is, and if you'll do exactly as I say, I think I can help you locate her."

"And what do you want in return?"

"Not so fast. I'll give the orders when I'm ready," he said. "Do you want to find your friend or not?"

"You know I do. I'm sorry, I'll do whatever you ask."

"Ally will sure be happy to hear that." His laugh was haunting. "She wants to see you."

"How do I know what you're saying is true? I want to speak to Ally," Jill pressed.

Ignoring Jill, he gave her instructions that she scribbled down on a notepad. "At ten o'clock tonight, go to Rock Creek Park—alone. Find the park bench where the two of you sat. Remember? This time, bring along a hundred thousand dollars in denominations of one-hundred-dollar bills, unmarked and locked in a briefcase. Got it?"

"Where am I going to get that kind of money on such short notice?"

"That's your problem, lady, not mine," he said. Then he lowered his voice and continued. "Slide the briefcase under the park bench and then take twenty steps into the grove of trees on the west side of the bench. You'll find Ally there."

"Tell Ally I . . . I'll be there," Jill promised, wondering where Rubric would find that kind of cash.

"Make sure you come alone so your little friend won't get scared and run away."

Click.

Jill pulled out Ally's home number and dialed, hoping the girl would pick up the phone. Then she could attribute this call as a prank. The phone rang endlessly before it was finally picked up.

"Cooper residence."

"Hello, may I please speak with Ally Cooper?" Jill withheld her name, not wanting to alarm Ally's parents.

"Ally lives in Washington, D.C., now. I can give you that number if you'd like."

"No, that's all right. Thank you."

Jill paced the floor and tried to decipher what the message meant. *Was this person watching when Ally and I met in the park?*

Or did she tell him we were there? Is this a setup? Jill was unsure if Ally was a willing participant or a victim. *Whatever the situation is, I have to be at the park tonight.* She recalled the day she met Ally at Rock Creek Park. She struggled to remember the exact location of the park bench. "What grove of trees?"

Jill tried Rubric's cell, praying he'd answer.

"What?"

"I think I've found Ally Cooper," Jill blurted out to him. She hated to sound dramatic. Rubric never took her seriously when she did.

"What?" There was so much noise and commotion. Jill tried to imagine where he was.

"I need to talk to you. It's urgent. Where the heck are you, anyway?"

"Griffith Stadium."

"Do you mean RFK?"

"It'll always be Griffith to me. My dad brought me here when I was a kid."

"Uh, that's nice, Rubric. How soon can you get back to the office?"

"Woo hoo! It's a base hit! Slide, slide, slide! Oh no! He's out. Wait, no . . . he's safe! Did you hear that, Jill? He's safe!"

"Rubric, did you hear me?"

All Jill could hear was the roar of the crowd in the background and a blaring version of Kool and the Gang's "Celebration."

Finally, after the screams of crowd, the song finished and Rubric asked, "What did you say you wanted?"

"Just meet me at the office ASAP," she said and hung up.

When Rubric finally arrived at the office, Jill told him about the mysterious phone call. "One hundred thousand dollars!" Rubric bellowed.

But after he calmed down, he readily agreed to make the necessary phone calls. Finally, at eight o'clock that evening the money was delivered to Rubric at the *Gazette* in canvas bags. The two of them stacked the bills into the leather briefcase.

"You know this psycho isn't going to have the girl there for you, don't you?"

"Don't be so negative."

"He's probably laying a trap for you."

"I'll take my chances."

"You're sure this girl's ransom is connected with Senator Brown's death, or am I just throwing the newspaper's money away to find some missing runaway?"

"If she's in danger, any amount of money is worth it." Jill stacked the rest of the one-hundred-dollar bills inside the case.

Rubric put his hands on his hips. "What happened to my spicy chili pepper? You're nothing but a blob of whipped cream now."

"But I'm so sweet. Don't you like the new me?"

"Sweet does not a reporter make. And I can't understand why you haven't questioned any of the people connected with Bio Tech Labs. If Brown was murdered, like you say, then that's where you'll find your killer."

"I'm working on it. Tommy Harrison can cut the red tape. He's making arrangements for—"

"Oh, great. A suspect controls your investigation."

"Not necessarily. I've got my radar up when it comes to Harrison. Don't worry."

Rubric gave Jill a disgusted look as he snapped the briefcase. "Go home and get some rest. I'll have one of my drivers outside your apartment building at 9:30 tonight. The code word is Annabelle. When the clock strikes ten, I want you sitting on that park bench, Little Miss Muffet. And don't be afraid, I'll be close by."

"Promise me no feds or police, Rubric. I don't want to be responsible for this girl's death. Promise me?"

Rubric nodded.

At the park that night, Jill took one step at a time. She looked around, walking quietly past the winos sprawled out on picnic tables or napping on the ground under day-old copies of the *Gazette*.

Near the rear of the park, she stopped. In front of her was the bench she'd shared with Ally. The memory of it made her shudder. She was relieved no one else was around. Noting the hands on her watch were at ten o'clock, Jill stooped down and slid the briefcase under the bench.

She began counting her twenty steps but stopped after ten to listen to the night sounds. After sixteen steps, she'd just stepped into the wooded area. "I'm coming, Ally, hold on," she whispered.

Jill stopped at step number twenty and called out, "Hello, I'm here. It's me, Jill Lewis. I'm waiting. Is anyone there?" She listened. The only audible sounds were distant sirens, crickets, and toads. No voices. She called out again in a whisper. "Hello? Ally? Is anyone there? I brought the briefcase you asked for, and it's under the park bench."

No response.

Jill took a few more steps into the wooded area. Even with a full moon, the awning of branches nearly shut out all light, casting shadows along her way. Walking on uneven ground was difficult even in running shoes. A bat swooped just above her, its wings swiping the hairs on her head, making her duck for cover. She bent down until the air was silent of fluttering wings.

"Ally?"

The wind picked up, creating a purring sound through the leaves. Clouds began to swipe the moon's face, blocking its light until Jill stood in total darkness. Thunder groaned in the distance. Now there was the smell of rain on the wind. A storm was quickly blowing in.

Jill looked at her watch—10:15. No one was there. Someone had obviously set her up, but she'd wait until daybreak if necessary. A whoosh of wind blew her hair around her face. Somehow she had gotten off the path. Lightning flashed long enough for her to see her way back to the trail.

Lightning flashed again, but the flash of light was too late to prevent her from walking head-on into an overhead limb. Knocked off her feet, Jill landed hard on her back. For a painful moment she lay still on the ground.

Now someone was calling her name. "Jill?"

It took a moment for her to recover enough strength to answer. "Rubric? Is that you?"

"Jill?"

"I'm right over here on the ground. Hey, I can see your flashlight beam. Keep coming."

Only a few yards away, Rubric stopped. "Oh no. What happened to you?"

"I ran into a low tree branch," Jill answered as she pointed up.

Rubric shined his light on the tree. Jill watched the beam of the light travel up to the tree, over the limb, and down to the base of the tree. Ally was propped up against the tree, blood clotted on her clothes, her eyes staring sightlessly. Jill screamed.

Rubric pulled Jill to her feet by her wrists. Homeless men and women began appearing out from the fringes of the woods. They moved in closer to Rubric and Jill, surrounding them on all sides. There was no place to run for escape.

Jill dug her fingernails into Rubric's arm and held on tightly. She screamed. Arms swinging, she began swatting Rubric, pushing him away from her.

"Calm down, Jill. They're only FBI agents."

Rubric turned his flashlight on Agent Masourian.

"Why would you bring in the FBI?" she said to Rubric.

"Don't be a wacko. How else was I supposed to get that kind of money?"

"But I was supposed to come alone! Alone! What if Ally was murdered because they knew I wasn't alone?" Jill railed as it began to rain.

"Jill, there's no way anyone would've suspected these agents. Even you were fooled," Rubric shouted back at her.

Agent Jimmy Allen ordered another agent to cover up the tracks with a tarp. "We'll try to preserve them and then take a mold when it's dry," he explained. "These footprints are relatively small, both the victim's and the person who killed her. The only other track we see is probably yours, Jill. Let's get a mold of your foot to compare with these prints."

"Definitely not Crew Cut's footprints," Jill noted as an agent carefully made a mold of both her shoes.

She turned to watch a cadre of other agents go about their tasks, cording off the area in yellow crime-scene tape and searching the outlying areas.

Lightning angled across the sky. By now the wind was violent, and the rain hit as bullets. Abe and Jimmy shuttled both Rubric and Jill in a golf cart to the nearby surveillance van.

"I know you're upset, Jill. However, in matters like this, your editor did the right thing by calling us," Abe explained.

"Believe me, we have much better luck bringing people back alive when the FBI is brought into it," Jimmy said.

Jill remained silent.

"While things are fresh in your mind, we need to ask you some questions. Do you feel up to it?" Abe asked.

"I'm fine. Ask."

"We've traced the call. It came from a pay phone at 9th and K Street. Are you familiar with anyone in the area?"

"That's not far from the Watergate."

"We know that, but Senator Harrison was in session at the time the call was made," Jimmy noted.

"I wasn't insinuating that he was a suspect."

"And why not? Everyone knows Senators Harrison and Brown were at odds," Jimmy said.

"Did you know that Senator Harrison had a heated argument with Brown on the day he died?" Abe asked her.

She acted like that information didn't surprise her. "That's no secret. Just because they were political enemies doesn't make Harrison a murderer." But yes, Tommy had failed to mention that little detail to her.

"Let's get back to this murder," Abe said as he turned on a recorder and prepared to take notes. "Do you remember when you first entered the park?"

"Don't you know every step I made?"

"We need your perspective, Jill."

She sighed. "Because of the moon, I could see pretty well, that is, before it clouded over and began to rain. I put the briefcase underneath the bench. Then I went straight into the woods, pausing only once to see if I could hear anything."

"Did you hear or see anything unusual?"

"Only your typical night sounds. Crickets, the wind through the trees, that sort of thing."

"Did you feel a sensation of being watched? Anything like that?"

"I did feel as though I were being watched. I mean, someone was coming for the money."

"That's not exactly what I meant. Did you sense anyone actually standing there watching you?"

Going back to her thoughts of when she first reached the park bench, Jill answered, "I did have a different feeling there than I did from when I walked through the park."

"Tell me about it."

"It felt as if someone were very close by. Yes, it was like I was being watched. It was as if I kept expecting someone to reach out and touch me. But I knew if I had been touched, there wouldn't be anyone there—at least no one that I could see. It was frightening. What made me stay was the hope of finding Ally alive."

The Washington homicide coroner drove up in a white van, and Jill watched as he and his team pulled out a black bag and a gurney.

In the torrid rainfall, Jill, Rubric, and the agents carried bureau umbrellas and tagged along behind the coroner. By now the park was lit up with floodlights. Someone was taking pictures of the crime scene, and when he was done, he gave a signal. Ally was laying on the ground now, and her head was tilted back, revealing a deep cut that spread nearly four inches across her neck.

The coroner took great interest in this. "It appears that she's been strangled, and then her throat was probably slashed for effect. I'll check to see if there's sign of tissue hemorrhaging when I get her back to the lab." He leaned over the body. "Oh, this is interesting. She's also been gagged."

The coroner methodically removed the gag. He pried open Ally's mouth and peered inside. "There's something down her throat," he said as he pulled a pair of tongs out of his bag. Everyone watched intently as he inserted the tongs into the corpse's throat. He took hold of an object and slowly pulled it out as if he were performing a magic trick.

Jill gasped. "A Saw-Scaled Viper!"

"Careful." An FBI agent swiftly stepped up and looped the snake with a long hook.

Fascinated with his discovery, the coroner used his penlight for a closer look. "There are teeth marks about three inches down—as though the girl's jaw was forced closed, and her teeth clamped down on it. Looks like the snake was alive when it went into her mouth."

The coroner opened the snake's mouth with a smaller pair of tongs and pulled out a piece of paper. "Looks like a note."

One of the agents bagged it, sealing it with evidence tape.

"I want to know what the note says," Jill insisted.

"We've got to get it to the lab first to check it for finger-prints and venom," Abe Masourian said. "There's a battery of forensic tests to be done on it, including handwriting analysis. Anything that isn't classified, you'll have as soon as we get the results."

Jill nodded her head. "If you have nothing else for me, I'm going home."

"That's it for tonight," Abe said. "But may I speak to you for a minute before you go?"

Exhausted and emotionally spent, Jill asked, "What is it?"

"Whoever did this went to a lot of trouble to kill this girl."

"I agree."

"The elaborate methods they made to brutally murder Ally Cooper. The killer did this as a warning to you . . . to back off this investigation."

"Well, I won't, at least not until Ally's killer is apprehended."

"That's all very noble, but you should know, he's going to come after you."

"Thanks for the warning, Abe. I'll be careful. Good night."

"Wait. There's one more thing . . . I think you should talk to someone. After tonight, I need to talk to someone myself," Abe admitted as he nervously fingered a silver cross that hung beneath his shirt. "If you know what I mean."

Jill nodded knowingly.

Rubric insisted on taking Jill back to her apartment himself. Before he left, he looked around her apartment, even peeked under her beds.

"Deadbolt this door when I leave," he ordered her.

After Jill told him good-bye, she followed his orders. She knew she should get her fingers on the keyboard to tap out the story for the *Gazette*. She couldn't, not now. It was impossible to shake the memory of Ally with her throat cut open. After a cup of tea, she finally forced herself to sit down and write the story. By 3:00 a.m. she had emailed it to the paper.

After that, she tried to get some sleep, but she was too restless. As an investigative political reporter, she rarely dealt with death in its unrefined form. With her work, she focused on crooked politicians, bribes, extortion, political maneuverings and manipulations, sexual misconduct, and other moral trepidations—but rarely death. Now she had Senator Brown's and Ally's deaths to contend with.

Maybe it was time for her to resign. Go back to Delavan and write the classified ads for porch furniture and obits of ninety-eight-year-olds who'd lived full lives.

Giving up on sleep, Jill climbed out of her bed. As soon as the clock crawled to a decent hour, she called Tommy Harrison.

"To what do I owe the pleasure of this early morning call?"

"I'm in no mood," Jill warned him.

"Fair enough."

"Have you seen this morning's headlines?"

"No, I'm on my way to an early session."

"Can we meet for lunch?"

"I can rearrange some things, sure."

"Make sure you read the paper before you come."

They set up the time and place, and then Jill hung up.

When she arrived for lunch, Tommy was walking in the door. He put his arm around her waist. "I read the paper. Are you all right?"

Jill pulled back before he could embrace her. "It was awful. The most gruesome crime I've ever witnessed." She sighed. "I can't help but wonder how God could let something like this happen to anyone, especially a young girl like Ally."

Tommy shook his head. "You can't blame God. There's evil in this world. Bad things happen. We have to do what we can to prevent it. And as far as I can see, you do that quite well."

Jill eyed the senator suspiciously. Tommy Harrison wasn't exactly the poster boy for Christianity, but she had to admit his words were comforting.

The waiter arrived for their drink orders.

"Jill, what will you have?"

"Iced tea, no lemon."

"I'll have the same with lemon, please," Tommy said.

In minutes the waiter had returned with their drinks and a basket of bread. Pulling out a pad, he clutched a pen and awaited their orders.

"I don't have an appetite," Jill confessed.

"You have to eat." He turned to the waiter. "What's your soup of the day?"

"Carrot-ginger bisque, as well as our usual French onion soup, tortilla soup, and broccoli cheese soup."

"I'll have the carrot-ginger bisque. Followed by a Cobb salad. What sounds good to you, Jill?"

"Chocolate mousse."

When the waiter left, Tommy reached across the table and put his hand over Jill's hand. Without a thought, she laced her fingers in his and held onto his hand tightly. Jill blushed when suddenly Tommy appeared uncomfortable. He reached up with his other hand and loosened the collar on his shirt as he wiggled in his seat. Perhaps it was because she had scolded him earlier when he called, warning him she was in no mood for his flirtations. Or maybe he was surprised at her behavior. After all, she was an engaged woman.

After the horror of the previous night, she felt desperate for someone to protect her and comfort her. This type of behavior was so uncharacteristic for Jill that she figured she should probably take Abe's advice and see a therapist right away.

Tommy broke the uncomfortable silence when he announced, "The more I've thought about my election to Senate minority leader, the more I believe it's not related to MST, nor was I handpicked by the people who murdered Brown. I don't believe it's a setup at all."

"I agree. The Democrats chose you because you're obviously the best replacement for Brown and the best candidate for the job."

"Thanks for the vote of confidence."

"It's all true. You're the only senator who can achieve the

Democratic Party's goals and get the important legislation passed that is necessary for the candidates to win their upcoming elections."

"I don't have a prayer of reelection, though."

Just then the waiter came over with the soup and Jill's chocolate mousse. Jill felt relieved that the food had arrived and used it as an excuse to slide away her hand.

"Okay, tell me about how you got into politics," she said after a spoonful of mousse.

He smiled. "Like most in the Bible Belt, I was raised in the church with strong moral and biblical teachings. I raised my children in the same way. You have a Southern mother, you must know this."

Jill nodded.

"But I never had a personal relationship with God. When my wife died, I asked, just as you did today, 'How could God let this happen?' The more friends and family tried to explain, the angrier I became."

"People react so differently. Losing my father is what drew me to God."

"Well, it had the opposite effect for me. I was so angry that I even stopped going to church."

"When did that change?"

"When I decided to run for Senate, a man I greatly admired offered to support my senatorial candidacy. He was a Republican, by the way. I was honored that he wanted to back me, but I was shocked when he put a price on his support. Because of his convictions, he told me he couldn't justify supporting a candidate who didn't serve God, but if I was willing to do that, I had his financial support as well as his endorsement."

"So you sold your soul for the election—not to the devil but to the righteous buyer. That's a switch."

"Well, that's not exactly what happened. I was flattered by this man's offer—until he began sharing his faith with me. I told him I was angry at his insinuation that I was a sinner. I told him emphatically, 'My conscience is clean, and I have nothing to repent of.'"

Jill laughed. "Did he tell you we're all sinners?"

"So you know the script?" Tommy chuckled before he continued. "After I left this man, I became even angrier. How dare he accuse me of being a sinner? But when I went to bed that night, God showed me a film clip in my head of all the bad things I'd ever done. After several hours of torment, I finally fell to my knees and begged his forgiveness for my million sins."

Jill couldn't keep the surprise off her face.

"Should I be insulted by that look on your face?" Tommy asked.

The waiter momentarily interrupted them when he brought Tommy's salad.

"Please go on with your story," Jill said. "I'm fascinated."

"Okay, so I got up off my knees and called this man around two o'clock in the morning and begged him to meet me at the Huddle House in town. By six o'clock in the morning, I had accepted Christ over greasy eggs and bacon, some gooey grits, and extremely bitter coffee."

"That's got to be a first."

"Yeah, right there in front of God, the short-order cook, and the waitress, I came home at last."

She found herself beaming at him. "That's a beautiful testimony, Tommy."

"Want another dessert?" He winked.

"You read my mind. This time I'll have coconut cream pie."

"I do love a woman with an appetite." Tommy smiled as he waved the waiter over to their table and ordered the pie for her and peach cobbler a la mode for himself.

When the desserts arrived, Jill said, "Let's talk about the investigation."

Tommy listened intently as Jill told him about the MST incident in Senator Brown's office. She also shared more of the details of the viper in the box of Krispy Kreme doughnuts.

"Jill, we've got to get some protection for you."

"I'll think about it, but Rubric's right. I need to get into Bio Tech Labs right away. Can you arrange for me to talk to the people there?"

"I'll take you there personally as soon as the Senate recesses. And I promise you, together we will find the killer."

20

*Kill the snake of doubt in your soul, crush the worms of fear in
your heart, and mountains will move out of your way.*

Kate Seredy

Jill awakened at midnight. Three days, a few deadly snakes, hundreds of vials of MST, one gruesome murder, and one absent boyfriend later equaled another sleepless night. Only tonight it wasn't the nightmares. She had been dreaming of Tommy Harrison. Holding her in his arms, he had kissed her fingertips. Then brushed her cheek ever so slightly with his lips. Thankfully she had woken up before anything else happened.

"You're engaged, remember?" she mumbled to herself and picked up the phone to dial John, praying he would answer. But no, she only got his voice mail.

Voice mail's not enough. I'm human. I need someone to comfort me, to hold me. Why aren't you here, John? Of course, it wasn't John's fault he was assigned to a case in Florida and couldn't be here for her throughout this horrendous investigation. Jill was angry with herself. She had placed herself in a vulnerable position with Tommy Harrison. "No more hand holding over lunch," Jill scolded herself.

She turned off the light and buried her head on the pillow, but sleep didn't come. Her thoughts ran rampant on the very subject she had desperately tried to avoid . . . Tommy Harrison. Was God trying to show her something? Was Tommy a con man who used his faith to entice her? Or was he the charming, sensitive man she'd grown fond of despite her attempts to dislike him?

Maybe the truth lay with the past. How did Tommy's wife die? Annabelle was unsure. Yet Jill had readily accepted her answer that it was a car accident, refusing to do further research because she was afraid the true answer might be one she didn't want to hear. If Catherine Harrison died in a car accident, was Tommy driving the car? Was it his negligence that killed his wife? She'd read somewhere that Tommy's father, like her own, was an alcoholic. So perhaps at one time in his life, Tommy had struggled with alcoholism too. Was he driving drunk at the time of the accident that killed his wife?

Discovery of the cause of Catherine's death would have to wait until tomorrow. Jill pulled the covers over her head and put Tommy out of her mind. But her thoughts of him bounced back again and again. Questions rolled around in her head. Had Tommy loved his wife, or was mourning a part of his act? Worse, was he involved in his wife's death?

Intrigued by the possibilities, Jill sprang from her bed at two o'clock in the morning and retrieved her laptop from its carrying case. If she had to pull an all-nighter to find the answers, she would. Cross-legged on the bed, she booted up her laptop and soon found an article describing Catherine Harrison's death and clicked print. Once the printer stopped, Jill snatched the papers and began to read.

While the Harrison family slept, a convicted criminal, who had escaped from a nearby prison earlier in the day, broke into their home after midnight. Authorities believed that Catherine likely heard a noise and confronted the burglar. There were signs of a major struggle.

At the time of the arrest, authorities found evidence of the victim's DNA on the man's body and clothes. The attacker also had a sizable amount of cash, as well as several pieces of the family's jewelry and silver in his possession. Jill was relieved that the convict, Cooter Orsen, was quickly convicted and electrocuted for the crime. Poor Tommy.

It would be a stretch to assume that Tommy had anything to do with his wife's death, but one of the facts of the crime nagged at her—Tommy was out of town on the night of the murder. It raised the possibility that Cooter Orsen may have been a killer for hire. This notion was preposterous, but then again maybe it wasn't.

If Tommy killed his wife, it would make sense that he could murder again, so Jill felt obligated to rule out any possibility of murder as an integral part of her investigation. To do that, she had to order a copy of the transcripts from Orsen's murder trial. But a trip to Alabama would further her research since she could get a copy of the transcripts and talk to the local folks about the murder as well. Jill was excited over the prospect of digging up the past for herself. She reached for the phone and booked a late-morning Delta flight, as well as a rental car.

Her arrangements made, Jill finally fell asleep, this time with Ally Cooper in her dreams.

Confident Rubric would approve her trip down south, Jill packed her suitcase and lugged it to work with her. Just before seven o'clock, she arrived at her office and pulled some additional information off the Internet about the Harrison murder. With several articles in hand she went straight to Rubric's office and knocked.

"Hey, Rubric, I came up with a couple of new leads."

"Before you spit them out, Abe faxed over the preliminary forensic reports on that note found in the snake's mouth. Want to hear it?"

Jill nodded. "That was fast."

"Yeah, but it'll take seventy-two hours to get the autopsy reports back from the lab. Anyway, here's what I have so far. There's the usual jargon on here as to the date and time and who did the initial lab work. No fingerprints . . ."

"Why am I not surprised."

"As to the contents of the note, here's what it says: 'If you want to keep the snake's mouth shut, keep your mouth shut.' That's all."

Jill slammed her fist on Rubric's desk. "If the killer thinks that snake has a deadly bite, just wait until I strike with my pen!"

"Ha! My spicy chili pepper has caught fire again." He sailed the report into the jumbled pile of papers on his desk. "Now tell me what you've got."

Pulling a file from her briefcase, she held up a photograph of the beautiful, smiling couple for Rubric to see. "Exhibit one."

Rubric studied the picture. "Who are the happy suckers?"

"Harrison and his wife, Catherine Delaney Harrison. Listen to this, Rube." Jill read aloud to him, "'A midnight intruder tragically ended the Harrisons' happy marriage when he murdered the wife of Superior Court Judge Thomas Henry Harrison.' Did you know about this?"

"No. I thought Annabelle said his wife died in car accident."

"She did, but if you recall, she couldn't remember the details, only that the death was gruesome. So she just guessed it was a car accident, but it was definitely murder."

Rubric's eyes lit up. "And just where was Harrison the night his wife was murdered?"

Jill continued reading. "'Judge Thomas Henry Harrison's life was spared, as he was attending a judicial conference in Washington.'"

"Ha! I'll bet my beloved ashtray that it was spared because Harrison hired someone to kill his wife, then arranged to be away on business."

"It gets better." Flipping through the papers once more, Jill read, "At the time of the murder, the Harrisons' son, Thomas Henry V, was away at a summer camp in North Carolina."

"How convenient." Rubric grinned, showing his gold tooth. "Was anyone ever arrested for the crime?"

"A local man by the name of Cooter Orsen. It says here, 'Mrs. Harrison caught the intruder by surprise, and he slit her throat to quiet her screams.'"

"That'll do it every time."

"There's one thing that bothers me about our theory. Would Harrison knowingly subject his eight-year-old daughter to such a horrific crime?" Jill wrinkled her nose, searching through the material until she found what she was looking for in the stack of papers. "'The Harrisons' eight-year-old daughter, Elizabeth, found her mother's body.'"

"Maybe his daughter wasn't supposed to be there, but something happened. You won't know until you ask. Go to Roanoke. You know how those Southerners love to talk. See if you can locate old Cooter's relatives too."

"My bags are packed, and I'm booked on the eleven o'clock flight to Atlanta. With your permission, I can be in Alabama by midafternoon."

"You naughty little manipulator." He scowled. "While you're in Alabama, go to Mobile and take a tour of Bio Tech Labs. Talk to a few key people there."

"But I've made plans to go to Bio Tech with the senator after the Senate recesses."

"Big mistake. By then, he could be our number one suspect."

Jill felt a little guilty for strongly hoping that wasn't the case.

"It'll do you good to get away, Jill. Time away might chase those snakes out of your nightmares. I'll call the FBI and tell them you won't be needing that protection they ordered for you yesterday." With that, Rubric disappeared out the door.

So Rubric had been afraid to tell her about the FBI protection. He had a habit of dropping a subject he wanted to avoid just as he was leaving. No doubt her life was in danger. At least she had convinced Rubric to let her go to Alabama. She would feel safe out of town.

Jill rolled her bag across the lobby toward the elevator. "Bye,

Landry," she said, waving as she passed the front desk. "I'll be gone for a few days, but I can be reached on my cell phone."

"Where're you going?" Just as Landry asked, Rubric and Annabelle zipped around the corner to take the elevator downstairs to their daily breakfast meeting.

With a big grin, Rubric answered for Jill, "She's going to Bio Tech Labs in Mobile."

I didn't convince Rubric to let me go to Alabama, Jill thought. *He tricked me into going to Bio Tech.*

On the flight to Atlanta, Jill loaded the Bio Tech personnel disks and studied them. Intrigued by the resume and bio of the director of the MST research, Dr. Kelly Arden, she added the scientist's name to her wish list of interviews. Since MST was Dr. Arden's "baby," Jill guessed that this woman would be as passionate as anyone to solve the murder and the investigation to advance MST.

Once her plane landed in Atlanta, Jill turned on her cell phone. She took a seat at the gate and called the CEO of Bio Tech to request interviews with several key people.

It was early afternoon when Jill walked out of the Atlanta airport. The temperature was soaring above a hundred degrees. The sultry heat was stifling as she perched on top of her suitcase to wait for the rental car bus. Shortly, the bus driver pulled up and helped Jill load her suitcase onto the rack, and off they went to the rental car company.

As she waited in the long, winding line for her rental car, Jill phoned her grandmother Muv to ask her if she could stay with her in Fairhope while she visited Bio Tech.

"I'm delighted you're coming to see me," Muv said. "I'll be here, so come whenever you can and stay as long as you like. Your mother told me you've been working too hard, and Point of View is the perfect place for you to restore your soul."

Jill smiled at the thought of a visit with her grandmother.

After the call, Jill walked outside with the car key and smiled broadly when she saw the red Mustang convertible. For the first time in weeks, she felt at peace. On her drive to Roanoke, she daydreamed about her visit to Muv's home, Point of View. When she and Kathy were little girls, they always referred to Muv's home as "heaven."

Her hair blowing in the wind, she sped down the highway with the top to the Mustang down. Suddenly inspired, she dialed John. Voice mail again, but this time she left a message. "John, I'm on my way to Alabama, and by the weekend I'll be at my grandmother's home in Fairhope. Since you're in Florida and it's not that far, can you meet me there? Call my cell phone. I really need to see you. Love you." She clicked off the phone and pulled out on the expressway.

Jill figured that seeing John was the best way to get Tommy Harrison out of her head and her dreams. She was sure that her vulnerability to Tommy was caused by the pressure of the case and John's constant absence.

Once she arrived in the small town of Roanoke, it was midafternoon. Jill took note of the change in scenery. Framed by running roses, a hand-painted welcome sign proudly heralded that this was Roanoke, home of astronaut Joe Frank Edwards Jr., the Ella Smith Doll, and, yes, her friend Senator Thomas Henry Harrison. At least this sign proved Tommy's hometown hadn't disowned him. That said something.

As soon as she reached the first gas station, Jill pulled over to fill up her tank. Not because she needed gas but because she needed directions. If she were going to get someone to talk to her, she'd have to buy some gas too.

In her best Southern accent, she addressed the attendant who cheerfully stepped up to wash her window. "Hello, sir. I've never been to a gas station that cleaned my car windows at the self-service tank. Thank you so much. This is such a treat. I just love small towns."

The man grinned and puffed out his chest. "I saw your Georgia tag and thought to myself that there is a big city gal. Where'd you come from, Atlanta?"

"That's right." She smiled flirtatiously. "Could you tell me how to get to Senator Harrison's house?"

The man's smile was replaced with a frown. "Who wants to know?"

Maybe getting these Southerners to talk wasn't going to be as easy as Jill had thought. She'd forgotten how they protected their own, especially when it came to outsiders. This situation called for a little creativity, and Jill had read that Tommy bred horses, so she replied, "My name is Miss Jill Lewis. I'm in the market for a horse, and I heard somewhere that the senator might have just the kind I want to buy."

The man tossed the bug-stained paper towel in a rusty barrel next to the gas tank. "What do you need with one of them good-for-nothin' little horses? For the life of me I never understood why the senator wastes his time raising those poor excuses for horses. You can't ride 'em. So tell me, now, just what in the heck are they good for?"

"Little horses?" Jill thought quickly, wondering just what kind of horse the senator bred. Probably Shetland ponies. "It's for my niece. How do I get to his farm?"

"Are you sure you want to waste your hard-earned money? Little girls do grow up, you know."

"Yes, but they have little girls too."

The man grinned and knelt down beside Jill's car. He pointed with a chewed-off fingernail that had trapped a half inch of mechanic's grease. "Take Highway 431 right out here and go left toward Wedowee for about six miles. Then you take a left onto Old Confederate Schoolhouse Road. Go about twelve miles until you reach the Tallapoosa River. Then just stop and look up to the right. You'll see his place up there on the hill."

"Uh, would you mind going over that again, sir?"

The man was happy to oblige. Jill thanked him and asked, "Do you know if the senator and his wife are at home?"

"You ain't from around here, are you? His wife's dead. Murdered.

But you can find her buried downtown in Cedarwood Cemetery. It's on the right just before you get into town. And as for the senator, I don't rightly know if he's at home or not. He stays up in Washington most of the year, and I haven't seen nor heard him around here lately. He trades with me sometimes. But if he is there, I best warn you, you'd better hold tight onto your shirttail, ma'am."

"I beg your pardon?"

The man threw his head back and laughed heartily. Once he stopped, his countenance became serious. "The senator's got an eye for a pretty lady like you."

Jill faked a giggle. "Thanks for the warning." She told the man good-bye and drove away. As she passed Cedarwood Cemetery on the way to town, she slowed the car and thought of Catherine Harrison, a wife and a mother, whose life ended so tragically. Was she happily married and in love with Tommy? Did he love her? Did he miss her terribly? She wondered if she'd find flowers on the grave.

Curious, Jill turned her car around and drove back to the cemetery to search for Catherine Harrison's grave. She pulled into the narrow grassy lane sparsely covered in gravel and parked her car in the shade of an old magnolia tree. The Harrison monument soaring above the others wasn't hard to locate. White roses rambled along an ornamental iron fence that cordoned off the family plot. The cemetery was eerily quiet until Jill opened an ornate gate that creaked and squeaked loudly. Her feet crunched across the marble chips spread over the plot.

Catherine Delaney Hadley Harrison's inscription read "Devoted Daughter, Wife, and Mother." There were two dozen yellow roses in a bronze urn on her grave. Unlike the artificial flowers on the other graves, hers were fresh.

As Jill calculated Catherine's age, she realized the deceased had been close to her age at the time she died. She quickly turned away from Catherine's grave to look at others.

Three graves were marked "Thomas Henry Harrison," apparently the father, grandfather, and great-grandfather of the senator, all buried with saintly wives, judging from flowery inscriptions on their tombstones. Except for Tommy's father's wife. Jill noticed that the date of this woman's death was blank, but her name and date of birth were already inscribed in the marble tombstone.

Jill left the cemetery and headed to town. In downtown Roanoke, Main Street was lined with purple crepe myrtles and neatly trimmed topiaries. Citizens of this little town obviously took a lot of pride in it. Just past the business district, Jill admired white verandas peeking out like ruffled petticoats under rainbow-colored Victorian ladies situated on rolling green lawns. Expensive cars parked under their porticos were a sign that some of the residents enjoyed the good life. On the outskirts of town, as she drove past shanty houses devoid of paint, Jill saw clearly that others did not.

Once she turned onto Highway 431, Jill was surprised at how desolate the roads became. The deeper she drove up into the country, the fewer people she saw. The perfect isolated setting for a murder?

Out of habit, Jill glanced into the rearview mirror. Before long she came to the twisted and unruly Tallapoosa River that crashed high above its banks. Just as the man at the gas station had directed her, Jill saw the house through the trees. Only it wasn't a house; it was more like a fortress that sprawled above the river, high upon a hill. She had expected an antebellum mansion, like what she'd seen in the newspaper article, but this house was a Gothic mansion lifted off the pages of *Jane Eyre*. What happened to the antebellum mansion? Jill figured it must belong to Harrison's widowed mother. She hoped to drive around town and find it. She'd recognize it from the picture.

"So this is the home of the senator. Impressive." Driving on the road alongside the property, Jill got a glimpse of the miniature horses prancing in the pastures. Just as the man at the gas station said, these horses were no larger than dogs, just the right size for her niece, Marion.

Although she itched to poke around, she decided to leave the property. It would take a little finagling to get inside. Besides, she'd get more of the kind of information she needed from the locals before she ventured onto the property and got thrown out of town.

Driving back to Roanoke, Jill realized the day was slipping away. Right next to Pizza Hut she saw a Best Western motel and checked in at the front desk. Once she was settled in her room, she felt hungry and opted for an early supper. Nearby was Gedney's Catfish Café. Folks sat in rocking chairs on the whitewashed porch of the restaurant, but she was too tired to question anyone tonight. Under the watchful eyes of the other diners, Jill feasted on a hearty supper of fried catfish, hush puppies, and coleslaw.

Her waitress, Bonnie, was friendly and would've chatted with Jill more if she hadn't been so busy with other customers. Jill was relieved, because she would've felt obligated to chitchat. She wanted to have a more definite plan before she started poking her nose into the lives of Tommy Harrison and his family.

Having missed so much sleep since discovering Ally in the park, she was in bed by eight o'clock, watching a sappy TV movie on the Lifetime Channel. By nine she was bored and turned off the TV and light. Tossing and turning to get comfortable in the strange bed, Jill thought about all the intricate pieces of her investigation, especially the details of tomorrow. Despite her suspicions, Jill closed her eyes and prayed she wouldn't find a murder in Tommy's past. Minutes later she was dreaming, but she couldn't make out the face of the man who held her in her dreams.

21

*It's a mystery to me how anyone ever gets any nourishment
in this place. They must eat their meals standing up
by the window so as to be sure of not
missing anything.*

Agatha Christie

The next morning Jill zipped through the drive-in window at McDonald's for a granola, fruit, and yogurt before she drove to the county seat in Wedowee eight miles away. She sat outside the courthouse in her car and ate her yogurt until the building opened for business. Inside the Randolph County Courthouse, Jill followed the signs to the offices of the circuit court.

A lovely Southern woman named Veronica Austin warmly greeted Jill. "Good morning. May I help you?"

"Good morning, I'm Jill Lewis, a reporter. I'd like to get a copy of the transcripts for Cooter Orsen's trial that took place in Randolph County about ten years ago."

Veronica smiled and shook her head. "Poor old Cooter was a regular fixture in our courts, but let me think. I suppose you mean his trial for the murder of his third wife. Are you from

Court TV? I've always wondered why Court TV didn't feature that trial. In my opinion, it was very intriguing and would be a great TV show."

"Oh, I'm not a TV reporter; I'm with a newspaper," Jill was quick to explain. "What I need are the transcripts for Catherine Harrison's murder trial."

Veronica's face fell in disappointment. "I just assumed, well, you look like somebody who'd be from Court TV."

Sensing the woman's disappointment, Jill asked, "Tell me about that trial."

Veronica smiled as she began the tragic tale. "Cooter and his third wife, Nadine, both drank. One morning they got into a fight in their vegetable garden. In a drunken rage, Cooter turned around and stabbed Nadine multiple times. Then he chopped off her head."

When Jill winced, Veronica politely paused. "I figured since you worked in crime you'd be pretty tough. I'm sorry if I offended you."

"I'm fine, just surprised that Cooter wasn't sentenced to die in the electric chair for such a heinous crime. He must've had a really good lawyer."

"Oh, he couldn't afford a lawyer. He had a public defender, but he had the best—Tommy Harrison. Tommy was just starting out as a lawyer."

Jill gasped.

"Ironic, isn't it? Cooter murdered the wife of the very man who saved him from the electric chair."

Jill quickly asked Veronica if she could copy the transcripts for both trials for her. Promising she'd be back shortly, Jill dashed out the door. Since her cell service didn't work in the area, she ran down the street searching for a pay phone. Finding one at the gas station, Jill hurriedly dialed Rubric.

"So you made it to the land of cotton."

"I just found out that Tommy Harrison defended Cooter

Orsen the first time he was on trial for murder—for killing his third wife, Nadine."

"Remind me, who's Cooter Orsen?"

"The man who killed Tommy's wife."

"Oh, you can bet they were buddies. Harrison hired Cooter to kill his wife. It's doubtful that Cooter escaped from jail as the newspaper reported. I'd guess Harrison got him out of jail so he could murder his wife for him. Tell me, did Cooter slit his third wife's throat too?"

"Worse, he decapitated her."

"Okay, two slit throats and a decapitation. We've got a definite crime profile forming here," Rubric said.

"And don't forget the death by MST, a drug manufactured by a company that just happens to be located in Alabama."

"Tommy obviously doesn't do his own dirty work. He hires the killers to accomplish whatever he's trying to do."

"To murder a wife or an opposing senator or anyone else like a poor file clerk who gets in his way? Let's think about his motives," Jill said.

"For Brown? It's known they were in a battle over MST and Bio Tech Labs. For his wife, I'm sure you can uncover that motive in Roanoke. And your little Nancy Drew's only sin was probably in obstructing his plans."

"Please show some respect and call Ally by her name."

"Whatever. Keep talking to people, and if Roanoke's like every other Southern town I know, you'll have your answers served up on a china plate right next to the fried chicken for Sunday dinner."

Jill walked back to the courthouse. She reached for the trial transcripts and dug into her wallet to pay for them. Before she left, she asked Veronica for the name and phone number of Cooter's public defender in the Harrison murder trial.

Veronica flipped through a card file and handed the lawyer's card to Jill and said, "Barney's office is right down the street on the same side as the courthouse."

Jill thanked her, but because she wanted to review the trial transcripts before she visited the public defender's office, she headed back to her motel to spend some time reading.

Back at the motel, Jill dialed Rubric again.

"Good work," he said. "Your next assignment is to find out if Tommy married the broad for her money. Also find out if the Harrisons were really in love. I'll have to tune in tomorrow for my next exciting episode," Rubric said.

"If the evidence continues to stack up against Harrison, we'll have a lot of questions answered," Jill said, feeling quite guilty over her silly flirtation with the man.

She spent some time holed up in her motel room, reading the transcripts. But she found nothing that would cause anyone to raise an eyebrow—except for the description of the grisly murders. The evidence against Cooter Orsen in the Harrison murder was substantial. His fingerprints were all over the place, the point of entry and the exit had his blood from where he cut himself on the knife and glass, and police found a large sum of cash as well as Catherine's jewelry on him. It certainly made it a slam-dunk of a guilty verdict for the prosecutors. If Tommy Harrison were involved at all, it was a murder for hire.

When she went to visit Cooter's public defender for the Catherine Harrison murder trial, the man was locked-lipped. It was obvious he resented Jill for poking her nose into this resolved trial.

"Veronica told me you'd be dropping by my office. I told her that I had nothing to tell you beyond what's in the transcripts, except off the record to say that Cooter Orsen was an evil man. This county is lucky to be rid of him before he could kill again. Too bad Thomas Henry got him off the first time."

"I'm surprised to hear you say this. You were Mr. Orsen's defense attorney."

"Just because I provided him with an adequate defense doesn't mean I don't have an opinion of him."

"Perhaps your opinion of the man was evident to the jury?"

He shuffled some papers on his desk. "Are you trying to accuse me of something?"

"Not at all. I'm just saying that guilt or innocence should be proven by a jury of peers built on evidence, not the conjecture of the attorney."

"Ma'am, the man was guilty. He walked into the Harrison home and murdered poor Catherine. He was arrested, he came to court, and he was convicted of his crime. I was given the daunting task of defending him in a county where the Harrisons are loved and revered. I provided Cooter Orsen with those services. At no charge, I might add, since the taxpayers picked up the tab."

Once the attorney's sermon ended, Jill left the building as quickly as she could. As she drove around searching for a place to have lunch later, she spotted a sign that read "Sassy Scissors." Jill had some time to spare. Nowhere else but in a beauty shop would she find enough gossip to curl her hair. Looking at herself in the rearview mirror, she thought she could use a makeover, especially if she might see John in a couple of days.

The girl at the desk absentmindedly waved Jill to a seat in front of a table piled high with old copies of *People* magazine. Jill read the woman's name tag and saw that the attractive blonde was named Ann.

"New in town?" Ann asked without looking up at Jill.

"Just passing through," Jill said, thumbing through one of the magazines.

"Where are you from, honey?"

"Washington. I'm here doing a piece on small-town murders."

"Oh my gosh," Ann said. She led Jill to the sink and fastened a plastic cape around her neck. "Is this like *60 Minutes* or *48 Hours*?"

"Not exactly, but you've got the right idea."

"We've had plenty of killings around here. Which murder do you want to know about?"

"Catherine Harrison's," Jill replied, leaning her head back into the basin. Surprised, the woman jerked the hose, and the spray of warm water splattered across Jill's face.

"Thomas Henry's wife?"

"That's the one."

"Oh my heavens, have you come to the right place! Everybody in here knew Catherine Harrison, isn't that right?" Ann looked to the other women in the shop to affirm her reply.

The bleached blonde seated at the manicure table heard the name and answered her. "Bless her heart, the woman's dead, but when she was alive, everybody in this town knew something about her—leastwise everyone had an opinion of her."

"Her murder must have been devastating to all of you," Jill said, putting an extra amount of sympathy in her voice.

"Are you joking, honey? The only tears that were cried at that funeral came from her next of kin," the manicurist replied as she furiously shook a bottle of bright red nail polish.

"Well, her husband sure was upset when she died," Jill said as if she knew firsthand.

"Where'd you hear that hogwash?" asked a large woman in stretch pants squeezing out a belly roll.

Before Jill could answer, the manicurist hollered, "Hey, Cindy, get your butt over here. This lady wants to know about Thomas Henry's wife. Tell her what you said right here in this shop the day we heard his wife was murdered."

Cindy, another blonde bleached from the same bottle, teetered over in a pair of four-inch stiletto heels to Ann's station, where Jill sat. Finding great humor in her friend's comments, she laughed. "The day we heard she was murdered, I told everybody in here that I'd bet Thomas Henry was throwing a party to celebrate and that the devil was trying to lock his doors to keep that woman out of hell."

"Poor boy," the large woman lamented. "He should've married one of our hometown gals."

"And whose fault was it that he didn't?" the manicurist reminded everyone. "That uppity mama of his. She's the one who pressured the poor boy to marry a rich girl just so she could live in the style she'd been accustomed to before old man Harrison drank up all of her money."

Ann bent over and said quietly to Jill, "In my opinion, Catherine was really okay. Not many gave her a chance. Folks around here don't have any use for outsiders, especially the ones who think they're better than us. The problem was her attitude toward us. This place wasn't good enough for her."

"She didn't think anyone in this town was a good enough hairstylist, so she drove all the way to Atlanta to get her hair done," Cindy explained.

"She said that was because she only liked for men to do her hair," someone else said. "I can't think of a man in this town who would be caught dead fixing hair, can y'all? So what does that tell you?"

"Oh, she had big fancy parties up there at her mansion, but did she ever invite anyone who lived around here?" The manicurist looked around the room at each face present. "Did she? Were any of you ever invited into that house?"

Right on cue all the women frowned firmly, shaking their head no, but one elderly lady said, "Catherine had our Sunday school picnic at her house. I can tell you one thing, though, the poor little thing didn't know how to make sweet tea."

"Honey, she didn't know how to cook up anything but trouble," Cindy said.

"She was a decent mother. I will give her that," the manicurist said begrudgingly.

A small uproar broke out in the beauty shop as a couple of women argued about the dead woman's mothering skills. "Y'all stop talking about Catherine Harrison, you hear?" the elderly woman ordered. "She was a fine Christian woman."

"What about Cooter Orsen's fourth wife? Does she still live around here?" Jill asked.

"Honey, she took her money and rode out of town on a big rig with that truck driver, Malcolm Lovingood," Cindy said.

"What money?"

"Should we tell her?" Ann turned around to ask approval from the patrons and other hairdressers. Some nodded their heads.

"Well, it's like this," Ann said. "After Cooter was fried like a catfish, wife number four, Fanny, started tooling around Roanoke in a big black Cadillac. Bought it brand new from Terry Cole over at Prestridge Buick."

"Don't forget her mink coat!" someone shouted.

"Oh, she wore that coat every Sunday right into spring," the manicurist reminded everyone.

"And the diamonds too," the elderly lady reminded everyone.

"Why would anyone marry Cooter after he murdered his third wife?" Jill asked.

"Well, honey," Cindy said, "there's some that believe Cooter didn't do it. Fanny was one of them people. In fact, there's some that believe Cooter didn't kill Catherine Harrison either."

"Who else would believe something like that?"

Cindy laughed. "I told everyone at the time that I didn't blame Thomas Henry if he'd done it himself."

"You think he killed her?" Jill couldn't hide the surprise in her voice. She couldn't believe that the knowledge she wanted was so forthcoming.

"Well, I can't say for sure, but a few people around here think he did."

"But what about all the forensic evidence? Cooter's fingerprints were everywhere," Jill pointed out to the women.

"Don't shed any tears for that old coot, honey," Cindy assured Jill. "Cooter Orsen deserved to die. He was bad to the bone."

"Some folks will swear to it that Thomas Henry gave Cooter a million dollars to kill his wife," Ann told her.

The manicurist chimed in. "Others say Thomas Henry slit her throat himself and then put Cooter's fingerprints at the scene."

"And don't forget Cooter's alibi," Ann reminded them.

The manicurist nodded her head. "At first Fanny told the sheriff that he was with her at the time of the murder, but she sure changed her tune when Thomas Henry pulled out his big fat checkbook."

"Once she came out with that on the stand, Cooter didn't have a chance of a not-guilty verdict," Cindy said. "Of course, who could blame Fanny for lying? She had three young kids at home, and Cooter never gave her a dime."

The white-haired woman put her magazine away and joined in the conversation. "I heard Cooter had been diagnosed with cancer the month before his trial and only had six months to live anyway." She raised an eyebrow. "What did he have to lose?"

"If the gossip's true, I reckon that was a pretty clever thing for Thomas Henry to do, and for the Orsens to accept," Ann noted.

"But wouldn't there be a money trail? Was that ever investigated?" Jill wanted to know.

"I guess nobody here ever cared enough to look." Ann shrugged. "Folks around here love Thomas Henry."

"Y'all hush your mouths," a woman ordered, pulling her rolled head out from underneath the hair dryer to offer her explanation. "If you're insinuating that money came from Thomas Henry, you're wrong. He had nothing to do with that murder, and you know it."

A saucy redhead spoke up from the back. "You're all wrong. I know for a fact that it was a certain lawyer in this town who gave Fanny that money. He made sure she got everything her heart desired, and his name wasn't Thomas Henry."

"Yeah," the hair dryer lady agreed and added, "Poor old Amos. He gave Fanny all that money, and she showed her appreciation by hightailing it out of here with a trucker. Whoops, did I mention his name?"

"It's not like you're telling us anything we don't know," the manicurist said as she paused her nail polish brush in midair, dripping red drops on the white towel. "Well, you all have to admit that poor old Amos never was much to look at, now was he?"

"It doesn't matter what he looks like. You girls are forgetting, Amos is rich," the hair dryer lady reminded them.

"Keep on talking, honey. Amos is getting better looking all the time," Cindy said with a chuckle.

"Where do Fanny and her truck driver live now?" Jill asked.

"She and Malcolm stay over in the valley, down around Lanett."

"How far is that from here?"

For a minute all the women just stared at Jill, probably wondering why she'd want to know. Jill squirmed.

Fortunately Ann spoke up for her. "She's one of them reporters. And she's doing a story about small-town murders."

"Well, if that's the case, I think she ought to go talk to Fanny, don't y'all?" Cindy suggested.

All the women nodded and the manicurist agreed. "Fanny would love that. She's always dreamed of getting her name in the newspaper. And the obituaries don't count."

"My cousin, she lives over in Lanett, and she says she sees Fanny every Wednesday in the Wal-Mart in West Point. She works as a greeter there," the hair dryer lady said.

"If she has so much money, why does she work at Wal-Mart?" Jill asked.

"In a small town, Wal-Mart is the hub of society, honey. Besides, Fanny is a big spender," the manicurist explained to Jill. "She enjoys the discount she gets there."

"I'll bet the old gal has spent every last dime Thomas Henry gave her," Cindy said.

"Maybe Thomas Henry was sweet on her. She's a good-looking woman, you know?" the manicurist said.

Cindy snorted. "Humph. Not likely, if you ask me. I don't know how anyone could've been in love with that woman."

Ann was eyeing Jill suspiciously and leaned over to whisper in her ear. "You can't fool me. You've got a little crush on him, don't you? You're writing a story about him, but you've been taken in by his charm and good looks. And I don't blame you a bit. He's good-looking, and he's fun. I'd want to check him out too, and there's no better place than right here in his hometown."

Jill blushed, but she decided to play along. "Well, a little one, maybe."

"I couldn't help but notice that honker of a ring you're wearing. You better watch out if you're engaged to another man, because you might just lose your heart to Thomas Henry if given half a chance." She scrutinized Jill for a moment. "You've got really good hair, by the way. Honey, if you like him, you go for him. Never mind about all our jabbering in here today. If they don't have anything to talk about, they'll just make something up." Ann cast a bemused look at the crowd of ladies.

"Why are you so sure he didn't kill his wife?" Jill asked Ann.

"That big old teddy bear? I've known Thomas Henry all my life, and I can tell you for sure, he's not capable of squashing an ant, much less murder. Besides, he wasn't even in town." Ann pointed a tall metallic can at Jill's head. "Hairspray?"

Before Jill could answer, her hair was plastered with the stuff. She thanked Ann and generously tipped her. Jill waved goodbye to the ladies before returning to her car. What she would've given to hear the conversation back in the beauty shop after she walked out that door!

22

We travel, some of us forever, to seek other states,
other lives, other souls.

Anais Nin

"Welcome to Wal-Mart."

Jill smiled. "Hi, you must be Fanny Orsen."

"Don't I wish? Have you seen that good-looking, truck-driving husband of hers?" the middle-aged woman with the big hair said.

"I haven't had the pleasure."

"Honey, he's a dead ringer for Elvis." Her chandelier earrings danced as she shook her head.

"Is that so? Is Fanny here today?"

"Fanny's at home. She's feeling a bit puny today, so I told her I'd come in for her. Frankly, I need the extra hours."

"Do you know how I can get in touch with her?"

"Well, I can't tell you 'cause it's against store policy, but I'll give a hint. You see that phone booth out in the parking lot?" The woman pointed. "You'll find the listing for Malcolm Lovingood in that phone book hanging on it."

Jill thanked the woman. Within minutes, she had her call

made. Ten minutes later she was standing at the front door of Fanny and Malcolm's neat brick ranch on West Point Street.

"Come on in, sugar. I was expecting to hear from you," Fanny welcomed her.

"You were?"

"Oh, honey, you just don't know. Sometimes folks around here tell me what I'm doing long before I've even thought about doing it. Ever since you got your hair done at Sassy Scissors. The skinny woman with the bright red hair, it ain't natural like mine, she's my third cousin. Although I don't always claim her," Fanny added, quite serious.

News doesn't just travel fast in small towns; it breaks world records. Probably breaks the sound barrier too.

"Come on in." Fanny, dressed in a pair of skintight jeans with a faded Grateful Dead T-shirt, opened the door wide, revealing her bare feet with red toenails and diamond toe rings on two of her toes. The same red polished her nails, and she wore rings on every finger. With red hair as bright as her cousin, Fanny wore hers pinned high on her head with long tendrils that tickled her cheeks. The women in the beauty shop had told the truth about one thing—she was a fine-looking woman.

Fanny led her toward the kitchen. En route, Jill paused at a grouping of paintings in the hallway. "Are these R. C. Gormans?"

"I don't know, but whoever painted them, I sure like them. They're Indians, and if anybody in this country got a raw deal it was them. My granny claimed we were part Cherokee."

Jill squinted at the pictures. Were they real or knockoffs? "Gorman is a Navajo artist who's become famous. Art critics dub him the Picasso of Southwestern art."

"They were given to me by an old friend. I thought they were pretty, and he took them off his wall and gave them to me."

Could that "friend" be Tommy Harrison?

Jill followed Fanny into the kitchen, where they sat down for coffee.

"My ex-husband, Cooter, God rest his soul, cut that woman's throat," Fanny said as she plunked a spoonful of sugar into her mug. "It was so embarrassing to my kids and me. We were relieved to move away from Roanoke so people would stop staring and pointing at us."

"I read the court transcripts. At first, you were his alibi."

"Yeah, but I had my days mixed up."

Jill couldn't tell if the woman was telling the truth or not.

"Cooter was drunk when he went over to the Harrison house that night. I'll never believe that he went there to kill her. He was just going to steal some jewelry. We needed the money. I figure Catherine woke up and tried to get her stuff back from him. Cooter didn't like anybody getting in his way. But I just don't think he would ever mean to kill Thomas Henry's wife, not after all that Thomas Henry had done for him."

"Do you know Thomas Harrison personally?"

"Know him? My mother was his mother's maid; we practically grew up together."

Interesting. "Did Senator Harrison give you any money after Cooter was executed?"

Fanny shrugged. "Yeah, but it wasn't the first time he gave me money. Thomas Henry paid my rent when Cooter wasn't able."

"Why did he give you money after your husband killed his wife?"

"I got real depressed and couldn't work after Cooter got fried. Mostly on account of my drinking, but I got that fixed at the AA meetings. Anyway, the money had nothing to do with Cooter or Catherine or anybody else—just a sense a loyalty between him and my mama and me, nothing more. My kids would've starved if it hadn't been for Thomas Henry. I suppose that's how these rumors got started. But Thomas Henry's very generous and does things like that all the time for a lot of folks around Roanoke."

"Did you know his wife?"

"I did, but it's no secret I didn't have any use for that uppity woman. Mostly, I didn't like the way she treated Thomas Henry."

"How did she treat him?"

She snorted. "You should've heard the way that woman talked to him. It was disgraceful."

"But the senator loved her, didn't he?"

"Maybe. I guess that just goes to show that you can't help who you love. Just like I loved Cooter. Everyone warned me to stay away from Cooter, but when he wasn't drinking, he was the sweetest man you'd ever want to know." Fanny stopped, tears welling at the corners of her eyes.

Jill touched her hand. "I'm sorry."

Fanny pulled a tissue off the cabinet to dab her eyes. "I've got a good life with a good man now, and I thank the good Lord for it every day. Malcolm is a fine-looking man, God-fearing and churchgoing too—and you should hear him sing. Want to see a picture of him?"

"Sure." Jill looked at the framed photo Fanny handed to her. He was a good-looking man—with so many tattoos you'd have thought his arms were ripped out of a comic book.

"Thank you, Fanny," Jill said, standing up from the table.

"I'm glad I could help. Is my name going to be in the newspaper?"

"I'm not sure yet, but if it is, I'll be sure to send you a copy."

After her visit with Fanny, Jill felt more confused than ever. The woman seemed sincere, and yes, she had gotten money from Tommy, but she claimed he wanted to help her. Help her? Paying a poor woman's rent was one thing, but why the pricey artwork, the diamonds, and the fancy car? Maybe they were from the rich lawyer in Roanoke, like the women at the beauty shop said.

Driving toward Mobile, Jill was just checking in with Rubric when she heard a beep, so she quickly switched over to the other line. "Jill Lewis."

It was John. "Jill, I got your message. I'm booked on a flight to Mobile tomorrow."

"I don't believe it!"

Jill gave him Muv's address and phone number before they said good-bye. She smiled. Now she'd have time to relax with John over the weekend before she had to face the Bio Tech folks on Monday. It was time to put work and the horrors of this investigation behind her for a few days of rest and romance.

Miles before she saw the gulf, the smell of saltwater filled Jill's nostrils. Flowers blurred in a profusion of colors as Jill meandered along the winding roads that led to her grandmother's home in Fairhope, Alabama. The saltwater draft coming through the window and memories of childhood summers at her grandmother's home made her giddy with anticipation.

Turning her car into the long driveway, Jill bumped along under a canopy of one-hundred-year-old oaks until she reached the entrance to her family's ancestral home situated on a half dozen acres on the Gulf Coast. Built in the 1850s prior to the Civil War, the house had only housed Winthrops inside its walls. Jill immediately felt safe.

Behind the antebellum home lay the expanse of the bay, wild and blue with cascades of seething foam. Jill parked in the splintered shade of an ancient mimosa tree that she had climbed as a child. She picked up a feather bloom that tickled her nose while she paused for a few minutes to admire the view.

After reaching out to take the lion's head doorknocker in her hand, Jill knocked three times until her grandmother's elderly butler, Charles, opened the door.

Jill found her grandmother on the back veranda overlooking the sea, sipping iced tea spiked with fresh mint. Muv gave Jill a big hug and a big welcome. She handed her a glass of iced tea and led her to a table bearing an array of tea sandwiches made with tomato, watercress, and cucumber slices. A cut crystal bowl held thick chunks of watermelon garnished with plump, juicy grapes and deep red strawberries.

"Mmm. This looks wonderful, Muv. And I'm so happy to be in your home. It's my favorite place on earth."

Her grandmother laughed. "I can remember telling your grandfather that I didn't want this decrepit old house. I wanted a contemporary one with lots of glass and no drafty old halls." Her grandmother smiled at the memory. "I told him I didn't want to see the ocean; I only wanted to see the city lights."

"I'm glad you changed your mind, but what persuaded you?"

"When I had your mother. Home and family suddenly became the most important things in the world to me."

"Now that I've met John, I kind of feel that same way."

"I can't wait to meet your young man. I'm delighted he's going to join us."

"He'll be here tomorrow, and he's looking forward to meeting you too. You're going to love him, Muv."

"If you love him, I'll love him. You remind me so much of myself at your age," her grandmother observed. "You know, your mother is worried about you. She thinks you work too hard."

"Right now I'd agree with her. This investigation is stressful. The harder I work, the more confused I become."

"Maybe you'll find the answers at my Bible study tonight."

"Tonight? Maybe your friends could pray for me."

By seven, the dinner dishes were cleared away, and Jill opened the door to elderly matrons wearing traces of youthful beauty in their smiles. A few of them leaned on silver canes, and another pushed a walker, whereas others seemed to do just fine on their own steam. Proper Southern ladies, they were all dressed in perfectly pressed linen dresses in popsicle colors of summer. Each carried her well-worn Bible in the crook of her arm.

Greeting Jill warmly, they acted as though it were an honor to see her all grown up, not because she was Jill Lewis, reporter extraordinaire of the *Washington Gazette*, but because she was Claire Winthrop's beloved granddaughter. It was a welcome change.

After the social hour, Jill's grandmother clanked a cut glass vase with a sterling silver soupspoon, and immediately the women came to attention, each silently taking one of the chairs in the front parlor to set in a circle. Muv's famous praline cookies arranged on embroidered cloths in silver cake baskets were passed as the women sipped chilled lemonade and shared stories about their families.

"All right, time for the Bible study to get down to business," Muv ordered the ladies.

After a time of prayer, the women all opened their Bibles to the book of John. Suddenly, a man's voice called from the foyer.

"Anyone home?"

"Who could that be?" Muv looked up with wide, curious eyes.

All the elderly women rose to their feet.

"Wait here. I better check this out," Jill suggested. She walked through the doorway into the foyer. "John? John!" Jill squealed as she saw her betrothed. She ran into John's arms and kissed him long and hard.

"I thought you weren't coming till tomorrow," Jill said.

"I wanted to surprise you."

"Well, you sure did. Come, I want you to meet Muv and her friends. They're in the middle of their Bible study." Jill turned around to see them all grouped together in the doorway. "Ah, here they are!"

Jill watched John as he shook each woman's hand. When he got to Muv, he gave her a big kiss. Turning red in the face, she politely welcomed him into the family.

Later that night, after Muv went on to bed, John and Jill sat cuddling on the wicker couch on the veranda, listening to the ocean sounds. For the first time in days, Jill felt relaxed, unburdened. John seemed at peace too.

"I wish time would just freeze on us so that this moment would last forever," Jill said.

John squeezed her hand.

Jill decided to keep her fears bundled inside of her head. "How long do you plan to stay?"

"Until Monday morning." He kissed her. "Tomorrow we'll have a whole day to be together. Relax."

"How can I relax when I'm driving over to Bio Tech Labs on Monday morning? If I don't find any answers there, I'm not sure what I'm going to do."

"What do you hope to find there?"

"Senator Brown's killer."

"Wow, those are lofty expectations."

"Brown fought furiously to close down a drug trial at Bio Tech, and we're waiting to hear from the autopsy to determine if he died from the drug in question or the venom that's used as a component in the drug."

"And you think someone connected to Bio Tech is responsible for his death?"

"At the moment, it's the only major lead I have. You'd have to agree that the people at Bio Tech certainly had a motive."

"Is that why you've been rooting around down here in the South?"

"That, and also an unofficial background check on Senator Harrison."

"What did you find out about Harrison in Roanoke?"

"I was trying to find out if he could've murdered his wife. I'm trying to get a sense of the man and what he may be capable of doing."

"Sounds like a good idea to me. By the way, I talked to my boss, Bill Tucker, and he said he met you in Senator Brown's office. He told me about the MST and the snakes in the doughnuts and finding the body in Rock Creek Park. What were you doing in Brown's offices, anyway?"

"I went there to meet with Eric Richter to get copies of Senator Brown's phone records. I've got them tucked inside my briefcase. You want to see them?"

"Eric gave them to you?"

"Not willingly, but I hammered him until he finally agreed. We were looking for the phone records when we found the MST."

"What are they supposed to prove?"

"That Senator Brown called me the day he was murdered."

"Didn't you already know that, Jill?"

"Of course, but his chief of staff refuses to believe me. But I'm looking for more than that. Like who else Brown was talking to in that same time frame. I had plans to go through the phone records but got distracted with the Rock Creek Park murder. Want to help me go through them now?" Jill took John by the hand and led him into the breakfast room and set up her laptop. "Would you rather use the laptop or go through the hard copies I printed?"

"I'll take the hard copies."

Jill eyed John. "I'm sure the FBI has already seen these, although they'd never tell me if they had."

Looking through the numbers, John commented, "These numbers are great, but you need to find out whose numbers they are. Then you might be able to put together some timeline as to his schedule for those days. But let it go for now; this is our time, remember? Come on; let's walk down to the beach."

Jill put away the phone records and went with John for a moonlight stroll. When they returned to the veranda, Jill fell asleep with her head on John's shoulder. She awoke in time to see the rising pink sun surfing in on the waves. Looking around, she didn't see John. She called out his name. There was no answer.

Jill ran up the steps to the guest room and saw that the bed hadn't been slept in. His bag was gone too. Jill pushed open the door to the adjoining bath. No sign of John there either. As she looked around, something caught her eye in the mirror on the opposite wall. There on the marble vanity was a dark leather dop kit. Jill hesitated. Should she open it? Finally convinced it wouldn't really be meddling, she pulled the kit open and found the usual array of the men's toiletries. Spotting John's cologne, she unscrewed the top and dabbed her wrists with it before putting it back. *Mmm, smells just like John.*

Inside a small pocket she found his business card and what looked like a plastic hotel key. She picked up the plastic card and slid it out of its paper sleeve to read it. Clarion Suites, Miami. Convincing herself she might one day need this key, Jill dropped the card into her pants pocket. After all, wouldn't he have to get another anyway? Eyes welling with tears, she stamped back downstairs and into the kitchen. On the dining table she saw an envelope with her name written on it with John's handwriting.

> Another urgent call from the bureau. Didn't want to wake you. Please tell your grandmother I enjoyed meeting her and I'm sorry I had to leave without saying good-bye. I loved being with you. And remember; I'll always come back to you. All my love,
>
> John

23

Have you ever studied a snake's face?—
how optimistic they look. They have an eternal smile.

Tasha Tudor, with Richard Brown

Jill crawled in bed to grab a couple hours of sleep. She'd just dozed off when her cell phone rang. Thinking it was John, she answered it. "Hello?"

"Jill."

She sat up in bed. "Tommy, hi."

"What do you think you're doing, snooping around Roanoke?"

Jill gulped. "Investigating."

"How dare you! You'd better not set foot in my hometown again."

"I can go anywhere I please, Senator."

"I'm warning you, Jill Lewis, if I ever hear you've been snooping around Roanoke again, I'll . . ."

"Are you threatening me, Senator?"

He was quiet for a moment. When he spoke again, his voice sounded even and controlled. "Don't be ridiculous. I just don't appreciate you stirring up old gossip."

"That's part of my job. I have to check to see how reliable my sources are, like any responsible journalist would."

Then anger returned to his voice. "If you ever try to go back to Roanoke, I'll have you arrested at the city limits."

"I wasn't aware that you had that kind of power, Senator. Does that power extend to getting away with murder?" Jill regretted it the moment the accusatory words tumbled off her lips.

For a moment Harrison didn't reply. "What are you insinuating?"

"Okay, I'll be direct this time." Now Jill was angry, and she blurted out, "Did you hire Cooter Orsen to kill your wife?"

"This is absolutely ridiculous, and I refuse to be insulted by you any longer!" The senator slammed down the phone.

"Ouch!" Jill said, rubbing her ear.

Jill drove into Mobile, worrying that her reception would be a chilly one because of her argument with Tommy. That is, if he hadn't already banned her from the place.

Once Jill arrived, it took fifteen minutes of security checks just to walk through the front door. In a few minutes a fiftyish woman appeared, introducing herself as the CEO's assistant. She led Jill into an office where a distinguished man extended both his hand and a smile to her. "Welcome to Bio Tech Labs, I'm Dr. Carl Johnson, the CEO."

"Thank you for seeing me."

"Thank you for coming. Everyone at Bio Tech is distraught over the news of Senator Brown's death. It was shocking to hear that MST or one of its components could be a factor in his death."

Jill got right to the point. "It's public knowledge that Senator Brown was no friend of Bio Tech, and you must realize his murder casts suspicion on your company."

Dr. Johnson seemed taken back by her brashness. "Ms. Lewis, are you aware that Senator Brown's accusations against our company and MST were totally unfounded? I assume Senator Harrison reviewed this with you?"

"He did, sir, and I've also checked it out for myself."

"Good. The negative publicity of Bio Tech has already cost the company millions of dollars. If MST or the Saw-Scaled Viper's venom is confirmed as the murder weapon in his death, truthfully, Ms. Lewis, I'm not sure our company can recover from the scandal. That's why we're dedicated to finding the truth as quickly as possible."

"Senator Harrison told me that the FBI has already subpoenaed your company records, but have they begun a full-fledged investigation?" Jill asked.

"Yes, as I've told them and I'll tell you, we'll cooperate and do whatever it takes to get this resolved. I've distributed a memo to my employees to make themselves available to both you and to the FBI."

"Are there any employees inside the company who would use the drug for their own profit?" Jill asked.

He shook his head. "I've personally reviewed the files of everyone in this company. There's no one I can pinpoint."

"Dr. Johnson, I've reviewed the Bio Tech files too, and I agree with your findings—there's no one person or group that fits the FBI profile in this company. Since we both have gone over the employee records and no one raises suspicion, do you have any ideas on how to proceed next?"

"I was hoping you'd be the one with the ideas."

"I've only read the employee records. I would like to meet with the employees department by department."

"Good plan. Let me tell you what we're doing on this end: we've begun the process by running a current credit check on all the employees to see if anyone is deeply in debt. I've not had a single employee refuse to have the credit check done."

"What about the officers in your company, your board of directors, and the majority stockholders?" Jill asked.

"We're reviewing everyone."

"I've gone over the records, but some of the names of the stockholders are hidden behind off-shore corporations. This is going to take months to investigate unless you can give me any direction there, such as names of the people you know are behind some of these corporations."

"They are all perfectly legal corporations."

"Oh, I'm not questioning that, I just need a list of names of the individuals behind them."

"I supplied the FBI with all the names. Don't they share their records with you?"

"Hardly."

"Then I'm afraid we have a problem. I'll have to get each board member to sign a clearance affidavit to reveal their name." Dr. Johnson stood up and sat on the edge of his desk and folded his hands. "And I must warn you, that could take some time."

"I'll wait."

"While you're here, I want you to speak with as many people as you can. Your first appointment is with the CFO, Bobby Hall. Follow me; I'll take you to his office."

"I'd appreciate that, Dr. Johnson." Jill picked up her things and followed, thrilled that he had been so receptive to her interview requests.

Once seated at Bobby Hall's desk, Jill started with her questions. "Dr. Johnson told me it could take time to reach all the stockholders. Is there anyone you suspect on the board, in the company, or within the stockholders?"

"Our stockholders have a lot more to gain if the drugs are on the market. Bootlegging the drug would make a fortune, but not as much if you combine their investment plus the profit they will make when the drug goes on the market, so I don't believe you'll find any suspects there."

"What about the employees?"

"We're doing everything we can to pinpoint any suspicious

employees. The FBI is checking them out as well. If you get a sense of any guilt from your interviews today, I would appreciate knowing."

"You have my word." Jill handed him her card. "Call me as soon as any of the stockholders' permissions come into your office."

Bobby Hall introduced her to the accounting staff, and Jill spent the remainder of her morning talking with them. With so much information, it would take her days of work to read through and understand everything she was handed.

Late in the morning, Dr. Johnson poked his head inside the door. "I've arranged for us to have lunch in the company cafeteria so you can meet several of our employees. I've told them you'll be circulating and that they are to give you all the time you need, Ms. Lewis."

"Thank you." Jill followed Johnson into the company cafeteria.

Lunch was pleasant, and all the employees, mostly Southerners, were cordial. After lunch Jill thanked Dr. Johnson and began her meetings with scientists who were responsible for developing MST. The next few hours at Bio Tech proved to be routine. Then she met with Dr. Kelly Arden.

"Ms. Lewis, how much do you know about MST?" Dr. Arden asked.

"Only the little I've garnered from my research, and a crash course from Senator Harrison."

"Most laymen struggle with the drug's chemical components and its scientific reactions. It would take years for them to learn everything about MST. Surprising that Senator Harrison has given you so much information."

"I'm a reporter. He brought me into the investigation, so he's obligated to provide the facts."

"I thought reporters were only concerned with the salient points?"

"We're interested in the truth, Dr. Arden. Sometimes that involves a lot of research before we arrive at it." Perplexed by the woman's demeanor, Jill tried to determine the cause.

"Yes, but wouldn't you agree that the senator has a way of making even business fun?"

Strange question. "That depends on your interpretation of fun," Jill quipped, sensing there was more than a professional relationship between this woman and Tommy.

"I think you know what I mean."

"I have a professional relationship with the senator, that's all." Jill quickly tried to nix any speculation on the part of Dr. Arden.

The doctor looked down at her watch. "It's late. Perhaps we should start fresh tomorrow morning?"

"That sounds good. I do have more questions to ask you." Jill pulled out her PDA. "Would 8:30 tomorrow morning work for you?"

Dr. Arden nodded curtly. "I'll see you at 8:30."

Driving back to Muv's house, Jill thought about her encounter with Dr. Arden. Knowing what a ladies' man Tommy Harrison could be, Jill was certain he had hit on Dr. Arden at one time or another. Did she love or hate the man? It was hard to tell.

Deep in thought, Jill jumped when the phone rang. "Hello?"

"How's my girl?"

"Oh, it's the guy who ran out on me."

"I'm sorry. It was unforgivable, but will you forgive me?"

"Of course, I forgive you. Hey, give me the mailing address of your hotel."

Instinctively, John rambled it off and then asked, "Why do you need it?"

"You left your dop kit at Muv's house."

"Forget it. Listen to me, Jill. I don't have much time. I need you to fly back to Washington early tomorrow morning so we can talk."

"But John, I've got interviews at Bio Tech. There's no way—"

"I'll explain when I see you. I've made reservations for you on the six o'clock flight tomorrow morning." John quickly gave Jill the confirmation number.

John certainly hadn't given her time to ask any questions. But she had recognized the fear in his voice. Fear for her life?

After the call, she wadded up the paper on which she had written the address of his Miami hotel. *Guess I won't need this anymore.* About to toss it into the trash, she stopped and smoothed it out. She folded the wrinkled paper around the hotel key card. Then, she slid it into her wallet.

24

Some questions don't have answers,
which is a terribly difficult lesson to learn.

Mary Astor

As she waited at the Pensacola Airport for her plane to board, Jill's cell phone rang. It was Dr. Johnson at Bio Tech Labs.

"Good morning, Ms. Lewis. I apologize for the early call, but I wanted to catch you before you drove into Mobile this morning." His voice sounded aloof, tense.

"Dr. Johnson, I'm glad you called. I was waiting for a decent hour to call you. An emergency's come up, and I'm at the airport now waiting to board a plane back to Washington. I left a message for Dr. Arden that I would have to reschedule our appointment."

"You've just made it easier for me to tell you what I'm about to say. I was calling to cancel your 8:30 appointment with Dr. Arden."

"Oh. Well, like I said, I hope to reschedule in a couple of days."

"Ms. Lewis, I'm afraid I can't allow you to return to Bio Tech

Labs at all, at least not until the cause of Senator Brown's death is resolved."

"But you said yesterday—"

"We've had some policy changes in the past twenty-four hours. Our general council has issued a ruling that prohibits our employees from talking to the media."

"Did the FBI release the results of the autopsy?"

"Not to my knowledge. The reasons for our ban on the media are strictly internal."

"But how can I help Bio Tech if I'm not allowed inside the company?" Jill felt deflated. "Wait a minute. Does this have anything to do with Senator Harrison? Did he call you?"

"I'm sorry, Ms. Lewis, but this is our company's new policy. If anything changes, I'll be sure to get in touch with you."

Dr. Johnson quickly ended the conversation, leaving Jill in a daze. As she boarded the plane, she thought to herself, *But of course it was Tommy Harrison. Why hadn't I thought of it right away? I'm just surprised he didn't stop me yesterday before I ever got inside Bio Tech.*

She knew that if she wanted to solve this case, she would have to make peace with the senator.

As the plane landed in Washington, Jill no longer thought of Tommy Harrison. Anxious to see John, she went straight to the office to await his arrival or a phone call.

"Rubric, I'm back!" Jill barreled into her editor's cluttered office. "Oh, I'm sorry. I didn't realize you had a guest." Recognizing John's boss, Agent Tucker, Jill said, "Hello, Bill." She glided across the room to shake the agent's hand. "Forgive me. I didn't expect to see you here. Have the results from Senator Brown's autopsy come back from the lab?"

"Agent Tucker isn't here about Senator Brown. He's here on another matter," Rubric explained.

"Oh."

"It's John," Rubric said quietly.

"I'm meeting John here today."

"Jill, I think you better have a seat," Bill suggested, standing to offer her his chair.

Slowly, a swell of panic began swirling around like a tornado in her head.

"No, I'd prefer to stand." Terror pricked at her emotions, rendering her weak. "It's John, isn't it? Is he okay?"

"John's been in an accident, Jill, but the doctors have assured us that he'll be fine in a few days."

She gasped. "What kind of an accident?"

Busily transferring newspapers from the extra chair, Rubric tossed them under his desk so Jill could sit down.

Bill began to explain the situation. "Let me begin by reiterating that John is alive, but during the course of an investigation, he was involved in a life-threatening accident."

"A car accident?" Jill blanched.

Bill hesitated. "John was bitten by a poisonous snake, but don't worry, he was taken to Ryder Trauma Center in Miami, one of the most renowned trauma facilities in the country. The doctors say he's going to make a full recovery."

"What kind of snake?" Jill asked, but she already knew the answer.

"A Saw-Scaled Viper. John was sent to Miami to inspect a shipment of exotic reptiles."

So he was working the same case. She clasped her hands together. "You're sure he's okay?"

"Yes, he's alive and improving every hour. I knew he'd want me to tell you myself before you had a chance to hear it elsewhere."

"Or worse yet, in the news," Rubric added.

"No news," Bill warned. "This is a highly classified case and must be kept out of the news at all cost. None of this can be printed, understand? I'm only here as a personal favor to John."

"Why didn't John call me himself?"

Bill hesitated for a moment. "I don't want to alarm you, but this snakebite is very serious. The doctors placed John into a drug-induced coma to prevent the poison from spreading too rapidly."

"Did John have surgery?"

"No."

"Are you sure he's all right?"

"Yes, he's in the best hospital and has the best doctors. If an accident were going to happen, it couldn't have happened in a better place."

Jill's knees felt weak, so she plopped herself into the chair Rubric had cleared off. "Tell me everything."

Bill sat down too. "It happened during a shipment check. John was on assignment with U.S. Fish and Wildlife in Miami. They inspect all the animal and reptile shipments that come into the country from abroad, and John accompanied the state U.S. Fish and Wildlife Commissioner inspecting several cartons of a suspicious reptile shipment that recently arrived in the Miami Harbor."

"Reptile shipment?" Rubric asked.

"The reptile import business is a big operation in the U.S. Many companies milk the reptiles to produce the antivenin, others to develop drugs. There are zoos, and also many hobbyists who keep snakes to enjoy, trade, observe, or whatever other bizarre reason an individual would want to have a poisonous snake."

Rubric asked the question that stuck in Jill's throat. "If snakes are big business, what made you think this particular shipment was suspicious?"

"First, the size of the shipment, the origin, and finally the destination."

"How large was the shipment?" Rubric asked.

"There were eighty dozen reptiles in this single shipment alone," Bill explained, "and an additional shipment is expected next week."

Rubric looked shocked, which didn't happen very often. "Nearly a thousand snakes in one shipment? Who would order so many snakes?"

"Bio Tech Labs?" Jill asked.

The agent nodded and continued. "We became involved in the investigation when a clerk at U.S. Fish and Wildlife called Bio Tech Labs to tell them the shipment would be delayed due to the size. Bio Tech Labs denied any knowledge of the order. The U.S. Fish and Wildlife Commissioner alerted us immediately, and we instructed them not to open the shipment until one of our agents arrived. We sent John immediately to Miami."

Jill gasped. "So that's why he had to rush off before our engagement party."

Bill nodded. "The day John arrived, he went right to work. He reported that he had discovered that the snakes were wrapped correctly, individually in bags, separated by dividers. A few of the snakes had died due to a problem with the ventilation, but overall there was nothing illegal about the shipment."

"Who sent the shipment?" Rubric asked.

"That's what we don't know. It came from Saudi Arabia, so naturally we were concerned. Because of John's extensive experience in the Middle East, we sent him on the assignment."

"How did John get bitten?" Jill asked.

"It was a freak accident. One of the U.S. Fish and Wildlife employees used a hook to pick up a snake that had escaped from its bag. Without warning, the snake whirled around and struck at the officer, causing him to swing the hook backwards, throwing the snake behind him."

"And John was standing right behind this guy?" Rubric guessed.

"The snake flew off the hook and onto John's shoulder and stuck its fangs in John's neck . . . about here." Bill pointed to the side of his neck. "He was bitten in a vulnerable location."

Jill pressed her eyelids closed. "What about the antivenin? Was it available?"

"To be perfectly honest, John wouldn't have survived without it," Bill explained. "We were very lucky, because there are so many species of the Saw-Scaled Viper, but the first one the paramedics tried, worked."

Unable to answer, Jill couldn't garner a mustard-seed-sized faith. "You're sure he'll recover?"

"Since the Florida Antivenin Bank has been established, there hasn't been a single snakebite fatality in the State of Florida."

"Has John's father been notified?" Jill asked.

"Of course. An agent from the Chicago bureau went to see him, just as I've come to see you. I'm sorry to be the one who has to deliver the news to you. It must be doubly disappointing since you were expecting to see John today."

Jill nodded her head, feeling numb. "Do you know why John was planning to fly back to Washington today?"

"No. I was going to ask you the same question. Last week he asked for a few days of personal leave, so I naturally assumed it was just that, personal."

"Personal?" Jill was perplexed. "I have no idea why he'd come home before his investigation was finished, but I'm going to ask him as soon as I get to Florida."

"That won't be possible, Jill. John is posing as an officer with U.S. Fish and Wildlife, and no one knows he's FBI. Until we know the origin of the shipment, we don't want to expose him." Bill stood up. "But I'm on my way to Miami to see John now."

"Thanks for coming, Bill. It means a lot to me." Jill started to give him a handshake and then gave him a hug instead.

"It's good to see you both. I'm sorry it had to be under these circumstances," Bill said as he left.

"Nice guy, don't you think?" Rubric said to Jill after Bill exited the room.

"He's the best. John has enormous respect for him."

"Are you okay?" Rubric asked.

"I'm fine. I will be, anyway." She headed out the door.

"Hey, where are you going?"

"Florida," Jill called back over her shoulder.

Rubric ran after her. "Jill. Jill! Come back here! Do you hear me?"

Jill didn't turn around.

"Don't you walk away from me. If you do, you're fired!"

She didn't even give him a backward glance.

"Take a few days off, then. What do I care?" Rubric turned and walked back to his office and slammed the door.

25

A man's illness is his private territory and, no matter how much he loves you and how close you are, you stay an outsider.

Lauren Bacall

Although Agent Tucker told her that John's plans to return to Washington were of a personal nature, Jill was unsure. She knew John so well, and by the sound of his voice, she knew there had to be something important he wanted to discuss with her.

Early the next morning, Jill's plane landed on Miami's airport tarmac. With only an overnight bag under her arm, she walked straight out of the terminal. Pushing through the double doors of the airport, Jill felt dizzy from the funnel of heat and humidity blasting her in the face.

After getting in the backseat of a cab, Jill looked out the window at the streets. The palm trees swaying in a hot spring breeze were welcoming. Why couldn't she be coming to Miami to enjoy these tropical pleasures with John instead of visiting him at a hospital?

After paying the driver, Jill found the hospital's information desk. Since John was working undercover, she had to be very careful about how she approached the desk clerk.

Jill took a deep breath and said, "Excuse me. How are you?"

"I'm fine. Do you need some help, or are you just interested in how I really am?" the young woman asked.

"Both. Can you please tell me on which floor the snakebite victims are treated?"

"Well, it's not on the maternity floor." The young woman guffawed at her own joke.

Jill laughed at it too, hoping the woman might relax before she continued her request.

"I was just joking. There's not a maternity floor in this hospital. Do you have a name of this snakebite victim?" the clerk wondered.

"No."

"Well, now, I can't help you if you don't have a name, can I? Especially since our computer lists our patients by name. Do you even know this patient, honey?"

"Actually, I know him very well, but it's a very complicated situation. Can't you just tell me where they take the snakebite victims?"

"And have you running around all over this hospital? No, ma'am."

A young orderly, who looked like he lifted weights in his spare time, stepped up to the desk and waited behind Jill.

"Please," Jill pleaded. "I've come a long way to see him. Isn't there a special floor for snakebite victims?"

"Well, he might be in intensive care," the young woman suggested. "Mmm, let's see. Or a snakebite victim could be on the first floor in the trauma units or the resuscitation rooms, or maybe even the procedures room. Depending on how long he's been here, he could be in the step down trauma care unit, right, Reggie?" The young woman looked up at the orderly, who plopped a Coke and a Snicker's bar on the desk in front of the young woman.

"Thanks, Reg." The desk clerk popped the can and ripped the wrapper off the Snicker's bar as though she were famished.

"What's up?" the orderly asked.

"Uh, this lady doesn't know her boyfriend's name." The clerk rolled her eyes at the orderly. "But she's looking for him. He's a snakebite victim. Do you know anything?"

"Nope, but I'll try and help you find him, lady," the young man said.

"Good, 'cause I sure can't help her. Miss, this is Reggie. Reggie, this is . . ."

"Jill, Jill Lewis." She shook Reggie's hand.

"Come with me, Jill Lewis." Reggie walked over to the bank of elevators and waved her to follow. "Well, Jill, do you have any idea when this dude was admitted?"

"Yesterday."

"Then let's first try intensive care."

"Where is intensive care?"

"I'll take you there." He pushed the elevator's button. "Let me get this straight, though. You don't know the dude's name? Do you know what he looks like, or is this one of those Internet matchmaking hookups and you haven't met him yet?"

"I know this sounds preposterous, but there are some very good reasons my fiancé had to be admitted under an assumed name."

"Why don't I walk around with you, and maybe we'll spot him. Let's start on my floor, intensive care."

Jill and the orderly strolled down the halls of the hospital, straining to see the patients in intensive care. Straight ahead there was a guard standing at a patient's door.

Turning to Reggie she asked, "Try there?"

"You think he's in there?"

Jill nodded. "It's just a feeling."

The orderly grinned. "Follow me. I'll get you in there, but first you'll need some scrubs."

Down the hall, they turned the corner and opened the door to a large supply room. It was filled floor to ceiling with shelves of linens on one side and custodial cleaning supplies on the other. A small window was at the end of the room facing the street. "Grab yourself a uniform."

Complying, Jill pulled an orderly's uniform on over her clothes. Then she placed the elastic of the pants low on her hips so the bottom of the legs would hide her high heels. The orderly clipped someone else's name tag on her. Next Reggie took her to the employee locker room, where they placed her purse and small travel bag in his personal locker.

Reggie grabbed a cart and quickly filled it with ice buckets. Like they owned the place, Reggie and Jill cruised up to the guard and flashed their badges to gain entrance to the room. She held her breath while the guard studied their badges. After a tense moment, the guard stepped aside, granting them access. Walking through the door, Reggie grabbed a fresh ice bucket off the cart and handed it to Jill. "Go on, have a look." He nudged her.

Tiptoeing to the bedside to make the swap, she set the bucket on the table. Taking a deep breath, she leaned over the bed. The patient was sleeping soundly with most of his face down in the pillow and the sheet pulled up over his right shoulder.

"John," Jill whispered, lightly touching his shoulder. One eyelid popped open as the patient pulled back the sheet. Stepping back, she caught the eye of an elderly man . . . definitely not John. Lunging at Jill, the prisoner was yanked back in place by his handcuffs.

Jill was quick to muffle her surprise. She backed away from the criminal and quickly left the room on Reggie's heels.

"You can't let 'em know you're scared of 'em. We get these old guys from the prison all the time. They're always carving each other up like Grandma's doilies, probably so they can enjoy hospital food. It's a heck of a lot better than prison food."

She wondered if Reggie spoke from experience. And she wasn't so sure she liked the flimsy security in this place, even though it allowed her to look for John.

"There're some more ICU rooms for high-profile cases at the end of the west wing."

The antiseptic odors in the corridor added to her nervousness. Doctors and nurses brushed past them without a second glance. Jill focused on the patterns of freshly mopped linoleum squares. Head down, she counted them, focusing on calming her nerves as she walked toward the last room at the end of the narrow hallway. Two guards stood at the door.

Jill and Reggie flashed their hospital credentials to the closest guard.

The guard shook his head. "You can't go in there."

"But the nurse said he needed some fresh ice."

"Mister, you've obviously got the wrong room," the guard said. "Move along."

"I'll keep it on the down low," Reggie said conspiratorially, "but isn't that snakebite victim in there? I was told to deliver this to his room."

The tight-lipped guard didn't respond, but the other guard said, "You heard the man. Get out of here."

Reggie motioned for Jill to come on and pushed the ice cart back down to the lockers. "How's your balance?"

Jill raised her eyebrows. "Pretty decent. I used to walk the high beam in gymnastics. Why do you ask?"

"Are you afraid of heights?"

"Somewhat, but I can handle it. Why?"

Reggie took Jill back to the employee locker room and got her purse from the locker. "This will cost you five Ben Franklins."

Obediently, Jill dug in her wallet and pulled out five hundred-dollar bills. "You've cleaned me out."

Reggie slid them into his pocket, smiling broadly. "Do you have any paper? I want to give you my cell phone number in case you need me."

Jill pulled a small leather notebook with a pen out of her purse and handed it to him. He scribbled his numbers down. "I'm noting the approximate times the nurses go into the rooms to check vital signs. I've also written down the approximate times we deliver the meals and the doctor's usual rounds."

Reggie moved closer. He took her by the hand and led her over to the window. Wedging between the shelves, Jill could feel Reggie's stale coffee breath on her. He pushed open the window. Sounds from the street were a reminder there was life outside this room.

"Go out this window."

"What?" She looked down and saw a ledge. Was he planning on giving her a shove as she crawled out of here? Jill looked from the street up into his face. Even though she was usually good at reading people, she sure couldn't read him.

"You can make it. Your man's on the other side of the building, the last in the hallway, remember?"

She gasped. "You mean I have to turn the corner?"

"Yeah."

"How will I get into the room?"

Reggie quickly looked around the room. He found a small six-inch crowbar in the tool cabinet and handed it to her. "This should do the trick." She hooked the crowbar onto her pants.

Before she could protest she found herself in the man's arms and being poked through the window. It was wider than it looked. Gently he held onto her as she found her footing on the ledge. She held onto the window frame.

"I'll leave this window closed so no one shuts it and locks it on you," Reggie said. "I'll check back here from time to time. But don't be too long."

Trying not to look down at the moving traffic, Jill slowly let go of the window frame and began scooting down the cement ledge inch by inch, holding onto the mortar in the bricks. Her fingertips started to bleed from the minute cuts she was getting, but she refused to loosen her grip. Now her pants began to drag under her heels. She yanked them up a bit.

She moved as quickly as she could, trying to reach the room before anyone looked up and saw her. They'd be sure to give her away, and what a commotion that would create. Fortunately, there were tall trees that hid her from view most of the time. Jill moved toward the first window; now she had to stoop so anyone inside wouldn't see her.

She moved along the narrow ledge. Upon reaching the corner, she stopped to figure out the logistics of climbing around it. Should she straddle both sides at once? Slowly Jill straightened her knees and hugged the building with her arms, one on each side of the corner. It was tricky to keep her balance while trying to swing one leg to the other side. Looking down, she saw the pavement. Paralyzed by the height, she closed her eyes to regroup. Opening them again, she noted that there were no trees here for cover so she had to move faster. One leg, then the other. Slowly she made it. She stood against the cool brick and panted hard. Fear set in along with the shakes. Now her legs began to feel like overcooked spaghetti.

She closed her eyes and imagined John lying only one closed window away. Her strength soared. Edging up to the window, she peeked inside. *That couldn't be John!* The head that faced the window was swollen and distorted. The poor man's face was crusty with something greenish. Yet she had to get a closer look and be certain it wasn't him.

Jill pulled out the crowbar and jammed it under the window frame, nearly losing her balance. What kept her from falling was the hold she had on the steel. She pulled down on the crowbar, and suddenly the window popped open. She slid the window open further, then pulled herself through.

She closed the window and then slowly turned around.

Inside the room, the machines were humming and beeping. Lines ran from the mystery patient's body to at least a dozen monitors. His chest rose and fell in perfect time with the oxygen apparatus that pushed air in and out through his nose. A bag of plasma hanging from a dipped hook channeled a large tube of red blood into his body. IVs were stuck in his right hand and anchored with tape.

Wrapped in white sheets and framed by silver metal bars, the patient was positioned on his back; his head was turned toward the window. Slowly walking over to him, Jill circled the bed and stood in front of his face, blocking the warmth of the sun that came in through the window. Sensing a sudden change in the environment, the patient's eyes fluttered open.

They were John's eyes. She stared at him and began to cry as she watched his heartbeat register on a high-tech screen beside him, its beats slow, hesitant, and prolonged—but all signs that he was alive!

John stared at her blankly, but there was no reaction, as if he couldn't see her. Hearing voices outside the room, Jill quickly ran to a small closet in the room and hid inside. She stood still, waiting, listening. Footsteps moved about the room, and she heard muffled voices. She thought she heard the nurse say it was time to change the bandages.

"I'll empty the urine bag while you do that," another nurse said.

A man walked into the room. It was evident by the sounds of the strides and the heaviness of the step. "I checked his chart, but there are no changes," he said.

"Thank you, doctor."

Jill remained in the closet several minutes after she thought they were gone, just to be sure. Once outside the closet, Jill gently lifted the bandage from the bite on his neck.

After half an hour, Jill knew she was pressing it with remaining here any longer. Besides, it was getting dark, and there was no way she could maneuver on the ledge if she stayed much longer. Out the window she went, closing it all the way. Again she sidestepped the corner, more sure of herself this time. Moving around the corner of the building, she got to her knees to pass along the bevy of windows and back toward the linen room window. It was a port in the storm when she finally reached it. As Reggie promised, it was closed but unlocked. In another minute she was inside. Jill slid down the wall and sat on the floor. The sound of a voice made her jump.

"How's your boyfriend?" Reggie said.

"I don't know. His eyes were staring at me, but didn't really see me."

"He's probably in a medically induced coma. They do that for snakebite victims to slow the poison. Here, I thought you might need these." With that he set down a sandwich, a bag of potato chips, and a Diet Coke.

"Thanks, Reggie. What do I owe you?"

"Nothing, it's on me. I get a discount down in the cafeteria. Are you going back again?"

"I don't think so. I need to get out of here before I'm discovered."

"Well, at least you've gotten to spend some time with him."

She took a swig of Diet Coke.

"Is there anything else I can get you?" Reggie asked.

"No, thank you," Jill replied.

Jill pulled John's key card out of her wallet. She'd swiped it from the dop kit John had left in Muv's bathroom. Carefully, she unfolded the paper wrapped around it with John's address at Clarion Suites. She had known this would come in handy.

"Thanks for everything, Reggie. Let me slip out of these scrubs and give them back to you." Before slipping out of the scrubs, she paused. "I wish I could see John one more time, but I'm not sure I can risk that ledge again."

"Mmm."

"I love it when you get that look in your eyes. Go on."

"I've checked out the other rooms near your boyfriend. There's a female prisoner in the room right next to John. No guards are posted at her door, because the nurse said she's a low security risk."

"What do you consider a low security risk?"

"She's in her seventies and has suffered a massive stroke that has paralyzed her and affected her speech. Believe me, she's not going anywhere, and if she sees you going out the window, she won't be able to tell a soul. Oh, and she's been in prison for forty years, so she doesn't have any family left. That means no visitors."

Still in the orderly uniform, Jill followed Reggie into the prisoner's room. Their eyes focused on the patient. She was sleeping, so Jill and Reggie went right to the window.

"I'll wait in her room for you, pretend to mop her bathroom or something. Just knock on the window when you're ready to come back in. If no one's around, then I'll open the window and let you back inside. If there is someone around, just sit tight and wait."

Jill wished Reggie had discovered the stroke victim earlier to save her the trouble of walking the ledge all that way. This shortcut was much easier. Once inside John's room again, she rushed up to his bed and took his hand in hers. Then she heard someone coming. She darted inside the closet again, barely getting the door closed before someone came inside.

"Dr. Graves, is this patient improving at all?" It was a woman's voice.

"In spite of how bad he looks, this patient is doing great. He got the best possible emergency care, and that's made my job much easier."

"Captain Al Crews and his team at Station 29?"

"Yep, they're the best in America when it comes to snakebites. We're lucky they had this antivenin too."

"What kind of snake was it?"

"The Saw-Scaled Viper." The doctor was quiet a moment and then said, "Look, the blisters are drying up and the reddish color is fading."

Dr. Graves and the nurse chatted a few minutes, and then it was silent. Apparently, everyone had left the room.

It was disconcerting to hear the shuffling pairs of feet within inches of where she hid. Slowly she opened the closet door to peek out just to be sure. When she knew it was only she and John, she walked over to him. Leaning down, she gently kissed his lips and squeezed his hand. She looked at her watch. Thirty minutes had passed; she'd better get back next door. As she whispered good-bye into John's ear, she heard voices again outside the door. Not taking any chances, Jill ducked back into the closet. From underneath the doorway, she could see that the light went off in the room. Why would they turn off the light?

A woman's voice said, "Okay, let's hurry."

Jill cracked the door ever so slightly, but the room was totally dark.

"I don't like stabbing anyone with a needle," the same voice admitted.

Odd thing for a nurse to say, Jill thought.

A male voice laughed. "You can wield a knife with the expertise of a butcher, but can't poke someone with a needle?"

Something was definitely wrong here. Before she could think of what she was doing, Jill opened the closet door.

"Oh, I'm sorry. I didn't mean to startle you. I was getting a blanket from the closet. Did something happen to the lights?" She walked over and turned them on, but before she could get a look at the two visitors, they were out the door. The male murmured something about the wrong room.

Carefully, Jill cracked the door and looked out. There were no guards. "Where are they?"

She went across the hall to one of the intensive-care waiting rooms, where she had a view of John's door, and dialed the nurses' station.

"The guards outside the door in intensive care room 3045 are missing," she reported.

"Who is this?" the nurse asked Jill.

"This is an emergency. This patient is under the protection of the FBI. You must go to his room immediately and stay with him until you can get a guard to his door."

"I'm sending someone right now, but I need to know your name."

Jill hung up the phone.

Next, she called the hospital security office. "I'd like to report a patient under FBI protection in room 3045. The guards are missing from outside his door."

"We'll have someone there immediately."

Stepping back into the linen room, Jill had a full view of the hallway as people ran to John's aid; security had guns drawn.

"How did this happen?" an angry suit asked. Jill figured he was FBI. Within ten minutes, there were two guards with assault rifles posted outside John's door, and from what she could tell there was a nurse placed inside his room probably around the clock.

"Run a tox screen for us. As a precaution we want to make sure no one got to him," another man in a suit said.

Dr. Graves spoke up to say, "I'll have the nurse draw some blood. I'm going to examine him to make sure nothing happened while the guards were away."

"It was only a few minutes," a nurse reminded Dr. Graves.

"A few minutes is all it takes," the doctor replied.

After all the commotion quieted down, Jill poked her head into the room next door. "I guess you heard all the commotion."

"Am I glad to see you," Reggie said. "I figured you were the cause of it, but then one of the nurses told me the guards were gone, probably to go get coffee or something. They're out of a job for sure."

Jill wanted to stick around and make sure John was safe.

What had happened to his guards? And who were those two people who had snuck into his room and turned off the lights? But she knew she couldn't stay any longer without looking suspicious.

After saying good-bye to Reggie, she wandered down to the waiting room on the first floor. She wanted to catch her breath and the headline news before leaving the hospital. A news alert on the television screen in the waiting room caught her attention.

John Roberts, CBS's chief White House correspondent, was on the screen. Finally the autopsy report had come in. The second autopsy confirmed Harrison's report and her suspicions: Senator Brown died from a massive ingestion of MST.

Right on cue, Rubric called on her cell.

"Hi, Rubric. By the way, with me out of town, who's going to write this article about the late-breaking news?" Jill asked him.

"Me, of course. Oh, here's Annabelle with her hand out. She wants to talk to—"

Annabelle's voice broke in. "What are you doing, sunning your skimpy little body on a Miami beach when I need you here, Lewis? You saw the news?"

"I sure did. Pretty exciting."

"Congratulations. This is big, Jill, and I need you to dive into this investigation right away. Uh, oh, by the way, how's John?"

"He's improving, but he looks terrible. I haven't been able to talk to his doctor, so all I really know is that they've placed John in a drug-induced coma to prevent the poison from spreading."

"If John's in a coma, then there's nothing you can do for him there. He's in one of the best trauma centers in the world. Is there any chance you could fly back to Washington tonight?"

"I can't. Not until I can find out more about John's condition."

"How soon can you do that?"

"Early tomorrow morning. If John's stable, I'll fly home afterward."

"Tomorrow's the best you can do?"

"I'm afraid so."

"Let's just hope someone's not sitting at your desk when you come back," Annabelle said and slammed the phone down.

26

Faith is a refusal to panic.

D. Martyn Lloyd-Jones

Jill took a taxi to the Clarion Suites closest to the port of Miami. It was only a couple of blocks from the hospital.

"Driver, I could be in there for an hour, but I still need you to wait for me."

"No problem, as long as you don't sneak out the back."

"I'll be back, and I'll pay you along with a big fat tip too."

Jill walked inside the motel. She located John's room, slipped the key card into the door, and opened it. First she looked through the small living area. There was nothing there except a *TV Guide* and an old newspaper neatly folded on the coffee table. Next, she inspected the kitchenette. She pulled out a jar of wheat germ, all natural peanut butter, and some vitamin supplements. *Hmm, it's disgusting what a healthy eater John is.*

Looking inside the refrigerator, Jill found several cartons of yogurt, some fruit, and a variety of juices and bottled water. Opening the freezer, she found Ben and Jerry's New York Super Fudge Chunk ice cream. *Ah, so John's human after all.* She pulled off the lid of the carton, stuck a large spoon down into it, and pulled up a thick, heaping helping. Then she returned it to the freezer and continued going through the suite.

In John's bedroom, Jill slid out the bureau drawers one by one. Just a few clothing items were inside of them, but they were neatly folded. The entire suite was immaculate. In the closet, John's shoes were carefully arranged in a straight line. Above them hung his shirts, suits, and a row of khaki pants, all painstakingly pressed. Going through his pockets, she found nothing significant. Over in the corner of the closet, she examined an empty suitcase on the floor below the ironing board.

Jill found his briefcase over by the desk, but she was disappointed when she discovered it was empty and that there was no laptop computer. Opening the desk drawers, she found them almost bare except for a stack of take-out menus and an old airline folder that had held a boarding pass. Reaching further inside, she discovered half of a Hershey bar shoved to the back of the drawer. Jill took it out and decided to break off a piece of the chocolate. When she did, she saw some numbers written inside the wrapper. The first few numbers had Washington area codes. The other had an area code that was familiar, but she couldn't say from where. Grabbing the phone book out of the drawer, she looked at the map in the front. It was an area code in Alabama. Could these numbers belong to someone at Bio Tech? So this is how her efficient fiancé hid his clues. Quite clever!

Jill pressed the button on her cell phone directory to see if they matched any numbers in her phone. She noticed that Bio Tech had a 256 area code, and this was a 334. Maybe the number belonged to Senator Harrison. Pressing the button again, she perused her contacts for Senator Harrison. While she didn't have a number for him in Alabama, she saw that the other numbers written on the paper perfectly matched his office number, his cell phone number, his number at the Watergate, and also another number, possibly the number at his home in Middlesburg because it was a Virginia area code. "What reason would John have to call him?" Jill wondered.

Looking around the apartment once more, Jill was satisfied nothing had been overlooked. Back out to the parking lot, she climbed into the waiting cab. Thinking about the numbers in her purse and all the sweat still left to do on the investigation, Jill thought maybe this was a good time to repair her working relationship with Tommy. She rummaged through her purse but couldn't find her cell. Suddenly she remembered she had taken it out of her purse to check the phone numbers and had set it down on John's desk.

"Driver, could you please take me back to Clarion Suites? I left my cell phone there."

"No problem." The driver spun the cab back around in the middle of the street, squealing his tires. Traffic was jammed, and when they finally arrived back at Clarion Suites, Jill jumped out of the car. "I'll be right back."

Jill ran up the steps instead of taking the elevator. On John's floor, Jill hurried down the hall to his room, reaching in her purse for the key card. Before she could insert it, Jill noticed the door was slightly ajar. Pushing the door hard against the wall, Jill called out, "Hello?" while hoping to see the cleaning lady.

Silence followed. Tenuously stepping into the room, she looked around. In the few minutes she'd been gone, the whole place had been ransacked. Suits had been turned inside out and then discarded on the carpet. John's shirts were tossed on top. The drawers had been yanked out from the bureau. A necktie hung on a lampshade near the bed. Whoever did this had come and gone, but just the same, she thought it wise to get out of there.

Jill ran over to the desk to search for her cell phone. It wasn't there. She searched again, working more slowly this time, really concentrating. No cell phone. She picked up the phone on the desk and called her cell. There was no ringing sound anywhere in this suite. Whoever had done this to the room had taken her cell phone.

Before she left the suite she thought of the candy bar. Had John put the numbers on the chocolate bar in the first place because he knew she had a sweet tooth and wanted her to find it if something happened to him? Suddenly she remembered the Ben and Jerry's ice cream in the freezer. She looked in there and saw that the freezer still held the carton. She lifted up the lid and saw something she hadn't noticed before: *Give this to THH. 2455882537. John knows me so well he can predict exactly where I will go . . . to chocolate. He's depending on me to help him solve this case. I can tell by the clues he's left for me. I can't disappoint him.*

Jill picked up the phone in the kitchen and dialed the number. A recording came on that said there was no such number. She went back into the bedroom and flipped through the phone book beside his bed, but there was no area code with the numbers 245. Maybe the numbers were a combination to a lock? But where was the lock? Or perhaps it was a riddle. She moaned. *I'm terrible at riddles. Maybe Tommy will know the meaning of these numbers.* It was probably too late to call him now, but she'd try him in the morning. Jill slid the numbers in her purse.

After she was satisfied that her phone was nowhere in the suite, she walked into the bathroom to wash her hands. She turned on the water and looked in the mirror. Dark circles lined her eyes, and her skin was too pale. She was one tired cookie.

Suddenly she noticed a light movement in the mirror. She froze, holding her breath. She turned off the water. The room was perfectly still. Looking back into the mirror, she saw the shower curtain move. Someone was behind the curtain. Quietly stepping out of the bathroom, she walked into the bedroom ready to hurry back to the living room and out the door when a man in a ski mask and gloves came out from behind the curtain and lunged at her.

Screaming, Jill fought him. Grabbing her hair, he dragged her across the carpet and threw her down on the bed. The man climbed on top while ramming his knee into her groin. He squeezed her throat while his gloves scratched and tore at her skin. Writhing, she kicked at him violently, desperately gasping for air. Slapping her hard across the face, the man snatched one of John's ties then began stuffing it down her throat. Jill began to choke. She mumbled a prayer for her life.

Her attacker's mistake was pausing to catch his breath. In doing so, he inadvertently loosened the grip on Jill's throat, giving her a chance to break away. Pulling out the tie, she gulped air, becoming aware of a familiar fragrance.

Someone pounded on the door. The attacker held up his gloved pointer finger to his lips, signaling her to be quiet. Jill looked from him to the door several times, trying to estimate her chances of calling out.

"Security! Open the door! Open the door now, or we're coming inside."

The assailant pulled something from his side, and then Jill felt the unmistakable sensation of a gun barrel at her neck. Yanking her to her feet, the man dragged Jill to the door.

"Hello?" Jill coughed.

"We got calls that screams were coming from this room. Are you all right?"

Her attacker pressed the barrel deeper into her neck and cocked the gun. Before she could attempt to speak, the security guards bolted through the door and into the room. Her attacker shoved Jill into them, causing them to fall. He scrambled to the opposite side of the room, where he slid open the door to the second-floor balcony and leaped over the railing to the street below. Now on their feet, both guards ran out in pursuit.

Soon the security guards returned, but they had no intruder and no information about him.

"We've called the police. They want your statement," one of the security guards told her.

Jill waited impatiently for the police to arrive. After they completed their report, they searched inside the hotel room but found nothing. As they left in their patrol car, Jill left in her cab.

"Do you want me to take you back to the hospital? It looks like you need one for yourself this time," the cab driver observed.

"No, take me straight to a hotel at the airport. Is there a Hilton there?"

"There's always a Hilton at an airport."

"Take me there, please."

"Oh, and by the way, there was a cell phone ringing in the backseat. Do you have two of them?"

"All that, and my cell phone was in here all the time," she muttered. *That's okay. I was meant to go back into that room. And God protected me through it all.*

Jill figured she could crash at the Hilton and take an early morning flight back to Washington. She'd wanted to see John before she left, but she wasn't sure she had the strength. With four guards posted outside his door, she knew he was safe. She'd call Bill Tucker in the morning to get a report on John's condition.

"I've got good news. Your fiancé's doing well," Bill told her the next morning. "The doctors plan to bring him out of the drug-induced coma today. By tomorrow, he'll be sitting up in bed talking to you."

"Are there any risks?" she asked. Her throat was sore and her voice raspy, the aftereffect of almost being choked to death.

"There are always risks, but it's a very small percentage. They'll bring him back gradually to avoid any risks. People react in different ways, but it's safe, and they have the best possible doctors at the Ryder Trauma Center."

"That's a relief. Thanks for all you're doing for John. Will you let me know as soon as he's safely out of the coma?"

"I will. Good-bye, Jill."

"Bill, wait—" Jill said, but she was too late. He'd hung up already. She wanted to tell Bill what had happened in John's motel suite last night, but it could wait until later.

Next, Jill decided to call Tommy Harrison and relay the numbers John had written under the top of the ice cream carton. He answered his personal cell on the first ring. "Hello?"

"Good morning, Senator."

"Jill?"

"Tommy, please don't hang up on me. I'd like to call a truce. I need to talk to you. It's important."

"What took you so long? I figured I'd hear from you last night when you heard on national news that Brown was murdered."

"That's not why I'm calling."

"Yeah, right. What happened to your voice? You sound very sexy, by the way."

"It wasn't easy to get this voice. Someone tried to choke me to death."

There was a long pause, and then the senator said, "Are you okay?"

"Yes. I'm sorry my trip to Roanoke upset you. And I don't blame you, but listen, I have an important message for you."

"What?"

"Can we meet this afternoon?"

"I have to check my schedule."

"All right."

"I'm looking at my agenda. I guess I can spare a few minutes this evening."

"Where?"

"My place. I'll have Ryan cook dinner for us."

"Fine."

"Is there anything you want to tell me in the meantime?"

She coughed a little to clear her throat before speaking again. "For starters, I found out my fiancé is working on this same case.

I found your telephone numbers among his things. Has John ever contacted you?"

"No, I've never spoken to him, but if it's important to you, I'll get my assistant to check the phone logs."

"I need to know why he had your phone numbers and wrote them in a place where he'd be sure I'd find them."

"I don't know," Tommy admitted.

Jill promised him she'd be in touch soon.

After boarding the plane for Washington, Jill settled into her seat and prepared for the flight. Her success at the *Washington Gazette* had afforded her this first-class status, and today she was grateful because she desperately needed sleep. She wrestled with the pillow until she finally found that comfortable position and closed her eyes.

Jill, I'll always come back to you . . . The words he had spoken to her last week sweetly returned. It was hard to leave John behind, but he'd soon be on the mend and perhaps coming back to Washington to finish his recuperation there. Anyway, John wouldn't want a girl who sat there twiddling her thumbs when she had an important case to investigate.

Before she knew it, the plane landed in D.C. As she walked through baggage claim at the airport, she heard a familiar voice. "Jill! Jill Lewis!" Jill turned to see Rubric galloping after her and waving his right arm up in the air.

"Did Annabelle send you to make sure I made it into the office? I have no other baggage than this." She chucked her bag at him.

"What in the heck happened to you?" Rubric hollered.

"I got beaten up."

"Who did this to you?"

"I don't know, the guy got away."

"Where did this happen?" Rubric asked.

"Last night in John's hotel suite. A masked man cornered me in the bathroom and then jumped me."

"Was there anything familiar about him? His voice? His mannerisms?"

"He never spoke, but there was one thing that was familiar. His cologne. I know I've smelled it somewhere before. Someone I know wears it, but I just can't remember who."

"Well, if it wasn't Old Spice, it wasn't me."

She wrinkled her nose. "It definitely wasn't Old Spice."

"Well, I'm sure thousands wear whatever cologne you smelled." His voice sounded flat. Not the usual Rubric. He slung her bag over his shoulder. "The limo is waiting outside for us."

"Wow, my investigation must have made Annabelle pretty happy." Jill hurried out through the glass double doors and easily spotted the limo. She couldn't help but smile, thinking of her last limo ride with John. That was only weeks ago. With all that had happened, it seemed like a lifetime.

Sliding into the backseat with Rubric, Jill was surprised to see Annabelle.

"What are you doing here?"

Annabelle's face was filled with surprise over Jill's appearance. "Before I answer that, tell me what in the world happened to you."

"I went over to John's hotel suite last night to see if I might find any clues, but someone jumped me while I was there."

"Who was it?" Annabelle asked.

Jill shrugged.

"Are you all right?"

"Other than this severe case of laryngitis and the bruises you see, I'm fine."

"You're very fortunate," Annabelle told her, turning Jill's chin with her fingertips to get a good look at her neck and her face. "Ouch, it looks like it really hurts."

"It does. I looked through John's apartment for any clues, wondering what the attacker was trying to find. I found Senator Harrison's numbers inside a Hershey bar wrapper." Jill pulled the paper out of her purse and showed it to them. "And these numbers were written under the lid of a Ben and Jerry's carton of ice cream."

Rubric and Annabelle didn't say anything in response to this information, surprisingly.

Jill shifted in her seat, feeling uncomfortable. "I'm surprised to see you, Annabelle. Did you come along so we could get right to work the moment I stepped off the plane?"

Annabelle didn't say a word, only turned away. Was she hiding her displeasure? Jill needed to convince this woman that she was fully committed to this case and there'd be no more distractions.

"Well, I'm back at work and ready to go."

Still Annabelle didn't look at her. She must be really mad. Fuming. Jill had no idea her little bedside vigil would irk Annabelle so much. Rubric was acting really weird too. Was she about to be fired?

Rubric and Annabelle exchanged glances.

"Jill, Annabelle and I are here for a specific reason. There's something we have to tell you."

Here it was. "Are you canning me? Annabelle, I'm sorry I ran off and left you in the lurch. Surely you understand why I had to see John. I knew when I flew out of here it might be a bad career move."

"Let Rubric finish, Jill."

Rubric looked down at his feet as he began to talk. "Jill, it's going to be hard for me to tell you this, but worse for you to hear."

Jill took a deep breath. "No, Rubric, you need to hear me out first. In the past, you know that I've never let my personal life get in the way of an investigation, but you should both know that now that John is in my life, he will always be my priority. This doesn't mean I won't do my job as well as I have always done it, nor does it mean I will neglect my work in any way."

Jill waited for their reaction, but neither of her bosses responded. Jill did a double take when she saw a big tear slide down Rubric's cheek. She had never seen Rubric cry.

As usual, Annabelle was making Rubric do her dirty work. Jill didn't want to lose her job; surely she could talk herself out of this one, so she continued to try. "Bill Tucker said that John will be out of the coma by tomorrow. His illness is no longer going to affect my work, I promise. He's fine."

"Stop it, just stop it," Annabelle said loudly.

"But I told you—"

"No, Jill," Annabelle said, softly this time. "John is not fine. He's anything but fine. Minutes after your plane left the Miami Airport, Bill Tucker tried to reach you. When they were bringing John out of the coma, he had a massive stroke. He's gone, Jill. John is dead."

27

*The sun has set in your life. It is getting cold. The hundreds of
people around you cannot console you for the loss of the one.*

Maria Augusta Trapp

"Let me out." Jill went for the door handle with one hand as she
covered her mouth with the other.

Annabelle grabbed her, wrapping her arms around her. "Whoa,
we're on the interstate. Not a good spot to exit the car."

Jill couldn't breathe.

"Quick, Rubric, find a brown bag from the bar area of the
limo. There should be at least one small one there," Annabelle
ordered when she saw Jill hyperventilating.

Rubric pulled down the latch and easily found what he
needed. "Here, Jill, breathe into this."

Obeying, she cupped the opening around her mouth and
nose. The sound of the crunching bag went in and out like an
accordion. She finally crumpled the empty bag and tossed it
down, closing her eyes.

She looked up at Rubric. "Rube, that can't be right. He looked
so much better last night. Bill Tucker told me he was fine just

a few hours ago. What happened?" Her words came in halting gasps.

Rubric's voice wavered a bit as he spoke. "About thirty minutes after you left, they began the process of bringing him out of the coma, and apparently there was swelling on his brain. He developed a hematoma. It put pressure on the blood vessels in that area of the brain, and it burst. The stroke was so massive that they just couldn't bring him back."

"But Bill told me the doctor said they were going to bring him out of the coma gradually."

"It was a freak occurrence. At this point, they're not even sure what happened."

"But couldn't they revive him? Why didn't they perform surgery to relieve the pressure on his brain?"

"I'm no doctor, but I'm sure they tried everything, Jill. You can talk to John's physician later. He said to tell you to call him as soon as you felt like it."

She felt numb. "Was he in a lot of pain? Was he conscious?" She could hear her voice speaking, but it seemed to belong to somebody else.

"No, he was unconscious. He didn't know what was happening. He didn't feel a thing."

She slammed her fists into the seat of the limo. "I should never have left him! I meant to stop by the hospital once more to see him, and I didn't. I didn't get to say good-bye."

"Try not to torture yourself with thoughts of things you have no control over," Rubric said as he put his arm around her.

"I shouldn't have insisted you come back to Washington." Annabelle squeezed Jill's hand.

"I just don't understand why God allowed this to happen. He allowed my father to be killed. Wasn't that enough? I never prayed when I lost my dad, so I guess I couldn't blame God, but I've been praying for John's protection every day. So why didn't God keep him safe for me?"

Annabelle and Rubric exchanged perplexed glances. Neither of them could proffer one encouraging word.

As they drove past the Potomac River, Jill watched the boats and was reminded of that evening when they had sailed the Chesapeake Bay—a young couple, laughing and dreaming together. Now John was gone, and Jill felt like she had aged fifty years in one short minute.

"I need to call John's dad . . ." Her raspy voice had now settled into a barely audible lilt as they approached her building.

Annabelle and Rubric insisted on helping her up to her apartment.

"I'm not leaving," Rubric announced. "I won't bother you. You won't even know I'm here, but I'm going to camp out in your living room. I can sleep on the couch."

"No, I need to be alone."

"I'm not leaving." Rubric was adamant.

"You're a survivor, Jill. Do you hear me? You are going to get through this," Annabelle told her.

Jill started to sob. "I can't do this. I can't. I want to fall asleep and never wake up."

"Jill, you've always said God has a plan for your life, and I've always given you a hard time about that," Annabelle said. "Beneath all your words, I always hoped there was something real. Here's the test, darling. Show me what you're made of. Is this God of yours real or not?" She gave Jill a hug and then quietly exited the apartment.

Jill walked aimlessly from room to room. Although Rubric made a lot of noise and left the TV blaring, he didn't bother her, as promised.

In her closet, she pulled the dress she'd worn when John proposed to her off its hanger. A chill ran over her arms. *At least I know John is in heaven with Jesus. I know he missed his mom so much. I feel comforted a bit knowing they are together, and he's with my father too.*

The light blinked on her answering machine. Jill pressed the button and listened to her mom's voice. "Darling, Jill, your editor called with the news . . . of John. I'm so sorry. Please come home, darling. You need to be at home with your family at this time. Call me. I love you. We'll get through this together."

Jill walked into her living room, where Rubric was sprawled out on the couch. "Blah, blah, blah!" she screamed. "Mom thinks her chicken soup followed by a walk next to the lake will heal my heart. She'll pressure me to move home, and together we can spend long evenings lamenting our dead loves. No way. Excuse me if I'm not fit company. I just want to be left alone. I don't want to see or talk to anyone."

"Hey, I didn't say anything. I'm just listening," Rubric told her.

She walked back into her room and crawled into her bed.

Jill remained in bed all the next day. The phone rang; she didn't answer. People knocked on her door; Rubric opened it and sent them away. Her mother called her several times—Jill assured her that she was all right and that Rubric was taking good care of her. There were messages from friends, all the women at the office, a few men, Helen from the newsstand, and several from Senator Harrison.

Then there were the flowers, a vanful from the office. John's father sent her a dozen red roses with a sweet card. His dad told her in his note that there would be no funeral. Instead he wanted to hold a memorial service for John in a few months. This news upset Jill. She needed closure, but she was only John's fiancée, not his wife, so her opinions didn't count.

A day later, the flowers got the best of poor Rubric. "I'm sleeping in a greenhouse," he complained after a fit of sneezing.

"Next time someone delivers more flowers, tell them to take them home to his wife or girlfriend, and if it's a woman tell her to keep them for herself or give them away. I don't care. Just keep the cards, because I know my mom will insist that I write thank you notes to everyone."

After several days of lying on Jill's couch, Rubric told her he thought he'd go home. "You have my numbers, so call me if you need me. But I think my dog needs me more than you do."

Jill gave him a big hug. "I know I ignored you, but I love you for being here with me."

When he left, Jill felt that she'd lost her security blanket, but at least now she could scream louder without the fear of disturbing him.

She knew Sunday had come again because the church bell chimed outside her window. Then the doorbell rang. And rang again. The caller was persistent, so she shuffled to the door and answered.

Expecting to see her mother when she opened the door, she was surprised to see Rubric standing in the hallway looking very uncomfortable in a dark suit. He even wore a tie.

"Rubric, what are you doing back here?"

"Someone is here to take you to church."

"Oh no, not my mother?" Jill looked up and down the hall, feeling panicked.

"No, not your mother. It's just me."

"You? Ha! Go away, Rube, please. I'm going back to bed."

Jill jumped at the sound of the door hitting the wall. "Leave your pity party and get yourself dressed right this minute! I'm here to take you to church, and you know how I feel about being late."

She rubbed her eyes. Rubric barged into her bedroom and began flipping through the rows of clothes in her closet.

"I'm not going," Jill balked.

Pulling out a black linen suit, he flung it at her. "Here, this one looks about right. It matches your mood."

"Didn't you hear me? I said I'm not going!" She crossed her arms in protest.

"Listen to me, young lady." Rubric got right up in her face.

"No one has gotten me into church since I was fourteen years old. But today I'm going with you! Don't destroy this big miracle in the making. What about my soul?" he cajoled dramatically, flinging his hand over his heart.

Jill couldn't believe her ears. She was refusing to go when Rubric, the avowed atheist, was offering to take her to church. It made her laugh for the first time since John had died. Okay, she'd call his bluff. "You win," she said. "Give me fifteen minutes to shower and throw something on. Just don't expect makeup."

"Fine. But please comb your hair."

Jill was ready with a minute to spare.

"Which way?" Rubric asked, looking up and down the street.

"We can go to my church . . . unless you have a preference?"

"Nope, yours is fine, especially since I don't have one. Progress has probably torn down my mother's old church by now."

"Oh, Rube."

They walked for a while in silence, then Rubric spoke up. "You haven't asked me what I found out about that phone number, but I played around with the numbers and finally got an area code."

"Where was it?" She tried to sound interested.

"Killeen, Texas. I called the number, and it was a pet shop, and I thought, 'Well, maybe this is leading somewhere. Maybe this guy is a reptile dealer or something.' But when I spoke with the owner, he said he and his wife bought this shop for their retirement, and they didn't carry any snakes because his wife was afraid of them. Besides, in Texas, you can walk right outside to pick one up."

"I hope you didn't just take his word for it," Jill said, feeling herself perk up a bit.

"Have you forgotten who you're talking to, Jill?" Rubric acted indignant. "Of course I checked them, but unfortunately for us, they're exactly who they say they are."

Rubric hailed a cab. Eight blocks later, the cab dropped them off in front of St. John's. Families walked in together as units, with couples following in step as well as those walking alone through the double doors.

"So this is the place," Rubric said, nervously wiping his brow and starting to show signs of panic. "Looks like a bunch of ants crawling into their anthill."

"You don't have to do this," Jill told him.

"Of course I do. I told you I would and I am. Let's go on in. I could use a nap since I had a late night at Diamond Jim's. Maybe your preacher will put me to sleep. But I hope he doesn't do long sermons; I want to get out of here at a decent hour. I'm already hungry."

"Reverend Perdue is the best. You'll see."

Arm in arm they walked into the church. Jill laughed to herself as she watched Rubric look around as if he'd landed in a new country. She was impressed that he stood to sing the hymns. Although her heart felt as though it were in a cold grave somewhere, it felt good to be here.

The young minister spoke about forgiveness of others, and forgiveness of sins. *Can I forgive God for taking John from me?* Then she heard the minister say something that was so truthfully simple it amazed her. "So many people ask, 'Why me? Why is there cancer? Why do people suffer? Why do the young die?' Let me remind you that this is not our world. We are strangers here. Our world is yet to come. This life is temporal. We are just passersby in this life, spreading the gospel. That is our purpose here on earth. We're not here to build our kingdom on earth. We are here to build God's in heaven."

"Amen," Rubric shouted, smiling at Jill and saying to her in a loud whisper, "Listen to what the man's saying, he's preaching this sermon just for you."

The churchgoers surrounding them tried to stifle their giggles, but one lady laughed out loud.

"Did I say something wrong?" Rubric asked.

Snickers arose around them again.

Jill leaned over and whispered, "This just isn't an 'amen' kind of church, and you're talking too loudly."

"Not an 'amen' church? Then it's not a church at all. I like those churches where you can get up and run if the Spirit moves you," he whispered indignantly before turning his attention back to the sermon. Shortly, he began sniffling.

"Is something wrong, Rubric?"

"No, of course not. I have a horrible sinus infection. With all this Washington wind and these cherry blossoms flying around the city, it gets me every spring. Remember last year? I was laid up in bed for a week!"

"I've never known you to be laid up anywhere."

"You're right, but I did lie down in my office for a couple of hours while I read some reports."

As soon as the church service was over, Rubric suggested, "How about I take you to Diamond Jim's for a nice lunch?"

"No thanks."

"Okay, okay, so you can't appreciate fine food. I'll take you to one of those fancy places you like. Think we can get in at the Palms without a reservation?"

"I appreciate the offer, but I want to get back home now."

"You're not going to bed again. I want somebody to go to lunch with me."

"I'd like to, Rubric. But I feel as though I'm going to collapse."

"Are you all right?" Rubric steadied Jill and directed her toward the cab he was flagging.

"No, I don't think I'll ever be all right again. Not in this lifetime."

28

There is a land of the living and a land of the dead,
and the bridge is love.

Thornton Wilder

Three weeks had passed since the news of John's death when Jill finally returned to her office. For two weeks she'd been on leave, and Rubric had given her permission to work at home the past week.

Taking a deep breath, she walked into the lobby of the *Gazette*, grateful no one rushed up to offer her sympathy. Like a zombie, she went to her office, took a seat behind her desk, and booted up the computer. There were literally hundreds of emails in her inbox. Unable to tackle them, she quickly got out of the program and went to the area code site. Checking the numbers again, she tried to rearrange them to see if John perhaps had made a transposition. If it were a riddle, she'd try to figure it out, but not now. Pulling out one of the Bio Tech CDs, Jill began to run through the employee files.

"Welcome back, Jill," Rubric said. "The coroner faxed over his report of Ally's death while you were gone. I thought you might want to—"

On her feet, Jill snatched it out of his hand. "I need a medical dictionary. I'm not familiar with all this jargon."

"Ha, I started out on homicide, so this is as easy as pig Latin to me," Rubric said, taking back the paper. "There were three snakebites inside of her mouth. Oh, there's even an autopsy on the snake that says it died of suffocation. Ally also aspirated into her lungs because the snake had been shoved into her mouth and down her throat. But the main cause of death is the snakebites. If they hadn't killed her, then the slash across her neck would have caused her to bleed out since it hit the carotid artery."

"So someone stuffed a snake in her mouth, then slashed her throat."

"You got it."

"How do you suppose the killer got out of there with so many FBI agents around?" Jill wondered.

"Probably went hours before the meeting time. The snake makes it related to Brown's death. Hey, are you still blaming me for this?"

"No, I'm not. Sorry I ever did."

"Good." Rubric dropped the report on her desk and left her office.

Jill scanned over the report again. It was so technical, making Ally an inhuman commodity. Jill stuck the report in a manila folder marked with Ally's name. Jill was thankful she'd never worked homicide. Give her politicians with their usual peccadillos any day!

Just as Jill picked up the phone to dial Senator Harrison, the temp receptionist beeped in on the intercom, "Ms. Lewis, this is Eva at the front desk. A John Lovell is here to see you. Do you want to come out here or shall I send him on back to your office?"

Her heart beat quickly. "John Lovell?"

"Yes, he says . . . hold on a minute."

Jill's heart raced. She paced back and forth. "I'm sorry, Jill. He said to tell you it's John Lovell Sr."

Her heart dropped. "Oh. Send him right back."

She watched the knob twist and the door open, first by inches, then by a few feet. Big John walked through the door. She closed her eyes.

"Jill, I'm so sorry."

"Mr. Lovell, Big John. I didn't expect you," Jill managed to say.

"I'm so sorry I didn't call first." Badly rattled by seeing John's father, Jill stumbled forward to give him a hug, but he only stiffened under her touch and quickly drew back as her tears splattered his dark blue sports coat.

Jill offered him a seat. The older man ambled over to the chair and collapsed in it, filling the frame of the dainty French chair.

After a few moments of silence, a nervous Jill began to blather, "I just want to tell you again how sorry I am about your son. It's been really hard for me. I know it's been very hard for you as well. I miss him so much; I know you do too."

He sat there quietly for a moment. "You're probably wondering what I'm doing here, but I felt this was something I needed to do in person. There's something I must say to you. It's a private family matter, but you need to know. It's not fair that you should . . ." His voice got whispery. Perspiration lined his upper lip.

Jill looked down at her hands. *Was it a family matter about a family heirloom ring? "It's not fair you should keep the ring" is what he wanted to say?* It was only right to give it back. After all, it had belonged to the older man's mother, and then his wife. Who was she to him now, anyway?

"I know what you're going to say," she said. "There's no need. It belongs to you." Jill slid the ring from her finger and set it carefully on the desk between them.

He seemed surprised for a moment, then cleared his throat. "Uh, thanks for being so gracious under these circumstances."

He was wrong. It was too soon to take her ring away. It was all she had left of John. Jill tried to still her shaking hands.

Scooping up the ring, Big John carefully examined it for a moment. Jill guessed he was making sure it was still intact. Then he tightened his fist around it. His demeanor quickly changed with the ring in hand; abruptly, he stood to his feet.

"Thank you for coming to see me," Jill said, trying to make the moment less awkward. "I just returned to work today. I . . . I hope you don't think I just jumped back into things without a thought about your son. I . . . I heard John was cremated."

Big John seemed to lurch forward. "Yes."

"Have you set a date for John's memorial service?" Jill asked.

"Maybe later, after I've recovered from the shock of my son's death. I can't think about it now."

How terse he sounded. Jill was taken aback. They had both loved John—why couldn't they grieve for him together? What had she done to make Big John treat her in this way?

"I'd better be going. Good-bye, Jill." He didn't even stop to give her a hug but headed right out the door.

Jill stood there in shock for a moment, then had the sudden urge to call her mother.

Luckily, Pearl answered right away.

"Mom, you'll never believe what just happened."

"Hi, dear, glad you called before I had to call out the infantry to make sure you were all right. Oh, by the way, did Big John stop by to see you?"

"How did you know about that?"

"I called him to tell him how sorry I was, and he's called me every day since. Since you haven't wanted to speak with me much lately, darling, speaking with Big John has helped me a lot, and I think I've really been a comfort to him. He even invited me to go along with him to Washington to see you."

"Good thing you didn't come. It was a quick trip."

"What do you mean?"

"He was here all of two minutes before taking back my engagement ring."

"Oh dear. That was insensitive of him. Men just don't understand these things."

"Wait, you said he calls you nearly every day?"

"Yes, every day since the accident."

"Mother, I wish you wouldn't speak to him. I don't think . . . I don't think he's a very nice man."

"Aren't you overreacting a bit, Jill?"

"No, I'm not overreacting."

"Not to change the subject, dear, but I have a surprise for you."

"A surprise?" Jill braced herself to hear what her mother's surprise was this time.

"Well, it's not a happy surprise. Did you know the *Lakes News* is for sale?"

"Max would never sell the *Lakes*."

"He has no choice. It's doctor's orders. Darling, I didn't want to trouble you in the midst of your own pain, but Max had a heart attack a while ago."

"You should've told me, Mother."

"I probably should have. By the way, Max has an offer from one of those big conglomerates. Miss Cornelia and your funny little friend Marge, the redhead, they'll both lose their jobs. Isn't that sad?"

"Max cannot sell it. It's not right," Jill said. "I wish I could talk about this some more now, but I've got to go."

Jill sat cross-legged on her bed later that day, staring into space. She thought about the mysterious numbers. She still couldn't make any sense of them, but perhaps Senator Harrison could. Wouldn't it make sense that he would know since John had written, *Give to THH*?

Jill hadn't spoken to Tommy since before John had died. Tommy had sent her flowers and had left a couple of messages, but she didn't have the heart to speak with him. Until now.

Within minutes Jill had the senator on the phone.

"Jill, I can't tell you how glad I am you've called me."

"I hope I'm not interrupting anything," Jill said.

"Not at all. I'm at my horse farm in Roanoke. I just came inside from doing chores. Did you get my messages and the roses?"

"Yes, thank you. The flowers were lovely."

"How are you feeling? Are you back at work?"

"Yes, and that's why I'm calling. John left some numbers for you, and I wondered if you might know their meaning."

"Phone numbers?"

"I thought so, but now I believe it's some sort of secret code."

"I'd be glad to take a look and try to make some sense of them."

"May I give them to you now so you can start working on them right away?"

"Sure."

Jill slowly read them. "Now that you aren't mad at me anymore, at least I don't think you are, would you arrange for me to get back into Bio Tech Labs? I'd like to question Dr. Kelly Arden again."

"Why don't you fly to Atlanta and drive to Roanoke, and we'll drive to Bio Tech together?"

"I'm sorry, but I can't do that."

"Why not?"

"I'm not interested in serving any jail time."

He laughed long and hard. "Maybe I overreacted with the threats. You're welcome to come to Alabama, Jill. I'll call you back as soon as I speak with Carl Johnson to make the arrangements for our trip to Bio Tech."

Within days Jill was on an airplane to Atlanta. Senator Harrison sent Ryan to the airport for her. He surprised her in baggage claim and carried her stuff out to the limo.

Once they got closer to Roanoke, Ryan lowered the window.

"I'm glad you've come to visit the senator," Ryan said, turning off Main Street. "I think he really likes you. You're different from the others."

"The trip is strictly business, Ryan."

"Maybe that could change." A note of hope rose up in Ryan's voice. "Once you get to know him, the senator's one of the nicest men you'll ever meet. I realize it's hard for you feminists to get past all his good-old-boy antics, but that's not really who he is."

"So you're a matchmaker who thinks I'm a feminist?"

"With your career, you'd have to be."

"Uh, okay." Ryan's definition of a feminist was sorely lacking, but she'd let it slide for now. "Let's change the subject while you give me a nickel tour of the town."

"Okay. Over here is the local newspaper, and that used to be an old hardware store." He pointed to the vacant building. "This is the Dairy Queen, and over there is Gedney's, a favorite seafood restaurant around town."

"Did you grow up in Roanoke?"

"No, but a small town like this, you get to know it pretty quickly."

On the outskirts of town, the car wound up and back down desolate country roads. Finally, Ryan pulled onto the long drive-way. Jill got her first close-up look at the gigantic fortress rising above the Tallapoosa River, whose waters churned and twisted in its hurry to reach the ocean. Gothic in design, the brick house looked like a castle with the river as its moat. In the back of the house was a circular drive covered by a portico at a massive back door.

Inside the house, the floors were constructed of wide planks with the same dark wood used for the trim around the windows. Massive beams soared above in the cathedral ceilings. It was a magnificent home filled with priceless antiques and valuable artwork.

"Welcome to the Harrison Hovel, Jill." Tommy smiled at

her as he walked through the front door. He wore blue jeans, a buttoned-down shirt, and a pair of cowboy boots. "I hope you don't mind, but we've had a change of plans. I've had something come up, so we won't be able to drive to Mobile today. The little bank in town has called an emergency board meeting this afternoon."

"And you're a board member?"

Tommy nodded.

Uh-oh, I was afraid of that. "That's a disappointment."

"Not really, because after the meeting I'll show you around Roanoke—unless you've already seen it all on the drive here. We can leave for Mobile around five o'clock in the morning."

"That's not a problem. I've got plenty of prep work I can do. Ryan can drive me back to Roanoke, and I'll get a room at the Best Western."

"Oh, I won't hear of it. You can stay right here. I've already had the maid make up the guest room for you. It's much more luxurious."

"Thanks, Tommy, but I don't think so."

"There's even a lock on the door, and I know from experience that it works very well."

"Sounds to me like there have been those who have used it," Jill chided.

"A few." Harrison laughed. "Listen, I'd never pressure a lady. I think I mentioned to you that I breed rare Caspian horses. I want you to have a look at the new foals. Ryan, take Jill's things up to the guest room. Do you ride, Jill?"

"I do."

"Get some jeans on then, and we'll take a ride before I leave for the board meeting, and I'll show you around my place."

Ryan looked at Jill. She nodded and followed him up the massive staircase that was carpeted in a mushroom-colored plush. Ryan carried her box of files and her luggage up to her room. He swung open the door to a room at the end of the hallway, revealing a cathedral ceiling, but the beams overhead had been whitewashed. It was a lovely room decorated with dark antiques and English chintzes, and it possessed a sunny view of the river through French windows. She smiled at the fresh roses in a vase on the chest.

It looked as though Tommy had probably planned this delay all along. But there was no reason to pout. It was a beautiful day, and it had been ages since she'd ridden a horse. A gallop through the countryside would be good for her body and spirit.

Jill spun around to inspect the rest of the room and saw that she had her own private bath, beautifully appointed with plush monogrammed towels, crystal jars filled with fragrant bath oils, and antique porcelain dishes that held French milled soaps. Fresh roses were in crystal vases on the vanity and on the ledge of the large Jacuzzi tub.

"Is there anything you need, Jill?" Ryan asked as he brought her last bag up from the car.

"No, I'm fine. Thank you, Ryan."

"The cook's name is Mary. She's made a fruit salad for you to eat before you go riding," he announced. "I'm off now, so I'll probably go home tonight. See you tomorrow. And Jill, give the old man a chance."

"Don't go there, Ryan."

Jill quickly changed into her jeans, a white shirt, and her running shoes. After she slathered on some sunscreen, she ran down the steps and went into the kitchen.

"Hello? Mary?" she called out in the kitchen.

The woman appeared. "Hello. You must be Jill. I've got your fruit salad on the table in the breakfast room. There's some iced tea there too."

"Thank you. It looks wonderful," Jill said, sitting down alone at the twelve-foot Jacobean dining room table. Jill scooped up a spoonful of cream and added a dollop to her bowl of fruit.

Tommy walked into the breakfast room.

"This watermelon's delicious," complimented Jill.

"Thank you. I grow the sweetest watermelons in Alabama. I like my watermelons just like I like my women—sweet."

"That's good to hear. I should be perfectly safe, then."

"What makes you say that?"

"I've told you before, *sweet* is not a word that would describe me."

"I disagree." He placed his hands on her shoulders and squeezed them.

"You'll see." She slapped his hands away.

"Ready to ride?"

Jill wiped her mouth with the linen napkin and followed him out the door.

Out back they walked into the meadow and headed for the stables. A huge sign arched above in capital letters, spelling out "Caspian Castle." With a closer look, Jill noticed it wasn't just one stable but several smaller stables, all interconnected by a main center residence where the foreman lived with some of the other ranch hands. This is where the senator housed the high-dollar horses and their foals, most of which were enjoying the warm summer day outside. Legs lifted high, they pranced, heads up with a regal air, seemingly cognizant of their pedigree.

As he took her on a tour of the stables, Jill noticed that Tommy became animated as he explained his passion for horses. "I've always enjoyed riding, but it was my late wife who got me interested in this breed. I was a Tennessee Walker man myself."

"I'm not familiar with the breed," Jill admitted.

"Caspians are an ancient breed, believed to be extinct for a thousand years. In 1965 they were rediscovered in Iran and brought to the United States. A handful of breeders have brought them back from the brink of extinction."

"They're exquisite."

Tommy and Jill stopped in front of one of the stalls. "This is

Ambrosia, by far my favorite." He rubbed the horse behind her ears and kissed her forehead. She nuzzled him.

"She's a beauty. Too bad you can't ride these horses."

"Children can ride them, and adults show them. What I love most about breeding Caspians is the knowledge that I'm bringing an animal back from extinction, but I have a few horses for riding, housed in our other stables."

With quick steps, Tommy led Jill to the next stable, where the groom had two horses saddled. The animals were anxious, ready to be let out of their pens for the day. Tommy pointed Jill to the Dutch Warmblood stretching her neck over the top rail. "Say hello to Tinkerbelle," Tommy told Jill, unhooking the latch and handing the reins to Jill. "I'll ride the gray, Gumshoe."

Jill took off on the horse, and Tommy galloped along behind.

"Do you have any trails on your property?" Jill asked when Tommy finally caught up.

"In the woods. You're going to be pretty sore by the end of the day," he warned.

Ignoring him, Jill headed to the trees.

Riding through the woods, Jill realized for the first time since John's death that she felt nearly happy again. After a while, Tommy rode up beside her. "It appears Tinkerbelle has taken to you."

"The feeling's mutual. I haven't had such an exhilarating ride in years. She's a great horse."

They began to ride back toward the house. She saw the familiar white and black stables in the distance. Reluctant to return, Jill took her time and slowed her horse.

Once back, Tommy and Jill looked at each horse and spoke to the barn manager, Jared, who doubled his duties as business manager of the farm. Half a dozen full-time grooms were running about seeing to their duties. There was also a full-time trainer on the staff who was in a ring working relentlessly with one of the horses.

Jill spent the better part of the afternoon reviewing the personnel disks from Bio Tech Labs, familiarizing herself with the employees while Tommy went to his board meeting.

By late afternoon, Jill's legs hurt from riding, and she was famished. After a good, long shower and fresh change of clothes, she met Tommy downstairs. He drove her into town in his pickup truck to Gedney's Restaurant, where they feasted on fried catfish.

"Hey, don't I know you?" The young waitress refilled their glasses with sweet tea.

"Maybe. I was in Roanoke a few months ago."

"Oh, I remember where I know you from. It was at the Sassy Scissors." The redheaded waitress smiled in remembrance and winked at Jill, who was squirming uncomfortably in the hard wooden booth across from Tommy.

Jill blushed, but thankfully Tommy ignored it. And they had a very pleasant meal, much to Jill's surprise. They discovered common interests in music, tastes in food, outlook on life, and faith.

Finally, she asked him what was really on her mind. "What helped you recover from your wife's death?"

"Something tells me you're asking that question more for yourself than you are for me."

"Does it get easier with time like everyone says?"

"It still hurts, but not as often. The pain comes and goes in spurts, a certain memory of something the two of you did together suddenly presents itself, and it's painful. But my children have helped me go on with my life."

"I wonder if it's better when you have children. It'd be comforting to know a part of your loved one lives on in them. I'm sorry; I shouldn't remind you of your sadness."

He waved a hand in the air. "This is cathartic for me as well. I don't mind discussing it as long as my comments don't show up in tomorrow's paper." He chuckled. "If I can help you through this difficult time in your life, I'm here. At least my pain serves a purpose to help someone else."

Jill smiled at him as the waitress plopped down two tall slices of chocolate pie with seemingly mile-high meringue.

Finished with dinner, they returned to the car and went for a drive through the area.

"I sure hate to bring up business when you look like you're having fun, but have you uncovered anything new on the Brown case?" he asked, shifting gears.

"Not really. I'm looking forward to our visit to Bio Tech Labs tomorrow. Once I meet more of the employees face-to-face, I hope to uncover some clues. If that doesn't lead us to someone, I'm not sure where we'll go from there. By the way, did those numbers I gave you over the phone mean anything to you?"

"Nope. If it's a phone number, it belongs to a small pet shop in Killeen, Texas."

"Rubic and I already checked out that pet shop."

"What did you find out?"

"The owner is a sixty-six-year-old animal lover with nothing in his lifetime but a couple of parking tickets on his record. And he's never carried snakes in his shop. His wife hates them."

"Sounds innocuous to me. I guess we'll never know what those phone numbers were meant to tell us."

They drove along, and an awkward silence separated them. Finally, Tommy spoke. "You've gotten quiet on me. Is something bothering you?" He pulled off to the side of the road at the cliff to see a panoramic view of the river.

"I'm sorry. It's just that suddenly the grief returns out of nowhere with such a vengeance it overwhelms me."

Without a word, Tommy reached over for Jill's hand. For the first time, she didn't pull it away. They sat in silence, holding hands. And then Tommy leaned over and brushed Jill's lips ever so slightly with his.

29

Be as shrewd as snakes and as innocent as doves.

Matthew 10:16

Tommy pulled away from Jill and sat back in his seat. Jill found his tender kiss comforting. There was nothing suggestive about it, yet Jill became consumed with guilt. She felt extremely disloyal and ashamed. After all, John had been gone less than two months.

At least Tommy didn't tease her about the kiss. She was grateful for that. In fact, he said nothing at all but merely started the car.

The silence became so uncomfortable that Jill decided to apologize. "Tommy, I'm sorry. I don't know what got into me back there."

"Sorry that you're human?"

Now she wished she hadn't mentioned the kiss, since it was obviously no big deal to the senator.

Fortunately, the senator's phone rang, distracting him. His smile dropped when he listened to the caller. "Yes? Call the vet and the police. I'll be right there." He flipped the phone closed. "I need to get down to the barn, now."

"What's wrong?"

Tommy pressed the accelerator hard. "It's the horses. With this rare breed, there's always the threat of someone doing harm to one of them. I have more security on my horses than my own children, and not because I care for one more than the other. It's just that the horse world is such a competitive one, and when big numbers are at stake, things can happen."

Dust blew up from the dirt road behind the truck as they entered through the back entrance of the barn. Stable hands had gathered together in large clusters then spread out as they saw the senator approach. Two squad cars along with the vet's truck were parked beside the barn.

Jared stopped Tommy a few feet after the entrance. Holding onto the senator's shoulders, he said, "It's Ambrosia, Tommy. She's dead. Dr. Shellnut's here, but it was too late. He couldn't save her." Jill saw the grief on Jared's face and in his eyes. Tommy looked even worse.

The local vet hovered over the Caspian. It was a sickening sight to see the magnificent creature lying stiffly in her stall.

"What happened?" Tommy's voice was rough. Looking to the vet for answers, he knelt beside the horse, stroking her head and running his fingers through her rough mane.

"I don't know, but she looks odd to me," Dr. Shellnut replied.

Tommy and Dr. Shellnut rolled the horse onto her side. Beneath her was a flattened snake.

The doctor knelt down and looked at the snake. "I've seen snakes all my life, but never one like this."

Tommy looked back at Jill. Stepping forward, she saw the unmistakable head with the wavy white stripe that started behind the eyes and extended to the rear. Tommy cleared his throat. "It's a Saw-Scaled Viper."

"There're no snakes like this one in this area. How did it get here?" the barn manager asked.

"There's only one way. Someone put it here."

Dr. Shellnut examined the horse. "This animal was bitten repeatedly. See all these fang marks? They explain why her death was so sudden."

"You mean there was more than one snake?" Jared was alarmed.

"Not necessarily. A lot of folks think once a snake bites, it has to wait for the venom to replenish, but that's inaccurate."

"Do you have any idea who'd do something like that, Senator?" a patrolman asked.

Tommy ignored the question. "Okay, this is what we're going to do. I'm enforcing a lockdown of all the barns and horses. First, scan the stables for any and all snakes or poisons or anything that even looks suspicious. Once it's determined the stables are safe, we'll bring the horses and foals in from the pastures and keep them under lock and key. Only the barn manager and I will have the keys."

"I'll get the tapes from the security cameras to see if there's anything or anyone suspicious on the tape," Jared volunteered.

"Ask one of the farmhands to review them first. I need you," Tommy ordered.

Everyone was given a job and set to work immediately, which included counting the horses outside, making sure all the stallions, mares, weanlings, and yearlings were safe. Tommy got on the cell phone and called in extra security.

"Jill, why don't you go back to the house?"

"I don't mind helping."

"I appreciate that, but we've got it under control. Don't you have some prep work to do for our appointment at Bio Tech tomorrow morning?"

She nodded her head. "I should probably review some of the bios of the employees we plan to question."

"I'll have Jared drive you back up to the house."

"No, don't bother him; he's got work to do. I'll walk."

Jill walked through the back door and into an empty house.

She spotted a note that said Mary had left, that she and her husband were at the grocery store in Roanoke. Jill strolled through the dark halls and in and out of the rooms belonging to the senator.

She felt oddly unsettled walking through the quiet house alone. She thought of Tommy's murdered wife and shuddered. *How does a person sleep in a house like this . . . the scene of such a brutal murder?*

Jill knew she should just head back to her own room and get some work done. But her curiosity got the better of her. She was curious to see where the murder took place. She wandered around until she found the master suite, then turned the brass knob on the door and walked inside.

It looked as though the room had been redecorated since the murder. Jill thought it looked more like a room in a medieval castle with its heavy drapes and dark woodwork and beams. She expected *Jane Eyre's* Mr. Rochester to appear at any moment.

Could Tommy have murdered his wife? With servants and his daughter asleep in their beds? But the master suite was on the first floor of the house, far from everyone else. Was it possible that what was meant for privacy also doubled for isolation? The thick walls assured the sounds would not travel far.

Jill wandered around the room. She found it unsettling that there weren't any pictures of his wife around to see. Throughout the rest of the house there were plenty of photos of the family. She wondered if Tommy had stashed them away in photo albums to avoid seeing his former wife's face. Was the reason his guilt or his grief?

She looked in his closet first but didn't see anything in there. Then she noticed an adjoining door, which was ajar, and peeked inside. It was obviously Tommy's office. A mammoth-sized desk sat squarely in front of the windows that were covered by shades in a khaki fabric. Jill pushed the door open and went inside. Looking around, she saw mocha-colored leather couches piled high with Apache print pillows. Two enormous wing chairs in striped Southwestern prints were arranged on the other side of the coffee table.

Jill studied the Southwestern paintings. Judging by the simple lyrical lines of the drawings, the artist had to be R. C. Gorman. Fanny Orsen had a set of Gorman serigraphs. Jill felt sick over the possibility of Tommy paying her off with them.

She still had a lot of snooping to do before Tommy got back from the barn, so she scanned the shelves for anything that looked like a family album.

Finally locating a neat stack of albums, she pulled them off and sat on one of the couches. Choosing the wedding album first, she hurriedly flipped through the pages, looking at the happy faces of the young couple, obviously quite in love with one another. Catherine wore her dark hair up in a classic French twist and was gowned in a beautiful dress. There were other pictures of them as well: Catherine Harrison pregnant with their first baby, then years later holding little Thomas while pregnant with their girl, the second and last child. There was one of all four of them on a beach together, ski trips, Christmases, birthdays. To her, they seemed like a normal happy family . . . very proper, bespeaking of wealth and impeccable breeding.

Deciding to return the albums to their rightful place, Jill closed them and was just stacking them back together when Tommy appeared at his bedroom doorway. At first he looked annoyed, but then his face broke into a smile. "Maybe it's *my* bedroom door that needs locking?"

Jill could feel her face turn red. "I'm sorry, Tommy."

"It's okay. You are an investigator; therefore, you investigate."

"I wasn't investigating you. I was only curious as to . . . as to your family. Look, I think staying here with you is a bad idea. Could you ask one of your men to drive me to a hotel? I'm imposing."

He answered with a gentle kiss. She reciprocated, then after a minute, she leaned into his ear and whispered, "I should leave, Tommy."

"Please stay. I don't want to be alone after what happened to Ambrosia."

She relented. "All right. How's everything down at the barn?"

"Well, we didn't find any more snakes."

"Looks like the bad guys have followed us here." Jill rubbed her temples.

"Don't look so worried. You're safer here than most places. Keep in mind it's hard for someone to hide in a small town where everyone knows everyone else and a stranger stands out like a pig among a litter of kittens. Besides, I told Jared to double the guards and take added security measures."

Tommy's confidence fueled both her confidence and determination. "Okay, what's next?" she asked.

"Tomorrow we'll drive down to Mobile and visit Bio Tech Labs. We leave first thing in the morning. Can you make it down to breakfast by five o'clock?"

"Sure."

"Go on to bed and try to get a good night's sleep."

He turned to go, but she put her hand on his arm to stop him. "Tommy, I'm sorry about Ambrosia."

"Thank you. I keep telling myself she was an older horse and wouldn't be around forever anyway. But I just counted on having her around a lot longer."

"I know. Good night, Tommy, and thanks for everything."

"Sleep tight. I'll see you in the morning."

In her room that night, Jill thought about Tommy's kisses. They comforted her at the time, but now she felt angry with herself. She ran her fingers over her lips to wipe the kisses away, wanting John's kiss to be the last on her lips.

There were many things that worried her about Tommy. Why had he given those paintings to Fanny Orsen? Was it a payoff, or were the two of them having an affair? She would've asked Tommy about the paintings, but after he caught her in his office, she wasn't going to risk alienating him—at least not until she got back into Bio Tech Labs. Jill had a hunch about Dr. Arden, and she was anxious to speak with her again. For now she'd have to behave herself.

Under a light summer quilt, Jill melted into a deep sleep. But after a few hours, she awoke from her usual snake-filled nightmare and jerked up in the bed. She turned to the clock on the bedside table: 4:30 a.m. She knew she should get up and get ready. *Just a few more minutes*, she thought as she slid back down beneath the quilt.

She thought she heard a strange sound. She stiffened. The unmistakable sound of the Saw-Scaled Viper rose from under the covers.

She lay there frozen. With everything in her, she wanted to jump from the bed screaming. But she knew she had to stay perfectly still and not antagonize the snake. Moments later the reptile stretched out as it crawled along the side of her leg, coming to rest just under her left knee. It stopped. Now the only movement in the room came from the hands of the ticking clock beside her bed.

It was nearly impossible to keep still when she longed to flee. Could she maintain her calm? She looked at the door to the hall-way, but she was certain she wouldn't be able to make it that far, not without getting bitten. She envisioned herself face down on the floor with her right hand outstretched toward freedom.

Jill took small, shallow breaths while fighting against the powerful urge to scream and fly off the bed. Praying, she fought with every ounce of her being to remain calm and relaxed. If she even flexed a muscle or inadvertently twitched, it could mean death. Sweat built up under her and began to run down her frame. Pictures of John lying bruised and filled with poison in that hospital bed became even more vivid to her.

Another tickling movement stroked the underside of her knee.

She wanted to scratch it, rub it. Instead she lay flat on her back with her eyes on the ceiling. Within minutes, a small ribbon-like feeling moved about on her skin as if it were drinking in her droplets of perspiration. Then it reemerged beneath her knee to rest.

After what seemed an eternity but was likely only a minute's time, the snake started to twitch once again and moved along her side.

Someone put the snake in my bed or near the bed at some point during the night. After I had fallen asleep? Tommy? Did he lure me to his home to kill me?

With all the security around the place it would be difficult to get past any of the guards. But wasn't the main focus of security put on the horses? If the culprit wasn't Tommy, maybe the one who placed the snake in the horse's stall went to the house at the same time? Was Tommy safe in his bed? Was he dead?

No one would come looking for her until five o'clock. Could she hold out that long? She didn't think so. Still as stone, Jill thought of all the people she loved and had pushed away from her just when she needed them the most.

I want to live. Please, Lord, give me another chance to show them how much I love them. I want to make a difference in their lives.

Suddenly the snake moved away from her body. The sawing sounded further away. Jill was undecided on whether to hop out of the bed or stay put. She decided to take her chances and hurled herself out of the bed.

She ran to the door of her room, flung it open, and quickly shut it behind her. She leaned against the door, her heart pounding furiously. *I made it! I'm alive!*

She couldn't stop shaking long enough to notice that Tommy had walked down the hallway and now stood beside her.

"Jill?" he said.

She screamed at the sound of his voice, then flung herself into his arms.

"Jill, what on earth is going on?"

It took Jill a while to calm down enough to tell him what happened.

Animal control came to the Harrison household for the second time in a twenty-four-hour period. They eventually found the snake in Jill's room and killed it.

Later that morning, Tommy showed her to the guest bath so she could take a shower and get ready for their trip.

Jill shut the door behind her and locked it. She turned on the shower but didn't have the energy to step into it, not yet. She sat on the vanity stool for a few minutes to compose herself and thanked God for sparing her life once again. The trip to Mobile to visit Bio Tech no longer seemed important to her. She was sorry she couldn't put John's killer away, but someone else was going to have to solve this crime. No man could chase her away, but the viper had.

"I'll call Rubric as soon as I get out of the shower, and I'll resign from my job," she told herself. "Mom and Kathy can help me pack up my apartment. I'll use part of my trust fund to buy the *Lakes News*, and live happily ever after as an old maid with my mother in Delavan."

30

Although the world is filled with suffering,
it is also full of the overcoming of it.

Helen Keller

Jill's nightgown lay in a cotton puddle on the marble bathroom floor. She hopped in the shower to wash away the snake's slimy tracks from her body. She didn't care if they were imaginary. She had to scrub her skin until the feeling was gone.

After the shower, she wrapped her hair in a towel, pulled off her jeans and shirt from the hook on the back of the bathroom door, and slipped them on. Then, still barefoot, Jill stepped into a menagerie of paramedics, policemen, and the local vet who were all going over the crime scene, some taking samples of fingerprints and others looking for clues.

Tommy smiled encouragingly at her. He looked as though he wanted to hug her, but she kept her distance.

"Do you still feel up to going to Bio Tech today?" he asked.

"Any place is better than here."

"Good. Because animal control has advised us to leave the house for the time being while they comb it for more snakes."

She shuddered.

"They've checked the other guest room already, so I put your stuff in there. You can go in there now to get changed."

"Okay." She started to walk away but then turned around. "Tommy, how do you think those snakes got on your property?"

"I wish I knew. Whoever put the snake in the stall had an open chance to set the other one loose in here when all our attention was focused on that end of the property."

Jill eyed Tommy suspiciously. If anyone had opportunity and perhaps motive for keeping her off the Bio Tech case, it was the senator. He ran things in his state.

She walked into the other guest room and saw her suitcase on the floor. But her files weren't there. She hurried back to where all the men were working at the crime scene. "Where are my things?" she demanded, addressing everyone in the room.

The frantic sound of her voice caused all the men in the room to stop what they were doing and look around at one another. Since no one answered the first time, Jill asked again. "I had a box of files here last night. Who moved them?"

All at once, everyone denied they had even seen a box of files, much less taken them. Just then, Mary, the cook, walked into the room to gather the last of Jill's belongings.

"Mary, did you take my box of files into the guest room?"

"No. I don't remember seeing any boxes. Where were they?"

"Right here." Jill pointed once more to the top of the empty desk.

"I didn't see anything there." Mary walked into the bathroom and emerged seconds later with an armload of clothes from the night before.

"Someone's taken my files! I need them!" Jill yelled.

"Ms. Lewis," one of the paramedics spoke to her, "I'll need to check your vital signs."

"That's probably not a bad idea," Tommy agreed.

"My vitals are just fine. I need my files." Jill began to look all over the room—under the bed, inside the closet, behind the bathroom door.

"I'll look for them myself. Just go to your new room so the paramedic can check you," Tommy urged.

"Nonsense, I wasn't bitten, or I'd be long dead. I need my files!"

"Are you sure you even brought them with you?"

"I'm not crazy, Tommy. Ryan loaded them in the car for me. Ask him."

Jill sensed she was getting nowhere with Tommy, so she went back to her new room. She dug into her purse, frantically searching for the paper where she'd written the numbers. Finding it, she breathed a sigh of relief. Putting it back safe and sound, Jill faced the window and sat silently on the bed as she waited for the paramedic to come into the room to check her.

He introduced himself as Smokey Cole. "Blood pressure's 110 over 79, heart rate 68. You're fine."

"I will be once I locate my files."

Smokey took the blood-pressure cuff from her arm. "You should go eat some breakfast to level off your blood sugar." He then turned to Mary and advised her to bring Jill a glass of orange juice.

The cook smiled and returned in minutes with an ice-cold glass of orange juice and a full breakfast of eggs, toast, sliced banana, watermelon, and strawberries in clotted cream. Jill gulped the orange juice, ate the fruit and toast, and left the eggs.

As she finished her last bite of toast, her cell phone rang. "Hello?"

"I'm sure glad to hear your voice. Are you okay, Jill?"

"Rubric! You don't know how glad I am to hear yours."

"I've been trying to reach you since yesterday, but a recording kept saying your cell phone was out of range."

"I know. Service is really spotty here. Is something wrong?"

"I'll say. Are you okay? I've been worried sick about you."

"Well, you should be. A Saw-Scaled Viper crawled up my body in bed in the wee hours of the morning. Someone planted it in my room. One killed a horse yesterday too."

"And I can tell you exactly who put it there."

"You're joking."

"I wish I were."

Jill plopped down on the freshly made bed. "Tell me what's going on, Rube."

"I've made in-depth inquiries into the senator's background. There's bad news. The senator is the majority stockholder at Bio Tech Labs."

"What? Well, I guess I'm not surprised." Jill sighed. "Wait until you hear my news . . . All my files are missing."

"Never mind about your files. Right now, it's much worse than that. You've got to get away from Harrison now. Go down to the hotel lobby."

"That's the really bad news; I'm not at a hotel. I'm at Harrison's house."

"What?" he barked. "Well, then pack your bags and get the heck out of there. Or better yet, just leave your things."

"I can't just leave. We're leaving for Bio Tech Labs any minute."

"Don't get in a car with that man."

"But how can I just leave without causing any suspicion?"

"Just walk out the front door."

She sighed in frustration. "I can't. Harrison lives miles from nowhere. I'm not even sure I'd know how to get to town from here. But wait, the paramedic is still here. I can tell him I'm not feeling well and insist on going to the hospital."

"You're brilliant."

"Ha! I'll remember you said that."

Rubric growled. "Don't trust anyone in that small-town hospital. They protect their own. Fake an anxiety attack. I'll call Tucker to see if he can send some agents over to the hospital."

"Once they check me out, they'll know nothing's wrong with me and release me."

"Just stay long enough until I get someone down there."

"Thanks. In the meantime, I'll act like a crazy person. At the moment, it isn't far from the truth."

"Remember, don't leave that hospital until I send someone for you. Do you hear me? The code word is Annabelle."

"Got it. The paramedics are about to leave, so I have to make my move right now. Bye, Rubric."

Jill glanced in the mirror. She noticed her hair needed brushing. She shook her head and messed up her hair even more, then stumbled into the hallway. Breathing hard, she thrust her hand dramatically over her chest. She knew that she had to put on the performance of her life.

"Somebody help me. I can't breathe. I can't breathe! I feel so weak. I feel like I'm going to faint." Just as she hoped, everyone spilled out into the hallway. Tommy ran up to her.

"What's wrong, Jill?"

"I feel so lightheaded and nauseous. I can't stop my hands from shaking." She panted for more breath. Truthfully, her performance was rendering her lightheaded.

"Her vital signs were all fine," Smokey said. "I don't understand. We'd better get her to the hospital."

"Yes, I think so." Jill shook as she glanced about as if she wasn't really sure where she was. "It's my head, Smokey, it's pounding. Take me to the hospital!"

"I don't understand it. Your vitals checked out just fine a moment ago. I'd better take them again."

"No! Don't touch me," she screamed. "Nobody come near me!"

"Maybe Jill really was bitten by the snake," Tommy said, worried. "And it's just taken the poison a while to get into her system."

"No, it works fast. Besides, she's not displaying any of the symptoms," the paramedic explained. "It's like she's paranoid."

"Let's get her to the hospital," Tommy replied. "Jill, I'll ride in the ambulance with you. Mary, call Ryan and ask him to get over to the hospital."

"Which hospital?"

"Do you think she should go to LaGrange Hospital?" the senator asked. "I don't think Roanoke can handle her in her present condition. And then there's the gossip."

Jill pushed herself into acting even more erratic by panting and putting on a fearful expression as she clung to the stairway railing with one hand and her purse with the other.

"Okay, I suppose so . . . if LaGrange is what you want," Smokey agreed.

Jill was strapped onto a gurney and rolled toward the waiting ambulance. She thought of Brown being transferred to a hospital and never coming out alive. And John too.

Tommy insisted on accompanying her, which definitely put a damper on her plans. Jill had to tell Rubric she would be at LaGrange Hospital, but she couldn't very well call him with Tommy at her side.

The paramedic insisted on checking Jill's vital signs, and she kept dodging him. By now she was sincerely getting worked up. An oxygen mask went over her face.

"Anxiety attack," she heard Smokey whisper to the senator.

Tommy held on to Jill's limp hand as the ambulance sped down country roads. Arriving at LaGrange Hospital, Smokey wheeled her into the emergency room. A nurse came into the room and checked Jill's vital signs while a doctor motioned for the senator to step out in the hallway.

"Hello, I'm the doctor assigned to your case. What are your symptoms, Ms. Lewis?"

"There was a poisonous snake in my bed when I awoke this morning," she quickly explained. "Maybe I was bitten, or maybe I'm just suffering from delayed anxiety syndrome or whatever it's called."

"That's post-traumatic stress disorder. How do you feel now?"

"My head hurts, and I'm having trouble breathing."

"Sounds like a classic anxiety attack to me, Ms. Lewis. I'm going to give you a mild sedative to help you calm down. You can relax now."

"No!" she yelled. "I don't want any drugs or needles in my arms." Before she could say more, the nurse pricked her arm with a needle. Jill fell back into her pillow and had no other choice but to allow the drug to do its work, sinking her into a dark hole.

A few hours later, the doctors declared her well—or at least sane—enough to leave. By now Jill felt like a zombie, and she was led toward the car. She thought it was Ryan who helped her in, but she couldn't be sure since the face was distorted.

Once in the car, she promptly fell asleep.

Through a fog she heard a voice say, "We're here."

Where? What were they saying?

She forced her eyelids open. Tommy sat in the backseat with her. She sat up straight in the seat.

"What's going on?" she demanded, her words sounding far away to her ears.

"Jill, you're awake," Tommy said, smiling at her. "We've stopped for gas."

"I would've preferred staying in the hospital a while longer and then checking into a hotel for the night." Her mouth and tongue felt numb.

"Why? What's the matter?"

"What's the matter? May I remind you . . . that I woke up with a viper in my bed, and then I'm drugged at the hospital, and now you drive off with me to who knows where? That's what's the matter with me."

"Relax. Nothing nefarious is going on here. We're just going to Mobile. You wanted to go to Bio Tech Labs, remember?"

It was hard to keep her eyes open. "Why did they drug me?"

"You were hysterical."

"I was not hysterical." Jill spoke in monotone while her eyes wanted to shut and stay that way.

"You just had an anxiety attack. The doctor said you'd be fine in the morning."

Jill realized there was nothing else she could do. She'd have to make the best of the situation for now. Sitting straighter, she noticed she still had her purse but couldn't find her other things. "Where are my bags?" she asked.

"I had Ryan put them in the trunk and bring them to the hospital. How do you feel?"

"Drugged."

While Ryan filled the car with gas, Tommy got out of the car, so Jill whipped out her cell phone.

Tommy walked over to Jill's side of the car and said, "Would you like to get out of the car and go to the ladies' room or anything? Or could I get you some water?"

"No. Excuse me, but I have to check in with my editor."

Fortunately, Rubric answered right away. "Jill, where the heck are you?"

"Driving toward Bio Tech Labs. We'll stay the night at a hotel in Mobile, and we're going to the lab tomorrow morning."

"I told you not to leave the hospital until the FBI got there. I talked to Bill Tucker personally, and he said he was sending two agents to Roanoke Hospital immediately. Didn't I tell you to stay there?"

"They took me to LaGrange Hospital, not the one in Roanoke."

"Why didn't you let me know?"

"I couldn't. The doctor gave me a sedative, and it knocked me out cold. I didn't want him to, but the nurse did it anyway. And then they let me go out of the hospital before the sedative wore off. I'm still feeling groggy."

Rubric was silent for a moment, which was an unusual occurrence. He finally asked, "Do you think he coerced the doctor into sedating you?"

"Ha," Jill laughed.

Rubric didn't laugh. "You didn't answer my question. Does Harrison have anything to do with this?"

"Probably. He's right over there." Feeling a bit loopy from her meds, Jill replied nonchalantly, pointing at Tommy standing outside the gas station.

"Do you know the name of the hotel where you'll be staying?"

Jill opened her door and called out to the senator. "Tommy, what's the name of the hotel where we're staying tonight? My editor needs to know."

"The Downtown Hilton in Mobile."

"The Downtown Hilton in Mobile," Jill repeated.

"Call me back as soon as you arrive. I'll call Bill Tucker and make sure he gets some agents over there."

"Thanks, Rube."

"You aren't staying in the room with Harrison, are you?"

"Give me a break." Jill shut off her phone.

Once they reached Mobile, Jill went right to her room. She told Tommy she planned to order room service for dinner and turn in early for the evening. In her room, she channel surfed. There was a knock at the door. *That better not be Tommy, trying to put the moves on me.* She slid off the bed, walked up to the door, and asked who was there.

"Hello, Jill. It's Agent Allen and Agent Masourian from the FBI."

"How did you get here so quickly?"

"We were already in Mobile to observe some of the personnel at Bio Tech Labs."

Unchaining the lock, she let them in and offered bottled

water as they each took a seat, one on the bed and the other on the chair. "What's going on?"

"We're not sure, but we discovered that Tommy Harrison is the chief stockholder in Bio Tech Labs. The FBI ordered surveillance for you," Abe explained.

"I know. So why didn't we pick up on this before?"

"Because it's not in his name but in the name of one of his wife's family's offshore corporations."

"Very interesting."

"Ms. Lewis," Agent Allen spoke up. "We'd like to wire you for the meeting at Bio Tech Labs in the morning. Our female agent arrives tonight, and she can stop by first thing in the morning to hook you up."

"That won't be necessary. I'm familiar with how to wear one," Jill said. Since the drug had worn off, she was beginning to feel like her old self again.

"Then we'll leave it with you, but we'll test it out before you leave the hotel in the morning."

"Sure, I'll call you when I'm dressed and ready to go."

"Don't leave this hotel without it," Masourian warned her.

"You have my word."

"We'll be in the next room if you need us." They left the wiretap along with a panic button that would immediately summon them.

When the agents left the room, Jill took out the coded message John had left for her and played around with it. Finally giving up, she dragged herself into the bathroom and took a shower. Then she opened her Bible to Psalms for comfort. She knew that whatever tomorrow held, she'd have to be spiritually strong.

31

The moment Jill stepped out of the hotel and into the motor lobby, the humidity entrapped a hot, wet blanket of heat and steam around her body. Melting the bottoms of Jill's sandaled feet, the hot concrete sent her hopscotching to the senator's waiting car in an effort to escape the morning's intense heat.

"Good morning." Ryan smiled as he leaned in to open the car door and helped her into the backseat of the car. Knowing her acting ability might save her, Jill chirped cheerfully, "Good morning, guys. I hope you haven't waited long for me."

"And good morning to you, Jill," Tommy Harrison replied. "How's your head?"

"My head?" Jill had almost forgotten she had falsely complained of a headache the day before in her quest to get to the safe haven of the hospital. "Nothing a good night's sleep couldn't cure."

"Are you still angry with me for taking you from the hospital?"

"I would've preferred to have left with a clearer head."

"How are you feeling this morning?"

"Better, and considering I woke up without a snake staring me in the face . . . I'm giddy with relief, but I still feel a bit drugged."

"That's definitely an improvement over yesterday," the senator agreed.

Jill turned her head in the opposite direction so he couldn't stare at her face while she closed her eyes. To Jill's surprise and relief, Tommy didn't press for conversation. In spite of the searing heat outside, an icy distance quickly crystallized between the two of them. Jill heard the rattle of a newspaper.

There were still so many unanswered questions in her head about the senator. First, how did the snake get into her room with so much security on the barns and residence? It gnawed at her. But, on the other hand, why would Tommy put a snake in his beloved horse's stall? If he wanted to throw her off track, why not kill a different horse? And where were her files? If Tommy didn't take them, who did? And why would he give her the information in the first place, just to steal it back? The possibilities were dizzying.

Jill realized she had to make the critical decision of whether to trust him or not. Her life would depend on the right choice. He spoke, drawing her out of her thoughts.

"I have a good feeling about today," he announced, folding the paper.

Jill opened her eyes and turned toward him. "Really? I feel discouraged since my files with the CDs were stolen. I've lost hours, weeks of work."

"It's my fault. I should've had equal security on the house and stables."

"Just how do you suppose the snake got into my bedroom—a bedroom with a locked door?"

"Maybe in the hubbub of Ambrosia's death, the person took advantage of the situation. Or maybe it was placed in your room when we were out riding and just worked its way into bed with you, seeking warmth during the night. I keep the air-conditioning turned down low."

"I suppose that's plausible."

"I talked with all the servants yesterday morning while you were getting dressed, and no one admitted they saw anything. Mary said no one even came to the door. The only people they saw all day were the police, the vet, and security people."

"Who had the key to my room?"

"The keys are kept in the maid's pantry."

The conversation ended there as they drove up to the security gate at Bio Tech Labs. When they arrived at the front lobby, the senator escorted Jill through security and into Dr. Kelly Arden's office. The doctor was waiting for them. She pushed out the chair from the desk and said, "Walk with me to my lab, and I'll show you the properties of the drug under the microscope. Ms. Lewis, I'm sure you know that pharmaceutical companies are always in pursuit of developing a miracle drug for cancer and a plethora of other diseases."

As they walked down the hall, Jill said, "Yes, my father was a doctor, and I'm familiar with the great strides made to find medical cures over the past thirty years."

"We still have no definitive cure for cancer, and today viruses are running rampant. You can only imagine our excitement when we found that our drug, MST, exhibited phenomenal success in laboratory mice for the treatment of brain cancer, which is normally a fatal illness."

"What exactly went wrong when MST was tested on humans?" Jill asked.

"I guess the senator told you what happened in the MST Phase I clinical trial?"

"He explained that the human subjects were far more sensitive to MST than the laboratory mice, and your dosage was off, so it proved fatal."

Dr. Arden did not hide her angst. "Before we could experiment and adjust the dosage according to the findings of our data, the FDA closed down our Phase I drug trial—at the urging of Senator George Brown."

"And all the remaining samples of MST were ordered to be destroyed under the auspices of the FBI," Tommy added.

"Do you know for sure that it was Senator Brown?"

"We can't prove it was him, but several reliable sources have confirmed it," Dr. Arden said, staring at Tommy.

"Were you one of those sources, Tommy?"

"No, but it sounded probable to me, especially since Senator Brown was on the Senate Subcommittee for Homeland Security. They're closely tied into the FDA through Bioterrorism and Counterterrorism."

"Who were your sources?"

"We're not at liberty to disclose that," Dr. Arden answered.

"You knew Brown had a motive, of course?" Jill asked. "He was protecting Creation Pharmaceutical, his largest campaign backer."

"Yes, of course." Dr. Arden added, "We were aware that he was trying to prevent its competitor, our new vascular-targeting drug, to go on the market. We'd just completed our Phase III clinical trial on that drug, very successfully. It was only months away from going into clinical studies trial Phase IV."

"I thought your vascular-targeting drug was already on the market," Jill said.

"That's true, but the pharmaceutical company is required to study the data and file its findings for a specified length of time after it's placed on the market," Tommy explained.

"I can only imagine how disappointed you were when they halted the drug trials," Jill said sympathetically.

Dr. Arden stopped walking. Jill was anxious to see the lab, and it annoyed her that every time Dr. Arden spoke, she stopped. "Disappointed is putting it lightly. I've spent my entire career developing MST. But I'm not the only loser. We were so close to a cure for brain cancer—a cure that probably could've been extended to other types of cancer as well."

"Since the cause of Brown's death has been officially ruled MST, the Feds will likely look at everyone at Bio Tech as a suspect," Jill reminded them.

"What are you insinuating, Ms. Lewis?" Dr. Arden glared at her and then at Tommy.

"Nothing, just stating the facts."

"Well, some people might say that Senator Brown got what was coming to him." The scientist's voice was riddled with bitterness. Dr. Arden froze the environment with attitude alone. "There'd be no reason for anyone to suspect a connection between MST and Senator Brown's death. Not until Senator Harrison got the *Washington Gazette* involved." Dr. Arden looked pointedly at Tommy.

Ah, so that's where the attitude comes from. "You can relax, Dr. Arden. We had a second source who made the same accusation," Jill revealed. "Senator Harrison wasn't the only one who came forward with information."

"But did you receive this other tip prior to the cremation?"

"Actually, I received it before I met with Senator Harrison."

With that knowledge Dr. Arden turned white. "Why wasn't I told about this?" She glared at Tommy.

Jill wondered what Kelly Arden had to hide.

"Dr. Arden, I know you disagree with my decision to come forward, but ultimately I had to follow my conscience," the senator said. "Besides, if we hadn't come forward with our history with Brown and this MST battle, there's a good chance we'd all be under suspicion for murder."

Dr. Arden glared at Tommy.

Jill found it intriguing that Tommy made his opinion known so readily. Had he told her about Brown and the MST just to throw suspicion off himself? Maybe, maybe not. It was entirely plausible that nobody would have known Senator Brown was murdered if it hadn't been for Tommy.

"Ah, here we are." Dr. Arden pushed open the double doors and walked into the lab.

It was an interesting conglomeration of mini rooms. Each room was unique with its own specialty. They walked into a back room filled with stacks of reptile boxes, labeled and placed one on top of the other.

"Don't tell me these boxes are still filled with snakes," Jill said. "I don't think I can handle staring another Saw-Scaled Viper in the face anytime soon."

Dr. Arden was patronizing as she explained that indeed all boxes were now empty, but that this area was once the lab where the venom was extracted from the reptiles and manufactured into MST.

"Where are the snakes now?" Jill asked.

"U.S. Fish and Wildlife came for them. Beyond that, I have no idea where they ultimately ended up afterwards," Dr. Arden told her.

"Um, sounds like we should visit the shipping department next," Jill said. "There would be lots of opportunities for someone in that department to get involved in the black market."

"Good point, Jill," Tommy replied.

"You don't really think someone is black marketing MST?" Dr. Arden asked.

"I don't know," Jill said, "but it's probably an idea we should consider. Most likely they're marketing the snakes. I wondered who ordered that last shipment of reptiles that recently came into the port of Miami."

"It was probably just an older order," Dr. Arden said nonchalantly.

"The size of the order puzzles me. If you didn't order that many snakes, how do you explain the size of the order? Bio Tech claims they never ordered a shipment of that magnitude."

"Ordering and shipping always has a high probability for errors. Are you familiar with the salary of a shipping clerk, Ms. Lewis? If Senator Brown hadn't been murdered, this would have just been considered a routine mix-up, wouldn't it?" The doctor was clearly exasperated with Jill's questions.

Jill decided to drop the subject. "Where do you think Fish and Wildlife disposed of the snakes in that last order?"

"They were probably distributed to medical labs and sanctuaries all over the U.S. for milking for antivenin," Tommy said.

Dr. Arden led them to the other side of the room, where she pointed to the dozens of tanks and cages containing rats and mice. Jill grimaced at the ones that the scientists had implanted with electrodes. Some of the mice had sores that had developed as a result of the researchers' injections of diseases or the chemicals that induced them.

"What's wrong with these mice?" Jill asked.

"They're called designer mice. The ability to breed genetically manipulated mice has led to tremendous advances in understanding the roles of individual genes in normal development, as well as generating animal models for testing therapeutic strategies," Dr. Arden explained. "Traditional breeding methods have resulted in the generation of many highly inbred lines of mice, which have been very useful in studies of the immune system, as well as other areas. Mice are also used in generating very specific antibodies, called monoclonal antibodies, which have been very valuable tools for research."

"Mice are popular experimental organisms with geneticists because of the size of their litters. It's not uncommon for some strains to have eight to ten in each litter," the senator added. "The fact that they are small mammals makes it easy and economical to house them."

And as one of the owners of Bio Tech, naturally, you would be interested in the economics of it. Jill knew there was no mistake that Harrison was the majority stockholder. It all made sense now. A senator, who was promoting an industry in his state, would never go to such lengths as Harrison had to familiarize himself with a company.

"Although other animals, plants, and bacteria have been extremely useful in many ways, no other single experimental animal offers such a wide variety of uses to science and medicine as a mouse." The doctor picked up a white mouse by its tail and dangled it in front of Jill's face. "This is why the mice are used in drug testing and experiments."

"Thanks for the biology lesson." There was a slight hint of sarcasm that leaked out of Jill's mouth as she turned away from the mouse.

Dr. Arden ignored her. "Just as the nutrition pyramid is being revamped, so we scientists are rethinking our chemical pyramid and reordering it. MST is near the top of toxic drugs. It's so highly toxic that, in the right dose, just a scrape of it on the skin can cause death within minutes."

"Thanks to Jill, this murder will soon be solved, and maybe then we can start working our cancer research again," Tommy said with admiration.

Jill cut her eyes to Dr. Arden. The doctor did not look pleased. "If you two are going to bring your personal relationship into my lab, I'd really appreciate it if you'd step outside so I can get some work done," Dr. Arden said as she slammed the door to her office.

32

If you see a snake, just kill it—
don't appoint a committee on snakes.

Ross Perot

"I get the strong impression that woman doesn't like me much," Jill said to Tommy when they were alone.

"You think so?"

"Yes, I do. And she has a motive for the murder."

"Kelly Arden isn't involved," Tommy said quickly. Too quickly.

"You're hardly a neutral party."

"What's that supposed to mean?"

"It's obvious there's something more between you and Dr. Arden than business. It's quite apparent in her hostility toward me."

"I think she assumed something was going on between us."

"You both can wipe that notion right out of your heads."

"We only saw one another a few times socially. After working together late one night, Kelly invited me to dinner at her house."

"That's it?"

Tommy shook his head. "She wanted something more. Kelly was more interested in what my position could do for her career than this good old boy from Alabama. My money didn't hurt either."

"The way you carry on with women, I'm not surprised she thought you were interested in her."

"I'll forget you said that."

"You said yourself Kelly's attracted to power. If anyone has a motive for Brown's death, she does, since he was about to put an end to her great discovery."

Their conversation ended abruptly as they walked into the shipping and receiving department. The head of the department welcomed them and told them that all the employees were briefed to spend as much as time with them as needed. After everyone was interviewed, Jill meticulously went over the shipping logs and tracked all the orders for the live reptiles with a couple of the key employees. Nothing appeared suspicious or out of order, so around five o'clock they thanked everyone and left for the day.

On the ride back to the hotel, the conversation was strained between Jill and Tommy. The senator broke the silence when he reached over and playfully patted her knee and then grinned at her. "Look behind us, it's Curly and Moe."

"Oh, who are they?" Jill played ignorant but knew he was referring to the FBI agents tailing them.

"Your friends. Remember?"

"Good, I'm glad you know they're there. Maybe now you won't get any ideas about slipping any more snakes in my bed."

"I'm not even going to respond to that ridiculous accusation." Tommy looked hurt.

"You're one of the few people who had access to my room," Jill reminded him.

"Try to be nice for a few minutes longer. After we drop you off at the hotel, Ryan's driving me to the Pensacola Airport and you won't have to deal with me any longer. You won't mind continuing the interviews at Bio Tech alone?"

"Not at all."

"Ryan will stay here, so he can chauffeur you to Bio Tech every day."

"I don't need a chauffeur. I'll get my own rental car."

"Whatever makes you happy." Suddenly Tommy grabbed her hand and held onto it tightly. "Jill, please, no more fighting. We've only a few minutes before we have to say good-bye, and there are some things I must tell you."

Jill lifted her eyebrow.

He paused for a moment, and then he fumbled with both his hands and his words. "I, uh, I genuinely care about you, Jill . . . deeply care for you. When this is over, I was wondering if I might see you . . . on a personal basis?"

Jill jerked her hand away. "I've just told you I believe you tried to kill me, and you're asking me out?"

"And I've just told you how much I care for you, and that's all you have to say?" He gave her a little smile.

"Senator, this is neither the time nor the place. John's been gone for barely two months, and I'm still very much in love with him. I'm still grieving." She raised her voice. "But if I were ready for a relationship, you'd be the last person I'd go out with!"

"Someday you'll have to get on with your life, Jill. And when that time comes, I want you to consider one thing—God brought the two of us together for a purpose."

"And that purpose was solving this crime." She moved farther away from him.

The sleek limo pulled up at the hotel, and Tommy helped Jill out of the car.

"Take care of yourself. And I'll stay in close touch."

"Don't bother."

"While you're still in Mobile, I consider you my responsibility. If you haven't called me by seven o'clock each morning, I'll call you as a safety precaution."

"Fine."

The senator walked her into the hotel lobby. When he left, she stood in the lobby and watched him drive away in the limo. Jill didn't know what to make of the man. Had this womanizer reformed and now genuinely cared for her? Or was he simply pursuing her to draw her attention away from his guilt? Jill shivered. *Is he the murderer? Why did I ever let this man kiss me?*

Jill hurried to her room and kicked off her shoes. With Tommy gone, she looked forward to a peaceful evening. But not for long; after a few minutes, there was a knock at the door.

"Who is it?"

"FBI," Agent Masourian's voice answered.

"Coming."

Jimmy Allen, the younger agent, walked in first. "Are you all right, Ms. Lewis? Agent Tucker sent us to double-check on your safety."

"Good news. The senator's gone. Will you be leaving now?"

"Not until we're officially called off the case," Agent Masourian explained. "Meanwhile, Agent Tucker ordered us to install these additional devices in your room."

"Isn't that overkill? I'll be gone in a few days."

"Sorry, we've got our orders," Agent Masourian apologized.

"Oh, all right." Jill watched the men install the bugging devices.

"Agent Sally Weinstein is here too. Call us if you need anything, Ms. Lewis," Agent Masourian offered before leaving.

Satisfied, the agents returned to their rooms.

The listening devices were rather invasive, but she had to admit, it was kind of Tucker to take the extra precaution. All this extra attention had to be costing the bureau a lot of money, but he had made John a promise to look after her. Obviously, he was determined to keep that promise at all costs.

Jill thought this day would never end. Exhausted, she looked forward to a nice dinner followed by a hot shower and a good night's sleep. With Tommy gone, it should be a peaceful one. She ordered a filet mignon, a salad, and garlic mashed potatoes with a pitcher of sweet tea from room service, adding a chocolate mousse for dessert.

Jill instructed the waiter to leave the food outside her door. He slipped the check through a crack in the door. She signed it, and pushed it back to the waiter. A quick phone call brought Agent Weinstein from across the hall with Jill's tray of food in her arms.

"Bon appétit," Agent Weinstein said as she set the tray on the desk.

Jill thanked her as the agent left. Ready to eat, Jill plopped down on the bed and leaned back against the pillows, swinging her legs up on the bed. She clicked on the TV for the seven o'clock news. With the tray on her lap, she unfolded her napkin and pulled the stainless steel warmer off her steak. It moved! Her food began to rumble. This was no steak. Whatever it was, it was definitely alive.

Jumping up from the bed, Jill knocked over the tray. The food spilled out over her blanket. Jill watched as two snakes slithered around the steak through the potatoes and another reared its head out of the salad. Were there more? Both escaped the plate and slid off the bed.

Jill flew out of the room faster than the snakes could wiggle their forked tongues in her direction. Still screaming, she collided with all three agents with their guns drawn. A look down the barrel of three guns only increased Jill's hysteria. Breathlessly, she explained, "I pulled the warmer off my food, and there were snakes inside the food . . . under the food!"

Agent Allen stayed with Jill in the hallway while the other two agents went inside her room and returned with the vipers in a container.

"Are you sure there were only two?" Jill asked.

"Yes. You can stay in my room tonight. Abe and Jimmy will talk to hotel employees and to the waiter who brought the tray. We have some additional agents on site, and I'll radio them to come and check out your room."

The details attended to, Sally escorted Jill to her room. Jill sat in the agent's room at the edge of a chair, swinging her foot back and forth until Allen and Masourian returned an hour later.

"No one knew a thing about the snakes. We questioned the young man who brought the tray, and he swears he picked it up in the kitchen and didn't put it down until he left it at your door," Agent Masourian told the women.

Agent Allen said, "The vipers were likely slipped in your food in the kitchen. We just don't know when or by whom . . . yet."

Agent Masourian folded his arms. "You're going home to Washington tomorrow, Jill."

"But—"

"That's an order. I don't want to have to send you back in a box."

When Agents Allen and Masourian left, there was a knock on the door to Sally's room.

"Who is it?" Sally spoke against the door.

"Agent Tucker," came the deep voice from the other side of the door.

Sally opened the door, and Bill Tucker walked into the room. It was the first time Jill had seen Agent Tucker since he'd delivered the news of John's accident.

Jill hugged him. Bill was her connection to John, which made her feel protected and safe. For a few minues they shared with one another how much they missed John.

Bill finally got back to business. "My team will fly with you to Quantico. You'll stay there until we've made our arrest."

"Arrest of who?" Jill asked. "And when?"

"A matter of days. We have hard evidence directly implicating

Senator Harrison in Brown's death, and we'll be picking him up within hours."

The last remaining ounce of strength left her body. Jill sank down into a nearby chair. "So Tommy's guilty after all?" She had always suspected him, but in her heart she'd wanted to believe in his innocence. She was never more aware than now that she had developed feelings for this man. Jill felt sick to her stomach.

"Is he also responsible for Dan's accident and Ally Cooper's death?" Jill asked.

Bill put his hand on Jill's shoulder. "Yes. I've hesitated to tell you this, but when all this is over, we'll probably discover that Senator Harrison was responsible for John's death too."

33

*I'd much rather see a snake in the road
than a snake in the bushes I can't see.*

Old Southern saying

In her room Jill felt like a prisoner in need of a jailhouse break.
Her blood was stirring as she stewed over the news of Senator
Harrison's possible involvement.

She tried to watch TV, but nothing held her attention. The
Animal Planet station was having a special on snakes, but Sally
quickly snapped that off. Next Jill picked up a book to read, but
she couldn't finish a single page. To make matters worse, she was
hungry and craved a Diet Coke.

"Can you walk downstairs with me? I want something to eat,
and I don't want to order room service," she said to Sally.

She and Sally stood in front of the vending machines. She
was so hungry that everything looked good. Jill poked her coins
into the slot and selected a Diet Coke, a bag of chips, and a
Hershey's bar. While Sally was making her purchases, Jill walked
back into the lobby. As she rounded the corner, she thought
she saw a familiar figure outside the window. Looking more
closely, Jill recognized Tommy Harrison standing at a new model

Jaguar convertible with the top up in the hotel's circular motor lobby.

But it couldn't be. Hadn't she watched Tommy drive away this afternoon? Either he lied to her or else had to come back for something. Jill skirted behind palm trees to inch her way back to the main lobby of the hotel so she could get a better view of him. It appeared he was arguing intently with someone. But it was so dark that Jill couldn't make out who was behind the wheel.

The car door swung open, and to Jill's surprise Dr. Kelly Arden stepped out of the driver's seat. Jill gasped as the doctor flung her arms around Tommy and kissed him. After a few seconds Jill thought he pulled away, but then she saw him smooth her hair, pushing a lock of it out of her eyes. Kissing the doctor on the cheek, Tommy left her standing beside her car and walked back into the hotel.

So there was something between the scientist and the senator. Were they in this together, trying to kill her? Jill inched back into the hallway to make sure the senator didn't see her. He walked toward the front desk and asked for his room key. As soon as Tommy was gone, Sally returned with her fruit, and they went back to Jill's room.

At Jill's insistence, Sally helped her push a dresser in front of the door. Jill then went through Sally's room like a crazy woman, looking for snakes and crawly things before she allowed Sally to turn out the lights. When the women were finally in bed, Jill said, "Thanks for putting up with my paranoia, Sally."

"After all you've been through, Jill, you've earned it. I know you were engaged to Agent Lovell and I wanted—"

"How did you know that?"

"John told me. He was so excited about your proposal that he and Tucker told us all about the yacht and the dinner in great detail. You see, we're a small division, and Agent Tucker has worked hard to establish a great deal of camaraderie amongst his agents. We're like family."

"That's evident. Bill's a wonderful man, and I know John loved him like a brother."

"We all love Bill, and we loved John too. So I wanted you to know . . . I'm really sorry about your loss."

"Thanks," Jill replied, wiping the tears with the edge of her sheet. "Sounds like John's death was a big loss for everyone in your department too."

"You've got that right, but it's been hardest for Agent Tucker. The two men have worked together since John first joined the bureau. And Bill's become so protective of us since John's death, it's sometimes hard to do our jobs." She was quiet for a moment. "Well, anyway, I just wanted you to know how sorry I am."

"Thanks, Sally," Jill said quietly, knowing tonight would be another of tosses and turns.

Jill rose early to dress, careful not to wake Sally. Whatever was going on with Dr. Arden and Tommy, Jill had a hunch it was crucial to her investigation, so she was going to sneak over to Bio Tech to question Dr. Arden before she had to leave for Washington this afternoon. Scribbling a note to Sally with a promise to return by noon, Jill tiptoed out of the room.

As Jill passed the hotel restaurant, she did a double take when she saw the unmistakable profile of Tommy Harrison. Ducking into the gift shop, she hid behind a rack of magazines and watched as the senator left the restaurant with Ryan.

Ryan accompanied Tommy and placed what appeared to be a room key on the counter of the front desk. As they were walking out to their waiting limo, she saw him. It was undeniably Crew Cut. She gasped. So they knew each other after all!

Jill walked closer to the exit for a better look, all the while trying to keep out of their line of vision. Ryan loaded the suitcases as Crew Cut allowed Tommy into the backseat first. Then he slid in beside him and shut the door. She pushed on the hotel's side emergency door, and fortunately the alarm didn't go off.

She crossed the parking lot diagonally, keeping low behind the vehicles, without calling attention to herself.

Reaching the rented Honda, Jill slid into the driver's seat, started the engine, and smiled down at the full tank icon. Staring at the men across the front drive, she watched as they began to roll out from the front of the hotel and turn left onto the street. She followed them.

Jill had a thought. Yesterday he'd told her to call him every day before seven or he'd call her, so it would be perfectly normal for her to call him. He may not answer the phone, but at least it was worth a try. To her surprise he answered his cell phone right away.

"I'm assuming you have something to report," he said without saying hello.

"No, I'm just keeping my promise." She smiled at the glint of the limo three cars ahead. If he wanted to play games, she'd be his opponent. She powered up the AC and pulled the sun visor down to shade her eyes from the sizzling glare of the sun.

"I decided not to fly to Washington. Ryan and I are on our way back to Roanoke."

"But I thought you left yesterday?"

"I was detained."

Tommy accented the word *detained* as though he was trying to tell her something. Jill looked up at the interstate sign where they were turning. The car was heading south, not north to Roanoke. Odd.

Jill pressed the knob on the radio to drown out traffic noise. In an effort to trap him, she asked, "How about I go to Roanoke with you? We could ride horses over the weekend, and then I can catch a direct flight from Atlanta to Washington. What do you think?"

"I think you're coming on to me. But this time, you're too late. We're already about an hour down the road." He emphasized the word *road*.

"Only an hour? Can't you come back and get me?" Jill tried to trap him with his words.

"You're serious, aren't you? I told you we were an hour down the road." Again he emphasized the word *road*.

"Wasn't it you who said I should get on with my life? I think a weekend at your farm, riding horses, is a great way to begin."

"And just who are you more interested in spending your time with—my horse or me?"

"I guess you'll have to come get me to find that out, won't you?"

"Looks like you're too late. You're on your own, kid. Besides, it looks like rain anyway. You don't want to ride horses in the rain, do you?" He hung up.

Jill glanced out her window. The sky was blue and sunny, not a cloud anywhere. She looked around and noticed that they had pulled off on an isolated secondary road. To remain unseen here was trickier.

Up ahead was a dilapidated one-lane bridge, only a few feet above a swamp marsh, where alligators and water moccasins loafed in the summer sun. A few of the gators reared their grinning heads above the algae-green water. Jill slowly rolled across the bridge. So many little roads jutted out from the main road, it was impossible to guess which one the limo had traveled, so Jill drove straight. When the road ended abruptly at the bayou, she slammed on the brakes, stopping at the edge. With no time to catch her breath, she pulled the gear in reverse and backtracked down the road, this time more slowly. Then she saw it—a sign that read Rain Road. *It looks like rain. It looks like rain.* Did Tommy's clue mean he was the victim, not the bad guy? Or was he luring her here to kill her? It was time to call Bill Tucker.

"Agent Tucker." He answered after three rings.

"Thank God I've reached you," Jill said, holding back her tears. Since John had died, Bill had become her safe haven.

"Jill, where are you? I've got agents out looking for you everywhere. Why'd you leave the hotel?"

"I'm okay, but—"

"You may not be for long. We've just learned that Harrison didn't leave yesterday as he said. We were worried sick he might have you."

"That's what I'm trying to tell you," Jill said quickly. "I followed Crew Cut and Tommy from the hotel. We're on Rain Road, off the Bayou La Batre Highway. You've got to get out here, Bill, and bring lots of backup too."

"Whoa, slow down. I'll get somebody out there, but I want you to promise me that you'll turn your car around and get back to Mobile and to the hotel. These men are armed, and they'll think nothing of putting a bullet through your head. Are you listening to me?"

"No, you've got to listen to me. They have another man by the name of Ryan too."

"Who's Ryan?"

"Harrison's assistant."

"Okay." Bill sighed. "Tell me exactly where you are, and I'll get some men and a chopper out there."

Jill hurriedly gave Agent Tucker the directions.

"Keep your cell phone hot, so we can stay in touch until I get there."

"I'll call you as soon I get closer and can see what they're doing."

"Wait, Jill. If I can't convince you to come back to Mobile, at least stay in your car until I get there."

"I . . . I'll try. Good-bye."

Jill turned into Rain Road and drove until she came to a turnoff and parked near a swampy clump of trees. She hiked down the road, sticking close to the woods. After nearly ten minutes of walking, she happened upon a small compound, a large warehouse surrounded by three smaller buildings, each with short chimneystacks—a crystal meth lab. Hidden deep in the bayou, these crystal meth labs had become a big business in southern swamplands over the last decade. Jill had read of the daring attempts the ABI and FBI had made to raid these labs.

And Jill knew exactly what this lab was being used for—cooking MST. She reached for her cell phone again. Only two bars left, and this morning she'd rushed out of the hotel without her charger. Not good. At least she had enough juice to call Bill a few more times. Getting his voice mail, she talked fast.

"Bill, it's Jill again. I think I've just found the location of a bootleg MST lab."

She slipped her phone back into her pocket and snuck around the building. There, the limo was parked right next to a green Navigator, this one with Alabama plates. A door banged open, making her dive for a mass of trees. From her hiding spot, she watched Crew Cut walk from the old factory and drive off in the limo.

After waiting for Crew Cut to disappear from sight, she slipped out of hiding. First, she touched the hood of the Navigator. It was cold, so it hadn't been driven in a while. The windows were filthy, covered with insect remains and smeared with an oily residue, and it was impossible to see through the glass.

A back door to the lab was hanging halfway off, partially ripped off its hinges. Jill pushed it aside, scraping it hard across the black soil, and slipped inside.

Inside the large warehouse, light poured in from all the windows. Six feet overhead, a wooden platform extended around its perimeter. Jill paused when she heard a noise coming from above—tick, tick, tick—and looked up at the ceiling. The sight was sickening—a corpse hung from a metal rafter, dangling from a rope suspended over a large hole cut out in the oiled pine floor. Jill felt like she was going to be sick. And then, out of the corner of her eye, she thought she saw the man move. A second time, she was sure she saw a hand move, then a twist of the head. He was alive. She recognized the face. It was Tommy.

Rigged by a series of pulleys and a timing device that dropped him a few feet at a time, more if he struggled to set himself free, Tommy was strapped into some sort of torturing device. Slowly, Jill made her way onto the platform. It squeaked and swayed under the weight of her body. Jill willed herself to look down in the pit, which was swarming with Saw-Scaled Vipers. How many, she wasn't sure, because they were all slithering and twisting together.

With a calm, gentle voice, Jill whispered Tommy's name. His head moved to look at her as his body whizzed down a few more feet. "Don't come any closer. Get out of here," he called to her.

Jill heard the desperation in his voice. She had to help him get down, but to get him down, she had to crawl out on the rafters high above the snake pit. Even in the best of circumstances, Jill found heights disturbing. Mix that fear together with a pit of snakes, and she wasn't sure she could do it. If she could climb the ridges at the side of the building without losing her footing, she could scoot across the metal rafter from which Tommy was suspended and undo the one rope that acted as the lever. This might stabilize him from falling any further, at least until Bill arrived. The thought that Bill was on his way comforted her, and it might encourage Tommy too.

"Agent Tucker's on his way. If I can stabilize you until he gets here, I think you'll be fine."

No response.

Jill took a deep breath and began her slow ascent up the side of the ridged walls. It was slippery, but there always seemed to be piping or a cross metal bar that she could grab hold of when one of her feet lost footing. Breathing hard, she kept moving until she reached the metal rafter. So far, so good, but now the tricky part—transferring herself from the wall over to the rafter. To do that, she had to push herself off the ridge toward the beam. She swallowed hard, daring to look down at the writhing snakes.

With one final thrust of her back leg, she pushed herself up and was able to hold on to the roof beam. She hung there for a moment and then, face down, stretched out on the beam. *Don't look down.* Dizzy-headed, she closed her eyes. Sweat dripped down her face, and she swiped it away with her hand. It had to be at least 110 degrees in there. Hard to resist the urge to lie there and wait for help.

Wearily, she got back up on her hands and knees. This movement forced her phone from her pants pocket. She let out a little cry as she watched it fall down into the pit. The twisting snakes that covered the floor made it appear as if the floor was alive, waiting to swallow up its victim. When the phone landed, the angry snakes lunged from every direction, striking at their cellular attacker.

Inch by inch, she moved swiftly along toward the spot where Tommy hung suspended. As though he sensed her presence, his eyes fluttered opened again.

"Don't move," she commanded in a voice above a whisper.

Tommy gave her a pitiful wave.

Before moving again, she stopped to study the apparatus tied around him—a rope with a lift, similar to the ones she used in sailing. She knew exactly how it worked, but it was knotted and impossible to unfasten. She knew she had only one option, and that was to cut the rope off of him. All this way, and now she had nothing with which to cut it.

"Do you have your Swiss Army knife on you?" Jill asked.

Tommy slowed inched his hand down inside of his pocket. It was there in the palm of his hand. But how could she reach it?

"Wait, I have an idea." She reached over to the free hanging rope to grab it, and swung off the metal rafter, straddling the rope. Her weight caused the pulley to slip down a few more feet, but luckily Tommy was still far enough from the pit. She shimmied down the rope a few feet, forcing the apparatus to slip downward even more. Tommy raised his arm high in the air with his palm up, cradling the knife. Jill reached down and snatched the knife out of his hand.

Instead of swinging back over to the rafter and forcing Tommy and herself downward any more, she began to hack away at the rope attached to the pulley right where she was. In minutes the contraption fell off of Tommy and banged into the rafter. Both Jill and Tommy clung to the remaining rope as they swung wildly back and forth. Jill prayed the rope wouldn't come loose from the metal rafter and dump them both into the pit.

"Tommy!" she called out to him. "Can you grab the rope and climb up?"

"I think so," he said weakly. Grabbing ahold, he began his climb up to her. Reaching the beam, he flung his leg up and over, climbing onto it.

He clung to the beam a moment, breathing heavily. When he caught his breath, he said, "I've never been happier to see anyone. And that's no come-on." He hugged her and planted a kiss on her mouth. She didn't fight him; her lips met his and they kissed.

"Come on, let's get out of here," he mumbled. "How did you find me?"

"I was getting ready to leave for Bio Tech this morning when I saw you get in the limo with Ryan and Crew Cut. I watched you leave. By the way, thanks for the clue of rain on the road."

"Hurry. We'd better get out of here."

"Wait! Where's Ryan?"

"With Crew Cut."

"Oh no." Jill's eyes grew wide with fear. "Is he alive?"

His silence spoke far more than any words could.

"I'm sorry, Tommy. He was so young, with his whole life ahead of him."

"Oh, he's alive, Jill."

"What?"

"Ryan's a traitor."

Jill couldn't believe it. But there was no time to process that bit of information. They needed to get out of there as soon as possible. She slid along the same way she came, on her belly, but now she was going in the opposite direction. At the edge of the beam, again she had to find a way to get herself back onto the wall. She held on to the beam as she swung her feet until they hit one of the ridges. Slowly she let go and grabbed on to the wall. She made her way down the wall but lost her footing toward the bottom. She fell the rest of the way down and landed with a thunk.

"Are you all right?" Tommy asked.

Jill sat up and then slowly got to her feet. "Yeah, just got the wind knocked out of me. As long as I didn't land down there, I'm fine." She pointed to the snakes.

Now it was Tommy's turn to stretch the distance between the beam and the wall. Tommy managed to span the distance with ease and in a moment was standing next to Jill.

"I have a car parked up the road. Let's go!" Jill whispered.

They began their jog just as the limo returned, winding around the corner. They ran for at least a half mile before Jill waved him into a small grove of trees. "I've got to stop," Jill huffed, collapsing on the ground. He sat down beside her.

"We can't stop for long. We've got to get to the car before they discover I'm gone or you're here."

"Wait just a minute," Jill said as she caught her breath. "You and I need to clear some things up."

"Is this really the time?"

"I saw you with Dr. Arden last night."

"Kelly means nothing to me."

Jill rolled her eyes. "I don't care what she means to you. I just want you to stop lying to me."

"You can't still think I'm a part of all this."

"Just because they were going to kill you doesn't exonerate you in my eyes . . . You could've double-crossed them."

"Jill, don't be ridiculous."

"Let me finish. If you were a part of this, you had every opportunity to push me into that snake pit, but you didn't, so no, I don't believe you're involved."

"Have you ever considered that I didn't push you in that pit because I love you?"

"So you are involved."

"No! This is crazy! Let's just get out of here." He pulled her to her feet, and they began to run again. It was also hard going on the uneven ground. A few times one of them stumbled, and the other would step in to help them back up on their feet. Teamwork. Still yards from the road, they saw a glint of the limo slowly cruising down the road. They dove for the ground. But it was too late. Crew Cut and Ryan had spotted them. The doors to the car opened, and the men were on their feet running into the bayou after Jill and Tommy.

Jill felt weak, spent from exerting all her energy in the climb. It was hard keeping up with the pace on uneven ground and leaping over fallen trees overgrown with vines. Frequently, her feet got tangled up in creeping plants. Her knees kept buckling. Stopping to catch her breath, she turned around to Tommy, but he was no longer behind her. Where was he? She didn't see Ryan or Crew Cut either.

Jill collapsed on a fallen log, trying to get her sense of direction. She wanted to call out for Tommy but decided against it; she didn't want to alert the others to her location. Suddenly the sound of another type of car engine rumbled down the road. She wanted to see who it was but also wanted to keep far enough back in the swamp not to be seen. Bit by bit she walked toward the sound.

Jill prayed quietly for God to protect her as she ran through the bayou, sloshing through shallow streams and hopping over tree stumps, keeping her eyes peeled for any sign of Tommy. When she got close to the road, she got down on her belly and slid forward in the grass and mud. She tried to spit out the thick maze of gnats that flew around her face.

Through the trees, she saw that the car belonged not to an enemy but a friend, Bill Tucker. She felt so relieved that she began to shake. She ran to him, sobbing. He saw her too and got out of his car.

"Jill! Are you all right?"

"How'd you get here so fast?"

"I took a chopper to a nearby field and had this car waiting for me there. Let me look at you." He held her out and looked her up and down. "Thank God you're safe."

"Where are your men, the helicopters?" Jill asked.

"They'll be along shortly. I just had to get to you as soon as possible, so I came on ahead. Get in the car, Jill."

Jill obediently slid into the front seat next to Bill.

He started the car. "Ready?"

"No! First we have to find Senator Harrison. Bill, the senator's not a part of this. They tried to kill him, and he's hiding someplace in the woods. His driver Ryan and the man I call 'Crew Cut' have been after us."

"Jill, I know you want to believe in this man, but Senator Harrison is guilty, and I have the evidence to prove it to you. Trust me."

"No, you must be mistaken. The other men tried to kill him."

"He probably double-crossed them."

"I considered that, but I really don't think . . ."

Bill pulled a revolver from under his seat and set it between them. He backed out of the drive. Both of them scanned the woods for Tommy as they cruised down the road. Jill spotted him coming through the brush.

"There he is!" Jill leaped from the car and flagged down Tommy. He jogged up to her.

"Agent Tucker's here. We're going to make it out of here alive," she said, pulling him by the hand.

"Quick, both of you, get into the car," Tucker ordered.

Jill slid into the backseat with Tommy. Back in the car, they found themselves driving down the grassy road right up to the lab.

"Shouldn't we get out of here?" Jill said as she looked up to see Crew Cut and Ryan walking toward them. "Please, Bill, they're coming! Let's go!"

With his eyes on the two men approaching the car, Tucker reached for his gun and held it on them. "Just stay where you are."

Carefully, Bill put the car into park and got out. He jerked open the back door of the vehicle and pulled Jill out by her hair, while keeping the gun firmly aimed on Tommy.

"Ouch, you're hurting me!" Jill yelled to Bill. A breeze in the bayou stirred the scent of cologne past her nostrils. *Wait, I know that scent. It's familiar. And the last time I smelled it was in John's hotel room!*

Trying to pull away, Jill screamed, "It's you! You're the one . . . the one who tried to kill me in John's motel room."

Bill shoved her onto the ground. She looked up into the faces of Ryan and Crew Cut.

Crew Cut raised his boot, pressing his toe into Jill's abdomen to keep her where she was.

Tommy lunged from the car toward Crew Cut. "Get off her!" Bill smacked his gun barrel against Tommy's temple with such force that it broke the skin. A blast of blood shot from his head and then began splattering down his face. Bill threw Tommy down beside Jill on the ground.

"Dump them in the pit," Bill ordered.

34

The more hidden the venom, the more dangerous it is.

Marguerite de Valois

Jill glowered at Bill as she tripped down the road. "Why are you doing this?"

Bill smirked.

"And what's your part in this?" she asked Ryan.

"Just playing my role as the senator's trusted sidekick. You sure made my job easy, Jill. Because of you, I got Ally Cooper's file."

"I suppose you killed Ally too?"

"That was a joint effort. You should've seen her eyes when I crammed that viper down her throat."

Jill jumped at Ryan, but Bill yanked her back.

"Did John know about this?"

"The kid was brilliant. It didn't take him long to figure out the whole plan."

"So you had to kill him?" Tommy said.

"No, fate stepped in, and the viper did that for me. At least, after I tripped the guy who had the viper on the hook."

Jill turned to Bill. "So you killed John? Who you said was

like a brother to you?" Jill shook with anger. She broke loose and smashed Bill's nose. Ryan pulled her off as Bill grabbed a handkerchief from his pocket. He dabbed up the blood while shooting her dirty looks.

"Please let me shoot them both right here, boss," Crew Cut begged.

"No, their deaths have to look like an accident. When the rotting platform caves in, the snakes will finish them off." Turning back toward the couple, he added, "It will appear as if you're the victims of your own investigation."

Crew Cut stayed outside for a lookout as Bill held the door to the lab and the men pushed Jill and Tommy inside. Ryan dragged the pair to the platform. "You liked that viper in your bed so much, I've got more of those vipers for you in the pit." Ryan pushed her head down for a closer look, but Jill pressed her eyes tightly closed.

Tucker shoved Tommy onto the platform next to Jill. "Any last words? Want me to give Kelly Arden your love, Senator?"

"Leave Kelly out of this."

"You don't think I could've pulled this off without Kelly?" Jill watched Tommy's jaw tighten.

"I have one last question. Did you kill Senator Brown?" Jill asked.

"Listen to the little newsmonger," Ryan said. "Still trying to snag an interview when she's about to drop into the snake pit. Planning to text message your story in to the *Gazette*?"

"Brown's goal was to cripple Bio Tech, to pay off a political favor to Creation," Tucker explained. "But he got a whole lot more than he bargained for, and then he got . . . well, let's just say that the senator developed an irrational fear over our little business deal."

"Fear? I'd prefer to call it a conscience," Jill said.

Bill and Ryan loosened the brackets on the already loose platform.

"I don't suppose you called anyone else?" he asked in a whisper.

"No." Jill berated herself for not calling Abe and the other agents. Maybe they were in on this too? The love of money made people do strange things—even commit murder.

Quietly, she began to recite Psalm 23 and thought of her mother. What would this do to her? She smiled when she thought of Muv, grateful she'd recently spent time with her. Next, she thought of her sister, Kathy. Jill hadn't been as close to her sister as she would've liked. Other family members and friends came to mind. She felt a profound sadness that she wouldn't be around for her niece's fifth birthday. Her thoughts finally settled on John, and she felt more peaceful. He'd be waiting for her. And so would her father.

Jill glanced over at Tommy and wondered how he felt. Tommy caught her eye and moved closer to her. He put his arms around Jill. As he kissed her, she began to weep. "I'm scared. I don't want to die . . ." She spoke in jerky sobs. "There's so much more . . . I never even got to . . ."

Tommy took her hand and squeezed it. "Be brave. We can do this, Jill. Not by our strength, but with God's strength. Close your eyes. It won't take long. And I'll be with you. I won't let go of your hand," he promised as he squeezed her hand more tightly.

Crew Cut suddenly burst through the doors, startling all four of them. "The Feds—they're here. They're coming this way!" he hollered and then ran away.

Relief was short lived as Bill picked up a piece of cement, heavy enough to break the rotted floor. He dropped the cement onto the platform, but the force of it caused him to lose his balance. In his rush, he hadn't judged how far out he was on the platform. With a look of horror and surprise, he reached out his hand to Tommy and Jill, but they were too far away. Bill frantically grasped at the platform as he dropped near the pit. Jill screamed and covered her eyes. Then the platform creaked and groaned as it started to break away from the side of the building and pitch toward the center of the space.

"Get out! Get out, Jill!" Tommy yelled at her as he let go of her hand. Jill opened her eyes and darted for a nearby window, where she climbed onto the ledge. She didn't see Tommy. Trembling, she spotted him near the edge of the pit. Why was he going after Tucker?

"No, Tommy, please, no! What are you doing?"

"I can't leave him down there to die!" Tommy yelled back at her.

"But you'll be killed yourself. Please don't go down there. Wait for the authorities."

"He'll be dead by then."

"Ryan, toss your gun down here," Tommy ordered as though Ryan were still his trusted employee.

Ryan reached for his gun, then stopped. "Wait! I can fire up the carbon dioxide gas. They use it to sedate the snakes prior to milking the venom."

Tommy hung a few feet above the snakes while Jill watched as Ryan opened a cabinet and pulled out a large canister with an attached hose. In less than a minute he cranked it up, and the gas began to blow. The platform creaked and swayed again. The gas flowed into the pit, magically mesmerizing the angry snakes. Tommy finished his drop into the pit out of Jill's sight.

The ledge she stood on began to sway. Quickly Jill hit her foot against the windowpane, hoping to break it. It took her three tries, and then the window was gone. Carefully pushing through the rotted frame, Jill jumped onto the grass. By now an army of FBI agents had arrived.

A doctor guided Jill to a gurney to check her vital signs, followed by a quick exam of her injuries. Then someone draped a blanket over her shoulders.

"Doctor, do you know . . . did the senator make it out of the building?" Jill asked.

"I'm not sure, Ms. Lewis. We'll find out for you." In a moment the doctor reported back, "Everybody's out, Ms. Lewis."

An army of FBI agents was closing in on the area, and helicopters were flying overhead. Jill finally spotted Tommy surrounded by an emergency medical team and watched as paramedics loaded someone onto a stretcher. Soon the ambulance zoomed away from the scene. Jill secretly hoped Bill Tucker was dead. She hated him for killing John.

Smiling, Tommy saw Jill and walked toward her. She jumped to her feet and ran into his arms.

"You thought I was nuts for going down after Tucker?"

"No, I thought you were brave. Did you get Tucker out alive? And did the FBI find Ryan and Crew Cut?"

"Whoa, slow down. The FBI has the ball now. They gave Tucker antivenin. He was on the verge of death when I carried him out of there. To my knowledge they haven't found Ryan or Crew Cut, but those helicopters will find them even in this bayou."

Jill shuddered.

Tommy put his arm around her. "Before the FBI comes for us, there are some things I have to say to you, Jill, starting with I love you." He lifted her chin and kissed her.

Jill knew Tommy was waiting for her to return those three little but powerful words, but she said nothing.

Her silence didn't hinder Tommy's declaration of love. "I want a lifetime with you, Jill. I want to be the reason for your happiness. Marry me."

"Marry you?" She thought love was a bit premature, but marriage? "Tommy, I . . ."

"I'm sorry. It's just that after all we've been through, life just seems so precious at the moment, and I don't want to spend even a second of it without you."

She pressed her hand against his cheek. "I do care for you, Tommy, but I need more time. After all that I've gone through these past few months, I've got to get my head on straight."

"Take all the time you need, but I know that we're destined to spend our lives together."

Jill saw a few FBI agents headed their way. "Uh-oh, looks like we've got company."

"Miss Lewis," an agent on the scene called out to her, "there's an agent who wants to speak with you."

"Okay. Where is he?"

"He's the special agent who masterminded this operation. His helicopter is landing now."

"Whoever he is, we owe him our lives," Jill said to Tommy. Filled with curiosity, she watched the helicopter set down. A form got out, and she strained to see his face. The manner of his movements seemed familiar to Jill. Holding on to Tommy's hand, Jill stepped closer as the agent ran across the field toward them.

At the moment she saw his face, she dropped Tommy's hand. First she moved slowly, not believing what she saw, and then she ran. He was running to meet her too. At last, they were face to face, close enough for Jill to throw her arms around him. She felt her body lift up in the air as he twirled her around in his arms, blotting her tears with kisses.

"John! I can't believe it! They told me you were dead. Or am I dead now too?"

John spoke in her ear above the roar of the chopper blades. "We're alive, Jill, and I'm here."

She touched every inch of his face to make sure it was true, that he was really there, and he was alive. "You're alive."

"Didn't I tell you I'll always come back to you?"

35

I have a theory that every time you make an important choice, the part of you left behind continues the other life you could have had.

Jeanette Winterson

Night after night Jill had cried for John. All these weeks he had allowed her to believe he was dead. Now he had returned to her, causing her heart to flip-flop between joy and fury. Combined with her near death in the viper pit, it was more than Jill could comprehend. And to make her life even more complicated, in less than an hour she would have to sit in a room across the table from both of the men who had taken up residence in her heart. Angrily, Jill rummaged through her purse for lipstick and suddenly spotted the plastic ring hidden in a side pocket. Her mood quickly changed. Feeling nostalgic, she slid the funny ring on her finger and closed her eyes, remembering the night John had proposed to her. The memories washed away her anger as she remembered how it was before she'd developed feelings for Tommy Harrison. But even though John had returned from the dead, Jill couldn't push the attraction she felt for Tommy out of her heart.

When Jill arrived at the FBI building, she saw John pacing

back and forth in the lobby, waiting for her. He appeared as nervous as she felt. She walked over to him and gave him a hug. "Good morning."

Instead of his usual smile, John hesitated before kissing Jill. "I've missed you, Jill," he whispered.

Jill pulled away. "Not here."

"I . . ." He stopped short and looked away.

"What?"

"Nothing."

"Well, I have a question for you. I found Harrison's phone numbers inside the candy wrapper in your motel suite in Miami and . . ."

Loosening up a bit, he half smiled. "But I guess you just weren't in the mood for ice cream that night, huh?"

"Me, pass up a spoonful of Ben and Jerry's? No way."

"Glad to hear your radar for chocolate is still intact. I knew it was a long shot that you'd figure out what I was trying to tell you."

"I knew exactly what you were telling me—to give the numbers under the lid to Senator Harrison. But neither he nor I, or even the super-sleuth Rubric, could connect the owners of the pet shop in Killeen, Texas, to the investigation. Was there someone—"

"What pet shop?"

"Wasn't it the phone number for a pet shop?"

"Oh no," John said as he slapped the palm of his hand against his forehead. "I guess I was in such a hurry that I failed to notice my numerical clue had the same number of digits as a telephone number. Those numbers were supposed to spell out 'Bill Tucker' on the keypad of a phone."

"I'm so sorry. We should've figured that out. How did the FBI finally discover that Tucker was the bad guy?"

"Luckily, the nurse in the ER at the trauma center took my hysterical pleas seriously and got the message to the FBI director for me." Suddenly John frowned when he noticed Jill's engagement ring was missing. He grabbed her left hand. "Did they take your ring?"

"Can't blame that one on the bad guys. Your father asked me for it."

"What? That makes no sense."

"It makes perfect sense to me. It's a family heirloom. Of course he'd want it back."

"Not to me. Dad knew I was coming back soon."

"What? Your dad knew? You told your father you weren't dead, and not me?"

"I didn't; the FBI did. He's my next of kin and—"

"And what am I to you? You say you love me, but you've allowed me to suffer, to believe you were dead all this time? It's obvious you don't trust me, do you, John?"

John reached for her arm. "Of course I trust you, but the FBI felt that because you're a reporter—"

Jill stepped back. "Get away from me."

"I'm sorry, I'll get your ring back for you right away."

"If you think I'm upset that your dad took the ring away from me, don't bother."

"Of course, I'll bother. We're engaged, remember?"

Jill was quiet for a moment. "The situation you walked out of isn't the same one you've walked back in to."

John looked at her intently with a small frown rippling his brow. "What's that supposed to mean?"

"It means I thought you were dead and . . ."

"But Jill, that was the only way the FBI could protect me. To stage my death and transport me to Quantico."

"Look, that was never an issue. What I don't understand is how you could have done this to me?" Jill couldn't keep the aggravation out of her voice. "A simple phone call or a note that you were alive would've sufficed. But no, you let me believe that you were dead. I mean, just put yourself in my place." Jill turned to walk away.

"Don't walk away from me, Jill." John blocked her way to the conference room. He took her by the hand into a small office off the hallway. "We have to talk about this. You know I didn't have a choice."

"Oh, you had a choice. You just made the wrong one," Jill snapped.

John barked back at her. "Then tell me, Jill, how do you explain your choices? Imagine how I felt when I stepped out of that helicopter yesterday and saw my fiancée in the arms of Senator Harrison—Washington's most infamous womanizer?"

"I was no longer your fiancée. You were dead, remember?"

"Well, you sure didn't waste any time after you thought I died, did you? Can you imagine how humiliating it was for me to see the woman I love, my fiancée, with another man in front of all my colleagues?"

"Oh, so this is all about appearances and your humiliation? Do you have any idea how much I suffered these past few months?"

"Well, you didn't look like you were suffering too much with Harrison by your side."

"Don't you dare judge me! And don't insult Tommy Harrison either. At least he stuck around to protect me while you played dead."

"This isn't about Tommy Harrison."

"Then what is it, John?"

"You! That you couldn't go without a man for a couple of stinking months. What a fickle woman you've turned out to be."

"How dare you, John Lovell!" She walked past him into the conference room, slamming the door in his face.

Red-faced and trembling, Jill strained to regain her composure and appear professional as she stepped into a roomful of agents. About to take a random seat, she spotted Tommy at the opposite end of the table.

He stood to his feet when he saw her and rushed over to her side with a barrage of questions. "Are you okay? Did you sleep well? How do you feel today?"

Batting tears with her lashes, she mumbled, "I've been better."

He gave her his monogrammed handkerchief. But before she could dab her eyes, the director of the FBI strode into the conference room, followed by a contingency of more agents, all except John.

Jill took her seat, and Tommy walked back to the opposite end of the conference table to take his seat.

Welcoming everyone, the director thanked the appropriate people. When John slipped through a side door, the director said, "Here he is. Come on in, John. Everyone, let's give Agent Lovell a hand."

Jill stood to her feet with the rest of them and clapped but refused to look in John's direction.

"Thank you, sir, and a special thanks to each of you for the exceptional work. This investigation has concluded much sooner than we ever thought possible."

Agent Masourian spoke first. "John, on behalf of our entire division, I'd like to express our deepest gratitude to you. We're indebted to you for your bravery and honor."

"Thank you," John replied. "I'd like to give everyone an update. Thanks to Senator Harrison, Bill Tucker survived multiple snakebites."

Tommy acknowledged the applause.

Without any emotion, John continued in a monotone. "The antivenin was administered to Agent Tucker at the location. Once stabilized, he was transported by helicopter to the naval hospital in Pensacola, where he's listed in critical condition. The doctors have confirmed Tucker will survive with only minor long-term effects from the snakebites. Once he's off the critical list, he'll be transported to Allentown, Pennsylvania, where he will be incarcerated without bail, awaiting his trial at the federal maximum security prison there. Accomplices John Corsini, a.k.a. Crew Cut, and Ryan Stiles were apprehended last night just before midnight. They're being held without bail at the Federal Transfer Center in Montgomery, Alabama, awaiting extradition to Washington for the murder of Senator George Brown and Allison Cooper. Dr. Kelly Arden is being held here in Mobile at an undisclosed location while she is undergoing extensive questioning. Before we proceed, are there any questions?"

"We're all in a state of shock over the news of Bill Tucker's betrayal. When did you realize he was a traitor?" Agent Masourian asked.

"I became suspicious over a few of his actions and comments, but Tucker was my boss and my mentor, so I dismissed these misgivings until the night before the attempt on my life. When I overheard Tucker tell someone on the phone that Jill Lewis was getting too close to the truth and had to be dealt with right away."

Hearing this for the first time, Jill turned her head toward John. He met her stare.

"When did Tucker first become involved with MST?" Agent Jimmy Allen asked.

"Our division was assigned to supervise the closure of the MST Phase I clinical trials. The assistant agent in charge of the operation, Agent Masourian, was assigned to spearhead the Bio Tech operations."

Masourian explained, "I was detained on a previous assignment, so Tucker agreed to sub for me at Bio Tech. When I was free, he insisted that he was too far along on the investigation and assigned me to a lesser role in the operation. Maybe I should've—"

"Don't beat yourself up, Abe. Bill's logic was perfectly reasonable, and there was no reason to question it," the FBI director assured him.

John continued, "Now that we've established the 'when,' I'll explain the 'why' and then the 'how.' When Tucker met Dr. Kelly Arden, the scientist who spearheaded the development of MST, she touted the miracle drug as a cure to all cancer. In Tucker, she found the perfect crusader for MST. Most of you know that he and his wife, Lynda, lost their four-year-old daughter to cancer a few years ago."

Jill winced. She didn't know the Tuckers had lost a child. But having worked a few cases where a parent snapped after the death of the child, she shared her thoughts with the group. "Most parents spend a lifetime searching for ways to justify their child's death or to escape the guilt that they feel over not having the power to prevent it. This explains Tucker's devotion to Dr. Arden with her cancer cure."

"Good point, Jill. What do you guys and girls say we hire Jill for the Bureau?" the director teased.

The laughter in the room seemed to relieve everyone's tension. Even John's attitude toward her seemed to soften as he gave her a friendly nod. "That's part of the motive, but there's even more. Dr. Arden told Tucker that she suspected whoever intervened to halt the MST trial had an ulterior motive. Since Homeland Security works closely with the FDA's bioterrorism and counterterrorism drugs, Tucker had full access to their headquarters and discovered Senator George Brown was the individual who initiated the closure of the MST clinical trials. Surprisingly, Tucker agreed with the senator's reasons to shut down the trials and encouraged Dr. Arden to forget MST, at least until the memories of recent terrorist attacks faded."

"Did the reports refer to the participants who died as a result of the MST trials?" Jill asked.

"There's a mention in the report, and Tucker sure used that information to murder Senator Brown, so his death would be deemed as a stroke, but this was not an issue for the FDA. Jill probably knows this one, but many of you may not know. The

Phase I of the MST clinical trial was blinded, which means no one but the pharmaceutical company knew the final results. The participants in the Phase I clinical trial died of a stroke. So I figured there was a high probability that Senator Brown was murdered with MST."

"If so many people died in the clinical trial, didn't you and Dr. Arden ever question that this may have been the real reason the FDA halted the MST trials?" Agent Allen asked Tommy.

"Dr. Arden explained that the real challenge of the Phase I trial is adjusting the dosage from laboratory rats to human beings. MST proved to be one of those drug experiments where the chemical reaction in human beings was different than what had been exhibited in the laboratory rats. Phase I clinical trials for cancer treatment are highly experimental, and the participants are always terminal. Usually they have less than six months to live. The FDA guidelines are far less stringent for these drugs used on terminal patients."

"You're saying the more terminal the participants, the more risks you're allowed to take?" Agent Allen asked.

Tommy answered. "I'm sure Senator Brown used this to show how lethal the venom was, but the reason the FDA halted MST was Brown's argument that it was a security risk. Dr. Arden immediately brought me the information about Brown and asked me to confront him, but without the identity of her informant, which she was understandably not willing to give, I explained that I couldn't confront the senator. We knew Brown wasn't really fearful of MST as a security threat, and we were eager to discover his motive, so I promised her I would look into the matter. When I reviewed a list of Brown's campaign contributions, I discovered Creation Pharmaceutical was his number one contributor. It was also the company that stood to lose millions as soon as Bio Tech's similar vascular targeting drug went on the market. I knew we had Brown then."

"So why didn't you come to the FBI immediately?" John glared at Tommy.

"In retrospect, I wish I had, but at the time, I was concerned the FBI would consider my ties with Bio Tech a conflict of interest and wouldn't take my accusations seriously. Besides, Dr. Arden assured me that her informant was in a position to file a report with the FBI. She was very excited believing this report would expose Brown and she would get her MST back into the drug trials. And she was correct, but then she cooked up what she deemed 'a better plan,' which we will get to later on in the debriefing."

"So we've got Brown's motive, and we have a partial motive for Tucker," John said. "Once Senator Harrison passed on his findings to Dr. Arden, she went back to Tucker with the information, and he was in the process of preparing a pre-report to open an investigation. In the meantime, Dr. Arden was preying on the emotions of grief he had for the young daughter he lost to cancer. Hoping to persuade him to black-market her wonder drug, she used her guile to seduce him. This comes as a shock to all of us who knew Tucker as a strong family man of the highest integrity, but the good Dr. Arden was a temptress, and Tucker succumbed to having an affair with her."

Shock and surprise filled the conference room with chatter among the agents around the table.

"Okay, let's move on," John said. "After she garnered his undying devotion and love, Dr. Arden was successful in her attempt to interest Tucker in the black market of the drug. He was easily able to retrace his paper trial and destroy all copies of his report to file charges, except for one that had been misplaced at the offices of the Department of U. S. Fish and Wildlife."

Jill gasped. "The file that cost Ally Cooper her life!"

John nodded. "With the exception of that one file, everything else was falling into place beautifully. Instead of disposing of the vipers at Bio Tech, Agent Tucker arranged to have the vipers transported to an old crystal meth lab he had raided a couple of years ago. So there the vipers awaited the start-up of his black market."

"And we all know the rest of the story. Except why Tucker killed Brown. Anyone care to speculate?" the director asked.

Everyone exchanged quizzical glances, appearing to have no clue. They waited for John to explain. "Although Brown refused to speak to Ally Cooper, one of his assistants briefed him on her many phone calls. His assistant dismissed them as a prank or a crazy person, but Brown knew they were for real. So he got her messages and feared he was about to be caught, so he contacted Agent Tucker to confess his crime and ask for a plea bargain. Oh, and Jill, we now know why the senator wanted to see you the day of his death. He wanted you to print the confession in the *Gazette*. Too bad he reached Agent Tucker before he met with you.

"Tucker went to see Brown right away with the intent to murder him. Now that his black market was well underway, he didn't want anything about Bio Tech or MST in the national media, so he had one of his thugs inject the senator with MST, believing it would mask his death as a stroke, a natural cause with no questions asked."

As John wrapped up the debriefing, the director stood to his feet and thanked everyone again. "I'm sure there will be plenty of questions in the weeks to come, but this gives you a brief synopsis of the crime."

As everyone filed out of the conference room, Tommy lingered to speak to Jill until John sat down beside her.

"May I speak with you for a moment?" John asked.

"Sure," Jill said tentatively as her eyes followed Tommy leaving the room. She turned her attention to John. "Congratulations, you did a great job."

"Thanks. I'm flying back to Washington this afternoon. How about you?"

"I don't know. I've got a big story to write, but beyond that, I haven't made any plans yet."

John stood up from the table. "Will you let me know when you get back?"

"Sure. Have a safe trip."

"That's all you have to say?" he asked her with a look of anguish on his face.

Jill didn't respond.

He sighed and turned around to walk out of the conference room.

Needing time to clear her head, Jill felt relieved to have John walking out of her life temporarily. *Or is it forever?*

36

No stair is too steep for happy feet!
Mary F. Robinson

Jill's sensational headlines appeared in almost every newspaper in the country, and her face appeared on all the networks and news channels.

Two weeks after the story broke, Rubric barged into Jill's office while she was stuffing dozens of unanswered phone messages from John, a couple from Tommy, and even a few from ex-boyfriend, David, into her trash can.

"Cleaning out your desk?" Rubric asked.

"No, just cleaning out my life," Jill announced as she ripped a few more messages to shreds and tossed them.

"What's next on your agenda?" he asked, squirming in his seat. "And tell Pearl, the next time she decorates your office, if she doesn't put some decent chairs in here, I'm going to hire myself another reporter, one with a couch potato décor."

"But everyone loves these chairs. They're antiques, and that silk fabric on them is Scalamandré. How dare you insult my chairs or my mother?"

"Scalawag, huh? So that explains it. Are you going to take any vacation time?"

Jill shrugged. "I don't know. Maybe. But first I hope to rid myself of the snakes in my dreams and in my personal life before I take a vacation."

"What? Now that the FBI has raised Prince John from the dead, I thought you'd be jumping the next white horse out of here for the land of happily ever after."

Jill put her hand on her hip. "They may have dug John up from the grave, but the man's got embalming fluid flowing through his veins."

"Ouch! I got a call from Prince John today. He asked me to persuade you to call him."

"You stay out of this."

"Why don't you just call him?"

"I will, eventually."

"Can you be a bit more specific?"

"In a couple of centuries, if he's lucky," Jill said, slamming her empty drawer.

"Looks like you need to hurry home and get a double dose of your mother's old-time religion."

Landry at the front desk buzzed in. "Jill, I've got the Pied Piper on the line. Do you want to take it?"

Jill couldn't hide her excitement from Rubric. "Another headliner?"

"Answer it." Rubric leaned forward.

Jill punched the button on the speakerphone. "What's in the Pipe-line today?"

The Pied Piper teased her. "A dead body? Or is a senator ready to unburden his soul? Best of all, is it a scorned wife seeking revenge? Take your pick."

"I'm there. Tell me when and where." Jill grabbed a pen and pad.

"Six o'clock tonight. The top of the Washington Monument."

"But it closes at 5:45—it's off limits at night. Do I have time to make it?" Jill glanced at her watch.

"Don't worry about it. I've got friends in high places."

"I smell money."

The Piper chuckled. "I'm feeling generous today. How about five hundred bucks?" The phone clicked.

Jill shut off the speakerphone. "An uncharacteristically low price for the Piper, don't you think?"

"Somebody's paid him generously to get you there. Are you up to it, kid?"

"You must be joking," Jill said, already gathering her things together.

"Then I'll get your money. Meet you in the lobby in five."

Jill arrived at the monument a few minutes after six. She handed the taxi driver a fifty. "Please wait for me."

Jill climbed the stairs two steps at a time until she reached the front entrance of the Washington Monument, where two security guards with arms folded blocked the entrance to the elevator. This didn't look good.

"Hi, I'm Jill Lewis from the *Washington Gazette*, and I'm supposed to meet someone at the top. Were you expecting me?"

Both security guards smiled at her. The younger one nodded and said, "The elevator's closed, but we'll let you walk up the steps. Can you make it in those shoes, or would you like for me to hold them for you?"

Jill looked down at her four-inch Jimmy Choo heels and then up at the soaring monument. Her eyes widened. The Piper had never given a cell number, so there was no way she could ring him to come down.

"You're young, and you look like you're in good shape to me, ma'am. Whaddaya think, Wayne? Think she can make it?"

"Sure, she ought to make it up to the top by about eight o'clock."

"Uh, thanks for the vote of confidence," Jill mumbled.

The older guard smiled, revealing a gold tooth. "Don't pay any attention to us. We're just having some fun." To Jill's relief the older guard turned around and unlocked the security gate to the elevator.

"Have a nice trip," he said.

The elevator shot up so fast, Jill felt woozy. When the doors parted she staggered out on the observation deck to look around. And there in front of her stood Tommy Harrison holding a bouquet of the prettiest yellow roses she'd ever seen.

Smiling, he presented the bouquet to her. "Hello, Jill. I hope you're not mad at me for getting you up here under false pretenses?"

Speechless, she took the roses from his outstretched hand.

"The florist told me that yellow roses mean friendship. I hope we're still friends."

Jill had never seen Tommy look so uncomfortable, so unsure of himself.

"I see a red rose in here too. Did she tell you what that means?"

"I love you."

"What?"

"A red rose means I love you."

"Oh." She drew in a deep breath. "Tommy, I'm so . . . so sorry. I know I've hurt you. You've done nothing to deserve this, and I feel terrible. You're such a wonderful guy and . . ."

"It's not your fault. This has to be as difficult for you as it is for me."

"I'm glad someone understands my predicament." She could feel tears welling in her eyes.

Tommy took the roses from her and set them down by the elevator. "It's too bad we don't live back in the old West so John and I could settle this with a duel, once and for all."

Jill's tears spilled over into a giggle. Tommy understood, even made her laugh in the worst of circumstances. But John, he expected to walk back into her life and take up where they left off, just like nothing had happened.

Tommy leaned over and kissed her. When he pulled back he said, "I know you're blessed with an overabundance of marriage proposals, but marry me, Jill."

"Tommy, you know I can't . . ."

"No pressure. I don't need an answer now. I only asked you here today to see how you were, and to tell you that in spite of all that's happened, the proposal I made in the bayou . . . it still stands. There's no expiration date on it either. Think it over, will you?" Tommy asked as he pressed the elevator button.

He carried the roses for her as they rode to the bottom of the monument together. Tommy helped her inside her waiting cab.

"Good-bye, Jill." Without giving her another kiss, he walked away. But he stopped for a moment, turned around, and said to her, "I'll be waiting."

It is often hard to bear the tears that we ourselves have caused.
Marcel Proust

A month later, Jill was at home with her mother and grandmother. The day after Jill arrived, Pearl rose early to cut flowers from her garden while the air was cool. Jill watched her mother arrange the homegrown blooms inside of a cut-glass basket. Finally, it was just right, down to the last detail with the feathery Queen Anne's lace looming over the primrose, orange lilies, larkspur, and iris. Minutes after Pearl went upstairs to change out of her gardening clothes, Jill watched Muv follow right behind her mother. One by one, she pulled the flowers from the vase, rearranging them in a French cobalt blue pitcher edged in gold. In minutes, Muv's bouquet replaced Pearl's on the breakfast room table.

Shortly, Pearl returned to the kitchen to prepare breakfast. Muv and Jill gathered around the table, where Pearl served them heaping bowls of oatmeal, fruit, and nuts. Linen covered a basket of English muffins, and nearby was a silver butter dish and a crystal jam jar. Jill poured orange juice as Pearl crisscrossed her, filling coffee cups. The women gathered around the table and held hands while Muv blessed the food. When Pearl opened her eyes, she noticed that a different arrangement was on the table. "What happened to my bouquet?"

"I rearranged it a bit," Muv confessed. "Don't you think it's more festive this way? And where did you get this exquisite French pitcher? It's so much prettier than that plain old basket. Don't you agree?"

Clearly displeased with Muv's interference, Pearl said, "It's lovely, Mother. But when I picked those flowers from the garden this morning, I had a vision for my arrangement."

"Well, your vision was a bit lopsided, and there were too many flowers in that tiny vase." Muv bit her English muffin. "This is delicious. Did you make these strawberry preserves, dear?"

"Do you like them?"

"Mm, I sure do, but they're a tad too sweet."

"I tried your recipe, Mother. Next time, I'll use mine."

"Okay, ladies. Time-out," Jill ordered. "We've got more important things to think about this morning. Like what we're going to give John at his party tonight? Any suggestions?"

"I think you should give him a pair of your father's gold cuff links," Muv suggested.

Pearl agreed. "That's a lovely idea, especially since John and your father became friends on the Burke investigation."

"Well, I'm glad you two can agree on something, and since I agree, where do you keep Dad's jewelry?"

"In the safe in my closet. If you'll clean up the breakfast dishes, I'll get the cuff links and let you choose a pair for John."

"Now, that's settled. But what shall we get him, Pearl?" Muv asked her daughter.

"A check."

"But that's so impersonal, darling. At least buy him a gift certificate."

"Well, with a check, he can buy whatever he wants."

"You give him a check, but Jill, will you drive me to the bookstore so I can buy him a book?"

"Right after I clean up the kitchen. Good choice, Muv. John loves books."

"I've got a better idea. Let's leave a bit earlier, and stop on our way to the Firkin," Pearl suggested.

Her mother and daughter both agreed.

Later that day Jill bounced down the stairs and held up a beautifully wrapped package to Pearl. "The cuff links. John will love them." Jill found a small bag in the pantry and dropped John's present in it.

"Leave it on the counter beside my purse, so you won't forget it."

Jill did as Pearl told her. On the way back to her room, she saw Muv in the upstairs hallway and complimented her. "Don't you look nice."

"Thank you, darling. May I see you for a moment?"

"Come on in my room, but watch your step so you won't trip over one of the bags. I haven't finished unpacking my things yet."

"Good heavens!" Muv frowned as she looked around the room at Jill's things spread out everywhere. "Well, come sit down, I have a little gift for you." Muv sat down on Jill's bed and patted the spot beside her. Jill took a seat. Muv handed her a package wrapped in Florentine paper tied with gold ribbon.

"For me? How sweet."

"Go on, open it."

Jill removed the wrapping and then opened the lid of the velvet box. Inside was a pair of vintage pearl and diamond earrings. "These are exquisite. I love them." Jill went to the mirror and tried them on. "Were these yours?"

"I wore them the day I married your grandfather, sixty years ago this fall. And my mother before me wore them on her wedding day, and so did your mother. I want you to wear them on yours."

"If I wait for my wedding day, I may never get to wear them. May I wear them tonight?"

"Of course. But with two fine young men in love with you, I'm predicting you'll set a wedding date soon."

"Not if I can't make up my mind who to marry. Besides, Muv, times have changed. A woman no longer needs a man to be fulfilled. She can find contentment in her faith, her work, her interests, and her family and friends. Marriage isn't for everyone, and I'm not so sure it's God's plan for me."

"Who are you trying to convince? God saw our need for a partner; he designed marriage for that purpose."

"In my life, I think he intervened to keep me from making a mistake. A part of me has always believed that his purpose for me in this life is to 'reveal the darkness to the light.'"

"That's very admirable, dear, but who says you can't have a husband and a family along with your career? There are plenty of young women who have it all."

"I know many of them too. And most of them only appear to have it all. Somewhere along the way, they seem to have lost themselves. But never mind about that; how can I even think of marriage when one day I'm madly in love with John, and the next day it's Tommy?"

"One day your heart will tell you who you love, and you won't just walk down that aisle, you'll run to meet the one you love, Jill."

"It all sounds so romantic, Muv, but I'm not ready, and I've come to realize that I may never be."

"Well, then, I can see you aren't ready. These young men will just have to wait until your heart speaks to you. If either one has a problem with it, send him to see me. And don't you dare let your mother pressure you either. Just because Pearl's bought her mother-of-the-bride dress, doesn't mean she can't return it or hang it in the back of the closet . . . if there's room. I've never known a woman with as many clothes as your mother." Muv checked the time on her wristwatch. "Excuse me," she said and hurried off to her room.

Half an hour later, all three women, dressed in pink, arrived in the kitchen simultaneously.

"We look like three bottles of Pepto Bismol," Jill quipped. Jill wore a sundress with a sheer organdy blouse over it. Muv was dressed in a prim linen suit piped in white, and Pearl looked svelte in her pantsuit.

In downtown Delavan, Pearl, Jill, and Muv went into the bookstore to buy a book for John.

Two hours of pleasant chatter later, Jill, Pearl, and Muv breezed through the colorful beaded curtains hung in the Firkin's doorway. The women oohed and aahed as they surveyed the tasteful décor of the restaurant. The place was crammed with a mixture of eclectic antiques and vintage prints, and the beamed ceiling in the main dining room was draped in twinkling lights that cast a night-sky glow over the restaurant. The women stopped at the bar covered with layers of wonderful food just for the choosing. While Muv and Pearl sampled the seared scallops with lobster mayo and caviar, Jill looked around for a familiar face but didn't recognize a soul. Then she heard a familiar voice behind her.

"Hey, you. I wasn't sure you'd make it. You look great. How are you?"

John didn't kiss her, but she had been terribly prickly lately, so she assumed he was probably too afraid to touch her. Admittedly, since the debriefing, she'd been tough on him, and rightly so. But seeing John tonight made her realize she still had strong feelings for him and maybe a future with him one day. "Congratulations on your big promotion, Special Agent Lovell."

"Thanks. I thought I saw you come in with Muv and Pearl. I'd like to tell them hello. Where are they?"

Jill looked around and pointed to Muv busily chatting with an older lady at the table. John waved at her and asked, "Where's your mother?"

They finally spotted Pearl with John's dad, Big John, cozy over the shrimp at the bar.

"Those two may beat us to the altar," John teased.

"Yuck. Let's hope not. I don't think I can deal with being your sister."

"Stepsister. Dad told me they've been seeing a lot of one another. That bothers you?"

"We'd be stuck together for every holiday, birthday, and all those family reunions. Think we'd survive it?"

"I wouldn't mind getting stuck with you every day for the rest of my life."

"Oh, you'd get tired of me, at least of my cooking. I'm improving, but so far I've perfected only three dishes."

"We can always eat at the Duck Inn."

Jill smiled that John remembered the first meal that she bought at the Duck Inn and pretended to cook for him.

"Wonder if we can find any plum duck over there?" John asked as he took Jill by the hand to the bar. "What looks good to you?"

"Mmm. Everything," she said as she piled her plate with Acapulco shrimp cocktail, caviar potato chips, and strips of salmon.

John took her plate to a corner table under Chinese lights, and pulled his chair close to hers. "I've missed you, Jill. I'm sorry for the way I've acted. I was just so hurt . . . so surprised. You were right. I was only thinking of my feelings, not yours. Can you forgive me?"

"It's okay. I understand."

"Ready to give us another try?"

She hesitated for a moment. "I need more time to get my head on straight."

"No hurry. But promise me you'll call when you get back to Washington. Maybe we could go out on a date . . . sort of start over again?"

"But I'm not coming back to Washington."

"Ever?"

"Didn't Rubric tell you? I resigned from the *Gazette*."

"He said something about a leave of absence."

"I think he prefers to call it that at least until he gets used to the idea I'm not coming back."

"Resigned, huh? Have you accepted another position someplace else?"

"Yes."

"Where? Wait, let me guess. I've seen you interviewed on all the cable news channels and the network news recently, and you did a bang-up job. I'm betting one of them offered you a job."

"You're right . . . I received multiple offers."

"I thought so. Now, I just have to guess which one."

"I never said I accepted any of the offers."

"You didn't?"

Jill shook her head.

"Oh, okay. So it's not TV, then, it's a newspaper?"

"You got it."

"Mmm. Since the *Gazette* is at the top of the heap for a political reporter, I think the only other newspaper that might come close is the *New York Times*. Or maybe you want to move closer to home. In that case, my guess is the *Chicago Tribune*. Unless you're fed up with cold weather, and then you're probably heading for sunshine and work in California at the *Los Angeles Times*?"

"Wrong, wrong, and wrong."

"Okay, I give up. Tell me."

Jill smiled. "Congratulate the new owner of the *Lakes News*."

MUV'S PRALINE COOKIES

Makes about 4 dozen cookies

1 ½ cups flour
1 ½ teaspoons baking powder
1 ½ cups brown sugar
⅔ cup solid shortening
1 egg
1 teaspoon vanilla
½ teaspoon salt
whole pecans or pecan pieces

Preheat oven to 350 degrees.

In a large mixing bowl, combine all ingredients. Blend at medium speed. Forms stiff dough. Drop by teaspoonfuls onto ungreased cookie sheet.

Bake 10 to 13 minutes until deep golden brown. Cool.

Top each cookie with a whole pecan or pecan pieces.

Praline glaze:
¼ cup brown sugar
2 tablespoons butter
2 ½ tablespoons milk
¾ cup powdered sugar

In small saucepan, melt butter, stir in brown sugar and milk. Add powdered sugar; blend to make a glazing consistency. Drizzle glaze over pecans.

Best known for the Match Made in Heaven series, **Susan Wales** is the author of over twenty books including *The Chase* with Robin Shope. Susan and her husband, Ken Wales, live in Pacific Palisades, California, and are the parents of a daughter, Megan, and a granddaughter, Hailey.

Robin Shope lives with her husband of thirty years near Dallas, Texas, along with their new cocker spaniel puppy, Cooper. They have two grown children, Kimberly and Matthew. A veteran teacher of twenty years, Robin currently teaches middle school. Robin has over two hundred articles in print in various Christian magazines and dozens of short stories published in such great reads as *Chicken Soup for the Soul*.